# THE ROSE TRAIL

## BY ALEX MARTIN

This book is dedicated to Jo for her constant belief and encouragement

Please note that this is a work of fiction. Any errors are entirely the author's responsibility. While extensive research has been undertaken about the English Civil War, so have many liberties. The battle of Roundway Down did take place on 13th July 1643 and the narrative in The Rose Trail is loosely based on actual events, with the major movers of the time given their real names, but the rest of the story and characters are entirely fictitious. This includes *all* staff members in museums, libraries, cafés and bookshops in Devizes, all of whom are helpful and charming in real life!

Please forgive any licence taken. It was artistic.

Note: The historical scenes use modern dialect but in fact would have sounded quite different. Families addressed each other with thee and thou in the 1600s and I played around with this but decided it detracted too much from the story and reverted to today's speech.

I am indebted to Jane at http://www.jdsmith-design.com/ for designing the brilliant cover picture from some pretty random ideas

Heartfelt thanks to Phil for his eagle-eyed editing and to Tom for his objectivity and insights

The right of A Martin to be identified as the author of this
work has been asserted by her under Copyright Amendment
(Moral Rights) Act 2000.
All the characters and places in this fictional book are a
product of the author's imagination. Any resemblance to people
or places is entirely coincidental. The author has endeavoured to
research historical facts accurately. Where they are not so, it is
hoped the reader will forgive any anomalies and grant the
author artistic license.

As a thank you for downloading The Rose Trail, you may claim your free gift (not available anywhere else) at Alex Martin's writing blog:

# www.intheplottingshed.com

# THE ROSE TRAIL

## PROLOGUE

## ROUNDWAY HILL

Robin dared me to do it. Ah, if only he hadn't...

And yet, I blame myself. Blame my thin skin between worlds. No, not worlds, time frames. It's the same old world spinning around now as spun hundreds of years ago but I wish I couldn't slip between those years so easily.

Robin was my first love and remains my last, ten years later. I loved him with my entire heart and soul and he loved me back. People called it a teenage crush but I know it would have lasted all our lives, except for that silly dare. We met on the very first day of secondary school. Our eyes locked on to each other during the registration ritual. His were deep brown, with a mocking twinkle deep-set at the back of them.

"Please team up with someone you don't know and talk about yourself, in turns, for a minute each." Miss Greenslade had a natural authority no-one dared challenge this early in the proceedings.

To my astonishment, Robin made a bee-line for me. Flattered, I listened avidly, pleased to be able to study his pleasant face without seeming rude.

"My name is Robin Braithwaite and I've just moved to Wiltshire. My old town was Halifax, in Yorkshire. My Dad's got a job down here and I don't know anyone at all." He grinned at me, showing white, even teeth and my stomach flipped over.

I was skinny then and tall for my age; very different to how I look now. I could tell he fancied me as much as I fancied him. By the time hormones budded my breasts and broke his voice, we were going steady. Our love deepened as our adolescence passed and we crossed the boundary into physical passion with a love so strong, it felt sacred, all because Robin made me feel safe.

I had never felt that before, as I had a guilty secret. I had been haunted all through my short life by spirits who'd passed on. My parents hadn't believed me when I'd told them I could see their ancestors, so I'd learned not to say anything much when I'd had a visit from the other side. But Robin was different; intuitive himself, he could sense my experiences were real. He could tell I'd been shaken up if it had been a rough encounter, as was increasingly the case after my sixteenth birthday. In my last nightmare, I'd woken up on my bedroom floor, struggling to breathe and clutching my throat, convinced I'd been strangled.

My bedroom window looked out on Roundway, an enormous hill studded with old earthworks dug by long forgotten tribes. In spring, the meadow on its lower slopes dazzled with buttercups and dandelions; their yellow pinpoints of sunshine supplanted in summer by the blanched froth of cow parsley, before bowing out via the rich warm tints of autumn into the barren winter.

I loved that view.

It had consoled me through a childhood fraught with taunts from my peers, until Robin silenced them. Now, anytime one of the cool kids teased me, Robin would step right up to them and stick his face in theirs. "If you've got nothing better to do than make up stuff about my girlfriend, you can shove off." Whether it was his tall, broad frame or alien accent, I don't know, but shove off they usually did, and I loved him all the more for it.

But that summer, ten years ago, phantom whispers infiltrated my solitary bedroom, coming through the window, disturbing me at night; sometimes even in the day. Sinister shadows crept about in the long grass on the hill in distorted shapes that didn't mirror their surroundings. At first I'd been fascinated by the strange energy patterns; they'd distracted me from revising for my GCSE's but the sibilant voices echoing up from the meadow increasingly kept me awake through the short summer nights.

Drawn by the inexplicable shape shifting and the hiss of faceless voices, I had taken to walking up Roundway Hill whenever I was alone, meandering along its time-worn paths, searching for something I couldn't name or identify.

I always took a book to revise from, more to keep Mum's nagging at bay than to study. One day, while searching for a secluded spot in which to dream away the sultry afternoon, I saw something glinting in the tall grass on the steepest part of the hill. Discarding my unread maths text book, I bent down to investigate. I found an old chain caught up in a gnarled tree root. Tarnished black and covered in layers of grime and dust, it was surprising I had spotted it at all but something intangible had lured me to it. I picked it up and held it in my open palm. Standing quite still, I stared at the exquisite intertwined metal strands, barely visible under the muck.

Immediately I heard  one of those indistinct whispers curling around my head.

*"Follow..."*

The silvery strand felt strangely warm and a tingle crept up my arm. I closed my fist over it. Instantly, the metal adapted to my blood heat, much quicker than it had any right to, so it felt part of me instead of a cold, inert object. The hovering whisper morphed into a low but recognisable laugh. Not a happy sound. It chilled every bit of me except my hand.

Shoving my book into my pocket, with the chain still curled up and hot inside my fist, I turned back to my house and ran upstairs to my room, shutting the door as quietly as I could, so as not to have to explain my muddy find to Mum, who'd become a hygiene freak since Dad died. I needn't have worried. I'd forgotten Mum always went to a WI meeting on Wednesday afternoons and often returned with cake. I licked my lips, which had gone dry, and re-opened my fist.

The pale chain lay coiled on my reddened palm, like a serpent.

I took it into the bathroom and used soap on an old toothbrush to clean it up. Dirt and bits of grass swirled down the plughole, making it burp and glug. I wondered what kind metal of it was made from. Could it be valuable?

I patted the metal chain dry on a towel and picked up my phone to share my find with Robin.

"You revising?"

Robin mumbled back in a sleepy voice. "Supposed to be, but it's too hot."

"I've found something on the hill. Do you want to come over and have a look?"

"What is it?" He sounded more awake already.

"Some sort of chain but I think it's connected to all the whispering I keep hearing."

"I'll be there in five minutes."

I took the woven metal rope down to the kitchen and laid it out on a clean tea towel on the Formica table.

Robin was as good as his word and let himself in through the back door of our old cottage in less than his allotted five minutes, looking pink with the effort of jogging over on such a warm summer's day.

He kissed me full on the mouth. He always greeted me that way when we were alone, and I never objected, but this time I pulled away quickly to show him the necklace.

"I'm sure it's moved. I put it on that tea cloth to dry and now its directly on the Formica."

"Don't be daft, Fay. Metal can't move itself. You must be mistaken." His broad Yorkshire accent was always more pronounced when he was hot and cross.

"I'm bloody not. Feel it, Robin. It's always warm to the touch."

Robin put out a tentative finger. "Feels cold to me. What's it made of, do you know?"

"No idea. Looks pretty old. Might be silver."

"Has your Mum got any silver polish?"

"Must have somewhere; she's got every type of cleaning agent ever invented." I rummaged in the under-sink cupboard and brought out some dusters and metal polishing fluid.

We settled down to work on the chain, one at either end. After half an hour's industry, the snake of metal shone silvery white against the red table top, revealing its beautifully worked intricate loops and twirls.

"This was made by a very skilled craftsman." Robin traced the pretty swirls with his blackened finger.

"I think it must be a necklace, Robin."

"Put it on, Fay."

"No. Never. I'm not wearing that round my neck." The very thought of it around my throat choked me.

"Ow!" I yelled in pain, as I pushed it violently away.

The silver chain fell on Mum's spotless kitchen floor.

Robin whispered, as he stared at the sliver of twisted metalwork, "What's the matter, Fay? It looked like it burned you."

I nodded but stayed silent, too scared to put my panicky thoughts into words and rubbing my scorched hands instead.

"Where did you say you found it, love?" Robin didn't look at me but continued to gaze, transfixed, at the necklace.

"Up on Roundway Hill, where the shadows shift and the whispers come from." My own voice was barely audible, not unlike those I kept hearing at inconvenient times.

"We must go back there and check it out." Robin finally looked at me, his dark eyes glittering with excitement.

"Not on your life. I'm chucking it out of the window."

"No, Fay, don't do that! It must be linked to the whispers you're picking up. We need to trace what the connection is, maybe sort it once and for all." Robin went to pick it up.

"Don't touch it, Robin!"

At this point my Mum sauntered in through the back door, laden with shopping bags. "Oh, hello, Robin, dear. Would you like some lemon drizzle cake? Mrs. Saunders had made a few and I couldn't resist buying one. Oh, what's that shiny thing on my nice clean floor?" Mum put her bags in the corner, bent down and picked it up, holding it in her hand nonchalantly, as if it wasn't evil.

"Nice necklace, Fay, dear. Have you cleaned it up yourself? It must have been dirty judging by the marks on that old tea cloth." She tutted, picked up the tea cloth between the thumb and forefinger of her other hand, carried it to the washing machine and chucked it in the drum.

I looked at the floor. There was no trace of a scorch mark on the pale floor tiles or on my sore hands but the teacloth had indeed looked filthy.

Mum was still holding the necklace, turning it over and over.

"Careful, Mum, mind it doesn't burn your hand."

"Oh, Fay, are you making up stories again? Silver can't burn you. Such a pretty chain too. Look, it's as cold as anything after laying on that tiled floor. Come on, let's brew up a cuppa and have a slice of this nice lemon cake." Mum filled the kettle and hummed a tune. Always a sign she was trying to divert me and it never failed to annoy.

Mum always ignored my 'fancies' as she called them. Robin and I exchanged meaningful looks in a tacit understanding not to pursue it and we shared cake and tea while Mum prattled on about Mrs Saunders' terrible varicose veins.

After Robin went home, I quietly took the necklace upstairs and stuffed it into my undies drawer and tried to forget about it, but the whispering episodes became more frequent and interfered with studying for my GCSE exams. I swear some of them emanated from that particular drawer in my bedroom chest but I dismissed it, preferring to believe Mum's pragmatic approach to my 'strange goings on'. I moved my underwear to another drawer and kept that one tight shut.

The term eventually fizzled out so we and our mates were off school on study leave and only exam time-tables disrupted our daily routine. I muddled through but all the testing of my distracted memory took its toll and I felt exhausted and wrung out when the examinations finally finished. I was dreading the results in August. With the exams over, the summer seemed endless, stretched out in front of us with nothing to fill it and I still wasn't sleeping well.

"I think we should investigate these whispers that are keeping you awake, Fay." Robin said, one day when I was too tired to do anything but flop on his bed, even though it was a lovely day outside and he wanted to go for a bike ride.

"No way, Robin. Just forget it, will you?" I closed my eyes and put my hands over my ears.

Gently, he pulled my hands away and lay down next to me. "Fay, it's not like you to be chicken about this sort of thing."

"It's that bloody necklace. I've stopped opening that drawer. I'm too scared. I can't even go to sleep, knowing it's in the room."

"Then I dare you to confront the voices by going back to the place where you found it."

"Oh, no, please, let's leave it." I opened my eyes again and stared at the dust motes dancing in the sunbeams slanting across the room.

"No, Fay. You'll never have any peace until you do." He kissed me softly on the mouth and stroked my hair. I could feel my resolve weakening.

"And I'll be with you. You know I'll always look after you, don't you?"

Hindsight is ever a marvellous thing.

Had I been sleeping better, had I fussed less over my exams, had I shut out the whispering, or thrown the damn necklace away, things might have turned out so differently. But it's no use. I would rewind that fateful night if I could and have done so in my head, oh, many times, but it cannot be changed.

We headed off to Roundway Hill, keyed up with nerves and excitement, on midsummer's eve. I knew the very spot we had to reach because I'd remembered it so many times in my mind's eye. We clambered up the steep slope and even though it was nearly midnight, the soft twilight of midsummer lit our way. We'd told our parents we were staying at each others' houses but really we planned to sleep out in the open at the top of the huge hill, with only the stars for company and of course, each other.

Making love by moonlight sounded very romantic to me and all week long I'd been picturing us cavorting under the stars, entwined and blissfully alone. A much more enticing prospect than solving the necklace mystery and I was confident my charms would make Robin forget about it, as I dreaded what we might stir up. And the night promised to stay warm, with a soothing gentle breeze, perfect for caressing naked limbs.

I giggled in anticipation and Robin, sensing my mood, reached over and kissed my eager lips as we set out.

"Nothing can harm us, Fay, in this world or the next, as long as we're together." Robin assured me and naïvely, I believed him.

Up, up we climbed, weighed down with torches and sleeping bags. Robin had insisted on bringing a little gas stove, some water and a billy-can. In another bag he had stowed the dried goods of powdered milk, teabags and biscuits. He was very excited about camping outdoors and had loved buying the equipment with his paper-round money over the previous few weeks. Anyone would think we'd been setting off for the North Pole.

I smile, even now, at our sense of adventure.

"Come on, love!" Robin's broad northern accent was unmistakably his, even in the glinting, deceiving shadows. The light was strange, with the sun barely setting, more like gloaming than true darkness. I looked up the path at his tall frame. He was constantly several paces ahead of me and I couldn't catch up.

"Can't you wait a moment for me, Robin?" I called up.

"No, I want to get to the top and suss out a spot to set up camp," Robin shouted back.

"Go on, then," I said, puffing with the effort. "Just look out for my torch if you can't see me, okay?"

"Yeah, alright. Look, I can see a perfect spot over to the side of that hawthorn hedge." Robin was obviously keen to find it and he put on a spurt of speed away from me.

"Where? Which hedge, Robin?" but he had gone.

The wind picked up and licked my face. Not now, not bloody now, I didn't want any apparitions while I was on my own, thank you. Too late, the breeze brought an unwelcome whisper.

*"You're nearly there; come, come."*

The familiar murmur drifted through the leaf-laden trees; the same female voice I always heard; her vocal pitch high, laced with a country burr. I could hear the disembodied words even more clearly up on the hill.

I willed her away, feeling triumphant when her hated voice was supplanted by the faint sound of a horse's hooves drumming in the distance. How odd. It was a bit late and much too dark for riding and my sexy plans for our al fresco night didn't include intruders.

I couldn't see Robin now. His young body had merged with the copse of trees on the hilltop plateau. He'd always been able to walk faster than me and I cursed my short legs, which hadn't grown any longer since the first year. Now I was the shortest girl in our form and no longer the slimmest. I worried about that. Persephone Godstock had grown tall and willowy and Robin was always chatting with her, exchanging looks at the youth club disco. It didn't help that her hair was naturally auburn (so she said) and fell in tawny, gold-tinted waves down her slender back.

More sounds of distant thundering hooves brought me back to the present and I looked around in all directions but couldn't see any animal silhouetted against the bulk of the hill.

*"Come... higher still...."*

The hissed command beckoned me on. I felt disorientated, turning in the direction of these phantom noises, then going the opposite way as the whispers slithered behind me.

Shaking my head free of the cobweb of sounds I couldn't locate, I tramped on and caught my foot in a rabbit hole, narrowly avoiding twisting my ankle. It hurt, making me test my weight gingerly before carrying on. I hitched my rucksack to a more comfortable position on my bent back. Whose idea was this anyway? Despite the gentle breeze, a dew had begun to pearl on the long grass at my feet and I shivered. I felt very alone and oddly queasy. Robin was nowhere in sight. What if he'd gone off at a tangent? How would I find him?

I never did.

It was the police who found Robin in the early dawn of the 22nd of June. He was sprawled at the foot of Roundway Hill, his arms outstretched and legs at an odd angle, directly below the sheer escarpment at its apex. I couldn't see his face, it was buried in the grass, and the policewoman wouldn't let me get any closer, however much I screamed and hit out at her.

9

## Squashed together

*"He was in the way and I had need of you."*

Life, after a loved one's death, goes inexorably on whether we like it or not. The world will insist on turning, unless we take matters into our own hands, which takes far more courage than I possess, though I can't say I haven't thought about it: often.

And my life, without Robin enlivening it, became grindingly tame and grey. I kept the silver chain from Roundway Hill in my pocket as a memento of our last night together, but it was no substitute for a living person. I had to re-invent myself as a singleton, for which I had zero appetite and I discovered, little appeal. Not only did I never gain height after the age of twelve, I was also born with enormous shoulders, which is unfortunate, as I remain only five foot two. I try to disguise my shape with scarves and big hats but only plunging necklines really work and then I have to be in the mood, which I rarely am. To cap it all, my surname is Armstrong.

And of course, my dear parents thought it might be nice to call me Fay – I mean, it might as well be Fey, mightn't it? Born and brought up in Wiltshire – obviously from sturdy yeoman stock – I yielded to my Mum's idea to escape my humble roots and my overwhelming grief by training to be an accountant. She thought it would be a safe, undemanding sort of career for her weird, sad daughter. She worried about me even more after Robin's demise crumbled me into a blubbering wreck. So it was Mum who'd found the course; Mum who worked out the qualifications needed, bought the text books and booked the train ticket to the training college.

I dimly remember the palm of her hand in the small of my back as I stumbled up the train steps, laden with cases of books and clothes.

"You'll be fine, Fay, dear. Just keep smiling at everyone you meet and don't go on about your fanciful stuff. No-one likes to talk about things like that. And join a sports club, won't you? Keep yourself fit and busy and everything will fall into place."

Mum stepped back from the train and waved until I couldn't see her any more.

Her words buzzed around my ears but I hadn't listened to them. I never did. I sat on that train and let the countryside blur past me and forgot every bit of advice she'd given me.

I now live in Swindon, where these dubious skills have taken me. It couldn't be more of a contrast to my bucolic home if it tried – and Swindon doesn't really try at anything. Except functional growth perhaps. But all the modern office blocks springing up like mushrooms, all the labyrinthian housing estates smothering the surrounding green fields, all the dual carriageways with their bossy signs obliterating the ancient lanes and woodlands, and certainly all the dreary accountancy exams, could not suppress the old souls who whispered around me, begging to be heard.

Already there were sniggers behind my back at the office. I was helping myself to coffee in the cupboard they laughingly labelled 'The Kitchen' one dreary Monday morning, minding my own business, when I heard two women whispering in the corridor outside.

"It's true. She thinks she can see ghosts."

"No!"

"Honestly. I don't know how I kept a straight face. She said she could see my old Nan behind my head. Can you believe it?"

"Frankly, no! Maybe she thinks it's makes her more interesting."

"That's what I thought. I mean, you wouldn't ask her advice about dress sense, now would you?"

More laughter ebbed away as my two colleagues wandered off.

You see, I still couldn't control these unwanted visitors from beyond the grave. The familiar dread would creep up on me, unbidden and unwanted. At first I would feel shivery and cold. Whatever the ambient temperature or however sunny the day, I would not be able to warm up. And then my surroundings would slip away and everything around me recede, thrusting me back into the lifetime of whoever had latched on to me. Very distracting, and not always as interesting as you might think or, as it turned out, convenient.

One day, I was driving along Salisbury Plain, in the middle of nowhere, admiring the view and singing along to Coldplay on the radio. I'd never had a problem with spirits when behind the wheel and was enjoying driving my old hatchback to Mum's house. Mum might be a nag but she was a dab hand with home-made chips and she'd promised plenty of them.

It was a warm, humid July day, well past midsummer, well past the tenth anniversary of Robin's untimely death. I had the windows down to create a breeze, confident it would blow any spirits through one window and out the other and do battle with my constant fatigue. Sure, I was tired but I wasn't concerned about anything, having just secured a new job in a faceless firm who manufactured computer parts. This time I wasn't going to let on whenever I saw someone's dear departed in the office. I'd had enough of being shunned. Plus, this position came with a better salary and I was planning to move to a nicer flat, one with a view other than red-brick terraced houses.

So, I was taken by surprise when the cold began to crawl up from my feet. I couldn't jiggle my legs while I was driving and I couldn't pull off the road either. I concentrated fiercely on singing 'Yellow' as loudly as I could but soon my arms felt frigid too and I couldn't feel the steering wheel properly. The radio DJ's voice faded and someone quite different whispered into my ear. The tarmac shimmered, its edges blurring until I couldn't tell where the grass verges bordered the road anymore.

My heart started to thud, trying to pump my cooling blood at its normal rate against the slow chill in my bones. I had to control this! I forced my mind to recollect the well-meaning self-help book I'd been studying the night before but my eyelids had drooped over its wisdom and I couldn't recall a single word. What had it said about mindfulness? I squeezed my eyes shut and opened them again, momentarily seeing clearly. I was entering a town; I'd forgotten where I was going by now but the road had become a street, strung with lamp-posts. I careered on, trying to judge where the pavement was. As my eyes flickered to the nearside, I glimpsed a lamp-post bedecked with tatty bouquets. Someone had died there. Was this who was trying to come through?

My hands were too numb to control the steering wheel and the car veered ever nearer the faded flowers. I pawed at the wheel, trying to pull it away from the pavement but I couldn't see where the kerb was, only the tattered blooms. The car stopped itself in the end, by bumping into the lamp-post, breaking the headlight and denting the front wing. The depressing tinkling of glass, after the jolt of the impact, imposed itself onto my fuddled mind and gradually I came to. Another car whizzed by, honking its horn in disgust at my crazy driving. Not a good Samaritan in sight.

I yanked the handbrake on and sat back against the driver's seat, shaking and breathless. I fumbled for the keys and switched off the ignition with clumsy fingers. The car engine hushed and I breathed out a long sigh of relief. Other cars swished past me, unnoticed. I rubbed my quivering hands over my eyes and rubbed the brain-fog away, recognising that I had nearly added another bunch of flowers to that lamp-post.

I had to find a way to manage these episodes before they were the death of me and *I* became a spirit interfering with someone else's life. Not for the first time, the black thoughts sneaked in. If I was dead, I could join Robin. God knew there were days when that was very appealing but the finality of death is just that, final, except for those tortured souls who can't or won't cross over, and I was as fearful of it as anyone else. And yet it never ceased to amaze me that Robin never came through. I'd had no contact with this dearest of spirits since he died. Was he as shocked as I was and finding it hard to adjust to being separate? Did the nature of his violent death mean he couldn't communicate? Or was it me?

I'd been going through another bad spell, mostly at night in the nadir hours. Maybe it had been the stress of the interview that had made me more vulnerable. I was getting exhausted and worried I wouldn't be able to hold down my new job and, after nearly killing myself in the car, decided enough was enough. I booked an appointment at my local surgery with a view to seeking some medical help.

I knew I'd done the wrong thing as soon as I set eyes on the GP. Red-faced, his paunch bumping against his desk, he wasn't the best advert for a healthy middle-aged man. It wasn't that the doctor was unkind, he was simply incredulous. How could I explain my dilemma to a man who reduced my symptoms to the rigid rules of logical science? He actually snorted his derision when I mentioned the word 'ghosts'. Snorted! And then converted it to a thinly disguised snigger. I'm not sure which was more insulting.

"Tell me, Miss, um, Armstrong, what do you experience during these episodes?"

"Well, I go very cold to start with."

"Yes, yes but do you have any visual disturbances?"

"I'm not sure if I'd describe it as disturbed, but certainly my eyes won't focus and my vision sort of blurs before I see who is reaching me."

"Do you have any memory afterwards?"

"Not always, although it's very vivid at the time."

"I see. And has anyone witnessed these experiences of yours?"

"My Mum says it looks like I'm in a trance."

"Aha! It seems to me, Miss Armstrong, that you might be suffering some form of mild epilepsy."

"Epilepsy?"

"Yes, these sorts of trances are sometimes called 'petit mal'. Have you ever suffered a fit?"

"A fit?"

The doctor sighed at my slow comprehension. As far as I was concerned, he was missing the point entirely. It wasn't me that was wonky. These episodes, as he called them, were entirely down to third parties but he obviously wasn't going to allow for that possibility.

He spoke slowly now, as if I was thick, or deaf. "Do you thrash about, find yourself on the floor afterwards, have any bruising or excess salivation?"

"No. Look, this is a mistake. I shouldn't have come."

"Nonsense. Epilepsy is a serious condition. I'm going to send you for some tests." He scrawled a note on a form, then

14

tapped on his keyboard. I couldn't see the computer screen. He might have been typing 'nutter alert' for all I knew.

I left the surgery feeling more depressed than ever. Tests. Then it would be medication I supposed, with attendant side effects making me more tired, grumpy and probably fatter than ever. Bloody doctors. They either want to clobber you with chemicals or chop your limbs off. I decided to go it alone and make a study of the paranormal my own way.

I took myself off to the local library's 'spiritual section' and scoured the internet for information on how to deal with all things occult. Some of the stuff I read made my hair stand on end, which only served to further emphasise its natural waywardness.

I decided to be methodical and kept both a journal and a folder on my computer in constant update mode while I assimilated all this new information and tried to get a grip on how to manage my unwanted visitors. After work each night, I would forego the mixed pleasure of escapism on the telly and settle down to study everything I could lay my hands on. Of course some of it was scam, some of it spam and a lot was sheer sensationalism trying to make a killing, not of ghosts but credit cards. Patiently, using the discipline that had got me through tedious accountancy qualifications, I waded and sifted through the minefield.

Gradually, I got an inkling that energy fields were involved somehow and took up Tai Chi, which seemed the most promising way to explore it. Under the tutelage of an eccentric old hippy called Ted, I learned to harness my own energy and feel the thrill of it flowing through my bones. My body remained disappointingly lumpy and too large but it gave my mind plenty of exercise. I learned to centre my energy and ground it. Interestingly, I never encountered the spirit world during these classes and my cynicism had to yield to being impressed by Ted's calm strength and ignore his wispy long white hair and bizarre clothing.

All this tinkering with New Age stuff did slightly ease the aching loneliness of life without Robin but it didn't vent my resentful grief, so a couple of weeks later, I also joined the local leisure centre squash ladder. There at least I could bash the hell out of the non-bouncy dead-ball and unleash some of my simmering anger. I wasn't very good at it but I made up for that with desperate enthusiasm. It was a way to meet people, although some were alienated by my aggressive but inept game and besides, it passed the endless time.

It was after a particularly bruising game of squash that I met my antithesis. I first saw the Barbie-look-alike studying the squash league table. I couldn't see her face as it was unnecessarily close to the lists of names, so I studied her form from behind.

The comparison between us was stark and clearly demonstrated the difference between female and feminine. We were both wearing 'leisure-wear'. Her track suit was made of soft dark-green velour; its simple lines followed her svelte contours like a glove. Legs up to her armpits were silkily encased in wrinkle-free stretch jogging pants that afforded the interested observer a fine view of her nicely rounded rear. The whole confection was crowned by flowing auburn curls that fell down to her feminine-sized shoulders in tawny waves.

I sighed, acutely aware of my own outfit, revealing spare tyres, the number of which I'd long since lost count, the ledge of my protruding backside, and my constant companions – the outsize manly shoulders. After my workout, I had no doubt, none whatsoever, that my complexion would be puce and my short, mousey-brown hair stuck to my head in sweaty clumps. Without Robin's tender affection, I had long ceased to care about my appearance.

"Can I help you?" I asked, not looking at her, as I too perused the lists for my next opponent.

"Thank you, I can't quite make out this name – Fog Armsling?" She was tracing the names with one long, perfectly manicured finger.

I hope my reply came with a disarming smile, "That'll be me – Fay Armstrong. Are we destined to play together?"

"Oops, sorry." A soft rose suffused the peachy complexion, as she turned to me with a ravishing smile. I noticed her eyes were an unusual moss-green colour, perfectly matching her expensive track suit. "Yes – we are – would you like to set a date? I'm Persephone Godstock-Wade."

Resignation settled upon me like a wet jumper in the rain. Persephone Godstock - and as immaculately beautiful as she'd promised to be all those years ago, when she'd been making doe eyes at Robin in the youth club. She obviously hadn't recognised me.

"Um, don't I know you?" I thought I might as well get it over with.

"Gosh, yes! Of course, I should have recognised your name. We were at the same school, weren't we?"

"That's right, in the dim and distant past. Different forms of course."

"Yes, you were with..."

"Robin Braithwaite. Yes, I was."

"Sorry, I shouldn't have said anything, I wasn't thinking."

"No." I swallowed, my constricted throat unable to squeeze out more.

She didn't reply but her delicately flushed face tacitly betrayed her embarrassment.

I cleared my throat but couldn't rescue her because of the lump in it.

But she managed well enough without my help by saying, "Can you forgive my slip up and get your revenge on the squash court next week? Tuesdays are my squash days."

"Fine – after work it'll have to be. I finish at five. Would half past suit you, as I walk to the leisure centre from work?"

"Oh, that's a bit late but yes, I could do it and be back in time to get supper together, I suppose."

"Right, but don't expect leniency."

I stomped off. So - Persephone Godstock-Whatever - now a domestic goddess; well she'd never been the sharpest pencil in the box. I wound my weary way back to work and routine and tried to forget about the stab of memory she'd knifed into my sore heart.

## Squished

*"How to bring you here? Ah yes, I shall use her; I can see a way."*

The following Tuesday, I made sure I finished work promptly and walked briskly up the hill to the leisure centre. The demanding climb warmed up my muscles nicely and I duly thrashed Persephone in an admittedly fierce game. Her Bambi-like demeanour belied a keenly competitive spirit. She could hit the ball hard enough for it to ricochet off the back wall and still reach the front one without bouncing. I found I had to step up my game by using my smashes and drop shots in every long rally.

I thoroughly enjoyed my petty triumph but then my guilty conscience prompted me to ask, after changing back into ordinary clothes, "Fancy a drink? I could murder a cuppa myself."

After all, Persephone hadn't killed Robin. I'd often wanted to kill her in my youth but it seemed I'd have to settle for the less dramatic slaughter of winning at squash.

"Um, okay."

Her lukewarm reply didn't put me off ordering a mug of builder's tea and a thickly buttered teacake in the bar-come-café upstairs, far enough away from the stale sweat of the changing rooms to restore my ever-ready appetite. Persephone sipped delicately at Perrier water, flavoured by a slice of fat-reducing lemon. I sunk my teeth into the teacake, its butter now melted and oozing messily onto my hands and chin. Scrumptious.

Watching the butter slip down my face with utter fascination, Persephone said, "So, um, Fay, isn't it? What do you do for a living these days?"

Slowly, without undue haste, I swallowed the last calorific morsel, wiped my greasy mouth with a scrumpled old tissue and answered, "Accountant." Brief but accurate.

"Ooh, how clever!" Persephone's eyes widened in admiration.

I sat up taller and took a glug of tea. "Well, not really, just need to know the rules and abide by them."

"I don't do anything."

"Lucky you! I wish I didn't have to grub about for filthy lucre. How do you fill the time then?"

"Play squash," Persephone twinkled.

"Obviously – but what else?" I took another slurp.

"Oh, you know – keep house, tend the garden, sketch and paint a bit – avoid coffee mornings!" She looked a little sheepish.

"Full-time housewife then?"

She nodded.

"Any children?"

"No." Her downcast features forbade further enquiry on that score. I cast about for a safer topic. "So, what does your husband do?"

"He's a photographer, mostly wildlife now." Her forehead creased into a tiny frown.

"Ah, interesting. He must be away a lot then."

It was a statement not a question but Persephone nodded.

I drained my mug. "School was many years ago. How have you filled your time since we last met, apart from squash and hobbies?"

"Well, I was a model."

No surprises there.

She hurried on, as if embarrassed, "And then I met Paul at a photo-shoot and we fell in love, then quickly got married - my full surname is Godstock-Wade now, I added my husband's surname to mine, you see. Um, then I moved to his family home and actually, I feel a little lost without having to work for a living."

"Surely you don't live in Swindon – it's such an awful sprawling place these days. You're not still in Devizes, near the school, are you?"

"No, just outside Swindon now but I like to come to a big town, even if it's just for my weekly game of squash, just to feel part of things." She squeezed her lemon slice into her water, making it fizz.

"Hmm. I must say I think I might stay away but then I don't get the opportunity. I live in Old Town." No need to add how grotty my flat was.

"Oh yes? We live out towards Marlborough way – at Meadowsweet Manor - on the downs, you know."

I knew. There was a swathe of swanky houses gracing the hills on the northern side of town. "Nice. Well, I must be off. Got some studying to do tonight." I picked up my holdall and with my usual clumsiness, missed one of the handles so the bag fell open, revealing a new book I'd just bought. Its graphic cover left no doubt about its subject matter of the paranormal.

I tried to shove it down while grappling with the bag but the damn thing fell out on to the floor instead.

"Oh, that looks an interesting book, Fay. Are you still interested in ghosts and things?" She laughed; a brittle sound. "You know, there was a rumour flying around school that you were dabbling with stuff like that, but of course I never believed that you were a witch or anything, like everyone said."

I ground my teeth and shoved the lurid paperback firmly under my damp towel. Zipping up the holdall, I turned to go. "Don't ever apply for a job in the Diplomatic Service, Persephone. See you around."

"No wait! I didn't mean to be rude, Fay, please believe me. I'm always putting my foot in it but I meant no harm, truly I didn't. Let me make it up to you. Look, um, Paul's gone away for a few days. Would you like to come to supper with me? I rattle around in the house like a pea in a bucket." Persephone laid her hand on my arm.

Too angry to accept, I shook my head, and her hand from my arm, and left without saying goodbye.

Almost a month passed without incident, a first for me in simply years. I felt I was making progress at last; felt I might even be able to have a normal life one day. The Tai Chi classes were definitely helping. I was even beginning to enjoy them. Studying the underworld of the paranormal yielded less positive results. I was going around in unproductive circles and wondering whether I shouldn't engage a medium to intervene on my behalf, but how could I tell who was genuine? The whole subject was littered with charlatans, some of them terrifyingly believable but none I wanted to connect with - or trust.

I kept up with the squash too, dreading meeting up with Mrs GodawfulStock again. I was careful to avoid Tuesdays and managed to steer clear. So it was a surprise when, on my new regular Wednesday slot after work, I found myself confronting her back on the court.

"I thought you only played on Tuesdays?" I bashed the ball against the back wall, just to warm it up. If she thought I'd given her a competitive game last time, she was in for a real shock. I would give her no quarter now after that witch remark. The old anger seethed through me and I felt hot and itched to begin the game.

"Oh, I swapped with someone at the last minute."

Persephone won the toss, annoyingly, and served first. We played silently, intensely, each concentrating on the next move. She was good, I had to admit and more focussed than last time, but I was fuelled by hurt pride. We were both sweating within ten minutes.

I had a narrow edge on the score when Persephone hit a demon soft dummy against the wall. I ran in for it and did the same, not bothering to run back to the central T-line afterwards, but crouching ready to scoop it up and slam it hard enough to hit the far corner, where it should drop dead and be unreturnable. Confident she was going to do another drop shot, I gathered my energy, my weight in my toes, anticipating winning another point. I smiled, relishing the moment. She didn't do another delicate drop shot. Oh, no. Persephone swung her racket back to whack the ball hard instead, catching my snub nose across its bridge and causing it to bleed profusely all over the wooden floor.

"Shit, my nose!" The pain was sudden and intense. I clutched at my ruined face while shards of lancinating pain encircled my head in great stabs. Blood spurted through my fingers and I sank to my knees, weak at the sight of it.

"Oh, my God! What have I done?" Persephone threw her racket away and came towards me.

"Get off!" I held my other hand up to ward her off but she wasn't having it. What was it with this blasted woman?

Blood was pouring out of my nose now. It was probably broken.

"Can I see, Fay? Are you feeling faint? Let me help you." Persephone knelt down next to me and peered at my smashed face.

Through the blood running into it, I opened my mouth and spluttered. "I think you've done enough, you idiot. Keep away from me."

"Come on," Persephone picked up our rackets. "We'd better get you to A&E."

"I can go on my own." I could only mumble my objections, as my head was threatening to split into a hundred pieces.

"No, you can't. Listen, it's my fault, I'll take you in my car." She helped me up to my feet and put her arm around my waist. I had no strength left to resist, as my knees were now unwilling to support me and I had started to shake all over.

She was right, of course, but that didn't make me any less cross. I sat on the bench in the changing room, holding a sodden tissue to my nose and quivering, and ignored the flapping assistant who offered to ring 999 for an ambulance.

Persephone, all calm efficiency, waved her away. "Thanks, but I'll take her to the hospital. My car is outside. No-one is holding you responsible. It's entirely my fault." She gathered up our things, stuffing jeans, shoes and towels into each bag with impressive speed. Before I could gather my scattered wits, we were in her flash Mini and whizzing along towards the hospital.

The panicky sports hall assistant had clamped an icepack on the bridge of my nose and the dull pain of it prevented me from further conversation. Not that I wanted any. The sooner this was over, the sooner I could go home and forget I ever met this stupid woman again.

Persephone drove quietly, expertly, the short distance to the hospital and guided me into the A&E department with discreet helpfulness. I hated her for that.

As I was still bleeding all over the floor, I was whisked away ahead of the queue and plonked in front of a harassed young doctor who prodded and poked at my face. It was excruciatingly painful until she injected an anaesthetic into the bruise. Persephone stood by me through the ordeal and, craven as I am to admit it, I reached for her hand when the needle, I swear it was the size of a knitting needle, appeared between my eyes, pointing its sharp tip directly at my poor nose. I think I must have passed out for a time because the next thing I was aware of was people in flapping white coats wheeling me on a trolley into the X-ray department.

"Lie still, please," said the radiographer.

No problem, I felt as weak as a newborn slug. Afterwards I was whooshed back into some clinical room where Persephone waited. She certainly was doggedly persistent. I didn't give a greeting.

An older doctor appeared, smiling gaily, which seemed both incongruous and unfair.

"Good news!"

"I fail to understand what is good about this situation." The anaesthetic was working and so was my mouth.

"No, really it is. Your nose is not broken. It's not even cut, just bruised. The bleeding was entirely internal and has now stopped. You'll have a black eye, maybe two, but once the swelling has gone down, you'll be back to normal." The doctor looked positively jaunty.

"No cauliflower nose to add to my normal good looks?"

"Nope. Give it a week, and you'll be as gorgeous as ever. Take these painkillers and get yourself home. You'll need to rest up, take some time off work for a week maybe but then you'll be able to forget this ever happened. Of course, if you do have unresolved pain or excessive bleeding, come back here."

"Thanks." I heaved myself upright and immediately felt giddy. Instantly, Persephone was at my side, as solicitous as ever.

Irritated, I shook her proffered arm away as we walked out of the hospital. The sunshine hurt my eyes and I raised my arm across my face to shield it from the dazzling light.

"I'm so sorry about your poor face. I've some sunglasses in my car, if you'd like?"

"And how the hell do you think I'd be able to wear them against my nose?"

23

"Sorry, sorry, of course. Sorry."

"Oh for pity's sake! Stop saying sorry, will you?"

She opened the car door for me to get inside and I stepped in, very gingerly, before slumping back against the leather seat. I felt distinctly unsteady.

Persephone climbed in far more elegantly and sat behind the wheel. She turned to me before switching on the engine.

"Fay, look, I am really sorry. Your lovely face is in a right mess and it's entirely my fault. If I hadn't been playing silly buggers with that drop-shot..."

I held up my hand to silence her, oddly touched by her compliment. I felt flattered and intrigued, while privately hoping she didn't think I was gay. People did – it was the shoulders - and, since Robin's death, I'd kept my own company, well, apart from the odd one night stand. And yes, okay, some had been women. I liked that side of femininity and envied female couples their co-operative intimacy but I didn't feel inclined to join the relationship club in any denomination.

"Please, Fay, let me make it up to you. You're in no fit state to look after yourself, unless, do you have a partner at home?"

I shook my head; pain shot across my face.

"Well, then, how about you coming to my house for supper, after all? I know you didn't want to when I asked you last time but I've got the house to myself and...well never mind all that...and I'd like to help." She ended limply.

What was she never minding about? Oh, what the hell. I felt too rotten to investigate. I speculated privately on the alternative agenda for the evening ahead. Microwave dinner, telly, shower and bed – or I could go mad and have a bath instead, except my tatty flat didn't have a bath.

Against my better judgement, against my intuitive nudges, out of sheer fatigue and pain, I agreed and opted for novelty. "Oh, alright then, if you insist."

Persephone brightened perceptibly. She started up the engine. My head throbbed with the vibration. Her brand new Mini-Cooper, slung low, hugged the road as she accelerated away from the hospital; very unlike my little hatchback, which had a habit of clutching, rather than adhering, to the tarmac.

Once we gained the main road, the powerful car zoomed up the winding hills towards the downs, while I gritted my teeth and surrendered.

I can't say I was surprised when she drew up in front of some impressive iron gates, one of which had been left open in welcome. Her Mini-Cooper scrunched across deep gravel and swept up in front of a beamed and thatched house whose three-pronged façade hid countless deep folds to the rear. Warm red bricks, in various shades of baked earth, jostled each other in herring-bone patterns between the silvered wooden beams. It was picture-postcard, chocolate-box beautiful and very, very large. It even had roses scrambling around the ancient front door.

The car engine hushed to the chorus of evensong from the garden birds. Persephone got out and fetched our sports bags from the boot and took them indoors, promising to come back and help me into the house, once she'd dumped them inside. I sat and waited in the silent car as the natural song of aeons past cascaded all around me in the momentary stillness. Out of habit, I fiddled with the silver chain in my pocket; my only keepsake from that last night with Robin. I never went anywhere without it. It comforted me, made me feel we were still connected somehow.

Wiltshire is a county that has long been inhabited by Homo sapiens. Stonehenge, Avebury and various white horses on hills are silent testament to that. As I sat in the quiet car, I sensed the humans who had preceded me. I witnessed them. History permeated my cells and something stirred within me. Ghosts from the past entered my soul, as they had before, and I had no strength left to resist them.

*"You are here at last. You are welcome in, but you can never leave."*

Still a little dizzy and now suffering a crippling headache, I tripped over the front doorstep and, in reaching out to save myself from falling, managed to knock over a pretty lamp standing on a small table on my left. The flagstone floor made an unforgiving target for its graceful ceramic base and shards of expensive pottery shot forth in all directions of the dark hallway. I had to admit Persephone couldn't have been more tolerant or kind. A dustpan and brush was rustled out of some deep cupboard in the hall's wainscot panels and the catastrophe swept into history, with the shade tucked back in the cupboard.

"Not to worry, I never liked it." Persephone smiled reassuringly.

Embarrassed by my habitual clumsiness, I followed my hostess into the biggest farmhouse kitchen that ever graced a glossy magazine.

A beamed ceiling sported baskets, jugs and dried hops above us and a royal-blue Aga hugged one wall. An elderly-looking cat opened a weary, hopeful eye as we ambled in and Persephone poured the shattered remains of the lamp's base into a discreetly hidden bin. All the kitchen cupboards were made of limed oak and solid granite topped the lot. A huge window behind the sink afforded a fine view of the walled garden and a large wooden table, with artfully unmatched chairs around it, supported a sumptuous basket of fresh fruit. The white walls were enlivened with some clever drawings, presumably sketched by my hostess.

Persephone welcomed me in and bade me sit.

I sat. A cup of Earl Grey tea appeared beside me but I wouldn't have recognised its delicate flavour, had Persephone not anxiously asked if I liked that sort of tea. I couldn't smell anything through my swollen nose.

"Are you hungry, Fay? You must be, after all that stress."

I grunted something about painkillers and rummaged in my handbag for the ones from the hospital.

She gave me a glass of fresh water in an instant. I chucked two down my neck and chased them with the tea, trying not to wince at the discomfort of swallowing.

I sat back and closed my eyes until the pain relief started to work its magic. When I opened them again, Persephone was wafting around the bright room in a vague but competent swish of activity, infusing the air with delicious aromas of garlic and saffron, rich enough even to penetrate my damaged olfactory system.

"Do you like prawns?" she asked, when she noticed I'd come to.

Feeling decidedly more human and even a little peckish, I told her that I like everything. My waist was a bit of a clue. Sitting back against the sofa, I watched in grudging admiration as she prepared a fragrant risotto. Within twenty minutes I was tucking in to a dreamy, creamy, heaven-scented meal and washing it down with a first-class chilled white Rioja that complemented the food to perfection.

Not being one to waste time on words when food this good – oh, alright then, any food – was being faithfully despatched to its rightful destination - my stomach, I ate in rapturous silence. Only when replete and after, out of courtesy you understand, a dutiful second helping had followed the first, I asked her how she could cook like an angel and still have the figure of one, not something I'd ever cracked.

"Oh, it goes back to my modelling days. You learn various tricks and I don't eat like this every day. Portions are important." And she grinned as I reached for a third helping, not wanting to waste the tempting little morsel left over in the saucepan. I let my hand drop guiltily. Persephone laughed out loud and relenting at last, I joined in, and the tension between us lifted.

"Are you feeling better now?" Persephone had a way of lifting her eyebrows when she enquired about something which was quite charming.

I nodded experimentally, delighted to find I could do so without pain. The combination of wine, pain relief and food seemed to have worked a little miracle.

"Would you like to change your top and have a little wash and brush up?"

I looked down at my polo-shirt and saw it was liberally splattered with blood. "That would be a good idea."

Persephone showed me into a swish cloakroom, off a utility room bigger and better fitted out than the kitchen in my flat. I splashed some water on my face, combed my disordered short hair and replaced my top with a clean one from my sports bag, carefully checking that my silver chain was still in my pocket. When I returned to the kitchen, feeling much restored, all the debris from our simple meal had been cleared away and I found Persephone had also changed out of her sports gear into fresh clothes.

"Fancy looking around the manor?"

She must have read my mind. We went on the grand tour. The old place was a labyrinth of antique corridors, ribbed with beams. I quickly lost my bearings after we climbed up the sturdy oak staircase that led off the dark hallway. The landing was narrow, with white plaster in smooth curves between blackened timbers. They'd obviously dispensed with a plumb line when they built it.

"How old is the house?"

"This part dates from the sixteenth century – the Elizabethan era, I think. Though it's been added to in a haphazard way ever since and the original hall was even older." Persephone marched me along too quickly for me to orientate myself so I just gave up and followed blindly. Walking about had made my head begin to thump again and I couldn't be bothered to concentrate.

"No planning applications needed in those glory days." I hoped my polite interest would be enough to pretend I cared, when all I longed for was a cold compress and a sit down.

She nodded her agreement as we went down a newish second set of stairs, ending up rather abruptly in a modern wing on the ground floor. My headache prevented me from being as curious as I might otherwise have been but I had the vague suspicion that we hadn't covered half the space in the manor house.

"This was added in the mid-seventies," Persephone said, as we stood together in a huge glass-fronted, vaulted extension on the west side of the house in which stretched clear blue water in a large, spot-lit swimming pool. It was nothing less than magnificent, if slightly reminiscent of shady seventies porn movies, but I couldn't admire it fully because of the pain now dominating my every thought.

"Could I trouble you for some more pain relief, please? The tablets are in my handbag." I grabbed the back of a cane chair, swaying slightly.

"Oh, you poor thing, of course. Sit yourself down and I'll fetch it."

She brought the bag and a glass of water from the kitchen. After I'd swallowed two more tablets, we sat around the pool watching the evening sun as it slipped down behind the trees. Gradually the throbbing in my face eased off and I started to relax, relieved not to have to force more polite conversation when I felt so whacked. When the evening shadows had lengthened across the velvet lawns, I broke the companionable silence. "Well, this is civilised."

Persephone smiled but looked a little strained. The phone rang and she jumped. I looked enquiringly at her but she just smiled again and trotted off to answer it. I was left to admire the surroundings in blissful solitude while ignoring her raised voice drifting in from the hallway. It was impossible not to notice the tone of the conversation, which sounded increasingly heated and angry, and I couldn't help wondering who she was arguing with.

"I tell you, it's true. No, I'm not lying!" Persephone's voice had become quite agitated.

I forced myself to focus on the golden orb of the sun sinking in a reluctant curtsey while the soft summer night stole the shadows. The dim lights around the pool beckoned to the moths, so I got up and slid the glass doors shut and inhaled the delicate aromas of honeysuckle and night-scented stock, which were strong enough to obliterate the all-pervasive smell of chlorine. It certainly beat my shabby flat in the Victorian terraced street where I lived, though I realised I ought to be getting back soon. There was the spectre of work tomorrow; I didn't feel the need for time off, now the swelling and the pain of my nose had subsided. Of course, the pain killers hadn't yet lost their effect.

Persephone returned from her phone call, her strained look only slightly masked by her lovely smile. "That was Paul, my husband. He's in Africa and has just found out the job is going to take longer than he thought. It came up suddenly last week but it was too good to turn down."

"Must be hard to tear himself away from here?"

She laughed nervously. "Yes. I wish he wasn't away so much but he loves his job." She still seemed on edge.

"I must take my leave." I peeled myself away from my cane chair. The movement jarred my head and made it throb all over again. I longed to climb into my own bed.

"Oh, must you go?"

"My country needs me. Work tomorrow and duty calls." I set my glass down on the glass table.

"But I thought the doctor said you would need a week off? And you don't have a car. I can't drive you home now I've had some wine."

Persephone looked crestfallen and a little petulant. This is a bit intense, I thought, perhaps she's bisexual after all. Better make haste because nice though she was, I really wasn't in the mood to oblige and, by the sounds of that phone call, her marriage wasn't in the best shape and I was certainly no counsellor. I started to shuffle towards the kitchen to get my things, muttering about calling a taxi. A loud crash interrupted my clumsy manoeuvres. Persephone jumped and grabbed my arm, pupils dilated and eyes wide in fear.

"Have you got another cat upstairs?" I asked. "I'm not allowed pets in the flat but we've got two at home. They are always jumping off the beds where they're not supposed to be and scaring the living daylights out of my poor old Mum."

Persephone didn't relax at my attempts at reassurance. "It's started early tonight. They must sense you're here."

"Who?"

"I don't know." Her voice cracked slightly.

30

"Is there something you need to tell me?" I sat back down next to the pool.

The moon was rising and casting its monochrome beams on the still water. I wasn't in the least perturbed. I'd grown up in the depths of Wiltshire countryside and knew that many odd nocturnal sounds could be assigned to animal behaviour of one sort or another. I remained determined to reject any other ideas. Persephone sat opposite me, her hands restless but her mouth silent, her teeth biting her lips.

I spoke into the awkward vacuum.

"I expect it's a fox prowling about the dustbins." My prosaic pronouncement produced a thin smile so I took heart and stood up.

"Well, I must be off, you know." I scrabbled in my jeans pocket for my mobile phone, which had the taxi firm's number on speed-dial.

"No! Wait, please. Would you like to stay the night here?"

I was quite surprised. "Err, I don't think so really, Persephone. It's very kind of you to offer but I need to change before work and sort my lunch out." I always took trouble over my packed lunch. Accountants have to break up their days somehow.

"I could lend you some clothes and make you lunch." Persephone's clutched her hands together, as if to control them from reaching out and making a grab for me.

I began to squirm. "No honestly, it's okay."

I turned to go, in what I hoped was a final and decisive manner. There was another crash from upstairs before I got half way to the door and this time, it sounded like glass breaking. The tiles echoed the noise in the moonlit cavernous space, magnifying its eerie effects.

Persephone screamed in a soft, strangled sort of way and finally, she did grab my arm. Recognising that fear, not my voluptuous charms, had prompted her invitation, my ego was damped down and my compassion rose up. I patted her trembling hand and it steadied us both.

"It's okay, Persephone. I am sure there will be a simple explanation for all the shenanigans."

"You don't understand," she whispered, pale as the moonlight, "this happens every night."

I felt the hairs on the back of my neck prickle and shivered. Swallowing in a throat that had suddenly become dry, I replied, also sotto voce, "Every night? No wonder you are scared."

She nodded, her face now drawn, as well as pale.

"The best thing is to investigate where the sound came from. I'm sure there will be a rational explanation. Would you, do you feel able, to check it out?"

"Now that you are here, I think I could manage it, Fay. I've always been terrified before."

My heart was beating pretty fast too.

Persephone softly stole up the wide wooden staircase that led up from the wainscoted hall. I followed, a reluctant investigator, with my heart still thumping loud enough to wake the dead and my squashed nose throbbing with a sickeningly synchronised beat.

## *"Now you will both listen to me."*

To say the hairs on the back of my neck were upstanding, as Persephone and I followed the direction of the sounds upstairs, would be a definite understatement. The ancient treads were made of oak, long beaten and worn by centuries of footsteps. They creaked under our modern trainers like a wooden sailing ship.

Persephone led the way to the back of the house, where a large, beamed bedroom overlooked the walled garden. Pushing open a heavy old door studded with iron nails, we peered into the moonlit room. An antique four-poster bed dominated the irregular space and heavy Jacobean tallboys graced the white walls.

All was silent. All was still. Our breathing eased a little. We looked at each other, confused and embarrassed. Had our imaginations run away with themselves?

As if reading my mind, Persephone said, "This isn't the only time this has happened. Paul says he never hears anything and it's true, it's all quiet when he's here. Sometimes I think I must be going mad."

"I heard it too, Persephone. But it could still just be a cat out on the tiles and thumping across the roof looking for love – or mice."

She laughed and relaxed. "Maybe you're right. Maybe I spend too much time here alone."

We turned to leave. Suddenly, a cold draught caught my sturdy legs. I flattered myself I wasn't the imaginative type.

"Do you feel that cold air?" I asked my hostess.

"No." She looked startled again.

I shivered. "Are there more old bedrooms in this part of the house?"

"Yes, this wing is all Elizabethan. Follow me." Persephone shut the bedroom door and led me further down the landing, deeper into the nether regions of the house.

33

Floorboards groaned and shifted under us again. The hairs on my neck rose upright once more. Every sense was alert.

"Be A Lert," I said, in a feeble attempt to lighten the atmosphere. "The country needs Lerts."

The old joke made Persephone chuckle quietly and she seemed to relax a little.

"Try in here." She pushed open another oak door and it gave out a long wheeze of rusty hinges. The temperature dropped dramatically as we softly entered the room. Again a four poster bed, as old as the original house, dominated the bedchamber, and an equally venerable trunk squatted at its foot. A few shards of glass lay in a heap on the floor next to the bed. This time Persephone didn't sweep them up as she had when I broke the lamp in the hall.

With my breath coming shallow and fast, I tiptoed into the room. Goose-pimples broke out in a rash all down my arms and I felt I had stepped into a freezer. Whether it was the coolness of the air or the sinking feeling in my heart, I at last admitted privately to being a bit frightened. A breeze stirred the bed curtains as if a hand brushed the fabric. A little dust fluttered into the still air, proving the shift of current about the bed. I sat down heavily on the wooden trunk and sighed.

I looked up at Persephone, wondering whether to confess about the depth of my dealings with the dead or not. I studied her face, thinking how little I knew her, though, in her desperation, she had obviously guessed the truth. After all, that's why I was in this situation. But she couldn't have known about my obsessive study of the occult or why Robin had died, could she? I reflected how keen she'd been to get me here. Had my squashed nose, I winced at my own pun, really been an accident? The words stacked up in my mouth contained my most private, innermost secrets. That cache of experiences over which I had plastered a concrete cover, fastened with reinforced steel and clamped down with a massive padlock, had never been shared with another soul since Robin's death.

Until now.

I sat, undecided, on the brink of truth. And there I dare say I would have left it, had the window, on this windless summer night, not blown wide open. Its rusty, simple clasp broke in the violence of its arc.

We both shrieked and, craven as it is to admit it, legged it back to the warm farmhouse kitchen where the electric lights hid no shadows and double glazing ensured that the windows stayed put.

We sat facing one another across the big refectory table, both instinctively clutching its reassuring, solid bulk and staring into each others' wide eyes.

Persephone broke the awkward silence first. My tongue had not yet rehydrated.

"Tea?" squeaked Persephone and I nodded, still mute with shock.

Over the bone china mugs, steam rising in soothing familiar wafts, Persephone was the first to confess after all. "Fay, I asked you to come back here to my house because I couldn't really face another night on my own with all the banging and crashing around me. I have been frightened witless. When I saw you at the squash court that first time and remembered you knew about ghosts and things, I knew I had to get you here somehow."

"Did you deliberately try to break my nose?"

"No, no! Of course not, but when I saw the book that fell out of your bag, I did decide to try and tempt you here. The accident was just that - purely accidental - but I wasn't sorry to find an excuse to bring you to the manor, and I did rearrange someone's game so I could play against you again."

"You rotten cow! Do you know how painful my face is? I feel I've got a bruised football stuck in my nose and the mother of all headaches." If it had been deliberate, I was out of there but then I remembered it was me that had got in the way by breaking the cardinal rule of squash by not returning to the 'T' in the middle of the court and some of my anger subsided.

"You must believe me, Fay. Honestly I never meant to hurt you in any way but truly, I'm not sorry you are here but of course I am sorry you are in pain. I was getting desperate. You see, Paul's been away for nearly a week now and it's just getting worse and worse. When I tell him, he laughs. Because he's never heard the noises, he thinks I'm being silly."

I made a mental note to tell this jerk a few home truths, should I ever be privileged to meet him.

I could no longer put off my own moment of honesty. "As a matter of fact, Persephone, you are right, this sort of experience is not new to me. I used to have them all the time as a child but that doesn't mean I'm a witch like the other kids said at school."

Persephone cringed under my angry glare.

"It wasn't just the kids at school, my family also thought I was nuts – a bit like your Paul with you, I suppose – and in the end I shut up about it. My mum insisted I train as an accountant – the most logical, dry and steady career she could think of. She wanted me to get busy and solvent and stop being so weird."

I decided not to elaborate on the isolation, ridicule and rejection I had suffered as a child before I'd met Robin, especially as she'd obviously joined in with it. As Persephone got up to refill the teapot, I seriously contemplated leaving. This wasn't my problem. I needn't stay. We had only shared a routine game of squash from the league table. I owed her no obligation bar a risotto and glass of wine. Oh and tea, I suppose. Trouble was, she was scared and I was lonely. The husband certainly didn't sound much cop.

I looked at the door. I looked at Persephone, hunched over the sink. There was no decision to be made. I held out my mug for a top up.

Persephone's dainty shoulders relaxed.

*"It goes well, she stays. Yes, sleep. Sleep here tonight. I have time, lots of time."*

There were modern bedrooms above the swimming pool extension and Persephone showed me into one of them. We had stayed up drinking cup after cup of tea and, even though we had switched to camomile, I had felt too wide awake for slumber until past midnight. I would be wrecked tomorrow.

There was no trace of chilly draughts on this side of the house, thank goodness. No intuitive hackles rose on the back of my neck and the bed looked inviting. I helped Persephone with the clean sheets and the ozone-rich smell of fresh linen relaxed me. Making sure I had all I wanted, including two more painkillers, she left for her bedroom at the front of the house. I turned back the cotton covers and slid between them gratefully. It had been a long day and there was much to absorb but I was asleep before any introspection could bear fruit.

I never saw the early August dawn, as my window faced west and it was quite late before I surfaced from my deep sleep. Shocked at the time when I looked at my watch, I used my mobile to phone the office and ring in sick. I was too knackered to work effectively anyway and my nose was still very sore and turning a dramatic shade of purple, which was rapidly spreading underneath my eyes.

Joan, my new office ally on the next desk to mine, picked up the call. For once, I had followed my mother's advice and kept my 'fancies' private at my latest workplace. As a result, Joan and I were getting along quite well, sticking to bland, safe topics like the weather and what was the special offer that day in the canteen.

"Morning, Fay, you're late."

"I know. Joan, I've had an accident playing squash and my face is black and blue."

"I've always thought squash was a man's game." She sniffed.

"Yes, well, I think I'll have to stay home today. I've got a thumping headache."

"You poor thing." Her smug tone didn't fool me into believing her sympathy genuine. Joan disapproved of all sports, preferring to get her exercise from using the stairs rather than the lift, with a martyred comment every time, while never failing to recommend I did the same.

"Would you tell Mrs. Burton for me?"

Our manager was a large, humourless woman who, like Joan, would never have understood why anyone would want to play squash in the first place. They'd have an enjoyable moment of self-congratulation over my injury, of that I was sure.

"Yes, no problem. You rest up now and get yourself well. A packet of frozen peas is the thing."

"Thanks, Joan, I really appreciate it. As it's Thursday, I think I'll take tomorrow as well. I don't want to frighten everyone in the office with my new colourful look. I'm on holiday next week anyway – so I won't see you until Monday week. Have a great weekend."

Joan signed off and I put the mobile down on the little side chest with relief. Days off were always welcome and I'd deliberately sneaked the bank holiday into my week's leave so I could take another day off some other time. The more the merrier. I hated my job with its mindless numbers and endless tax laws to get your head around. I could do it and it paid well, but it didn't exactly give me a reason to live.

But here, right now, someone really needed me.

It was an unusual feeling.

Maybe I *could* help Persephone. Maybe I could forget her flirting with my Robin after all, even if I could never quite forgive her.

***

The rich aroma of coffee guided me unerringly to the kitchen. A percolator bubbled in one corner as Persephone welcomed me with a dazzling flash of her Persil-white teeth – there had to be dentistry involved there. And had those bee-sting lips had a tiny injection too?

"Good morning, Fay. I hope you slept well?"

"Like a top. It's beautifully quiet here compared to my town flat. I bought it when I first moved to Swindon and was broke and somehow I just haven't got round to upgrading."

"I'm glad you were comfortable. Would you like some coffee? I've put a pot on." She retrieved something from the Aga, wearing oven gloves.

I sat down at the table. "I know – its siren call drew me from my slumber. Smells delicious - I'd love a big mugful please."

Persephone immediately poured some into a large bowl-shaped cup. "Milk or cream?"

"Persephone, don't tempt me with cream this early in the day! My resistance is still weak and anyway, I prefer it with milk and lots of sugar."

"Would you like croissants with it?" "Are you speaking in the plural?"

Persephone laughed, "Of course, if you are hungry enough?" She put the pastries down in front of me. They smelled heavenly.

"As you get to know me better, Persephone, you will learn that is usually a rhetorical question," I said, lunging for one of the golden croissants in the willow basket.

"They should still be warm, I popped them in the oven when I heard you get up."

"Hmm, very good," I spoke through a mouthful of pastry and chased it down with the delightful roasted coffee before asking, "Columbian?"

"No, actually, the coffee is from Peru – organic, of course."

"Oh, of course." I nodded through the ethical Peruvian steam. "Did you hear any more bumps in the night?"

"No, thankfully. Though I must admit I didn't sleep well because I was listening out for them."

"How long has it been going on? The bumps, I mean." I helped myself to a second croissant and spooned some strawberry jam inside. "Is this home-made?"

Persephone nodded. "There's not much else to do around here."

"Time well used," I said, just catching a juicy red berry before it slipped T-shirt-wards. "Mmm. Yummy."

Persephone looked pleased and then serious. "It's been going on ever since I came to live here after we got married last year. I moved in last March and very soon after, Paul was called away to a location in Siberia for a photo-shoot about tigers."

"Did they find one? I thought they were getting extinct." I ladled on some extra jam.

"No, that was the point. They didn't. He wasn't too happy about it when he got home, having frozen half to death in some Godforsaken outpost in outer Russia, and I didn't like to bang on about the noises and the furniture moving about."

"The furniture has been moving about?" Replete from my croissant guzzling and with caffeine organically waking up my sluggish brain, I sat up to listen.

"Yes, while Paul was away in Siberia things got quite out of hand. Heavy chests were hauled across the older bedrooms - really heavy ones - that couldn't possibly be moved accidently unless there'd been an earthquake." She tucked a strand of her hair behind her ear. The lobe sparkled with a single diamond stud. Expensive.

"And you didn't tell your husband about this?"

"Well," Persephone shifted in her seat, "I did, eventually, but he just laughed it off. As I said yesterday, it never happens when he's here, only when he's absent. So I can't blame him for thinking it's all a figment of my imagination."

Silently, I thought I could, but said, "Go on. What else has happened, Persephone? Look - on that note, do you have a nickname? Persephone is a bit of a mouthful, if you don't mind me saying so?"

Persephone laughed. "That's just what Paul said. He calls me 'Phoney' because we were always on the phone to each other before we married and," she look embarrassed, "I have had a little help with my, um, outline."

"Ooh really? Do you mean breast enhancement? I could never put myself through that – although I'd be better off with reduction surgery all around." I felt a secret satisfaction in this confession. After all, no-one could look that perfect without some help and added, with more truth than diplomacy (never my strong point), "Seems a bit mean for a nickname."

"Do you think so? I thought that, but I didn't like to say so to Paul." She fiddled with her wedding ring and another diamond sparkled above it on her finger.

"Why ever not?"

"Oh, he wouldn't like it."

"So what?"

Persephone stuck out her full bottom lip at my confrontational tone.

"Well, I'm not using that," I said. "I shall call you Percy; wasn't that what you were called in school? I remember the boys teasing you about it. Would that be alright?"

"Oh, yes, I'd like that, Fay. I never minded that school nickname."

I'll bet she didn't. I remembered how it had got her even more male attention at the time. "That's settled then."

"More coffee?"

"Love some." I held out my mug. "By the way, Percy – have you had breakfast?"

"Yes, thanks. I had a vegetable juice after my morning swim."

I spluttered coffee across the polished wood of the table, spraying the last remnants of croissant in a liberal sweep. "How long have you been up?"

"Well, I couldn't sleep." Percy wiped the table with her pristine dishcloth.

"Do you exercise every day?"

"Yes, it's a habit from my modelling days." She went to the butler sink and rinsed the cloth under its brass mixer tap.

"Do you polish your halo as well as this table?"

She laughed and said, with refreshing asperity, "Modelling can be very lucrative, Fay. I was pretty motivated. The agencies are ruthless, you know. They're always wanting you to shave off another centimetre from your hips while inventing new expenses for themselves out of your fee."

"Sounds painful on both counts." I pulled down my jumper which had ruckled up over my belly.

"It is. You have to negotiate with parasitic bread-heads until you find a decent representative who won't rip you off. People always assume all you have to do is laze about on car bonnets or beaches in paradise. It's a much tougher life than you might think and the lush-looking locations are usually studios with false backdrops in some grotty part of London." She wrung out her cloth and draped it over the tap.

"Point taken."

"And now it's brought me all this." Percy waved her slender arm in a semi-circle. "If I hadn't met Paul on a photo-shoot I wouldn't be living here."

I added to myself, or be lonely and scared.

I traced my finger on the rim of my mug. "So, how come you and Paul can afford this place, if you don't mind me asking? Must be worth a bomb. I hadn't realised modelling was *that* lucrative."

"No, I don't mind. It *is* worth a fortune. Paul inherited it from his mother's side of the family. I don't even know the family surname on her side, to be honest, because he never talks about her. He's an only child and she had become very eccentric, apparently. I never met her, you see, she died before we met."

"What about his father?"

"Oh, he died much earlier, under a bit of a cloud, I think. Paul is very tight-lipped about it but I sense that he bears his mother a grudge about his father's death, as if she were to blame in some way."

"Curiouser and curiouser. Percy, do you think Paul's father might be the source of these nocturnal goings-on?"

Percy raised one delicately arched eyebrow. "It had crossed my mind, then I dismissed it because, surely, Paul would feel it too, if it was his own father?"

"Not necessarily, in my experience. The closer you are sometimes, the harder it is to reach them." Especially beloved boyfriends who'd died tragically early.

"Them?"

"People who've died but, for want of a better expression, not passed over." I wriggled in my chair. We were entering what I considered to be forbidden territory.

"How much experience have you had of," Percy hesitated and looked out of the window at the garden, "of...of ghosts?" She exhaled the last word in a whisper, as if not daring to label something or someone from the spirit world.

I sighed, thinking, here we go again. I was about to cross that murky threshold once more; this was the turning point beyond which I just knew I could not return, once committed. But, I chided myself, I had already made that commitment last night. It was time to go for it.

I let my eyes rest on the well-kept garden, enjoying its neutrality and order. There was a huge weeping willow tree in the far corner; presumably next to a stream or wetlands. The willow's long fronds lifted and sighed in the summer breeze. Had this giant tree witnessed the lives of those souls who were not at rest here?

"I don't like the term ghosts," I began. "They're just people like us, usually unhappy ones who did not find peace after they died. When I was a girl, I used to chat to them. Like your Paul, I was an only child, so my mother wondered who I was talking to. The doctor said a lot of children have imaginary friends and told her not to worry."

I looked at Persephone and she gently nodded me encouragement. After a moment's hesitation, I continued. "After my Dad died, I could chat to him for a little while and then, when he was confident I could cope, he passed over and I've not heard him since. He remains the only close person I've ever reached. Mum found that really weird but it seemed natural to me. Dad was overweight – I take after him – and loved his food. He was chopping wood for the fire one day and had a massive heart attack in the garden. It was a long cottage garden and he was out of sight of the house."

My mouth had gone dry so I gulped some coffee down, spilling a little on the table as I replaced my mug. "He was completely cold by the time we found him. He hadn't come in for his dinner, you see, and that, as you might imagine, was completely out of character. He was just fifty. My Mum worries I'll go the same way if I keep stuffing my face, so I took up squash to keep fit."

Percy had looked sympathetically sad while listening to my tale but she smiled at my last comment and sat down in front of me. She poured herself a cup of coffee and drank it black, unsweetened and calorie free. "I'm sorry about your Dad."

"Yes, so am I. He was a good laugh and kept my Mum from getting anxious." I added another teaspoon of sugar to my mug and topped it up.

"But you said he wasn't the only ghost, I mean, deceased person, you'd had, um, contact with?" Percy's face was soft, without judgement, unlike some of my past friends – and enemies. Under her current benign gaze I had to force myself to remember that she had been a member of that vindictive clique at school.

I stirred my sugar, enjoying swirling the grainy sludge at the bottom of the mug until it dissolved, and avoiding her gaze. "No, far from it. Of course, I couldn't keep telling Mum about them after Dad died, she'd have had a fit, so I got more secretive. Friends at school, I'm sure you heard the rumours, thought I was strange too and kept their distance, so I learned to tell jokes and shut up about my other, shall we say, acquaintances? I could trust my boyfriend, Robin, but he died very young, about ten years ago. I think you said you remembered it?"

"Yes, of course. The local papers left no-one in ignorance of his accident." Persephone rearranged the fruit in the bowl on the table.

"I know, we had journalists camped on the doorstep for days, trying to wheedle the sordid details out of me, but I didn't talk to them, or anyone else. The gossips could say what they liked, I no longer cared what anyone thought. Still don't."

"I'm sorry for what you went through. You must miss him very much. Children can be very cruel." Persephone topped the pile of fruit with some grapes, taking one to eat.

"You were quite popular, as I remember?" I changed the subject back to her, not wanting to share more about Robin with the girl who'd caused me so much anxiety. "Especially amongst the boys. You were in the year below me, weren't you?"

"Yes, everyone thought I was older because I was such a lanky kid. I didn't really bloom until I was well into my teens and learnt how to make the most of myself. There was a bit of jealousy when I got my first modelling gigs but then I left home and went to London, so it became irrelevant."

I envied her this sangfroid at such a young age. I must have been in the sixth form college down the road by the time she left school and struggling with life without Robin. I couldn't remember anything about that black time.

Percy brought me back into the present. "But, Fay, please answer my original question. I want to know more about your communications with – what do you call it? The other side?"

"It's corny but actually not a bad description," I answered, reluctant to return to our earlier theme. I still felt cautious sharing this stuff but, having decided to help her, despite all the mixed feelings these memories had conjured up, I went on, fingering the chain in my pocket for comfort, as was my habit.

"I see it as a parallel reality. We're here - warm blooded, needing food and drink – some more than others. We can touch this wooden table and feel its solid mass. We can feel the rain and sun, hear music and move about. Well, they can't do any of those things but they can still see us, sense how we are feeling and their own feelings are still very much part of them. They have no shape or real form unless they decide to project it but that takes a lot of energy; a lot of emotion."

"Have you seen them, then?" Percy shivered, despite sitting next to the warm Aga.

"Oh yes, many times but not for long – it's too exhausting for them but very interesting to see how people looked, what they wore from different eras. Quite comical sometimes."

"But weren't you frightened?"

"No, not really. Maybe because I'd always had these conversations. They were as real to me as this one. Until Robin....you know. That's when I stopped encouraging them and turned to dull, humdrum accountancy."

"What really happened that night, Fay?"

I felt angry she was pushing at my memories. "Don't want to talk about it."

Percy's forehead creased into a frown. "Why?"

"Damn it, Percy. Must you keep on about it? Listen, it was horrible and it did frighten me. Just as in this world – our daylight everyday normal world – there is good and evil – so it is after death. That night I tasted evil and I never want to again." I looked back out of the window, noticing that the willow fronds were waving in the breeze, wishing I was outside next to it, instead of being interrogated.

"I see, I'm sorry to keep on." Persephone was straightening the table mats now. Had she got obsessive compulsive disorder?

"No, I can see you are very worried and I have been studying how to deal with my visitations lately;  though I wouldn't say I'm anywhere close to being able to control what happens. You saw that book that fell out of my bag, didn't you?"

I looked up at her, surprised at how white she had gone.

"Yes, Percy, of course, I do realise that's why you asked me here - I'm not as stupid as I look. But I must warn you, maybe *you* don't understand what you are taking on."

"Yes, yes it is the reason I asked you here, but if you don't want to confront my ghosts, I would understand." Percy looked crestfallen and alarmingly distressed.

"Did I say that?"

## *"It lies outside; come, come"*

"So, Percy, if we're going to make any progress, you'll need to tell me more about your encounters here at the manor," I said, as we sat over the remains of another light but delicious lunch.

Percy's obvious unease had finally persuaded me to stop over for a few days and, despite my own fears, I was intrigued by the disturbances she'd witnessed. I hadn't booked a trip anywhere else for my week off, only planned some DIY that I'd be very pleased to avoid. When I'd taken a taxi home to pick up some clothes, and my car, earlier that morning, the comparison between my little flat and the grandeur of Meadowsweet Manor had been stark. I luxuriated in the warmth of its big kitchen, the contented rumblings of my stomach and my new unexpected friendship. When my own anxieties about why I was invited here punctured my smugness, I ignored the butterflies trying to over-ride my mood.

Later that afternoon, we wandered around the manor's lands. I was surprised to see how far they extended beyond the immediate walled garden. The large weeping willow stood in the corner like a green fountain and hid a decaying wooden gate set in the moss-covered stone wall. When Percy unlatched it, with some difficulty due to its rusty hinges, a big meadow stretched out in front of us. Once through the gate, we walked past the weeping willow to a tumbledown chapel, whose broken walls looked forlorn in the unkempt field. Marsh-grass grew in an erratic pattern towards a line of ordinary willows of upright habit, standing a few hundred yards away.

"Very boggy ground by the looks of it," I said. "This whole area feels sad and neglected."

Percy looked at me, her green eyes inscrutable but sharp. "It's funny you should say that, Fay, because I hate this corner of the garden. It gives me the creeps. You can't walk over it in the winter, it's too wet and there's an odd smell too."

I sniffed. "Hmm, you're right. Reminds me of bad drains. Must be the waterlogged soil." I pointed to the heap of stones around the damaged building. "Was this the village church in years gone by, do you know?"

"Paul says not. It was just for the people who lived in the manor house, the ones who re-built it in the 1600's."

"Pity no-one maintained it." I wished Percy hadn't mentioned the fetid pong. Now I was conscious of it, the noxious odour seemed to be all pervasive and getting stronger by the minute.

Percy went around the back of the ruined chapel. "See here? That line of boggy marsh-grass weaves its way towards an old pond over there."

"Oh yes, maybe they were trying to drain the water away from the little church." I drew my muddy foot out of thick mud with a squelch. "I don't think they quite got the engineering right. Not enough of a slope."

"The boundary is over there, Fay – see that stone wall?" Percy pointed to a ramshackle wall about two hundred metres from where we were standing. It formed an uneven circle around the field.

"Was that the original boundary?"

"I don't know. I doubt it. I've always assumed that the manor had a large farm with lands attached but I've never delved into the local history books."

"I think we should." I tried to ignore the fact that the smelly mud had got inside my porous trainers and between my toes. "It would be fascinating and might shed light on who is trying to communicate with us – or you rather."

"Oh, I don't think they are trying to connect with me specifically." Percy looked alarmed.

"They aren't talking to anyone else, are they? Your Paul seems totally incommunicado."

Again, Percy looked cross at the criticism of her husband. I decided to change the subject. I noticed her white trainers were still unblemished and relatively dry. How had she managed that?

"Do you think anyone was buried here? Members of the family perhaps? Or did they use the village churchyard?"

"Again, I don't know. Paul has never shown any interest in this area of the garden, except for photographing the wildlife. There are lots of dragonflies in the early summer and he loves all the meadowsweet over there."

"Ah, is that meadowsweet? I'm clueless about plants. I assume it's always grown here in abundance as the manor is named after it. How lovely." Privately, I wondered how anyone would want to spend hours in this stinking swamp, however fascinating its insects might be. "Shall we investigate the village church records and find out?"

"That would be interesting, but maybe tomorrow. It's starting to get a bit chilly and I think it must be time for supper." Percy turned back towards the house.

"You're talking my language, Percy." I attempted a jump over the boggiest looking stretch of marsh only to land heavily in more mud. The brown sludge sprayed up the legs of my jeans in an ugly stain. "Bugger," I swore under my breath.

Percy walked towards the house in long-legged strides but when we reached it her pale blue chinos hadn't a single mark on them.

"I'll go and change before supper, Percy. I seem to have brought half the garden with me."

Percy laughed me away and turned to the kitchen sink with a motherly smile which only irritated me further. After scrubbing my jeans and trainers in my swish en-suite bathroom and hanging them over the shower to dry, I returned to the kitchen wearing fresh clothes and shoes, sniffing the spices in the stir fry Percy had rustled up.

Now I sat, clean and replete, ready to earn my keep with some focussed attention on the problem at hand. "Right then. Let's make a start."

Percy answered my queries patiently. "Okay. The – encounters – as you call them, began the first time Paul was away, like I told you. To start with, I thought it was just an old house creaking and noises I could reason away. Then, just like last night, I felt cold draughts on warm days and things moving to places I hadn't left them."

"Anything else? Did you hear any voices or see any human shapes?"

"No, nothing like that, but there *was* something else."

"Oh? What was that?" I felt a gentle tingle in my spine. I hadn't had one of those in years, not since that concrete lid was clapped down.

"Well, I'm not sure if it's connected, but every time a major incident occurred, I smelt – only faintly, you understand – a hint of roses."

"Roses?"

"Yes, I have aromatherapy massages regularly and it's my favourite essential oil so I know I'm not mistaken."

"Aren't there roses growing against the front door?" I was determined to remain rational for as long as possible.

"Yes, and under the sitting room window, but they don't flower in winter!"

I liked it when Percy asserted herself and wondered how often she did that with her absent spouse.

"No, of course not, you're right. So these spooky happenings were a regular thing throughout the time you've been here then?"

Percy looked a little irritated. "I told you, Fay, only when Paul's away but yes, consistently since I've lived here."

I nodded, hopefully sagely. "Have you done any research on the history of the manor house?"

"No, not really. To be honest, I didn't want to find out. I dreaded discovering that someone had been murdered here or some other tragedy had caused the disturbances. I kept wondering if it was something to do with Paul's parents and that's why he won't discuss it. But why would they try to come through me instead of him? Then I decided if I did find out anything it would just make me more frightened and I tried to ignore it." Percy switched on the dishwasher and it purred into life.

"That's perfectly understandable. Would you mind if we did some now? Have you got a computer here?"

"Yes, there's one in Paul's study."

"Good. And I assume you've got broadband?"

"Of course, there's the router, behind your head."

Strangely, I hadn't bothered to even try surfing the 'net while I'd been there and had not had any desire to check my

50

emails, for once. I had to admit it had felt good to be off the hook.

"Great, I could use my phone, but it's always easier with a larger screen, then you can follow the threads using multiple windows."

I followed Percy back through the hall where the wood panelling made it dark; womb-like. The tiny diamond-shaped windows around the door lent little light and the late summer evening was fading fast, with looming clouds making it feel more like autumn. Percy showed me into a room at the front part of the house which looked as old as the hall.

We entered a small study. A disproportionately large fireplace of carved local stone faced the door and laden bookshelves lined the walls on either side of it. There were lots of black boxes amongst the books on the shelves, presumably full of Paul's camera equipment, and the surface of the large desk was obscured by the untidy mound of papers that lay upon it, laced with dust. The monitor of a desk-top computer rose above the debris, its keyboard buried under the clutter.

"Paul doesn't like me to move any of his stuff so I never bother to clean in here. I hope the computer still works. I haven't switched it on in weeks so it'll probably go into frantic updating mode and crash. He takes his new tablet everywhere he goes and I just use my phone usually." Percy touched a couple of buttons on the old-fashioned computer and its lights blinked alive.

"Yes, handy aren't they? Well, we can resort to them if this doesn't fire up." As if to contradict me, the computer screen flickered into life.

Percy sat down in front of it and typed in its password, 'meadowsweet'. I lifted off a pile of photography magazines from an ancient wooden chair in one corner, blowing the dust off its seat before placing it next to Percy and sitting down to squint at the screen.

The computer updated itself and pinged it was ready.

"What shall I type into Google then?" asked Percy, her fingers poised over the keyboard.

"Hmm, try your password. 'meadowsweet' wasn't it? But add 'manor' and 'Wiltshire'. Let's see what comes up."

Percy used the index finger of each hand to fulfil my request and up came dear old Wikipedia with a wealth of facts about stately homes in the county.

"Bingo!" Percy turned and grinned at me.

I rummaged in my tracksuit jacket for my reading glasses but, by the time I'd carefully propped them on my bruised nose, there was a loud bang and the computer screen went black.

"Oh! What happened?" Percy stared at the blank screen.

"Has all the power gone out?" I got up to try the light-switch. Nothing.

"Oh dear, it must be a power cut. I hope it hasn't damaged the computer, Paul will be furious if it has."

"Never mind Paul. Do you often get power cuts around here?"

"No, I've never had a full one before, although the lights have flickered on and off a few times. Fay – do you think? Surely, it can't be connected to, to...them?"

"Dunno. Wouldn't be surprised. They're pretty good at interfering with electrical stuff."

Percy shivered. "I hope we haven't lost any data on the computer's hard drive."

"Worried about your husband again?" I asked, trying not to sound sarcastic and fearing I hadn't succeeded. I rarely did.

"Hmm, very." Percy looked genuinely worried.

"Doesn't he have external hard drives for storing stuff?" I said, trying to mollify her.

"Ye-es, but he says it uses so much space because they're all photos. It's alright for the new ones because these days they don't take up so much storage and they're stashed on his new computer, the one he's taken with him. He's told me he's got loads of old ones on there he still hasn't backed up. He'd be furious if he lost them."

I checked my next caustic comment about Paul's apparent inability to use cloud storage for his precious archive of pictures and addressed the practical issue of the moment. "Listen, Percy, show me where your fuse box is. Let's see if we can get the electricity back on and then we can test Paul's computer to see if it's okay."

"Yes, good idea. It's this way."

Back we went into the gloomy hall. Percy went to the wainscoting and opened the same panel into which she'd shoved the broken lampshad on my arrival. I hadn't noticed how large the cupboard was, hidden under the stairs. Using her phone as a torch, she bent double and went inside.

"Aaagh!" she shrieked, jumping backwards and cracking her head on the low architrave.

"What is it?"

"The biggest spider I've ever seen!" Percy's eyes were wide with dismay.

I laughed with relief. "Is that all? I'm not afraid of crawlers. Where's the fuse-box?"

Percy pointed a shaking finger into the black hole of the cupboard. With my heart thudding, I switched on the torch on my own phone and clambered inside. The cupboard was huge and smelt of mice. Dusty crates huddled under the slope of the stairs to my right and on the left was an ancient Bakelite fuse-box, caked in cobwebs. I blew them away and the resulting cloud of dust and detritus made me cough and sneeze.

"Are you alright, Fay?" Percy's pale face loomed into the cupboard. The beam of her phone torch distorted her regular features into odd flickering shadows.

Not being as ladylike as my hostess, I wiped my nose on my sleeve, wincing at the pain, and answered, "Yes, fine, just about to tackle this ancient set of fuses. Has Paul never heard of re-wiring?"

"Heavens, I don't know. I leave all that side of things up to him."

I switched off the main power switch and then prised off the cover of the Bakelite fuse-box which revealed a row of old-fashioned fuses standing to attention. I reached out and carefully removed each one using the light from my phone, which I'd balanced on the top of the box, and tried the trip switch. Nothing. I worked my way along the row examining each one methodically but they all looked fine. As I rummaged around in the cavernous hole, I stubbed my toe on a metal toolbox. "Eureka!"

"What is it? Can you get the lights back on?" Percy's voice held more hope than I liked to hear.

"Give us a chance! I've found a toolbox and ah! yes, a screwdriver. That might come in handy but I can't see another fuse-box anywhere. Is there another trip switch?"

"Oh, I hadn't thought of that. Paul did show me. Look on the left of the fuse-box."

I worried that both our phones would be running low on their batteries if we kept using them as torches. I speculated whether Percy had any battery-powered torches in the old place, as I groped the wall on the left of the box. I didn't feel quite brave enough to turn my phone light off and used it to cast about for a switch within the depths of the cupboard. My fingers touched a protruding plastic knob and I focussed the light on it. This big black trip switch was also up, as it should be if the electricity was on. I flicked it down and then up again. Nothing.

I didn't find another fuse-box but deep in the recesses of this wooden cave my dwindling torch picked out something shiny. My eye had been caught by the faint glimmer of yellow metal. Hoping it might be the modern fuse-box we so desperately needed to re-instate the electricity, I explored its bumpy surface with tentative fingers. The fading beam of light revealed a hefty book fastened tight shut by a metal clasp. I lifted the heavy tome up, surprised by its weight, and stepped out of the closet into the dark hallway.

Percy had disappeared. I placed the book down on the hall table, narrowly missing a vase of roses.

"Hell's teeth!" I exclaimed, frightened I might have drowned it in rose water.

Percy came hurrying back into the hall. "I've found another torch but the battery is fading already. Oh, it's that rose smell again. Fay, are *they* here?"

"What? No, don't be silly! It's this bowl of roses. You must have put them there yourself."

"No, no I didn't." Percy shone her weak torchlight on the hall table whose polished surface was now empty, apart from the dusty book, which smelt more of mice than of flowers.

"But I saw them! Clear as day, they were. In fact I thought I'd knocked them over and was worried they'd spill water on this old book I've found."

"Clear as day? How can you say that when it's pitch dark? I think you must be imagining things now, Fay."

I shook my head to clear it of the image of the rose bowl. "That's really weird. Never mind, look at this old book. I think it might be a bible. The perfect start to our research. Now all we need is some modern illumination. I'm going to look again in that cupboard for another fuse-box. That ancient one can't be all there is."

"Okay." Percy didn't even bother to look at the hall table where the bible was waiting, solid and real. I wondered if she thought I'd imagined that too. Well, electric light would reveal all. I stepped back inside the fusty cupboard and laboriously explored the entire space, spitting out cobwebs as I crawled about.

"It's no good, Percy. I can't find anything or see anything wrong with the fuses. I can't understand it at all. Have you another, brighter torch?"

"Of course, how silly of me not to fetch the garden one. It's by the back door in the utility room. I'll get it now."

Percy darted off again and went through a door on the other side of the hall to the study. I stood impatiently watching for her return. I couldn't wait to get my hands on that bible and see what secrets it might reveal about the mysteries this old manor house had hidden.

And I had not imagined those roses.

*"The soft darkness hides my shadow but I am reaching her. She sees through a veil, a veil too dark for me to pierce. I will crush my roses for her to smell my scent."*

Lit by Percy's rather feeble torch, I carried the bible into the study and tried to clear a space for it on the cluttered desk but it was so huge it wouldn't fit amongst the hardware and papers. I pushed the computer to the back of the desk and laid the age-worn book down on the leather-topped surface I'd exposed.

Rain pattered gently against the mullioned window pane. Summer seemed to have disappeared with the daylight.

I was alone.

For the first time in my life, I decided to invite the deceased into my head instead of resisting them. Using the calm I had cultivated through Tai Chi, I quietened my mind while letting it become open to communication. After a few moments, the familiar chill crept through me and my skin broke out in goose-bumps, but I resisted shivering, instead welcoming the dreaded iciness into my veins and accepting it spreading through me without a whimper of complaint. My thumping heart was less easy to control and I had to content myself with ignoring the rush of adrenaline countermanding my attempt at a truly meditative state.

I laid my hands on the unopened bible and emptied my mind. The room was silent, apart from the tapping of the rain against the old distorted glass in the windows, now muffled by the drawn curtains. Memories, centuries of them, shifted into my receptive fingers. The skin of my hands rested on the tanned pigskin. I settled myself in the chair and its rush seat creaked a little.

The room hushed around me and was still.

A strange smell assaulted my nostrils at first. I sniffed. The scent was not of roses this time but blood. Fresh blood, unmistakable with its unique animal aroma. My own drained away and then I did shiver in the chilly room. I shut my eyes and concentrated. My fingers trembled on the book's cover as the tang of iron-rich blood grew stronger. Then I heard a confused jumble of men shouting and metal clashing against metal. Frustratingly, no pictures came to my mind's eye as they usually did, unbidden. Was I hearing a battle? It was too tenuous to be sure, without images. I waited, sensing I mustn't rush this.

Through the thin skin of my eyelids, the darkness lifted. With my eyes still shut, I thought I was beginning to see the pictures that would colour in the sounds of conflict.

A sudden pain jolted me out of my reverie. Hot wax had spilled on to my cold fingers. I gasped in surprise as my hands jumped away from the bible in reflex. I opened my eyes and the smells and sounds evaporated into a pool of yellow candlelight.

Percy had returned holding an antique candelabra aloft and its bright flames confused me for a moment. I tried to hide my disappointment in a smile but it was probably just as well we didn't have harsh electrical light, for I doubt my face would have convinced anyone.

"Oh sorry, Fay, I didn't mean to burn you. The garden torch is missing. I looked everywhere but I couldn't find it. I hope these will be enough to see by." Percy placed the candelabra down on the desk. The three tall candles looked a little wobbly in their silver cups but they illuminated the bible with a good, strong light and brought me back into the land of the living.

"It didn't really hurt, Percy, don't worry. Those candles are great. I can see much better now." No point telling her about those strange sensations unless I had to. I had a feeling more would come once we read the pages of this big book. And anyway how could I trust this first experiment? How could I know I hadn't projected those sensations from my subconscious?

Percy settled herself on the chair next to mine. "Shall I open it?" She spoke reverently but I could hear the excitement underneath.

"We won't find out much if you don't."

Gingerly, just using the very tips of her long, slender fingers and thumb, Percy unclasped the brass latch and lifted the embossed leather cover. The spine cracked and groaned with reluctance. We looked at each other. Percy looked as wary as I felt.

"Go on, Percy, turn those pages. They're not alive you know."

White lies don't count, do they?

She swallowed and nodded. The next page was beautifully inscribed with old-fashioned letters and I read its legend out loud.

# THE HOLY BIBLE
Containing the Old Testament
And The New
Newly translated out of the old tongues
IMPRINTED IN LONDON
BY ROBERT BARKER
Printer to the King's Most Excellent Majestie
## ANNO 1613

"Blimey, 1613; that's over four hundred years ago." I peered closer to read the date.

"It is hard to believe," nodded Percy in agreement and gently turned the next crinkly page of parchment.

The genealogy tree of Adam and Eve was drawn on the yellowed parchment in exquisite detail. We gazed at them cavorting under its branches, stark naked and unabashed in the Garden of Eden.

"Our idyllically happy forebears," I chuckled. "If only life had remained that simple and she hadn't snacked on that apple. It's not as if she looks hungry. Look at the size of those thighs!"

Percy laughed and broke the tension that had built up ever since the computer had blown the electricity supply. "So, you wouldn't have yielded to temptation then, Fay?"

"Touché." I acknowledged the hit with a nod.

Percy turned over the next leaf in the bible.

"Aha! This is what we are looking for." I read the next bit out loud.

In a much less even hand, was written the title,

# HEREIN LIES THE RECORD OF THE FOULKES FAMILY - THEIR HOLY UNION AND ISSUE

The first entry was a joyful one.

### The Marriage of Lord Edward Foulkes
### of Meadowsweet Manor
### to Eleanor Margaret Brynne of Brambleton House
### this day of our Lord the 5th of May 1615

"Look, Percy, Lord Edward Foulkes must have started the bible when he married this Eleanor."

"Yes, how lovely. Then she must have become Lady Eleanor, like that old folk song. I love that song. What was the name of the group who sang it?"

"Oh, yes, some bearded hippies, wasn't it?"

"Didn't they have a name from the north, something quite romantic?"

"Lindisfarne?"

"That's it." And Percy broke into song.

Her voice was surprisingly tuneful and melodious. I didn't join in, knowing that mine sounded more like cracked ice. I confined myself to reading out the next, less happy, entry when she had finished singing:

### Given to us this day of our Lord the 7th June 1617, a
### daughter, baptised Eleanor Joan Foulkes
### Taken by our Lord the 9th June 1617, the said Eleanor
### Joan Foulkes

"Oh how sad! Their baby died two days after it was born!" Percy looked really upset.

"The next one lived though." I read out,

**Given to us this day of our Lord 12th August 1618, a son, baptised Ralph Edward Foulkes**

"But then they lost three daughters in a row." Percy shook her head sadly.

"Yes, Juliet, born in 1619; Mary, a year later, and then another girl, Lucy, in 1621. See, they all died within a week of being born. How exhausting for the Lady Eleanor. It hardly bears thinking about - a baby every year. There must have been a genetic problem with the female Foulkes line because look, the next one's a boy and he seems to have survived, like Ralph."

Percy read the next line:

**Born this day of our Lord, the 25th September 1622, a son, baptised Will Harold Foulkes**

"So, she had two boys then but no girls, poor woman. Look, she loses another two a few years later," I pointed to the record of another daughter who died shortly after birth in 1633.

"Poor woman indeed, Fay, the next entry is really sad, look, she had another daughter but Lady Eleanor must have died during childbirth and then this last little girl died only two days later, like all the others."

"What a shame. All that giving birth and she copped it with the last daughter. What a tragedy."

"At least Sir Edward had his two boys to console him." Percy sat back from the desk, her shoulders slumped.

"Yes, now I wonder what happened to them?" I leant over her to turn the page. "That's strange. Look, Percy, the next page has been torn out."

"Oh, yes." Percy ran her finger down the inside spine of the bible, where a ragged edge showed where the page had been ripped away. "Now why would anyone do that?"

"To cover something up? To hide ugly facts?" I felt irritated we could go no further.

"Or maybe it was too painful – a scandal?" Percy's already large eyes widened.

"It's so frustrating; there's no further reference to the Foulkes family." I flicked over the next few pages and found the history of the house continued right through Georgian and Victorian times with a different family and written in a different hand, labouring under the unedifying surname of Slaughter, ending with a sad entry in 1917 when the last surviving child perished, living up to his name in World War One aged 19, without issue, ending their line forever.

"What a horrible name," Percy said.

"Perhaps they'd made their money from butchering and took over the manor from the Foulkes. It's funny, I thought families kept their bibles with them, rather than leaving them in a house, but I suppose, if they'd died out... The Slaughters don't seem to have had much luck with having children, either. Look - only one child, seldom two from each generation." I turned the remaining pages to see if I could find out any more but it was just standard bible text after that. It was beautifully printed with the first letter of each paragraph carefully coloured in and its enlarged print drawn with a fat, italic nib but it told us nothing more.

"Maybe there is a loose page amongst the bound ones? And I wonder why the Wade family never made entries in this bible? Perhaps Paul's mother's maiden name was Slaughter, but then the name died out when that David Slaughter was killed in World War One and the females married and took different surnames. I suppose there might have been a cousin who inherited." Percy picked up the heavy volume and very carefully held it along its spine with the open pages facing down towards the floor.

She gave it a gentle shake, but the only thing that fell out was a single rose petal.

*"I made a real petal; unlike the rose bowl, it remains on the floor. Pick it up, hold it. Feel my presence. Smell my scented rose."*

I bent down, picked up the little pink petal and held it out to Percy. It sat, quivering a little, in the palm of my hand. I laid it on the desk beneath the soft candlelight. We stared at it as if we had never seen a flower petal before; as if it could speak.

"The scent is overpowering. What does it mean?" whispered Percy.

"It might mean nothing at all but you did say you had smelt roses before and I definitely saw a whole bowl of them on the hall table, even though they mysteriously disappeared afterwards."

"It must be a clue to who is trying to talk to us."

"I suppose it must be but what on earth is the connection to roses? There was no-one of that name listed in the family bible."

"Fay, wasn't there a War of the Roses? I haven't a clue about it but I seem to remember a lovely rose emblem at the beginning of that programme on the telly last winter."

"Yes, that's right." The image prompted my rusty memory. "Richard had the white rose from the house of York. Henry the seventh took the Lancastrian red rose and combined it with Richard's white one as the new Tudor emblem."

"Presumably he was just before the eighth one with all the wives?"

"Yes, he was his father. He had a good reign but then he was succeeded by his thug of a son, Henry, as you say, of the six wives. His only son, Edward, didn't survive long, so his daughters inherited. The eldest being Bloody Mary – a right psychopath – and then clever, stable Elizabeth the First, but I don't see how its connected to roses here."

As I said the word 'connected' the rose petal lifted, as if someone had blown on it.

Percy grabbed my arm. "Look, it moved. The petal moved, Fay. Holy shit, this is scary."

"Now, let's not get this out of proportion, Percy. The wind has picked up outside; it could simply be a draught from the gaps around the window pane."

Percy gulped and nodded but her eyes never left the little rose petal.

Neither did mine, as I registered the fact that the candles hadn't flickered at all. So, no draught then.

"Percy, let's look at those first dates in the bible again. Do they correspond with the Wars of the Roses?"

Percy turned the stiff pages back to the one with the earliest entries. "It starts with the wedding of Edward and Eleanor in 1615 – is that during the Wars of the Roses? My knowledge of history is very patchy."

"No, that was earlier, much earlier. Now let me think. Elizabeth Tudor died in 1603; now, who succeeded her? James, that's it - James the First – bit of a dodgy character but I've a feeling he was the one that had bibles printed en masse. Have you heard about the King James' Bible? This must be one of them - wow." I flicked back to the title page. "Yes, he's his most holy majesty, I'll bet. Oh, I wish the computer was working!"

"Try my phone." Percy held out her mobile. "I've still got quite a bit of charge left."

"But the wi-fi will be knocked out, Percy. Do you mind using data-network, because it'll cost you?"

Percy giggled. "Paul pays the bill, so go ahead."

I gave her a conspiratorial wink. "Good, okay then, type in King James I, followed by bible."

Percy duly tapped the keys.

"Oh, yes, you were right, he had bibles printed for everyone to read in English. Very radical for those days, I suppose. Wasn't it all in Latin before?"

"No idea, but if so, this would have got people thinking, those who could read of course."

"What's the date of this bible again?"

I flipped back the cover. "Anno 1613, two years before Edward and Eleanor married. Maybe it was a wedding present.

They must have been some of the first people to have obtained one. Momentous really."

Percy looked thoughtful." Wasn't his son Charles the First?"

"Yep, that's right."

"And wasn't it during his reign that there was a civil war, based on religion?"

"I follow your thinking, Percy. Google the English Civil War and see what comes up. No, wait, type - date of Civil War in England but I can't see any connection to roses, but we've got to start somewhere, I suppose."

Percy screwed up her eyes and punched out the question with a tremulous index finger.

"Percy, do you need reading glasses?"

Percy grinned at me. "Yes, I do! But I hate wearing them."

I passed her mine. "Borrow my ready readers, you idiot."

Percy took my heavy-rimmed glasses and placed them tentatively on the bridge of her nose. She looked very studious as she concentrated on the answer that came up, laboriously slowly. "It says here that the Civil War started in 1642."

"I thought so, that's much later than these bible entries."

"Let's see now." Percy frowned. "What was the name of their first boy? Ah yes, Ralph was born in 1618, so that would make him - how old - when the war started?"

I did a quick calculation, "Twenty four, plenty old enough to fight."

"Yes, and the younger brother, Will, he was born in 1622, four years later – so how old would he have been at the outbreak of fighting?"

"Um, let's see – I make it nineteen as the war began in August 1642 and he wasn't twenty until nearly the end of September."

"Did they fight that young?"

"Young boys have been slaughtered on battlefields since time immemorial, sadly."

"Oh, Fay, bad pun after that last entry."

"Sorry." I shivered, wondering if it was David Slaughter's blood I'd smelt earlier.

"It's almost as if the bible was abandoned after that page was torn out and before the Slaughter family moved in and used it again. Who knows what might have happened in the interim? The ghosts could well be associated with the period that's blank, or any of the ones who came after. There's nothing to connect these roses with the Civil War, not really. We must go to the village church tomorrow and see what records they have kept; at least then we can identify the ones we find; maybe even find the ones between the entries - perhaps the missing occupants grew a rose garden here but I can't say I've noticed one. And we're only assuming that the Slaughter family were butchers - they could have been rose growers with a rose as their family emblem."

"Yes, the churchyard would be interesting and we could explore your garden too. Are there any wood carvings of roses in the house or garden? I did a project on heraldry once and it's amazing what you can deduce from a family crest."

"No, I can't think of any, which is surprising in a place this large and old, but then, I've never looked. We'll make it a priority in the morning." Percy closed the bible and fastened its clasp.

"Yes, and look at any of the old portraits and in drawers for medals and such like. Surely there's an old desk rammed with such stuff somewhere? Hmm, I wonder how long the Foulkes family lived in Meadowsweet Manor? Perhaps they were still here during the time of the missing pages? Does Paul have a connection to either Slaughter or Foulkes?"

"His name is Wade but he inherited the manor through his mother's side and I told you, I don't know what her maiden name was. It could well have been Slaughter and who could blame her if she didn't keep mentioning it?"

"Next time he rings, you must ask him. Just because we've found this bible, doesn't mean the people from its pages are responsible for your nocturnal visits. It could still be Paul's parents or anybody in-between."

"Um, okay." The flat tone of Percy's reply hinted hesitation. "I doubt he'll ring again for ages because he's out in the real wilds now. That was why he called last night, to say he'd be out of range of a phone for a few weeks."

"That cuts that avenue of research off for now then." Annoying. Everything I'd heard about Paul Wade annoyed me.

Percy picked up the little rose petal and cradled it in her palm. She bent her tawny head and sniffed it delicately.

"It's the same rose fragrance, Fay. Much stronger scented than one little petal has any right to be. I can feel the pull of it, just like I've felt it before, when it usually led to panic. Now, with you here, I'm not so frightened, well, I am a bit, but I sense someone desperately trying to tell us something, don't you?"

"Yes, yes, I do. But who?"

"We must explore the connection to roses. I don't know, somehow I don't feel it's that boy in World War One because it's the poppy that's associated with that, isn't it? But what woman doesn't love roses? Could be any of the women in that bible."

"It could be a man, for all we know. Could be a gardener who created a new strain of roses."

Percy sniffed the petal in her hand again. "I can't see that, somehow. Maybe Lady Eleanor or one of the Mrs Slaughter's grew roses? Maybe they loved them and had them around them all the time?"

"Could be, I suppose it does suggest a woman's touch."

"Yes, my aromatherapist says the rose is the queen of oils and good for all female complaints."

I wondered if Percy suffered from some, hence her sensitivity on the subject of children when we'd met. Was that why it was her favourite essential oil? Or was there something in this house that hindered every female occupant's ability to conceive and bear healthy children?

I kept my reply as neutral as I could. "Does she? Maybe one of them used rose oil too. It seems any mother of this house had plenty of reason to complain about her feminine duties, especially Lady Eleanor."

Percy smiled but it was a forlorn smile and held no joy. "Didn't she just? Poor woman."

I was jotting down the dates of the families in the bible on a scrap of paper, trying to work out how they fitted in to my sketchy knowledge of history, when my mental mathematics were rudely interrupted by Percy shrieking loudly next to me. I turned around at her shout to see that Percy was rigid with fear and staring at her open hand in which nestled the rose petal. The petal had shrunk to almost nothing. It looked as dry as dust and as old as the house that sheltered us from the rain, now hammering against the window.

"It's drying up right before my eyes!" Percy stared through my reading glasses at the scrap of flower she held.

The petal shrivelled up some more and within seconds all that remained was a desiccated wisp of organic material. Percy sniffed her hand.

"There is only the merest hint of scent now," she said, her voice low.

"That was extraordinary." I gaped at her hand, awed at what we had witnessed. "It was like a speeded up film of the ageing process. You know what I think?"

Percy dragged her gaze up to mine and shook her head silently, her mouth open in a perfect circle.

"Percy, I think we are dealing with someone who died here in your house. They manifested that rose petal but it's used up all their energy. We must find out what they are so keen to tell us, but I don't know what danger that might bring or whether we'll be able to handle it. Do you want to continue, knowing that it might bring other spirits here? That it might uncover something awful from the past?"

"How can we leave it here? I feel this poor soul is in distress. Why else would she be trying to communicate like this? Fay, I'm so glad you are here. I feel we were meant to meet up and I'm so relieved you have experience of this weird stuff."

"Yes, they meant us to link up."

I was thoroughly convinced that I had been called here for a purpose. I was less sure where it would lead, and still less, whether we would be safe.

## *"I will not rest until you hear me."*

"That wind is getting up," I said to Percy. "Look at the candles guttering."

"Yes, we must be careful they don't splash wax on this beautiful old bible." She lifted the big book on to another little table, away from the candlelight.

"Well, Percy, seeing as you said you are prepared for anything, I might as well tell you what I saw – no, that's wrong, I didn't *see* anything - what I *heard* when I held the bible earlier."

"Go on, Fay, I'm all ears." Percy looked more composed than I felt.

"It wasn't much but I smelt fresh blood and heard sounds of battle."

"What did you hear?"

"Sounded like the clash of swords - with lots of shouting – all male voices and the smell was unmistakable." The memories came clear and sharp to my mind.

"That does sound like a battle. Can you be sure it was swords - were there no sounds of gunfire? Because that would really date it and point to David Slaughter's death. Could you do it again? Should we do more research through our phones on-line?" Percy's oval face was very serious.

"I could try holding the bible again, I suppose, see if some pictures come this time."

Before we could agree on the next step in our investigations, we both gasped out loud. Something had crashed to the floor in the room above us.

"What was that?" Percy grabbed my arm.

"Probably something the wind blew over," I said, without any conviction.

"Oh, Fay, I'm not sure I want to go and look tonight with no electric light to chase the shadows away."

"Come on, Percy, we can't fall at the first fence. I told you it could get scary. Grab some more candles from that stash you have in the dining room. Have you any more candelabra like this one?"

Percy folded her lips together and nodded, "Come with me this time?"

I chuckled. "Come on then scaredy cat. By the way, where is your moggy?"

"Arthur? Probably hugging the Aga as usual, especially on a wild night like this. That wind is howling now, just listen to it."

Percy led the way back into the dining hall.

"Wow! This is a beautiful room, Percy." I stood still, just staring at the big room.

Even by the dim light of three candles, the grand dining hall was impressive. Its vaulted ceiling was supported by ancient beams arching in graceful curves high above us. A minstrel gallery commanded the best view from the opposite end and, in the centre of the flagstone floor, stood a vast refectory table. I could see the shine of hundreds of years of polish gleaming on the wood through the flickering gloom.

"Yes, it's a bit overwhelming, I find. Too formal for me and so much to dust and polish!" Percy shrugged.

I wondered why she didn't have hired help in the house. Was her husband a bit of a miser? I had enough to do investigating past lives from this house and decided to refrain from comment about the current owner. "Is this the oldest part of the house?"

"Yes, Paul said the house originated here way back in the mists of time as a single hall and then they built out from there."

"They probably had cows and pigs next door in those days."

Percy rummaged in the drawer of the massive sideboard. I picked up an aged wooden candelabra that dominated the big table. It was rather heavy and cumbersome but boasted five candle holders.

Percy handed me some beautifully carved beeswax candles.

I sniffed them. "These have a wonderful aroma, Percy, just like honey, but it seems a shame to light all five."

She carried on inserting the candles into each holder. "To hell with that. I want all the light we can get if we're going to brave it upstairs."

"Fair enough." I used one of the beeswax candles to take the flame from hers, now half burned down, and lit mine. Immediately, the room's shadows receded and I found a store of courage I sorely needed. "Want to go first, or last?"

"Neither!" Percy's mouth teetered on a smile that withered before it was born.

"I'll go first then, with my lovely bright candles."

I led the way back into the hall and kept the light high above my head. It was no mean feat lifting the candle holder, as its ironwork made it heavy, but I soon forgot its weight when the welcome light illuminated the corners of the creaking staircase. I was breathless once we gained the landing, and not just from the climb.

"Which way, Percy? Which is the room above the study?"

"Over there." Percy pointed towards the front of the house.

"Of course." I forced myself to continue walking in that direction. The floorboards groaned under our feet but the gale outside moaned louder. The hairs on the back of my neck rose once more to upright and stayed that way. The door of the front bedroom opened reluctantly to my hefty push and its lower edge scraped against the wide planks beneath it. Years of rasping had scoured out a quadrant scar, carved deep into the wooden floor and I tripped on its sunken edge. I nearly dropped the heavy candlestick. Hot beeswax sank through the denim of my jeans, where it quickly congealed.

"Careful, Fay."

"You could have warned me about the bloody hole in the floor, Percy!"

"I forgot it was there. I rarely come in here. We use it as a guest room."

My arm was getting tired and I looked about for somewhere to place my candles. An old table stood under the biggest window so I put the weighty candelabra down on it and rubbed my cramped biceps.

"Another enormous room, Percy. It's quite some place you have here," I said, as I admired the wide, leaded windowpane on the east wall, with an inviting window seat set deep into its recess. Two smaller windows flanked it on either side, giving a balanced aspect that I found both restful and pleasing. I could easily imagine myself curling up with a good book within the embrace of that brightly lit alcove.

"Yes, in the daylight this room is very bright as it faces due east and catches all the morning sun. Although we have a bed in here, I think it must have been someone's study or office years ago, don't you?"

"Could be, though it's quite large for a study and I'm not sure they used rooms that way when the manor was built. They had to be a bit more multi-purpose. Perhaps it was a morning room back then." I sat down at the table against one of the side windows, wondering who else had sat there writing their letters, armed with a feather quill.

Immediately, I felt that all too familiar frisson up my spine. My stomach flipped into butterflies. We were getting closer to that insistent spirit again and, while that was the reason we were here, I dreaded making new contact. The familiar creeping cold spread up from my feet, chilling my bones.

"Are you alright?" Percy peered at me.

"Sit down, Percy, I, I think I'm reconnecting. I'll have to go quiet, so don't mind me, okay?" Already my vision had blurred and I gripped the table to steady myself. As I shut my eyes again, my voice tailed off and I was no longer in the twenty-first century, or even aware that my new friend had obediently sat down in the deep window-seat from where she could watch without disturbing me.

The room was flooded by daylight. Not the strong yellow sunshine of summer but lit by a pale winter sun. A boy sat in the window seat under the biggest window. A bright fire blazed in the hearth opposite and a woman sat hunched next to it, as if she couldn't get warm. She looked delicate and faded. Her skin was very white and blue veins showed through on her tall forehead. Her hair was drawn back under an elaborate lace headdress that looked as light as the feather atop it, but the way her head drooped made it seem like the pearls decorating its edges were too heavy for her weary head. A few twists of hair peeped out underneath; their coils showing strands of white here and there. Her long gown, beautifully embroidered, was of rich silk with wide, slashed sleeves and finished with a stiff white-lace collar, high up to her neck, almost choking her. Her belly was swollen by the child she carried. The scene was a peaceful one; I sensed harmony between the woman and the boy. They shared similar facial characteristics – underneath the long forehead they each had soft, brown eyes and a generous mouth. The woman smiled at the boy, who was playing chess, balancing the board on his knee.

Suddenly an older lad, in his teenage years, burst into the room, knocking over the little boy's chessboard with his flapping cloak. The younger one looked up and his pale face flushed red with anger.

"I give you good day, Mother." The older boy smiled, baring white, even teeth in a ruddy face.

"Ralph! Oh, you are clumsy, you've spoiled your brother's game! And look at your boots–they are covered in earth and filth." The woman's face looked as cross as the little boy's but her soft and mellifluous voice undermined the sharpness of her words. She dabbed at her mouth with a lavender scented handkerchief; its aroma as clear as the daylight. She kept coughing into the dainty linen square, as if terrified to infect either of her sons.

"But it is only a game, is it not, Will? You can play another. Better pick up the pieces, little man." And, ignoring his mother's protestations, the elder boy leant over her and gave her a smacking kiss, right on the lips.

Ralph laughed as he pulled away from his mother's shocked face. Will looked up from the floor, where he knelt to pick up the ivory chess pieces, his young face a study in resentment as he stole a look at his brother, standing so tall with muscles already bulging into sinew - the epitome of rude health. Will carefully placed the chess pieces back on the board. His hands were white and delicate, like his mother's, whereas Ralph's were broad and strong and looked capable of anything, so tanned were they by the sun, even in winter.

Will turned his attention back to the ivory chessboard, probably looted from the orient by some old crusading knight in an even earlier century. He seemed to remember exactly where each elaborately carved pawn, king and castle had been in his solitary game.

Already Ralph looked restless and bored in the warm room, tapping his booted foot against the stone hearth, like a stallion impatient to bolt. "Mother, Father has sent me to ask if we may invite our nearest neighbours over for his birthday feast next week?"

"Is it so soon? 'Pon my faith, I must go and tell Martha. Tell your father that of course he may invite whomever he wishes." A cough quelled the bright tinkling music of his mother's laughter.

Ralph appeared not to notice and kissed her again, more respectfully on her white forehead this time, before she had finished her coughing fit. "I am glad you will entertain them, Mother. I'll ride out there this afternoon, right away."

"Aye, go Ralph, and tell the Charltons they are welcome, but make sure you issue the invitation to the elders, rather than their offspring." She smiled and waved him away with a waft of lavender.

Ralph banged the heavy oak door shut, leaving a trace of frost behind him. The fresh air cut a swathe through the stuffy room; a postscript of Ralph's zestful energy that lingered for a moment and then, like him, was gone.

## *"You see well; I can use you easily."*

I thought, oh, so the bottom of the door didn't scrape on the floor then and suddenly, I was jolted back to the present. I snapped my eyes open. With the beeswax candles burning so near to me, my eyes shuddered at the adjustment. I blinked and rubbed them and felt Percy stroke my arm. I had forgotten I was not alone. It always took a while to come to.

"Fay? Are you alright?" Percy's face loomed into mine. She looked anxious and scared.

I rubbed my eyes to free the fog that clouded them. "I'm fine, Percy. I think I know who I saw."

"Really? Who was it? What did you see?"

I told Percy what I had witnessed and that the entries we had found in the bible corresponded exactly to the scene.

"What did they look like, Fay?"

I described how different the brothers were and how delicate their mother had looked. I added, "I think the mother must be Lady Eleanor and, not only was she pregnant again, but I think she had TB or a chest infection; she was coughing the whole time into her handkerchief. It was scented with lavender. Have you smelt lavender anytime when you've had funny goings on?"

"No, never, only rose."

"Interesting. So, it's not Eleanor who's restless."

"Did you see any reference to roses?"

"No, it was definitely lavender. So maybe it'll be you that solves that clue."

"Me? Oh, no, I don't think so." Percy retreated further into her window seat.

"Let's face it, Percy, you've had a lot of things going on here before I ever turned up, haven't you? And you are very sure about the rose scent that comes every time."

"That's true, Fay," Percy nodded slowly, "but I don't have psychic abilities. I've never gone into a trance like you just did. It was fascinating. I've never seen anything like it."

"Psychic abilities come in all sorts of media. Some hear voices, others smell things; lots of people see stuff, some just sense it. There aren't any rules, you know." I eased my back in the upright chair, relieving the muscular tension that had built up.

"I had no idea," Percy said, in a hollow voice.

"You are a lot more sensitive than you think. Tell me, do you sometimes know before the phone rings who's about to talk to you?"

Percy nodded, that tremulous smile tinkering at the edges of her mouth again.

"And do you think of someone just before they send you a letter or text you?"

Another sheepish nod.

"Can you call up a car space in a crowded car park when you need one?"

"I thought everyone did that!"

"Nope, you are one of the lucky few." I stood up and went over to her at the window-seat. The rain was still pelting against the old, distorted glass.

"Me?"

"Little old you. Something bigger than us has thrown us together, Percy. I'm convinced this is all happening for a reason. There's something unresolved, something unhappy, even tragic, in this house and we must find out what it is. Are you game, because I think you are crucial to solving the puzzle?"

Percy gulped audibly, "Yes, I want to help these poor, dead people find peace."

I patted Percy's hand and found it cold and trembling.

Ralph ground his teeth as he strode towards the stables. Why did his mother never return *his* kisses? She was always stroking Will's hair and pinching his cheek but had looked relieved when Ralph left. And it was ever thus.

"Saddle up Lodestar, Young Peter. And do not tarry."

"Ay, sir." Young Peter scurried off. He'd not forgotten that last thrashing then. Servants were like dogs; they needed to know who was master of the pack. His father would have done, had done, the same many times. It was the natural order of things.

That's why Will irritated him so much. He behaved like a girl, keeping guard over their mother all the time. It was a shame that Lady Eleanor couldn't bear live daughters but that was no reason for Will to behave like one. It embarrassed Ralph to see how Will followed his mother around like a lap-dog, staying inside in those stuffy rooms, never seeing daylight in the winter. It wasn't healthy for one thing.

Young Peter led Lodestar up. The young mare's hooves slipped on the wet cobblestones. His newest acquisition looked nervous and as fired up as himself. Good, they'd have a fast gallop over to Charlton House. Ralph mounted the big chestnut horse easily and nudged her into a trot. Once outside the manor's gates, he used his spurs to galvanise her into a fast gallop. Leaning low over the horse's withers, he pushed the young animal as fast she could go. Lodestar was a fine beast, fleet and big-boned, if a little highly strung. They thundered down the lane at full pelt. Villagers jumped out of the way when they saw him coming.

He whooped with sheer joy when they cleared the stream that divided the village from the manor lands. Sweat glistened on Lodestar's gleaming coat; but she didn't falter, just lengthened her stride across the wide meadow bordering the stream. Sooner than Ralph would have liked, Charlton House reared up in the distance, it's square stone walls angular and pale against the patchwork of fields surrounding it. He could have ridden his new horse all morning but the thought of seeing Rose was the perfect compensation for his short ride.

And there she was; out in Charlton Park riding her pony with one of her brothers.

Lodestar slowed to a lumpy canter. "You cannot unseat me so easily, my beauty."

Lodestar snorted and Ralph laughed. Soon they were in hailing distance of the two Charlton children. How alike they were with their black curly hair and lively brown eyes. In another life, in other clothes, they could be mistaken for Romany gypsies.

"Halloo, there."

Ralph's shout was rewarded with a returning wave.

"Good day to you, neighbour." Rose's eldest brother, Tom, was barely two years younger than Ralph, though it felt like more, but then Ralph had had a very busy year exploring the delights of adulthood, so he felt much older. Still, he liked Tom enormously and looked forward to initiating him into some of the new tastes he had acquired. You could rely on Tom; he might only be thirteen years old but he'd take a fence on his pony like a man. He would have been a better brother than bookish Will, although even Tom was not quite ready for some of the more intimate sports Ralph had recently discovered, but there was no need to mention those in front of Rose.

"May I ride with you, neighbour?"

"You are welcome, Ralph."

Tom and Rose drew up alongside him.

Ralph checked Lodestar's longer strides into step with the two ponies, as they slowed to a walk. "I have ridden over to ask if your family would honour us with your company next week. My father turns forty on Friday and has sent me to welcome you to mark the day at the manor."

Rose's face lit up. "A party?"

Ralph and Tom laughed.

"Aye, a party." Ralph looked at Rose. How pretty she was when she smiled. He'd not noticed those dimples in her cheeks before.

"Of course we can go, brother?" Rose turned in her side saddle to look at Tom. "We'll have to ask Mother and Father but there is no reason for them to refuse such a delightful invitation, and I thank you on their behalf, Ralph."

"We shall be glad to have you, Tom. Even so, I had better go into the house and request their presence."

"Aye, Ralph, better had, or our mother will scold." Tom gathered his reins. "But let us have a race first!"

"Can you hold your pony in check on your own, Rose, if Tom and I have a gallop?" Ralph chivvied Lodestar into a trot.

"By my troth, I can." Rose looked indignant. "Better than that, I'll gallop with you."

And, before they could gainsay her, she was off, cantering towards the house across the field.

"Rose, be careful!" Tom dug his heels into his mount.

Lodestar's big strides soon caught up with Rose's plump little pony, Bodkin, and Ralph leant over and grabbed the reins.

"Unhand me, Ralph! I can ride perfectly well on my own." Rose stuck out her pink bottom lip.

"And a very good rider you are," smiled Ralph. "But, think on this, if we get to the house too soon, I'll have no time with you."

The pink lip retreated and spread into a wide smile. Ralph laughed at the coquettish look on Rose's face. On the brink of womanhood and already a flirt. Ralph felt a surge of sexual attraction rush through him.

Tom caught up with them and scolded his little sister. "Rose, why do you not take more care, riding off like that? Mother would never forgive me if you took a fall."

"I didn't fall, though, did I, Tom? I can ride just as well as you. And you are only two years older than I. Come on, I shall race you to the orchard!"

And off she went again. Ralph let her have her head. Rose was right, she had as good a seat as any man, better if you counted the side-saddle. He wasn't sure he would have managed so well in that awkward position. Tom started chasing after his sister but Ralph restrained him with a hand on Tom's saddle.

"Let her win the race, Tom. She's safe enough." He cantered behind Rose, so he could admire her horsemanship from a safe distance.

When Rose reached the orchard a good ten lengths ahead of her male companions, she wheeled Bodkin round to face them, flushed with triumph. "See - I won, I won! Your two steeds are so slow."

Ralph bowed from the saddle, "Brave work, my lady." He took off his plumed hat and waved it to her in acknowledgement.

Rose beamed her pleasure.

By the time it was Sir Edward Foulkes's birthday, Will had long forgotten the odd sensation, like a shiver of ice on a hot day, that time in his mother's morning room, after Ralph had slammed the door and left to visit Rose Charlton.

Will's father got roaring drunk on the day he turned forty. Will, when his eyes didn't linger over Rose's animated pretty face, watched his mother's flushed one with anxiety. He could see, as no-one else could, the strain behind her forced smile.

Ralph, his restlessness temporarily quenched, teased Rose Charlton throughout the long feast. Will longed for a tongue as quick as his brother's.

Rose wore a gown as pink as her name. Now nearly eleven, she'd always been a precocious child, and the only girl amongst the Charlton family. She had inherited the sharp wit and striking good looks of her mother with the intelligence of her more reserved father. Will, so often the observer at these gatherings of the two neighbouring estates, wasn't the only one who found it an irresistible combination. On the few occasions she had noticed he was alive he had revelled in her lively company. For Rose had eyes for no-one but Ralph. She laughed at all Ralph's coarse jokes, letting her big brown eyes dwell on his face, laughing up at him and peeping through her long lashes. Ralph chased her around the great hall in a game of tag with her brothers and claimed a kiss every time he caught her.

Will joined in but could never run as fast as his long-legged brother so he didn't even get a peck on the cheek. Rose's father, Roger Charlton, drank far less than his host despite the acid comments about sobriety by his wife, Agatha. She kept up, glass for glass, with Sir Edward, her red face testimony to the quantity she put away. As they mellowed, Agatha and Sir Edward exchanged their favourite vulgar tales with great gusto. The noisier they became, the quieter were their spouses.

Roger and Eleanor withdrew to the fireside, at the opposite end of the vaulted hall to the minstrel gallery. Agatha and Sir Edward's flushed faces looked warm enough without the fire, as they sat at the long trestle table in the centre of the vast room, with flagons of wine and the remains of a haunch of venison between them. Sir Edward was cracking walnuts between quaffs from his goblet and Agatha let him put the bits of nut straight into her mouth, accompanied by squeals of laughter louder than those of the children running around them.

By the fireside, as if in a different world, Roger leaned his head closer to Eleanor's pale countenance, his long forehead creased with solemn attention, as he listened to her softly spoken words. Eleanor glanced surreptitiously at her husband and, seeing he was engrossed in feeding their neighbour's wife, smiled at Roger as he pulled a small, leather bound volume from the depths of his fur-lined gown. She and Roger then read from it to each other, their faces serene and contemplative. Will thought, not for the first time, how much easier life would have been for them all if his elders had married the other way around. He knew which set of parents he'd prefer.

Will had been caught out early in the game of tag and went to sit at his mother's side, from which vantage point he watched the other children dart about the hall. Under cover of their shrieks of laughter, Roger and Eleanor were discussing the new book Roger had bought. Will looked at the slim volume; its vellum pages occupied his mother's full attention so that, for once, she didn't notice her younger son.

"How did you procure such a treasure so soon after its publication, Roger?" asked his mother, her lovely voice full of awe.

Roger Charlton's face suffused with pleasure at her question. In his deep bass voice he replied, "I was fortunate enough to know George Herbert before his untimely death and visited him at his rectory at Bemerton. He was kind enough to share some of his poetry with me. It touched me deeply, dearest Eleanor. It gives me great pleasure to share it with you now, knowing you will comprehend the depth of his profound work."

And Roger proceeded to read aloud while Eleanor listened, apparently enraptured.

*"You, whose sweet youth and early hopes inhance*

*Your rate and price, and mark you for a*
*treasure;*
*Hearten unto a Verser, who may chance*
*Ryme you to good, and make a bait of*
*pleasure.*
*A verse may finde him, who a sermon flies,*
*And turn delight into a sacrifice."*

Rose bounced up to Will then and grabbed his willing hand. "Come, Will! We are starting a new game and I command you to join in!"

Will did not need asking twice and readily gave his hand while instructing his heart to stop fluttering like a trapped bird. He tried his best not to be caught; to win the prize of Rose's kiss but her brother Tom stole up behind him and tweaked his ear and Will sat out the game once more.

The Charltons left before dusk could hinder their short ride home. Sir Edward became morose in the silent aftermath. Eleanor went to sit next to him while he grumbled into his pewter cup. Will was glad when his father eventually smiled again at his wife. Soon after, Sir Edward took her upstairs and Will did not see them again that evening.

He went to bed early himself. The long winter nights lent themselves to slumber and he was tired after the games of tag. He left Ralph lying with the dogs in front of the fire, a silly smile playing on his kiss-full lips.

Will and Ralph's chamber was next to their parents with the thick walls of their manor house between them. He climbed into his little truckle bed against the party wall. Ralph had claimed the four poster bed for his territory, refusing to share it with his younger sibling, declaring him to be all elbows and knees. Will hadn't minded. When he was younger, he'd suffered bouts of illness and had liked his little bed next to his mother's room, feeling her close by, knowing she'd come to him if he was unwell in the night, even though Martha had tut-tutted at the usurping of her role as nursemaid. Even though he was older now, and had grown out of those childhood illnesses, the bed and Will had stayed put and no-one had thought to change it.

Tonight he was glad to have the big room to himself. He lay back against his pillow, his hands behind his head, and remembered how Rose had smiled at him. Just the once across the table, but it had been a really big smile and he was sure it had reached right up into her huge, brown eyes. Will had smiled back, feeling his mouth stretch wide enough to touch his ears.

And they had touched hands when she had invited him to join in the game. Rose's slender fingers had the feel of the flower she was named after, silky-soft and gentle. He wished she wouldn't smile at Ralph so often.

His mother's cough, usually too quiet to penetrate the stone wall, interrupted his thoughts. He supposed she was tired too after the festivities. His father shouted something. It was too indistinct to make out the words but was followed by a crash as if a chair had fallen over. Will sat up straight and listened hard. A muffled scream made his heart thump. Should he go in and rescue his mother? His father could be rough when drunk.

Soon a rhythmic grunting noise told Will he would not be welcome. He knew what that meant. There were enough animals on the manor farm who made that noise in pairs. Poor Mother! Half an hour later, snores replaced the grunts. Will, too tired to keep vigil, drifted off to sleep and rosy dreams.

In the morning, after the late winter dawn had woken him, he went downstairs to find Ralph stretching before the fire.

"Did you sleep there all the night long, Ralph?"

"Aye, the hounds kept me good company."

"Ralph?"

"What is it?" Ralph said, scratching his head.

"I think Father was drunk last night. I, I heard him shouting at Mother."

"Of course he was drunk! Why shouldn't he be? Turning forty is enough to make any man drown his sorrows."

"But Mother..."

"Oh, you, and your mother! You are a fine pair of whimpering ninnies. Both of you would fret over a sunny May morning. I'm going out for a ride."

Ralph stretched his long body and walked towards the kitchen in search of breakfast. Both the hounds loped after him.

Will poked the fire back into life and slung a log onto the dying embers. His mother would be cold when she came down. The smell of fresh baked bread from the kitchen wafted into the hall. Ralph had found someone to provide his breakfast.

Will went to seek his own. The big kitchen was warm from the bread oven and the servants were guzzling their morning meal at the long table. Will nodded to them and his stomach grumbled in sympathy. Martha, his old nursemaid, greeted him by pinching his ear.

"Good morning, young mannikin. I trust you slept well?" Martha's shrewd eyes betrayed that she'd heard noises in the night too.

"Is Mother abroad yet?" asked Will, in answer to the look.

"Not yet, no," said Martha quietly.

Will had finished his bowl of milk and bread by the time he heard his mother's cough. He jumped up and went to the hall to find her. Will stopped dead in his tracks when he saw his mother's face. One eye was closed up and the other bulged purple with a bruise. She walked, as she often did, with her hands resting on her swollen belly.

"Oh, Mother! Your poor face! What's happened to you?"

"Upon my faith, William, don't make a fuss. I slipped on my train last night on the stairs. It was foolish of me wasn't it? Fetch Martha for me, there's a dear lad and she'll bring me some salve. I'll just sit here by the fire awhile."

Will was fuming as he ran back to the kitchen. Martha looked mighty incensed too, when she saw her mistress.

Eleanor waved Will away, as he hovered around the two women. Martha was tutting and mopping at the same time.

Eleanor said, through gritted teeth, "Run along and play, William."

## *"Listen to ME, not them!"*

I returned to the high backed chair and slumped against it, completely drained from my dip into the past. My head ached, especially around the bridge of my bruised nose which only contributed to the brain-fog that always followed one of my episodes, as the doctor had called them. If only he'd seen what I had.

"Percy, I'm going to lie on the bed for five minutes and rest."

"Are you unwell?" She half got up to come to my aid, but I stood up and waved her back down.

"No, I'm always wiped out after one of my little trips but I quickly recover, as long as I give in to it. Do you mind?"

"No, of course not, go ahead. I've got lots to think about. I'll stretch out here on the window-seat and have a doze myself. It's getting late anyway."

I nodded, willing but unable to speak, and stretched out on the modern divan in the opposite corner. I immediately slipped into a deep sleep. I could not have resisted if I'd tried.

I didn't try.

My dreams were vivid but disorganised. My tired brain could construct nothing from the chaotic scenes in my head. They gradually faded into black nothingness. I could hear my own snoring but was in too deep to stop it. The night pressed into the old room, sucking me into fathomless slumber.

I always knew when I'd slept well because I would wake refreshed to find both my arms flung backwards behind my head in total, vulnerable abandonment. Big mistake this time. Into the velvet blackness of my slumbering brain a sharp pain, knife-like and severe, cut into the soft flesh of my left underarm. The pain intensified so much that the dream of a dagger slicing through flesh imprinted on my mind's eye and woke me. I opened my eyes and saw, not a madman with a dagger, but Percy standing over me. Her green eyes blazed into mine. She looked ugly, her regular features distorted by naked hatred. In her right hand she pressed a large twig against my arm and its sharp thorns cut my skin. A slow trickle of blood meandered towards my elbow.

Triggered by the pain, I lashed out with my lacerated forearm and belted Percy away from me. An arc of my purple venous blood sprayed across her once-lovely features and she fell away off the bed and landed spread-eagled on the hard floorboards.

I sat up and swung my legs out, grateful to make contact with the floor's solid mass. My arm throbbed and I fished in the pocket of my jeans for a tissue. Finding a relatively clean one, I clamped it to my wound; now pumping quietly and ominously, in sickly heartbeats.

My brain, fuddled from sleep and awoken too violently, struggled to absorb the sight of Percy sprawled on the floor, still clutching the branch of a rose bush in her scratched fist. Her breathing was odd. She was sucking in air like a woman drowning, making whooping noises at the back of her throat in deep, gravelly growls.

All the candles in Percy's holder had burned out and only two of my remaining beeswax candles lit the big room. Clutching my bleeding forearm to my body, I slipped off the bed and knelt down next to the woman who had cut me.

"Persephone? Percy?" I dimly remembered seeing a First Aid video at work and shook her shoulder in the prescribed manner. No response. Her breathing was still jagged and rasping. I rolled her, one handed and awkward at first, on to her side, in an approximation of the recovery position. It wasn't easy, as I had to revert to using both hands and then quickly staunch my blood flow between movements, but somehow I managed to get her lying with one knee up and her airways clear.

Percy's horrible rattle abated as soon as I laid her on her side, and her face resumed its normal docile expression as she slipped into sleep. I laid my ear against her chest. Her breath now came softly and regularly. I sat back on my heels and clamped the sodden tissue harder on to my bleeding arm.

Once my dizziness had eased, I decided I had to find a bandage. I picked up the candelabra and took out one lit candle, leaving one for Percy should she wake. With only a third of their length left to burn on each of them, the candles wouldn't last much longer. I held my other arm elevated to stop the flow of blood and went out of the room with my hands in the air as if asking for mercy from a gunman. Indeed, I felt in as much danger.

Despite feeling both terrified and quite faint, I had to find a bathroom and some sticking plaster. Then I needed more light to sort this mess out. Percy looked out-for-the-count and no use to anyone.

I wish I'd memorised the geography of the house, as I peeked around dark corners of the corridor that led back to the landing and stairs.

I could guess the location of the stairwell by the dense black pit that yawned away from the banister and the dread in my stomach as I looked down its wide, beckoning vacuum. No, I wouldn't attempt descent in the treacherous darkness. I turned away into the long corridor ahead, lifting the candle higher still to shed more light. I only had ten minutes at the most left of the beeswax candle, however beautiful and aromatic it might be. With my hands still held above my head, aching now as the blood drained from them, I felt my way along the uneven wooden floor with my feet, stumbling each time I hit the fringe of a rug.

I would have to be logical and systematic. I still had my phone in my pocket if the candle gave up the ghost. Silly expression; I amended it - if the candle gave out. I took a deep breath, disappointed to find it uneven. Come on, Fay, no hyperventilating.

Progress was slow but I managed to open every door along that endless corridor. They were all bedrooms, a couple furnished with modern cheerful bedroom suites, the others crowded out by curtained four-poster beds. I shut the door on those promptly after a quick peek. Eventually I reached the end of the passageway. There was a door facing me. This had to be a bathroom, surely?

I lifted the latch and went in. My candle was guttering now and casting unreliable shadows everywhere I didn't want to look. I ignored the cramp in my arm and lifted the candle stump higher. When the wax burned my fingers, I ignored that transient pain too, now eclipsed by the gash in my arm, as it stabbed me with bruised, glutinous pulses. Thanks to the white tiled floor, the feeble light reflected back, and I could see that I had, at last, discovered a bathroom. I judged it had been constructed in Victorian times from its roll-top bath and throne-like toilet with its old-fashioned pull-chain. I turned around and joy of joys, finally found the answer to my quest. A bathroom cabinet hung on the tiled wall above the sink. The mottled mirror and wavering light reflected someone whose two enormous eyes, surrounded by purple bruises, stared back in a white, bloodless face. It took me a couple of seconds to recognise it as my own. I looked so scared, I was surprised my hair was still flat on my head and not standing upright in stalks.

I placed the candle stump down on the sink under the cupboard and longed for some bright electric light to help me find the bandages I needed so urgently. My arm was numb from being held above my head for so long and I fumbled with the magnetic catch of the cabinet door. Eventually it yielded and an array of methodically organised medical kit stood before me in neat rows.

"Thank God!" I said out loud. My hand shook with relief as I pulled out a box of plasters. I used both hands, just letting the blood drip into the sink. Thankfully, it was easing now and beginning to coagulate. I pulled out the biggest plaster I could find, and ripped off the layers of fiddly coverings that the modern world demanded, while swearing my head off. With the plaster in place at last, I relaxed a bit and had another rummage in the cabinet. To my relief, I found a box of ordinary white candles, obviously kept there for emergencies.

The stub of my beeswax candle had just enough wick left to light the new one, so I lit two, feeling wildly extravagant, and set them on the sink while I swished away my precious red blood in their benign glow. I found a sling amongst the tidy paper packages, tore off the cover and tied it around my neck as best I could, before sliding my aching arm inside its cradle. Its support felt wonderful.

I filled the tooth-glass with some fresh tap water and drank it down in one go before sitting down on the elaborate loo seat and telling my knees to stop shaking.

Toilet seats are great meditation tools.

And I had to think. What on earth had come over Percy? She'd behaved totally out of character. Why had she attacked me with that vicious thorn twig?

I drank some more water.

My brain woke up.

Ah yes, roses have thorns, don't they?

The parson, a shrivelled old man with a quavery voice, hurried on the meaningless words as if he too could sense the imminent rain. He gathered speed with his prayers, his rheumy old eyes flicking up to the sky in anxious darts. Against the autumn trees, the sky blackened into an angry storm cloud. Will might only be thirteen years old but he could tell when a soaking was on its way.

Will twisted his mother's handkerchief in his hands, round and round and round. He quaked at the ripping sound when it tore in half. He glanced around furtively, hoping no-one else could hear it against the wind that lashed them all, as they stood together in the family graveyard. He had no wish for another beating from his bereaved father. The little scrap of lace-edged linen was sodden with his tears; tears he choked back as his father glared at him with red, swollen eyes across the huge hole in the ground. Its hungry mouth gaped open, eager to gobble his mother's coffin and swallow it down.

Their servant, Old Peter, whose gnarled knuckles showed white with the strain, gripped the band of leather supporting the wooden coffin. Old Peter nodded at his pimply son, Young Peter, who took hold of a similar band at the other end. They both grunted as they took its weight and, bending their knees, slid it across the freshly unearthed mud into the deep pit. Rain had puddled at the bottom of the grave and the coffin made an undignified plopping sound as it hit the water. The wooden box wavered, settling and sighing into its final resting place.

Will pictured his mother lying inside, with his newest little sister curled up next to her. He envied little Elizabeth the safe cradle of her mother's arm about her tiny, still body. Not quite a man and yet no longer a child, he was missing that gentle touch already.

Ralph would be alright. He was the apple of his father's eye. Ralph was four years older than Will. Older, louder, stronger, tougher. Ralph stood with his legs planted wide apart; long, muscular legs that showed no sign of buckling under him, as Will's threatened to do. Ralph's long hair whipped about in the wind against the big white collar at his neck and his arms were folded across his chest in a mirror image of his father's stance. Will looked at them standing together, feeling the distance between them and him. They two were at the head of the grave, separate from the rest of the motley crew that huddled together, hunched against the gusts of wind that buffeted them in sudden, vicious tugs.

Will dared another peek at his father to see if his infamous temper would flare at the unseemly rush. But Sir Edward's eyes were open and strangely unseeing. He stared, unblinking, as Eleanor and little Elizabeth received clods of earth from each mourner in turn. Will picked his up with distaste. The soil was cold and damp. He didn't like to think of his mother covered in the dirty stuff. Eleanor had always been so fastidiously clean and meticulous. A faint whiff of lavender had always clung to her thin frame like the memory of summer, whatever the season.

Then the two Peters shovelled all the earth back into the grave, until it was full.

Will caught the elder Peter muttering about the ground being too wet. "Should never of diverted that stream. 'Tis asking for trouble, burying bones in marsh."

"Hold your tongue, Old Peter," Martha said through her teeth, her eyes on Sir Edward. "Don't 'ee let the master hear you say such things."

Old Peter grunted but said no more, as he heaved the heavy clay back into its sodden pit.

The ancient cleric turned to Sir Edward and said, his voice trembling more than ever, "Would you like to say a few words, Sir Edward?"

"What?" Sir Edward seemed to return from another place. His eyes didn't focus on the little quaking churchman for a minute or two.

Reverend Biggot swallowed. Will watched his Adam's apple bob up and down before he repeated, "A few words, sir? About your wife, Lady Eleanor?"

"I know what she's damn well called, you dolt!" Sir Edward said.

Will heard a gasp from Martha, who held his hand. Martha was never keen on blasphemy and to hear it at the graveside sent a shockwave through them all.

Ralph stepped in, as decisive as ever. He was only seventeen, but spoke with the confidence of a fully-grown man.

"God speed you, Mother and sister. May your souls rest in peace."

Ralph's young voice hit just the right note, serious and solemn, but composed. Will wished he could think of something to say. Edward clapped his elder son on his shoulder approvingly. No one thought to ask Will if he might say a few words.

Sir Edward pulled his cloak about his tall frame, turned away from the grave and started walking back to the house in long strides. Everyone else followed dutifully, some of the servants running to keep up with their master. Ralph kept pace with his father easily at the head of the little cavalcade. Will watched them, until they'd all passed through the gate into the garden that surrounded the manor house.

Only he stayed behind. Martha had tugged at his hand to get him to join the others, but he'd resisted, and she was too scared to disobey Sir Edward. When they were all out of sight, past the willow trees that bordered the kitchen garden, Will sank to his knees, and blurted out all the love that had been squeezing his heart dry since his mother had died.

Even when the threatened storm broke with a clap of thunder, young Will Foulkes did not move. The storm inside him was no less violent than the one that raged about him, spitting hail and rain at him with spiteful accuracy.

## *"I'll hurt you again, if I have to."*

I had to piece the evidence together. It seemed likely that Percy was a vessel for this ghostly character. A right piece of work she was turning out to be, or he for that matter. Who knew what they might get up to next? Lots of energy there. I'd have to be careful. They might harm Percy, as well as me.

And who was coming through me? I still had no clear identity in the story that was unfolding. I pulled my phone out of my pocket and was dismayed to see I only had a fraction of charge left in the battery. Researching the internet would have to wait until we had a power supply. Annoying. Before switching it off I checked the time. 3.15 am. The nadir of the night.

Dawn was still far too distant for my peace of mind. I decided I'd had enough for one session. The best thing to do would be to grope my way back to the morning room, where Percy lay, and if she was alright, for us both to get some sleep. I grabbed the packet of plasters and the box of candles and stuffed them inside my fleece jacket. I picked up both the lighted candles and held them before me in my free hand, tilting the dripping wax away from my fingers. These utility candles burned brighter than the fancy beeswax ones, for which I was deeply grateful.

Moving slowly and extremely carefully, I inched my way back along the long, dark passageway from west to east. The wind outside had eased, replaced by the drip of persistent, dogged rain. Its steady thrum formed a softer soundtrack to my shallow breathing than the earlier roar of the gale but the flame from my pair of candles still danced on the wooden panelling, shaken not by draughts from the storm now, but by the trembling of my hand.

I was concentrating fiercely on the whereabouts of the stairwell and remembering the turn I must take to get back to the room where Percy lay, when a scraping sound distracted me. I didn't want to stop, I really didn't, but something or somebody was moving furniture in the room on my left. I stopped in my tracks, not sure if my courage was still strong enough to investigate. My heart joined in the drumbeat of the rain with a blood-thick thump.

I didn't have to open the door, did I? After all, I really ought to check on Percy, make sure she was alright. And I was tired. It was the middle of the night, for God's sake! These ghosts might not need sleep but I damn well did; but being sensible was like being an accountant: not the real me.

More light. I had to have more light if I was going in there. I quickly turned back to the bathroom and put the two lit candles in the tooth mug and added two more that I lit from the others. Why hadn't I thought of that before? No hot wax to drip on my fingers and twice the illumination. Pleased with myself, I walked more quickly back to the passageway and halted once more by the bedroom door. All was quiet. I was just about to shrug and move on when the door creaked open. On its own - I swear I hadn't touched it. The aperture beckoned me inside. Drawn by its magnet, I entered the bedroom. It was one of the rooms with an old four-poster bed; in fact it was the one with the broken window. Shards of glass still lay scattered on the wooden floorboards but I barely noticed them as the door, slowly and quite gently, shut behind me.

I swallowed, grimly aware I wasn't alone, although I could see no-one in the closed room. No-one living at any rate. Resolving to keep calm, I carefully placed my makeshift light on to the trunk at the foot of the bed. The big box looked very heavy with its iron-studded lid; too heavy for any one person to shift. I liked its reassuring bulk and sat down on it, gripping its sturdy edge with my free hand and settling my wounded arm in its comforting sling. I willed my breathing to slow and calm, and shut my eyes. They had invited me in and I was going to return the favour. Immediately, my body cooled in that familiar manner I hated so much.

Quicker than I'd ever known before, images spilled into my head. Not one, but two young men stood before me. I recognised them immediately, as Ralph and Will Foulkes. Not boys now but full grown men and not happy bunnies either.

They were arguing. I couldn't follow their old-fashioned language. Ralph's handsome face was now sporting a beard, neatly trimmed and triangulating to a point at his chin. He also wore a pearl earring in one ear and a wide-brimmed hat, adorned with a sweeping pheasant's feather. His fair hair curled against the collar of his pale blue jacket, belted at the waist and wide at the thigh. His boots almost touched the hem of his coat with their stupidly wide leather tops. I wouldn't like to try and run in those. Vicious looking spurs were clamped to his heels. I shuddered to think of their sharp spears digging into innocent horse-flesh. A long sword jangled on one hip. To me it just looked like a further impediment to movement but Ralph looked every inch the horseman, so I doubted he ran on his own two feet very much.

By contrast, Will was much more soberly dressed in soft brown wool. His tan leather coat was narrower, as was his tall plain hat, decorated with a single buckle. No sword clanged at his side and his breeches were narrower and fitted inside his long, slim boots. His hair was shorter than his brothers' and cropped right up to his ears. He was clean shaven and his big brown eyes looked sad in his serious young face. Though not as handsome as his brother, his face had an intelligent sincerity that Ralph's lacked.

Will had filled out since I had seen him as a young boy and the brothers shared broad shoulders now. Although Ralph remained the taller, Will had the lithe look some slim men have, hinting at a steely strength. I wasn't sure who I'd back, if it came to a fight.

They glared at each other like rutting stags, poised for violence. Ralph had his hand on his sword and Will squared his shoulders, almost as if ready to take the blow. Then Will turned towards me, thrust out both hands in appeal and looked me directly in the eye. His brown eyes held such depths of sorrow, I struggled to return his stare, startled to be included in the scene. What was he trying to tell me? Will pointed to his brother, whose face suffused with an ugly red colour, and mouthed something at me I couldn't catch. His voice was distorted and distant and I strained to listen. So much so, I didn't hear the door opening, and couldn't understand it when the images faded as quickly as they had appeared, leaving me glaring at a cold, empty fire grate.

"Fay? Are you in here?"

Who was talking? Where was I? Where had the brothers gone? I wanted to follow them, to hear what they had to say, find out what sorrowed Will and made Ralph so incandescently angry. My eyes watered and I rubbed them with my hand. Someone took it in theirs. I blinked and saw a beautiful young woman standing before me. Her auburn hair was in a mess and her lovely face crinkled on one side where she had lain on her arm. I didn't know who she was.

"Fay? Fay, can you hear me?"

The woman's voice was as distant as Will's but not distorted this time. My fuzzy head refused to clear and I rubbed it, then brushed my hair away from my forehead, wondering why I only had one hand.

The woman squatted in front of me and held me by the shoulders. I remembered who she was and drew back in fear. This was the face that had come at me with hatred in its eyes, whose clawed hand had cut me.

"No, keep away!" I pushed her. She fell back on her haunches with a yelp.

I wanted to go back, back in time. She was getting in the way. She made Ralph and Will go away. I hated her for that.

She scrambled back to her feet and shoved a candle flame in my face. It made me blink; made my head hurt so much I thought it would burst. My body juddered with shock and I slumped against the bedpost behind me. My solar plexus felt sore, as if someone had punched it, and all the air went out of my lungs. I sucked in oxygen with rasping breaths, feeling it permeate my veins, before it reached my head and cleared my sluggish brain. I felt a bit sick and clamped my free hand over my mouth. My fingers felt real again, attached to me, warm and alive. I sat up and looked about the room, and saw Percy sitting on the floor in front of me, looking frightened.

"Fay?"

This time I recognised my name and her face.

"Yes," I replied, glad to hear my voice working normally.

"Oh, thank goodness!" Percy scrambled to her feet and held out her hand. I took it and she heaved me upright.

She hugged me close for a brief moment and I felt surprisingly safe in her slender arms.

"Fay, what happened to your arm?"

"Don't you know?" I withdrew from her embrace, fuelled by the sudden memory of our last interaction.

She shook her head.

"Let's get out of here, Percy, before I tell you,"

"Good idea. We'll go down to the kitchen and hug the Aga, shall we?"

"That sounds like heaven."

I gave her three of the candles from the packet in my pocket and we added them to her holder. Guided by the flames, we braved the stairs and fumbled our way into the warm kitchen. Old Arthur opened one eye, stretched and yawned and went back to sleep, unfazed and uninterested.

Percy filled the kettle and placed it on top of the Aga with a shaky clatter. She left it to sing into a boil and filled a pot with tea, spilling the black, dry leaves with unsteady hands, then setting it to warm nearby before gathering up two chintzy mugs from the dresser. "Biscuit?"

I nodded wearily. Soon, we were scoffing chocolate digestives, yes, even Percy, and sipping hot builder's tea together. With two sets of candles on each side of us, the cheerful kitchen was reasonably bright and beautifully warm. I let out the breath I'd been holding and, by the third biscuit, my knees stopped quivering.

## *"Rest, yes; I will wait."*

I woke with a crick in my neck. Percy and I had decided to sleep on the kitchen sofas where the warm Aga and Arthur's purrs melted away unwanted spirits. The sofas were old and lumpy in the style of crumpled shabby chic that humbler homes hid for shame's sake. However charming the effect, I missed the mundane practicality of a sprung mattress and my back was in knots, though when I touched my face with tentative fingers, my nose, at least, was less tender. These aches and pains were eclipsed by the soreness in my left arm. I didn't like it when I saw the way the plaster bulged with congealed blood, but I didn't dare take it off, in case it starting bleeding all over me again. It was all very distracting when I needed to think. I looked across at the other sofa, where Percy lay huddled into a foetal position under her fleecy blanket. Arthur slept in a perfect circle at her feet. I envied her his warmth. My feet were distinctly chilly, but at least they weren't being cooled by the spirit world, just the frigid air. I wriggled my toes and got some life back into them, sat up and rubbed my eyes. I had dispensed with the sling before going to sleep and was grateful to have two functioning hands once more.

I looked at the clock. It was coming up to midday and we'd slept for about six hours, which would have to do. I didn't feel as tired as I might have expected, given the circumstances, and once I'd stretched out my cramped muscles and got some coffee on, I felt almost human. Thank goodness for the Aga.

As the aroma of coffee wafted across the big room, Percy stirred and stretched, kicking poor Arthur off his cosy perch. He was soon coiling himself around my legs and mewing for his breakfast.

"Where's the cat food, Percy?" I asked, as she sat up and blinked at me.

"Under the sink and good morning to you, too."

"Sorry! Cats never stand on ceremony do they?" I leaned down into the cupboard.

"Hmm, that coffee smells good. I'm in dire need." Percy yawned.

"No protein shake today then?" I said, spooning out gloops of cat mush.

"No, I'm going for the hard stuff." Percy sat down at the table, propping her head on her elbows before reaching for the cafétière. She didn't look quite so pristine today, and I suspect neither did I, but that was much less abnormal.

We sipped silently for a few minutes, both deep in thought and nursing the bruises we had inflicted on each other.

Percy cleared her throat. "Where do we go from here, Fay? I'm totally out of my comfort zone with all this. You look like the walking wounded with all those bloodstains on your clothes. Are we still in danger, do you think?"

"I'll mend." I tried not to wince as I poured another cup. Neither the origin nor the organic state of the coffee seemed important this morning, just the caffeine. "I think the first thing we need is an electrician. If we had power, we'd feel much more in control and we could do some useful research on the internet; follow up what we found out from that ancient bible."

"Good thinking, I'll get on the phone right away. It's in the hall; Paul hasn't installed a hands-free one yet. It's a real nuisance. Landlines still work in a power cut, don't they?"

"Usually, yes." I looked out of the window. "Everything seems much less frightening in the daylight, doesn't it?" The day was dull, with a grey, grumpy sky, but it was better than the pitch black of the countryside at night without city street lights. I had missed those during last night's hectic activity. "Looks like more rain on the way, judging by those clouds building up to the west."

"And we can't even check the forecast without power," grumbled Percy. She thumbed through the yellow pages of her phone directory, squinting. Silently, I handed her my reading glasses.

"Thanks." She put them on without a trace of vanity. I thought they rather suited her and said so.

"Really?" Percy looked up at this, her eyebrows raised in surprise. "Paul can't bear to see me in them."

This time I forbore to comment on her fatuous spouse. "Have you found a sparky yet?"

"Yes, here's one and not too far away. I'll give him a bell." Percy got up and went into the hall.

Toast, I thought, this is definitely a toast situation. I found the bread bin, cut a satisfyingly thick wad and reached for the toaster, forgetting there was no power. Disaster! My need was urgent.

When Percy came back, I said, trying not to whinge, "I need toast, Percy, but of course the toaster won't work."

"Ah, but you can use the Aga. Look, just lay it down on the hot plate and it'll be done in seconds. I'll just top up the fuel first," and she opened the fire door and shook in some more coal from the nearly empty hod.

I slapped the bread down on the hotplate and watched gleefully as the toast caramelised before my eyes. Good job it was a solid fuel cooker. Whilst waiting for it to cook on the other side, I enquired about her phone call.

"Yes, I found the electrician bloke alright but he's booked out solid until Tuesday. I tried a couple of others but only got an answerphone, so we're stuck for now. Typical it's happened over a bank holiday."

Even buttering my hot toast did not allay the sinking feeling at this news. "So we have four days without electricity? In this day and age? Surely someone is available? What about the electricity board?"

"Good idea; I'll give them a try." And Percy hopped off back to the phone in the hall. I'd succumbed to another piece of toast by the time she came back. "Honestly, Fay, these bloody call centres! It took ages to plough through the options and then I had to listen to Bohemian Rhapsody for ten minutes before I finally spoke to an idiot who didn't know which way was up."

"No go then?" I licked the jam spoon.

"They said they'd try and get someone out within twenty-four hours but I don't have much confidence. I think I need some toast too."

Greatly cheered by her crumbling discipline, I offered to do it for her. "We'd better get some coal in and keep this Aga topped up." I cooked the bread and handed it to her.

Through a mouthful of toast and marmalade, Percy said, "I'll have another piece of this, Fay, it's yummy and then we'll tackle the coal shed together."

I hummed a tune while I toasted another slice, thinking, I'm getting to like this girl.

Within the hour, we'd hauled in a mini-mountain of coal and stashed it in several buckets in the kitchen. We couldn't have showers because of the lack of an electrical pump to power the water up to the first floor but, by using the kettle, we had comfortable wash and brush ups in our individual bathrooms from jugs of hot water we lugged upstairs. Even without power, I couldn't claim I was really slumming it, as I donned fresh, unstained clothes in the shiny, tiled bathroom.

We reconvened at the kitchen table, both looking spruce and refreshed. I had brought pen and paper to the summit meeting and drew up a list of what we knew about our ethereal co-habitees.

"Right, it seems we can discount the Slaughters, as I've seen the lovely Lady Eleanor and her two bickering sons. Agreed?"

"Well, we don't actually know that they are haunting the place. It could be one of the Slaughters or someone entirely different. Just because you've seen these guys, doesn't mean they are the ones that have been bothering me, does it? And there has been no link with roses through them. There could be other ghosts than the ones you've seen."

"Fair point, Percy, but it's all I have to go on so far. None of these Foulkes characters have actually done any poltergeisting, or tricks with roses, but they are the only ones I've seen. Until something else comes up, I'd like to recap on that, for now. Okay?"

Percy nodded. She looked tired, I noticed, and I felt much the same.

I took a deep breath and continued. "Okay, so we know that Eleanor and Edward Foulkes lived here in the 1600's and had two surviving sons, Ralph and Will. We also know their neighbours went by the surname of Charlton. So far, so good. I've seen Eleanor and the two boys, but nothing to connect with roses. Neither have I smelt any rosy scent but you have. When you attacked me with the rose thorns, Percy, were you aware of what you were doing? Have you any memory of it?"

Percy shook her head. "Nothing at all, I'm afraid. I don't even know how I got hold of that twig. I'm terribly sorry I hurt you."

"Don't worry about it, it wasn't really you, but this is the dangerous bit: if someone was acting through you, as I suspect, we don't know what else he or she might do. You looked really angry, as if you hated me, but who did you think I was? It's a pity you can't remember anything."

"Fay, is there any way you know to help me remain conscious if the ghost comes through me again? You know, so that I retain some control and remember it afterwards?"

"Intriguing question, hmm, let me think. Now, what do I do? I always have extremely clear pictures of what I see. They are like incredibly crisp photos or videos with more clarity than I have normally. And I never forget them, even if I wish I could sometimes, but I don't have a method for it. It's just how it's always been. I've never questioned it before or invited them in, which is pretty scary to be honest, or indeed, shared the experience with a partner, except for Robin," and I scratched my head with the end of my pen.

"So, am I being...possessed then?" asked Percy, her eyes wide with fear.

"Ooh, that's a strong word. We're not talking 'The Exorcist' here – have you seen that film?"

Percy shook her head.

"Just as well, forget I mentioned it. Let's just say that someone is borrowing your body for a while but remember, they can't do it for long. It's really hard for them to gather enough energy to do that, so they are probably also draining yours. You went straight to sleep afterwards and were out for the count for quite a while. It must take it out of you, too."

"Yes, I slept so deeply on that hard floor. Was it you who put me in the recovery position?"

"Yes, I did a first aid course at work. Everyone has to do it at the office. Let's hope I don't have to keep relying on it."

"Quite." Percy absentmindedly poured more coffee into our mugs. We sipped in silence, once more deep in thought.

Percy broke it first. "I think we should pop over to the other side of the village and go to the church. We could try and find the vicar and ask to see the parish records, maybe search the gravestones for names. What do you think?"

Actually I didn't fancy the graveyard much but fibbed, "It would be nice to get out of the house and have some fresh air, I suppose. Good idea."

The gusty wind tore into our jackets as we splashed down the puddly lane and on past the village green to the little parish church. Solidly Saxon, it squatted in the lee of the downs, looking smug as it sheltered from the stiff breeze. Percy tried to open the arched door but it was locked. That left the graveyard.

"Shame we can't get in," she said. "Come on, let's read a few headstones."

"Okay. Maybe the vicar will turn up in the meantime." I wouldn't mind a bit of ecclesiastical support right now.

"Maybe." Percy looked doubtful.

"Do you know him, or her, for that matter?"

"No, never met him, I'm ashamed to say." Percy tucked her hair behind her ears as it flapped about in the wind.

I shoved my cold hands in my coat pockets and resolutely began reading the headstones surrounding the snug little church.

"We'll work from left to right, shall we?" Percy looked quite happy amongst the stone slabs but then, she'd not had the same experiences as I'd had.

I shoved the memories away, wishing they weren't inscribed so indelibly on my all too susceptible mind. The first autumn leaves danced in giddy circles about my head. I watched their chaotic swoops and dives, concentrating hard on following their balletic whirls until they settled on the wet grass, taking my unwanted thoughts with them.

There were the usual family groups commemorated in varying styles competing with other graves, depending on the fortunes they'd left behind. As always, the local hierarchy was evident with the dominant landowning gentry building monstrosities of marble, piled high against the devil's incursion. These contrasted sharply with the simple crosses etched with loving words by their subordinates. When we met in the middle, having covered the whole graveyard between us, we agreed there was one glaring omission.

"Not a single Foulkes, is there?" Percy said.

"I didn't find one, certainly, or Charltons, but plenty of the Slaughter family, who also seem to have lost more children early on than is fair. It's a dead end."

Percy's winced at my unintended pun. "It certainly is."

"Hah, yes, sorry, but still no vicar either, dead or alive. I'm not a church sort of person but I gather they often have to run several parishes on their own these days."

"Right, well, we might as well get back home before the light goes."

"Yes, wouldn't it be sod's law if the electrician is there knocking on the door and we've missed him?"

We hurried back and Percy's phone pinged a text from the electrician as we walked. He was sitting in his van outside the gates when we arrived, looking none too happy at being kept waiting.

"Hello, please come in," said Percy, and showed him straight into the hall and to the fuse-box under the stairs.

Miraculously, the lights flicked straight on five minutes after the electrician disappeared into the wainscot.

"Fantastic!" I grinned at the dour middle-aged bloke, as he dusted off strings of cobwebs, after he'd clambered back into the hallway.

"Awkward cupboard, that."

"You've fixed it." Percy beamed at him.

No smile came in response. The man shook his head. "Nothing to it, just needed to flick the trip switch."

"But I tried that." He looked at me that way that workmen do to women when they claim to know technical stuff.

"Oh yeah? Well, love, it's sorted now."

Percy slotted her credit card into his little machine and bundled him out of the door before I had a chance to explain more fully.

The electrician hunched his collar higher around his neck and ducked his head down, as he walked across the drive in the rain and sped off in his van.

We turned back into the house.

"Thank goodness, electricity again. I'm going to put the heating on, right now." Percy marched off into the utility room at the back of the kitchen. I followed, trying to be grateful rather than cross at the speed with which the electrician had fixed the power supply. I *had* flipped that switch, I know I had. It just didn't make sense.

"Here comes hot water and warm rooms!" I heard Percy switch on the central heating with a sharp click, and then all the lights went out.

"Blast! They were only on for five minutes. That damned electrician should have tried switching the heating on before he left." She stared at the business card he'd given her.

"That is bloody annoying. Switching on the heating and hot water must have overloaded the circuit and tripped it out again," I agreed, and returned to fumbling inside the cupboard under the stairs, but however many times I flipped the trip switch, there was no welcome return to power. I went back to a kitchen once more lit only by candlelight and slumped into a chair.

Percy got straight back on the phone and, after a quarter of an hour of impatient fuming, was told that we'd missed our chance for the electrician to return today and would have to wait until Tuesday for another call out. "And," she said, coming back into the kitchen, "they are still going to charge me megabucks for the engineer coming out, even though he didn't do a damn thing! And it's a bloody bank holiday!" She threw the card into the Aga and held the fire door open while it flared into a bright flame. Percy kicked the little flap shut.

"Hey, don't break the Aga, it's the only comfort we have left and we could have used that business card you've just incinerated."

"Too true." Percy flopped down on the settee again. "Oh, just think of all that fruit in my freezer. It'll be ruined."

"It'll probably last quite a while," I said, without any idea of what I was talking about, not being domesticated, unlike my hostess.

"Twenty-four hours, max. But... we can raid it now for ready meals."

I perked right up at that and we both felt better after a solid meal and a glass of wine each.

When Percy offered me more wine, I refused. "No thanks, alcohol and time travel don't mix well," and corked the bottle.

Percy nodded her acceptance. "I'll go and ransack all the drawers that might have candles. Luckily, I bought a shed-load the other day."

I washed the dishes, relishing the warm water from the kettle.

Percy came back with armfuls of candles, including two big boxes of tea-lights, and we stacked the hoard on the kitchen table. "If they're all stashed here, we'll both know where they are in an emergency."

I fervently hoped one would not arise but kept the thought to myself. "You must have been a Brownie when you were a kid. Isn't their motto 'always be prepared?'"

Percy laughed. "You know, that is perfectly true, I *was* a Brownie! I went on to be a Girl Guide, too. I loved all that."

"Good training for a ghost-buster." I counted up the candles. "Got any more torches - with newer batteries, too?"

"No, not really and that other one was pretty useless, wasn't it? But here's a some new batteries – only one set though - and a couple of boxes of matches. I've dug out some empty jam jars for the candles and we can make handles out of string, like this." Percy demonstrated some nifty handiwork, tying the string around the jar tops, but I didn't attempt to help her. Dexterity is not my forte.

"Excellent, though it's a shame we can't recharge our phones. That's the best torch I ever had, really bright, but no use now."

"Fay?"

"Hmm?"

"I'm dreading tonight," confessed Percy, her voice low.

"Well, I can't say there isn't anything to worry about, judging by last night's performance, but at least we won't be caught out unawares if we have any more visitors."

"But now this spirit has found a way into me, won't it just get more aggressive?"

"I don't know, is the simple answer. You must try and stay in the present, even when they're there."

"How do I do that?" Percy lined up her makeshift lamp holders.

I tested her string handles. They stood up heroically to my tugs. "These are great, Percy, but you're right, we need a plan. I wish we'd been able to do more research, so that we knew more of the background.

I checked the batteries in the torch. "Dead as a doornail, these batteries. I'll put the new ones in." I fumbled with the back of the torch, not seeing it clearly, as the memory of my last encounter intruded. I spoke my thoughts out loud, "You know, the image that remains with me, is the sadness in Will's eyes. He looked directly at me, as if he could see me."

"Wasn't that frightening?"

I shook my head, "Not at the time, I just wanted to ask him why."

"You may get the opportunity tonight," Percy said, with a barely perceptible tremor. "Is that what you want? Personally, I quite fancy a bland, clean modern hotel room to sleep in – with the lights left on all night."

"That's not without appeal, I admit." I smiled with a reassurance I was far from experiencing.

Will was enjoying himself. He drove his axe into the ash-wood and it sprang apart into logs. He'd dispensed with his jerkin hours ago and sweat beaded his spine, as he bent to lob the cut logs onto the pile that had grown steadily all morning. He relished the warm September sunshine on his bare skin. The physical release of hard work was welcome too. He hadn't thought of Rose once this morning, he realised, as he stopped for a rest and a swig of ale from the jug Martha had given him.

He looked at the mound of logs, now as tall as him, and felt a real sense of achievement. His father would frown at this manual labour, calling it demeaning for one of his sons to sweat over such a menial task, but it suited Will.

It was typical of his father to hold on to this feeling of superiority over his fellow man. Just like the way he clung to the altar remaining at the east end of the church. Will had tried to persuade him to reposition the communion table among the congregation in the new inclusive way, but his father wouldn't hear of it, and neither would their timid parson, who would never countermand his squire anyway. They were just mortal men, the same as any serf, what right had they to instruct others how to worship?

Tomorrow being the Sabbath, he'd determined he would go and hear one of the sermons over at Stickerton that the new preacher was giving. He much preferred these gadding sermons and felt closer to God in the open air, away from the distractions of the fusty chapel at the manor. If he left early, his father would be none the wiser. Sir Edward was rarely up with the lark these days and often complained of a sore head. Will thought anyone would have a sore head with the amount of mead and brandy his father put away each night.

Will picked up his axe again and plunged it into the heartwood on his block. As he flung the split logs to join the pile of others, he heard the sound of a horse neighing nearby. He glanced up and saw Ralph riding towards him through the woods. His chestnut mare was flecked with foamed sweat and her eyes showed white at their edges. Ralph was riding her far too fast between the tree trunks. The horse could obviously sense the danger even if her rider could not. Poor creature, to be ridden by someone with less sense than her. Will turned away to gather more wood.

He didn't even look up when Ralph pulled up hard alongside, with scant regard for his mount's mouth, as he sawed at the reins. Will tried not to wince as the mare chomped uncomfortably at her bit and blew out her heaving chest.

"What's this, little brother? Labouring like a serf? Are you a woodcutter now?" Ralph doffed his wide-brimmed hat in a way that implied insult rather than respect. How did he always make Will feel a fool, and so quickly?

"There's nothing wrong with honest work," Will said, carrying on regardless, with a careless swipe that missed the log and nearly chopped his leg in half.

Ralph roared with laughter. "Methinks you need more practice, Will! Why not leave it to Young Peter? He has the muscle power that you so obviously lack."

"Peter has other work to do and no doubt your bones will be glad of a warm fire when winter comes."

"I? I never feel the cold."

"Nor hunger? The kitchen will need wood to roast one of your deer, after you have killed it."

"True, brother mine, but surely you can find something more suitable to do?"

"What is more suitable for a man than to cut wood?" Will felt ridiculously pleased when his next stroke split the wood like butter.

"Oh, I see clearly now, this is all part of your Puritanical nonsense, is it not? The humble lord being equal to everyman on God's earth. Such pompous tripe; it sickens me."

"You do not have to stay here to witness my labours, Ralph." Will kicked the logs out of reach. "Go on and fritter your day away, as usual, and be neither use nor ornament to anyone else. Why change your ways just because the world is changing around you?"

"Damn you and your sanctimonious preaching. A true gentleman can do what he likes. He need not sweat in the field like a miserable peasant!"

"Who said I was miserable?" Will looked up at last and smiled broadly.

Ralph dug his spurs into his mare's tender belly. She leapt forward with a snort of pain and tried to rear, but Ralph's strong hands pulled her neck down so hard, she thundered back to the ground before she could unseat him.

Ralph looked down at his sibling and said, through his teeth, "If you are so content in your labours, I shall no longer keep you from them. I bid you good-day, little brother."

Will waited until the cloud of wood shavings settled back on to the sunny timber yard before plunging the axe into the greenwood once more. The log split asunder with a loud crack, such was the force of the metal blade upon it.

An executioner could not have done better.

## *"I must reach him through her."*

I watched Percy lean forward and throw another log on the fire. She soon had it roaring up the chimney and the flames helped to light the small sitting room opposite the study, on the other side of the hall. This room was surprisingly cosy and I was glad of it. Who needed a vast echoing chamber when your heart wouldn't stop pounding erratically in your chest?

We sat in comfy wing armchairs on either side of the fire, toasting our toes on the brass fender. Percy had lit tea lights in colourful glass holders around the snug little room. They glowed in rainbow shades of reassuring, primary colours; their gaudy glitter wonderfully cheerful and modern.

I relaxed back into the embrace of my cushioned seat and exhaled my tension. I felt sleepy after the exertions of last night. Percy was content to read. She sat, hunched over her book, with her candelabra reinstated on the little side table next to her and my reading glasses perched once more on her dainty nose. She'd found a book about the English Civil War and was deeply engrossed.

I was happy just gazing into the core of the fire. The logs shifted as they burned, making sparks fly up the chimney. The woodsmoke was aromatic, reminding me of incense, and my thoughts meandered by association to the little village church. How odd that the family who lived in this beautiful manor house, and who must have owned most of the other houses in the village, wasn't represented there.

Not having any matchsticks to hand to prop my eyes open, their lids grew heavy and so, inevitably, did my head. I snuggled it into the wing of the armchair and slipped into a doze.

Was I snoring, or was Arthur purring very loudly? The drone of whatever it was drilled into my head. Instead of waking me, it drew me further down into velvet sleep. Giving up the struggle to stay awake, I surrendered to fatigue and allowed my mind to drift.

Through the murk of my subconscious, muddled dreams, a pair of deep brown eyes bore into my head. Full of sorrow and wide open in silent pleading, they drew me away from inspecting gravestones, draped with purring cats and being pestered by angry electricians. It took a few moments, or longer – who knows how time operates during a dream – to identify the serious face before me as belonging to Will Foulkes.

He was alone, hatless and sitting cross-legged like a pixie, in a wooded glade. His solemn face was bare, marked only by a deep gash on his cheekbone. The trees were in full leaf so I guessed it was summertime. Will's cropped hair made him look vulnerable without his tall hat. He wore an ankle-length white shirt with full sleeves, untied at the neck, revealing a light brush of chest hair and well worked delts and pecs. In fact, he looked downright tasty, except for that solemnity. What was it that made this attractive man so sad?

Will opened his mouth and spoke in that old-fashioned dialect again. He seemed to understand that I found it difficult to follow and slowed down his speech. I concentrated, forgetting I was asleep. I had rarely felt more awake.

"Rose," Will said. His mellifluous voice was surprisingly deep and added to his sex appeal. I felt emotionally stirred by him, unsettled.

"I need to see Rose," came the rich brown voice again.

"Why?" I asked, wondering if he could hear me.

"I must explain."

"Explain what?"

"Why I had to go."

"Where did you go, Will?"

"Time, I haven't time to tell ye, I need Rose, before I..."

"Rose isn't here," I said. "I am not Rose."

"I am here, sweet Will," came a voice, very close to me.

"Rose? Rose, my love?" I watched Will reach out with his hands and caught my breath as I saw bruises the colour of blackberries all along his arms where the soft cambric shift-sleeve fell away.

"I cannot see you! Rose, Rose, where are you?" His voice was laced with anguish.

"I'm here, Will!" Percy's arms stretched out and clasped mine. I jumped awake, and saw her kneeling in front of my armchair, with her back dangerously close to the fire.

I felt her jumper. It was red hot and scorching. Strangely, I felt calm this time and instantly alert. "Percy, come away from the fire." I pulled her forwards.

Her arms went rigid. "You shall not stop me this time. I can hear him, I can hear my Will. He's calling me. Cry you mercy, get out of my way!"

"Persephone. Wake up! Percy, it's me, Fay. I am not stopping you doing anything. Will's dead and gone. Come on, Percy." And I shook her shoulders, gently but firmly.

Percy's eyes opened. They were cloudy and unfocussed. I held her shoulders and kept looking into her eyes, until her pupils became less dilated and attuned to my face. Recognition came slowly but I held on to her until it did, waiting for a blow that, thankfully this time, did not come.

"Fay?" Percy whispered my name.

"Yes, it's me, Fay. Are you alright, Percy?"

She nodded. I let go of her and guided her to her chair opposite mine. I poured her out a glass of water from the jug we had brought with us.

"That's it, Percy. Drink up. Thirsty work, this." I poured a glass for myself. The water slipped down my throat, cool and real and welcome.

After a few minutes, when I could see Percy was once more in the land of the living, I said, "I think we should congratulate ourselves, Percy. We got some useful information then and didn't end up knocking seven bells out of each other."

Percy gave me a rather wan smile. "Well, that's something, then. Heavens, I'm hot."

"Your back certainly is. And you need a fireguard in here! Let's compare notes. I saw Will in a forest of some sort. He was on his own and looked injured and as serious as ever. He was asking after someone called Rose."

"Was he? I could hear a man's voice calling me. It was a lovely voice actually. Rich and deep, but the language was strongly accented and hard to understand. He was definitely calling for Rose though, that was quite clear."

"Don't you see what this means? It must be Rose who is coming through you."

"Yes, of course, and Will is in love with her. And I must remember that isn't me."

"Yes, you must, that's very important. You see, I've never hosted anyone the way you are with this Rose person, so I don't know what the implications are. I only see people – as if they were in a movie or a dream. I don't *become* them."

"Well, I wish I bloody didn't," Percy said, without a trace of her earlier smile.

"Let's recap. We know that Will is trying to make contact with Rose but is finding it difficult."

"Ah, yes, but we still don't know what Rose's relationship is with Will."

"Don't we? I felt such love for Will just then. I'm sure they were lovers." Percy's voice softened as she said this.

"Then why can't they reach each other?" I took another sip.

"Maybe if they did, they'd find peace and stop haunting this place." Percy looked pensive and sad.

"That would be no fun at all." I held my glass against my hot cheek.

"You are not serious?" She stared back at me with an appalled face.

I laughed, "Not in the least."

"I'm glad to hear it, Fay, because you might be enjoying yourself, but I really am not."

"I've just remembered something important." I put my glass carefully down on the little table.

"Oh?"

"Something you said, just before I woke up. You said I couldn't stop you reaching Will this time."

"Did I? So who is preventing the two lovers getting together?"

"I don't know, Percy."

"I wish I could see Will, too." Percy's wistful tone and the longing in her strange, green eyes made me feel distinctly uneasy.

Feeling oppressed by the unseasonal heat of the early autumn day, Rose wandered into the still room to think about her new situation. The stone chamber was cool and dark; infinitely soothing. Inside, surrounded by herbs, she felt calmer. She looked up at the bunches of plants drying above her head. There was lavender, the tops of its grey stems blossoming into fragrant heads of flowers, now fading from bright purple to a delicate shade of violet, still reminiscent of hot June days when bees busily harvested their scented nectar. Rose squeezed the petals and a few dropped on to the stone floor. She crushed them under her feet and breathed in the clean scent but it did not clear her head.

She recalled that rosemary was a tonic for the brain. She walked to the next bunch of herbs drying above her, pulled some of the spikes down and ate them. Their sharp, piercing taste was slightly bitter and astringent. Rosemary, for remembrance; just what she needed to sharpen her dull wits.

Which one of these healing plants did Ralph resemble? Ralph had always smelled of frost and horses, leather and sweat, when they were children. Rose had always looked up to Ralph. The gap in their ages had made him seem so much more grown up. Now she was older, she felt she had caught up with him. They were both of marriageable age and he was confident that she would be his bride, as predestined by their mothers. Ralph's kisses were deep, hard, and exciting. Ralph, experienced and teasing, enjoying her hunger, would kiss her until she was breathless. Then he would drop his hands and look at her through eyes dancing with mischief before pinching her chin and pulling away. The adult Ralph's aroma was more intoxicating, like summer jasmine; richly aphrodisiac, full of musky sweetness and belonging to the night.

And what would Will smell of? Which one of these herbs most resembled him? Would it be soft, round camomile? Safe to give to children, calmer of digestive upsets, soother of headaches? No, Will was more complex than that. His fragrance was mixed up with dust and books, soap and candles. Will thought about things deeply. His solemn brown eyes rarely sparkled with mischief and yet they held more warmth, more – dare she call it, love? – than Ralph's sky-blue ones. Will reminded her of expensive saffron. The deep orange threads of crocus that turned the milk possets she gave to her dyspeptic father from white to deep yellow. Elegant, yes, and concentrated. Deep. Yes, that was what Will had – depth – something you could never suspect Ralph of possessing. And now Will had grown up too, filled out and hardened since Lady Eleanor's death.

Truth be told, she wanted them both. Rose sat on the still room stool and laid her arms across the wooden bench. She had spent many a tedious hour here, sorting herbs for winter storage away from her mother's busy, sharp tongue. Late rose petals lay, fading gently, on a wicker tray in the cool room. Rose lifted her hand and picked some up, letting the blood-red petals of her namesake trickle through her hand. They needed longer to dry completely. When she crushed them the flowers did not crackle like paper. Their complex scent still lingered on their velvet skins. Clutching some in her hand, Rose held them to her nose and inhaled. She still wore the pomander Ralph had given her when she had promised to marry him. She lifted its shiny lid, added the new petals to the dried-up ones within and shut it with a snap. She was no nearer a decision, despite the tranquillity of the quiet still-room.

Why had she acceded to Ralph's proposal? Did she have to follow the dictates of their parents like a lamb to its slaughter? Her face suffused with the same delicate shades of the petals she held in her hand. She held them to her nose again and their scent whirled her back into that giddy moment, when Ralph had held her in his arms, and made her yield up her answer through breathless gasps.

"Answer me, Rose," Ralph had commanded, between butterfly kisses that he fluttered across her breasts. She had both dreaded and longed for his tongue to reach inside her straining bodice and lick her nipples. They stood, erect and stiff, urgently begging him to find them, as if they had a will of their own, beckoning him lower across the lace-edged boundary. Rose's mind, she remembered with a blush, had struggled to discipline their wayward demands. Usually such a sharp instrument, one she could rely upon in most situations, her brain had gone dizzy with excitement as the insistent yearning between her legs dulled its edges.

"We can make everyone happy today, Rose," Ralph had whispered, as his lips now brushed her ears, leaving her tingling nipples disappointed. "I want you so much, more than any woman I've ever known."

Rose's mind had quickened at that point, "And how many would that be, Ralph?"

A deep chuckle emanated from Ralph's throat and entered her mouth, as he laid his lips upon hers again.

"Enough to know you will be the best bride a man could have on his wedding night. In fact, why wait till then? I can tell you long for our union now, as much as I do, don't you, Rose?"

Ralph had pushed her down on to the rose garden's grassy floor then, and laid his lean, corded body against hers. Oh, it would have been so easy to yield at that moment; to let her body have its desires and satisfy Ralph's.

"Just think, sweet Rose, our fathers would be ecstatic for once and united, after their years of bickering, as we would be in the most profound way. I could make you feel like a queen. Indeed, you are the queen of my heart already."

Rose wandered around the still room, her memories more vivid than the bunches of herbs she brushed against. She fingered her throat, around which Ralph's pomander now hung on its strong silver chain, and recalled the sudden constriction in her breathing when she'd heard her mother's voice and had thrust Ralph away from her.

She had stood up and quickly straightened her clothing, feeling mortified when her mother gave her a knowing look. Her noisy breathing could not be quietened or slowed quickly enough to fool Agatha. The game had been given away.

"What are you about with my daughter, Ralph Foulkes? And in my rose garden too! Have you not heard that roses have thorns?" Agatha's ever-sharp words had been softened by an indulgent smile.

Ralph had smiled back and slid a possessive arm about Rose's waist. "I'm kissing my future wife, Lady Agatha."

Rose had started to protest, "I've not agreed to this!" but Agatha had swept towards them and caught his hands in her own.

"My dear boy! It is what I have always wanted! Ralph, you will be as beloved to me as my own sons. I welcome you into the family."

Agatha, not one usually given to warm gestures, had stood on her toes and kissed Ralph on both his ruddy cheeks. Ralph caught his future mother in law by her waist and spun her around, shouting his joy.

"Ralph Foulkes! Unhand my wife!" Roger Charlton strode into the arena, presumably drawn by the noise. "I command you to give me an explanation, young man!"

Ralph had taken off his feathered hat and in one graceful movement and made an elaborate bow to the older man, casting it wide enough to include Agatha into his obeisance. "I humbly beg your pardon, sir, and also the hand of your beautiful daughter, who has just agreed to marry me, if you will give me your blessing."

Roger had immediately looked to his only daughter for confirmation. Before Rose could speak, her mother stepped in once more, "Of course we give our blessing, don't we, husband? What could be better than this alliance of our two houses?"

Ralph had taken something out of his pocket then. "Then let us seal it with this gift!"

He'd turned back to Rose and quickly placed a necklace over her head. Its silver pomander lifted and fell on her breast; her breathing quickening as fast as the events around her.

Rose had put her hand to her chest and felt the weight of the filigree container. It was beautifully worked; its chain delicately patterned yet strongly made.

Agatha had been in raptures. "Oh, what a wonderful gesture, Ralph!"

Ralph had stood aside as his future mother-in-law embraced her daughter briefly, before falling on the trinket, fingering its silver filigree where it lay on her daughter's bodice.

"Oh, it must be Italian! Is it Italian, Ralph? Such workmanship! What is inside? Or shouldn't I look? Is it a lover's secret?"

Agatha's titters had grated on Rose. This should have been *her* moment. Her mother had stolen it again. She looked at her father. He was as solemn, and as silent, as ever.

Ralph had opened the pomander, even though it still lay across Rose's breast. It felt too intimate with his hand there, as well as her mother's. Rose had blushed at her parents' witnessing the breach of etiquette but their silence condoned it. With two pairs of hands pawing at her, Rose had felt stifled.

Ralph had tipped the open pomander towards Agatha with a grin and the sharp tug on the chain around her neck had made Rose feel as if she was being strangled.

"Empty as yet, my lady Mother-to-be. What could be better than rose petals for my Rose? And here we are in your beautiful rose garden! We shall gather some now, to celebrate our union. Which are the most fragrant?"

Ralph and Agatha had fallen to searching for the best blooms with great enthusiasm.

Rose had felt cheated then. No one had actually asked her what *she* wanted to do. She had looked from one to the other as each face registered joy and pretend surprise and their feigned anger receded. Her previous lust ebbed away too and Rose's mind once more took charge. It was not happy that her body had subdued its dominance. Her father, Roger, dodged her eyes when she sought his. Why did he never stand up to his wife? Had she *no* advocate?

The net had tightened when Ralph's father was apprised of the news, after they all rode over to the manor later that afternoon. Sir Edward had joined in the celebrations with equal enthusiasm. Everyone but Rose wanted a quick wedding but in this at least, her wishes had been respected and the betrothal put off until her nineteenth birthday. Rose had pleaded she had always wanted to be married in the merriest month and, with the country at loggerheads over things she didn't understand, she asked the two families to indulge her and wait until things had settled down.

"Of course you must marry in the May-time, my dear, if that is your desire, but you need not wait quite so long." Sir

Edward had patted the paunch he had acquired since Eleanor's death and puffed out his red-veined cheeks. "Although I suppose it will give us ample time to prepare your new quarters at the manor. We will give you a bedchamber fit for a princess, hey, Ralph?"

"I would rather it were sooner, Father." Ralph had looked at his bride through eyes bright with desire.

"Indulge her in this, Ralph, and I'm sure she will reward you in time," said Agatha.

Rose had looked at her mother and again felt that faint revulsion at her coquettish tone, as she conspired with her future husband. The joy Rose expected to be feeling had eluded her. She'd felt confused and strangely alone. And quite angry.

Several days later, after the apples in the orchard had been gathered in and the warm September had fulfilled its promise of a good harvest, Rose had thrown off her doubts and decided to ride over to Meadowsweet Manor and surprise her betrothed.

She succeeded. Having given Bodkin's successor, a black mare called Inkwell, to the stable boy, Rose walked through the apple orchard which lay between the manor house and the stables. The branches of the apple trees looked forlorn without their ripe, round fruits and discarded apples lay rotting amongst the bruised turf. At the far end of the orchard, some pigs rooted amongst the decaying fruit. Rose was relieved to see they had been fenced in. She lingered under the largest tree and remembered how the grass in the rose garden at home had felt under her when she had lain with her future husband, gasping with pleasure as his knowing hands had burned her skin through her velvet dress.

Out of the corner of her eye, she saw another skirt flapping in the autumn breeze and Ralph's unmistakable profile next to it. This dress was grey, not made of rich velvet but drab wool, that bore no lace. Rose held her breath and slid noiselessly behind the sturdy tree trunk, glad that her riding habit was russet brown and not easily seen in the dwindling twilight.

She did not want to look but could not drag her eyes away, as Ralph laid another girl down on a different grassy sward. The plump servant girl looked much the same age, or maybe even younger than Rose. She too was panting hard and clutching at Ralph's doublet, just as Rose had done. Rose sank to the ground, unconsciously gripping Ralph's pomander in one hand while steadying herself against the solid wood of the apple tree with the other. The servant girl wouldn't or couldn't stop Ralph. No-one's mother came to intervene this time, as he lifted her skirts and pounded out his frustration.

Rose waited until it was over. Ralph left first, casually slapping the girl's rump before disappearing with a swagger and a blown kiss to her. The girl smoothed her rough gown and replaced her white coif, tying it under a chin that trembled upon a guilty smile. Then, after looking around, she too quitted the quiet, darkening orchard. Rose was left alone to witness the final splendours of the September sunset through moist, narrowed eyes.

She whispered her secret vow into the bark of the tree.

"Well, now, Ralph Foulkes, two can play at that game."

## *"We will meet again, I assure you."*

I don't think anything or anyone, even that wretched hussy Rose, could have woken me that night. We returned to our respective bedrooms, having both agreed that a proper sprung mattress could no longer be denied, even for restless spirits.

I crawled under the clean white linen and cravenly covered my head with the downy duvet. I think I was asleep before my head hit the pillow. Maybe our forebears were also exhausted, because it was the prosaic sound of my own snoring that woke me many hours later. I blinked my eyes open, surprised and relieved to see sunshine peeking around the edges of the expensive-looking tapestry curtains.

I got up and drew them across, marvelling at the sight of the morning mist rising up from the boggy ground beyond the garden wall in regular, everyday wisps. The world looked rational, normal, and the right way up. The gash in my left arm was still swollen under the plaster but my nose was definitely returning to its normal snub shape and size. I touched it gingerly, delighted to find the tenderness almost gone. I opened the modern window. It creaked as it swung out to greet the morning. I stuck my head outside and breathed in the fresh air, luxuriating in my renewed sense of smell.

There was a hint of autumn in the air; that first nip in late summer which warns against frosts to come but is strangely invigorating. I inhaled and filled my lungs with oxygen; fuelling up for the day ahead. I wondered if Percy had slept as well as me. I grabbed my fleece dressing gown and tied it around my sizable middle. I didn't care a jot how unflattering it was. The fluffy material encased me in a warm, comforting embrace. I shoved my feet into equally unfashionable slippers, schlepped down the corridor to the older part of the house and knocked on Percy's heavy bedroom door.

When no answer came, I unceremoniously opened it and entered Percy's private chamber. The four-poster bed was rumpled by a recumbent form. My heart began to thump as I approached the heap of bedclothes. I reached out to touch it with a tentative finger and prodded the mound.

"Aagh!" Percy shrieked and sat up, all in one go. Her hair was all over the place and she clutched the bedclothes to her chest in an instinctive gesture of protection.

Mortified, I sought to reassure her. "It's only me, Fay. Just wondered if you'd slept alright?"

"My God. You frightened the life out of me!"

"Well, I was worried when you didn't answer my knock, so I had to check. Are you alright?"

"I think so," Percy lowered the bedclothes and looked down at her slim body then around the room and back at me.

"Thank goodness for that. I slept like a log. How about you?"

"Don't remember a single thing, so I suppose I must have done." Percy brushed her long hair out of her eyes.

I slumped onto the bed as the tension eased from me, and smiled. "Shall I make tea?"

"I'll get up and help. You'll never manage that Aga."

"Oh ye of little faith."

I left her to get up in privacy and went downstairs, feeling quite sprightly. The morning sun was bright in the cheerful kitchen and Arthur jumped down from the sofa nearest the stove and wrapped his sinuous grey body around my bare legs. I felt ridiculously touched that he had recognised me, if only as a food provider, as if I was in my own home. Then fond memories of yesterday's morning's toast downgraded him on the priority list. Ignoring his miaows, I opened the spinwheel of the Aga to make it draw, before opening its door and throwing a couple of lugs of coal on to last night's embers. They caught immediately and my sense of wellbeing increased tenfold.

I ran the tap into the kettle and set it on the hob before turning back to Arthur, who's voice had become strident.

"Alright, old feller, let me find the cat food." I felt even more at home knowing where to look for his breakfast and doled out the brown gloop into his dish. I watched him gobble it up and turned to fetch clean mugs for the tea.

"My goodness! You've got everything under control already." Percy wafted into the kitchen in a silk robe whose turquoise folds exactly matched her eyes. She had combed her long auburn hair and donned dainty silk slippers, embroidered with Chinese dragons. She could have done justice to a photoshoot right there and then. I hoisted my rope-like waistband a bit higher. It had sagged and slipped with bending down to feed both the fire and Arthur. I pulled it tighter with a resigned tug.

"I hope you don't mind me treating the place like home?" I said, rummaging in the bread bin.

"Not at all," Percy's fine-boned face lit up with a bright smile. "Feel free. To be honest, it's lovely to have someone giving a hand." She nudged Arthur out of the door into the garden with the toe of one of her pretty slippers.

"Good, sit yourself down then, Percy, and I'll make some toast."

"Oh, not for me today, Fay. I think I'll revert to a smoothie."

I was disappointed. I'd felt we'd bonded over the caramelised toast, dripping in butter and jam, yesterday morning. It wouldn't be nearly so much fun chomping away on my own.

The kettle sang into boiling and I made the tea.

"No idea how to make a smoothie so I'll leave you to sort that out on your own."

"Oh, I've just thought, we still haven't got electricity, so I can't use the liquidiser."

"Shame. Toast?"

"Oh, go on, then." Percy laughed. "I do fancy some stodge, actually."

"Excellent!" This was turning out to be a splendid morning.

When several slices of toast were safely tucked inside us and we were sipping our second mug of tea, I felt replete enough to take stock.

"So, Percy. Our bellies are full, which is always important, and we've had the benefit of a good night's sleep to boot. I suggest we capitalise on our sense of wellbeing and tackle some proper research in a well-lit museum."

"Yes, I agree. We could go to the library too and use their computer."

"It would be good to get out of the house, don't you think?"

"It certainly would."

We set off as soon as we were dressed.

"What a wonderfully normal day," I said, as we got into Percy's smart Mini.

She laughed. "Yes, those phantoms seem to be largely in my imagination now and not real at all."

"Really?" I was surprised. I hadn't forgotten her sticking that rose thorn in my arm. How could I, when it still throbbed painfully every time I reached up?

"Well, no, not really, but they certainly seem less scary today in this beautiful sunshine and they aren't going to bother us when we're away from the manor, now are they?"

"No, how could they?" I smiled back at her and relaxed into the seat.

Percy was a good driver and I felt safe as her passenger. I watched the downs speeding by and looked forward to using my brain instead of my over-sensitive intuition in a nice neutral environment with Rose, Will and Ralph safely left behind us.

Fool that I was.

# Stickerton Common 1641

Rose looked up at the sound of hooves clopping steadily along the track that ran between her home and the village. She was sitting in her favourite perch on an oak tree root, hidden from her mother's inquisitive eyes, in a wooded glade on the edge of Savernake forest. Being just off the thoroughfare, screened by trees, it was easy to see if anyone was coming who might wonder what she was about, but far enough from Charlton House that no-one could find her. Inkwell, placid as ever, chomped contentedly at the blades of grass at her feet.

Today, her journey was legitimised by a charitable errand for an elderly cousin, and she'd stopped off along the way for a quiet moment to herself. She'd taken to frequent solitary rides lately so she could think about her betrothal to Ralph Foulkes. When he smothered her in kisses, her pulse raced and her heart pounded and there seemed only one solution to quieten them; one which Ralph was only too eager to supply, should she consent, but, as soon as he left her, she hated him for it and a deep sense of dread enveloped her.

Much as her body craved his, her mind felt suffocated by his desires, beyond which she sensed no harmony between them. Would they, once married and burdened by children, become as estranged as her own mis-matched parents? Having witnessed her betrothed seducing that plump servant girl at the manor, she could see how fickle he might be and how unlikely he'd remain faithful to her. Didn't she deserve more than that? If he couldn't keep his breeches on while they were engaged, she had little expectation of his retaining them while she bore his children. Rose wanted a man who would adore her, and only her, and who was interested in more than her body. She was beginning to feel she'd rather not marry at all than become a thwarted, neglected harpy like her mother.

But all the time Ralph baited her, bringing her to the point of submission before withdrawing with a teasing smile of forbearance. He seemed to enjoy taunting her. Perhaps it was no wonder he sought release elsewhere. Truth be told, she felt trapped, betrayed by her own physical desires for a man she suspected she could never truly love.

A brown hat, with a single buckle adorning it, could be seen through the branches of the trees that hid her. Rose stood up, brushed some twigs from her russet velvet riding habit and straightened her elaborate lace collar. The rustle of her skirts disturbed a nest of fledglings. They rose up in a cloud, squawking their protest and causing the rider to turn and look across at her secret hideaway. Inkwell also played her part in giving her away, by whinnying to the other horse.

Her cover blown, Rose came out from her hiding place to see Will Foulkes, checking his distinctive piebald mare, who had started and faltered at the sudden flight of birds. She heard him pat her neck and whisper reassurance. The fact that Sir Edward had two sons presented an interesting situation, now she thought about it.

"Who goes there?" Will called out in his strong, calm voice.

Rose stepped out on to the narrow lane, pulling Inkwell along by her reins.

"It is only I, your neighbour and friend, and I will not rob you, Will Foulkes."

Will's whole face lit up with his rare smile. "Why, Rose, you are as fair as this May morning and do not resemble a robber in any guise, but 'pon my faith you should take care in these woods. It is not safe for you to be riding alone."

"I do not fear, Will. Inkwell is fleet of foot and the villagers know us of old. Where are you going on this beautiful spring day?"

Will shifted in his saddle and looked uneasy. Rose had heard of his Puritan leanings and how much Ralph and his father, Sir Edward Foulkes, disapproved.

"I am riding out to Stickerton Common." Will's smile faded.

"Father said there is a gadding sermon there today." Rose hoped her answering smile would encourage further confidences.

Will hesitated. "That's right, Rose, and I'm going to listen and pay my respects, though my father would not approve."

"May I journey with you?"

"I shall be out for hours, Rose. Won't your parents be wondering where you are? Your elders would not consider it seemly for you to attend a non-conformist sermon."

"I was on my way to visit Cousin Margaret, who lives near there. Mother has asked me to take her these possets, as she has been unwell. I will not be missed." Using the milestone as a platform, Rose mounted her horse.

"Have you no servant to accompany you?"

Rose settled herself in the saddle and gathered up Inkwell's reins. "Nay, Alfred could not be spared from the farm. There was a difficult calving and he stayed to help. I don't mind riding alone and Mother was busy in the still-room. Father is forever buried in his beloved books these days, so no-one will miss me," she repeated.

"Where is your brother, Tom?" Will asked, as their horses fell into step beside each other.

"Tom has gone out with your own brother, Ralph. I'm not sure where. Riding their horses into the ground, hunting deer, I expect." Rose let her horse amble at an easy walk, pleased to have Will as her only company; pleased to test the strength of her female powers; pleased for the opportunity to compare him to his brother.

"Would you not rather be with your betrothed?"

Rose was silent. She supposed she should be with Ralph, but he would merely laugh at her curiosity about Puritans and cover her lips with kisses, until coherent thinking became impossible. Will, on the other hand, always made her feel peaceful. It was a pleasant contrast to his insistent brother. Will's silences were never awkward but compassionate. Those big brown eyes of his held sympathy, not the laughing derision of Ralph's blue ones. So she remained silent, hoping her inner monologue would commune with Will's in that uncanny way he had of reading the minds of others. She relaxed into the saddle, letting Inkwell set the pace, and enjoying the respite away from her mother's shrill commands and Ralph's pressing desires. Will, as she had hoped, picked up on her mood, leaving his question unanswered and they rode together under the trees, content with letting the birds sing them along their way.

"Tell me about the preacher, Will. Have you heard him before?"

"Nay, but I've heard he's worth listening to."

"So, tell me, what is it that has drawn you into attending these meetings?"

Will's brown eyes lit up with a sombre passion as he spoke in his sincere, straightforward way.

"It all started when Father sent me on a mission to our forest ironworks. He wanted the foundry to make more ammunition for King Charles and I was sent to instruct the workers. On the way, I was set upon by vagabonds."

"Oh, Will, were you hurt?" She peeped at him from under her lashes, seeing if it drove him mad, the way it worked so well on Ralph.

She was gratified when Will couldn't drag his eyes from her face. "Far from it, Rose. When they saw my purse, to be sure, they relieved me of it, but they did not harm me."

"Forsooth, why not? I've heard these vagabonds are vicious and kill for the love of it." Inkwell tripped on a stone so she pulled her up and smoothed her neck until she settled again.

She noticed how Will watched and smiled at her handling of her horse before continuing at his usual measured pace. "That is a black rumour spread around to turn folk against them. Instead of fighting, I talked to them, and found learned men amongst them who had rejected the old ways. These are the people who have come to live in the forest and there are many others who also wanted to escape the laws of the land."

"Outlaws, you mean?" She reached out with her gauntlet and touched his thigh. "I would have been greatly afeared, Will. It is a brave heart to have courage thus."

Will looked down at her hand, and flushed. "They live outside the law, 'tis true." Will bent his head under a hanging branch but it still clipped his hat which fell off and he caught it deftly with one hand.

Rose regarded his bare head and thought how exactly his chestnut hair matched his hazel eyes. She was sorry when he replaced it on his head.

"But they are not wantonly violent men. They do steal from those rich enough to have coins to spare but they do not keep it for themselves. Rather, they distribute their pickings to the poorest amongst society - for this is what drives them, Rose. They seek to create a more equal society everywhere and speak passionately on the subject. 'Twas these outlaws, as you call them, that made me think differently for the first time."

"Do you think differently, Will? Different to whom?" She let Inkwell sidle closer, close enough for their legs to touch now and then.

Will coughed but he didn't move away. "Yes, Rose, I have come to think very differently to my father's unswerving loyalty to the Crown. Think you, why is it that we landowners have so much when poor peasants who labour in the fields all day are made to give us, who have done none of the work, such a large share of their harvest?"

"Is it not so their lord will protect them in times of trouble?" She'd heard her father muttering about his obligations many a time.

Will's attractive voice strengthened as he became impassioned with his subject. "But who is protecting them now? The King didn't even protect Lord Strafford, once his favourite and Lord Deputy of Ireland. Did you know he was executed last week?"

She shook her head, annoyed with her ignorance.

"And did you also not know that John Pym, the leader of the House of Commons, has published new Institutes of the Laws of England?"

Instead of being angry, as she would be if Ralph had questioned her knowledge, she asked, keeping her voice low and submissive, "No, I don't. Tell me, what is that, Will?"

Will smiled. "Have you heard of the Magna Carta?"

"I think so. Is it not very old, dating back to the time of King John?"

"Aye, that's right." Rose was gratified that he acknowledged her educated guess with a graceful nod. "John Pym has re-interpreted those true words and overthrown the might of the King, thus enabling any man to be free and unoppressed by the law of Rex."

"Rex meaning the King?"

"'Aye, 'twas written 'Rex is Lex' before, which means 'The King Rules' but this king does not know how to manage his kingdom with any wisdom. I am glad he can now be overruled. Only God can claim any right to divinity." He turned his head to face front again and she noticed his jaw clenched in anger.

"Are you really glad royal law can be overturned, Will? But," Rose paused to think, "won't these radical ideas turn our world upside down?"

"Aye, Rose, they might well do that."

Will chucked his horse into a trot, making conversation difficult. Rose kept pace, pondering the enormity of Will's words and dwelling on his eloquence. How handsome he had looked as he talked. How different could two brothers be? How unsettling he was; how much more interesting than she'd realised.

They rode on towards Stickerton Common and Will refused to leave her alone when they reached Cousin Margaret's house, which stood in the village next to it. He insisted on paying his dues to the deaf old woman while Rose deposited her mother's possets in the cool scullery and instructed Margaret's maid on their storage.

They stayed and listened to Cousin Margaret's bellowed complaints. Rose listened with ill-contained patience to the shouted ramblings, thinking, like most deaf people, Cousin Margaret assumed no-one could hear her words, simply because she couldn't hear them herself; but Will bore it all with his usual good nature. This surprised and impressed her as, the longer they lingered, the more of the sermon he would miss.

Pleading being needed at home, Rose kissed her cousin goodbye and they returned to the Stickerton road. The horses, having rested, were willing to canter, and they soon made up the time they'd lost at Cousin Margaret's.

It was easy to find the preacher. He stood on a little hill above the common land, where a crowd of silent worshippers listened with intense concentration to his fervent oratory. Will and Rose looped their horses' reins by a willow tree next to a stream and left them to drink their fill, while they quietly walked on foot up the slope and joined the throng. Rose noticed how plainly dressed the congregation was. The better dressed women wore simple white linen caps, grey dresses enlivened only by white collars bearing no lace and the men also went unadorned in severe garb; others simply wore rags. She felt overdressed and overtly wealthy against them and a few of the women looked askance at her favourite russet brown riding habit.

Rose focussed on the preacher and soon forgot about fashion. "Yea, and I walked through the valley of darkness for many years before I saw the light, brethren! You may yet walk there but you will see the light of God in your souls, if you but let Him enter. Every man, every woman, every child, has a right, indeed a duty, to find their own way to God, as I have. Once you have seen that light, my dear children, you will never look back, and all are entitled to this. Let no man deny you. We are all equal in the sight of God. Yea, we are all God's children, and no one of us is less or more than the other."

Rose listened as intently as any in the group of devout Christians. She caught the whiff of sincere piety that the pockmarked preacher evoked in those around her. There were nods and grunts of approval at his eloquent speech. Will's face shone with an inner spirit, and when she saw it mirrored in those next to him, she wondered at how a few words could have such a deep effect. She saw how the rough-looking speaker echoed Will's words on political equality and sensed the ripple of change running through everyone present. After the crowd had dispersed and she and Will rode home through the dimming light, Rose was alternately deep in thought, then blurting out questions to her companion, while she absorbed all these new ideas. Will answered them all with sober patience.

"I remember being as thunderstruck as you at first, Rose. There is so much unrest abroad caused by King Charles' unfair taxes and the dismantling of the wool trade in these parts, I think rebellion was bound to happen. People want to uphold their beliefs their own way, but they also want to be free to trade and prosper, and all is hampered by those in power. People will not tolerate this forever."

"No, I see that change was inevitable but Will, a war will not make things right!"

"I see no other way to settle matters."

They parted at the gates of Charlton House and Rose rode to the stables, weary at last and glad to dismount. Her mother, Agatha, was in the great hall, arranging flowers.

"You did take some time at Cousin Margaret's. I know she can talk, but she rarely listens. Was she very ill?"

"What? Oh, no, not really but as you say, she likes to talk."

"Not for that long. What really kept you, daughter?"

"I, I just enjoyed a long ride, that is all, Mother."

Agatha gave her a shrewd look. "Did you ride with Ralph by any chance?"

"No, I didn't, Mother! I need to speak to Father. Where is he?"

"What do you need to speak to him about? Do we need to bring the date of the wedding forward, perchance?" This was said with a snigger.

"Oh, Mother. Do you think of nothing else?"

"Nay, not about a lass of your age and I'll bet that's the same for Ralph Foulkes, and who could blame him? Such a handsome, virile swain as you have. You cannot keep him at bay forever, child."

"I assume Father is in his chamber?"

Agatha snapped off a bloom that had withered on its stem. "Aye, where else would that man ever be but with his long nose in a book?"

Rose knocked softly on her father's chamber door and waited for his invitation before entering. Roger Charlton did not like to be disturbed. Now she was grown, he would never raise his voice to her, or indeed his hand, but his aloof withdrawal when displeased could wound her just as deeply.

Rose continued to stare at the studs on her father's door until she eventually heard his deep voice issue the command, "Enter."

"Ah, Rose, you have found me contemplating deep matters. This book of George Herbert's has such pearls of wisdom, familiar to me as it is, I discover something new every time I pick it up. Have you something to discuss with me, my child?" Her father didn't actually put his book down but marked the page with a quill and closed it, keeping it in his furled hand as if still connected to the words it contained.

Rose could see his mind remained within its yellow pages, as he looked at her with his solemn brown eyes that remained unfocussed, their pupils still large from reading by candlelight. "Yes, Father, if I may?"

Roger sighed and folded his lips into a thin line. With exaggerated, slow precision, he carefully laid the book down, smoothed its cover and, with reluctance, brought his gaze back to his only daughter and eldest child. Making a church steeple with his hands, he leant his elbows on his desk and at last gave her his attention.

"Father - I have just listened to one of those gadding preachers and..."

"You have done what? Without my permission?"

"I, I wasn't alone, Father. Will Foulkes came with me."

"Will Foulkes is fast becoming a dangerous man to know. If you must be with any of that family, it should have been his elder brother to whom, may I remind you, you are betrothed."

"Yes, Father, but what do you think is going to happen? Will all this unrest lead to war, think you?"

"God's truth, girl! What has any of this to do with you? I have heard no rumours of war breaking out. Things are a little unsettled, 'tis true, but then they always are and there are always gossips to spread rumours, no matter what the season. If you seek deeper thoughts, you could do no worse than to read George Herbert's poetry. Now there is a refined mind, there is true spirituality."

"But, Father, isn't it unfair that the peasants till the fields and pay us for the privilege?"

"Enough of this, Rose! There is much unrest abroad and it is well to keep your counsel."

"But will it lead to war, Father?"

"I trust not, child."

"But if it did, would Ralph be for the King, or Parliament?"

## *"There is nowhere to hide from me."*

"Library first?" Percy parked her shiny Mini-Cooper in one of the central car parks.

"Coffee first," I replied quickly, "and cake."

We stepped into the little café to the tune of its tinkling bell and I felt my ever-ready stomach relax. It was all so delightfully ordinary. We sat by the window and ordered our drinks and my carbs from the young waitress. The aroma of coffee pervaded the cheery place and the chink of china acted like a balm on my frayed nerves.

"This is nice." Percy echoed my thoughts.

"Very."

We sipped our coffees silently; hers black, mine with a triumph of foam atop its wide cup. Percy had, of course, refused patisseries but I chomped contentedly on an almond croissant, relishing its sweet reassurance.

When our cups and my plate were empty, Percy looked at me and smiled. "Better?"

"Much."

"So, where do we start?"

"I still think the library's the best place. At least they'll have computers there, presumably."

"Yes, even Devizes has entered the twenty-first century. Sure you don't want another croissant, Fay?" Percy's lovely mouth creased up into a smile.

I decided not to over-react to her teasing and, after arguing over the bill, we left together amicably and headed off to the library a couple of streets away.

The library was housed, not in one of the graceful Georgian buildings that lined the large market square, but in an ugly sixties cube down an obscure side street. It was surprisingly gloomy inside and the librarian no less so. A cursory glance was all the welcome we got.

Undeterred, I asked the woman, a short, slight female in her sagging middle years who looked as dried out as the pages of any book, if she could point us in the direction of books on the Civil War.

"Do you mean the English Civil War?"

"Yes, that's the one."

"In the 1600's?"

"Yes, please."

She sighed. "We don't have that much but I suppose you're welcome to look in the history section. It's over there, fifth shelf on the left."

"Thank you. Do you know if there is any local history of that period?"

"I'm not a historian, I'm a librarian. I suggest you search the shelves yourself."

"Right. I see, thanks."

Percy, unmoved by this exchange, probed further. "And are there any computers we could use?"

The librarian narrowed her eyes behind her batwing glasses. "We have two."

"Lovely, and do we need a password?"

The woman pursed her lips and passed over a miniscule scrap of paper with some numbers on it.

"Thanks." Percy picked it up in her manicured hand and bestowed her sumptuous smile upon the husk of humanity behind the desk. No answering smile came back.

"Come on," I said to Percy.

The librarian raised a finger. "One moment. I would remind you that this is a library and silence is mandatory. At *all* times."

I simply nodded, not prepared to waste another second on this diminutive autocrat.

We walked, ever so softly, trying not to giggle like schoolgirls, to the fifth shelf along the left. Sure enough, there were some hefty tomes on the Civil War amongst the plethora of books about the two world wars.

"So much war. Will people ever stop fighting each other?" Percy whispered.

"I doubt it. We're a warped species." I looked at the volumes in despair, not knowing where to start.

Percy was more decisive and scooped up every book on the subject and staggered with the pile on to the nearest table, dumping half on each side.

"Let's get started then," she said with a grin, forgetting to whisper.

From nowhere, the waspy librarian appeared, again with her finger raised, this time against her lips. "Sshh!"

Percy averted her eyes from mine and bent her sleek head over her pile of books but I wasn't deceived; I saw her dainty shoulders shaking with suppressed mirth.

Frowning, the librarian turned away and started filing books back in the romance section. I couldn't help noticing there were some torrid book covers in her hands. Surely reading must broaden the mind?

We couldn't speak, Madam Librarian was well within earshot. I cleared my throat, smothering the laughter threatening to break through it and concentrated on the matter in hand.

The first book I flicked through had some colourful pictures of the fashions of the time. I instantly recognised the different costumes of the two brothers, confirming my theory of their fighting on opposing sides.

The King's men, or cavaliers as they were known, looked very fine in their colourful outfits. Broad hats sported huge plumed feathers, skirted jackets bloomed over silken breeches and should have looked feminine, especially with their long hair worn down to their shoulders but their war-like faces brayed their gender by yet more hairy embellishments. Pointy beards imitated Charles the First, as had Ralph's, and handlebar moustaches trumpeted their machismo. They all seemed to espouse those ridiculously wide leather boots with vicious looking spurs on their heels. To a man, they carried swords, great shafts of steel in decorated sheaths. It looked very awkward to me and I knew I'd trip over mine should I ever be unfortunate enough to wear one.

I turned the page. The Roundhead soldier depicted there looked grim by comparison. Stern, too, and full of purpose. His metal helmet hid no flowing locks and was unadorned by feathers, or anything else. He looked ready for battle with his metal waistcoat and orange cummerbund. He also carried a sword that meant business but without the bejewelled scabbard. His leather boots were even taller, again wide at the top; didn't they chafe his thighs? No facial fur on this weathered face, just harsh and uncompromising furrows behind the metal bars of his helmet. The orange sash splashed the only colour in a diagonal line across his impressive chest.

Yes, it was pretty obvious which side Ralph and Will had each been on when I'd seen them arguing in the bedroom at Meadowsweet Manor.

I dared to look up and over to where our dear helper had been organising shelves. She was nowhere in sight.

"Psst! Percy," I whispered.

Percy looked up, her eyes screwed together to try and see. Really, this girl needed glasses. Next stop the chemists for some ready readers.

"Look, Percy. See these uniforms? This was what Ralph was wearing, but in sky-blue - very fetching." I turned the page. "And this was the type of gear Will wore, except he wasn't in battle dress like this guy, but you can tell it was the same style of uniform in tanned leather."

Percy blinked and studied the contrasting drawings. "So it *was* brother against brother. How awful." She traced the outline of the Roundhead with her finger.

I retrieved the heavy book and turned it round to face me again. "Bit of a misnomer, Civil War. Looks damned *un*civil to me."

There was a loud cough directly behind me. I didn't need to turn around to guess who'd made the noise. We put our heads down again and, like contrite children, perused the account of the dramatic times that led to England chopping off the head of its own king. It was engrossing stuff and an hour passed without my realising. The librarian, having secured our silence, left us in peace and Percy and I read in mute harmony.

I was wrestling with The Ship Money trial of 1637 and thinking, as any decent accountant might, that tax was bound to raise its ugly head with a man who thought he ruled by Divine Right, when I noticed a trickling sensation down my wounded arm. I had taken off my coat, as the library was a lot warmer than its frosty reception might indicate. My jumper was a pale cream one, cabled like a cricket sweater. I looked down at my arm, alarmed to see a red stain oozing through the wool. Now I thought about it, my arm was throbbing with a dull pain, almost as if the wound had re-opened. Almost as if, but no, that couldn't be...almost as if someone was digging into it with another thorn. Another *rose* thorn. I shivered in the cold draught that swirled around my legs.

The room receded.

Feeling slightly sick, I looked down, my eyes inexorably drawn to one of the pictures before me, entitled 'The Battle of Edgehill', 23rd October 1642. The still forms began to move on the page. They fleshed out into three dimensions. The horses neighed and galloped across the paper, their riders yelling and brandishing swords. Again I smelt the tang of iron as metal found flesh. Smoke threatened to choke me from the muskets popping nearby. The racket of the horses' hooves thundered in my ears. I rubbed my forehead to clear it from the chaotic noise of battle. Round metal helmets turned towards me; the faces inside alternately terrified and angry. Closer they came. The screaming of the cavaliers around me intensified. The soldier next to me stood up in his stirrups and yelled, "God Save The King!" His sword pointed horizontally towards the Roundhead in front of him. The Parliamentarian stared back, then dropped his gaze, hauled his horse's neck around and pounded away in flight.

Someone shouted nearby, "After them, my lads!" The horses found extra speed from somewhere, gathering their long legs up, nostrils flaring, chests heaving, as they chased the retreating Parliamentary cavalry.

My breath came in gasps and something, or someone, was shaking me violently.

"Fay! Wake up!"

An agitated hand joggled my shoulder. They were trying to wobble me off my horse! I elbowed them in the belly, I wasn't going to miss this rout.

"Ow! Fay, you must wake up!" A sharp exhalation had accompanied this command but I wasn't having any of it.

"What is going on? I thought I had made it quite clear that this is a no talking area!" Another female voice joined in but I didn't recognise either.

"I'm sorry, my friend isn't well."

"What's wrong with her?"

"Um, she's sort of..."

"Is she having a fit?"

"In a way..."

The battle ebbed away from me. I could no longer hear the stampeding hooves, the clash of steel, no longer smell the sweat of the straining horses, or the shouts of my triumphant comrades. I blinked and swayed and reached out my arms to stop myself falling - only to find the solid mass of the plywood table and a blob of old chewing gum under its edge. I opened my eyes and stared into two alarmed ones behind batwing glasses.

Percy abandoned our books, grabbed me and our coats, unplugged our charging phones and we staggered out into the cold air. The hard pavement dipped and swayed in waves before me and I resisted the urge to throw up. I clutched Percy's arm and did not argue when she marched me back into the cheery café where we'd enjoyed our coffee earlier.

"Sit down, Fay."

Percy pushed me down into a corner seat and poured me a glass of water from the carafe on the table. "Drink this. Go on."

I drank. The water clinked with ice-cubes and the cold liquid jolted my senses back into the present. I blinked and the nausea receded.

Percy was staring at me intently, her creamy forehead marred by a frown.

"Back again already?" The young waitress of this morning's carefree break stood smiling at us, notepad in hand.

"Could you give us a minute?" Percy said. "We're not quite ready to order."

With a look that said, 'not surprised, you only had coffee a couple of hours ago,' the girl retreated behind the counter of cakes. It was looking at that splendid array of sweet delights that brought me round.

I let out my breath in a long whoosh. "Sorry about that, Percy."

"That's alright, Fay, but what happened?"

I told her about my foray into the battle of Edgehill.

"But that means... Oh God, Fay, that means we're not safe wherever we are! I thought the ghosts could only reach us at home."

"I'm sure it was just my overactive imagination," I said, half convincing myself.

"But you weren't daydreaming, Fay. You were in one of your trances, just like those I've seen at the manor. That was no flight of fancy. You were living it. And look at the state of you. You can't tell me you're not shaken up."

I couldn't deny it. I didn't even fancy eating any of that marvellous food.

"And, oh no, your jumper! Your wound is leaking. We should get that sorted out."

My arm did ache. "I felt someone was poking the cut with another thorn, just before I morphed into a cavalier."

"Ugh, that's creepy," Percy's wide mouth turned down at the corners.

So Rose hadn't been manipulating her then.

I cleared my throat as well as my mind. "We'd better go to the chemist's and get more plasters - and see about getting you some reading glasses. I saw you squinting in the library." And it would be a nice, prosaic errand. Nice and run-of-the-mill.

I felt a rumble of hunger. Sanity had returned.

"Now, Percy, what do you fancy for lunch and don't bloody say salad!"

Will studied his father's face as he perused the broadsheet.

"By thunder, these images from Ireland sicken me." Sir Edward shoved the parchment away from him and glugged from his pewter tankard.

Will took up the paper. His eyes widened at the disgusting scenes depicted there.

"Surely these cannot be true? Children roasted on spits before their parents' eyes? Such widespread rape and torture? Can we verify them, Father?"

Ralph looked at him with scorn. "Difficult for a milksop like you to imagine such lusts, I suppose, Will? Where was your God in Ireland?"

"Ireland was ever a wild place," Sir Edward muttered.

"There is lust and there is depravity." Will could not believe his brother would condone such behaviour.

"We do like to cut a fine line, don't we, brother?"

Sir Edward grunted. "Catholics, the lot of them. Always a barbarous lot. Look at Queen Bloody Mary - she didn't get that nickname for nothing." Their father looked from one son to another, his eyes sad and bloodshot.

"That's as maybe, but Pym is now refusing our King his royal prerogative to send an Irish expeditionary army to quell the rebellion. How can the man have become so powerful?" Will could see a vein pulsing on Ralph's forehead as his brother spoke.

"And this Grand Remonstrance Pym's concocted. How dare he remonstrate with our sovereign? What is the world coming to? We had none of this in my day. King James might have kept unsavoury company but he kept the country together. Now it's coming apart at the seams." Sir Edward took a swig of ale.

"You are strangely silent, Will." Ralph looked across the table where Will sat, his eyes still resting on the crude depictions of battered children.

Will felt shaken to the core by the grotesque images and an anger had ignited somewhere deep in his bowels, thankfully still intact, unlike those poor innocent children.

"I am praying for those poor Irish Protestants."

"Praying, praying!" Sir Edward stood up and banged his tankard onto the table. "What use is praying, boy? It's religion they're damn well fighting over!"

Sir Edward swept out of the room, calling out for Young Peter to saddle his old grey horse.

"So, Will, my dearest, well, my *only* brother, where do your sympathies lie? Would you support the King and help crush this ugly rebellion or would you rather join in with the mealy words of John Pym and give his Majesty a public humiliation?"

"Happily, Ralph, I do not have to make that decision. I cannot condone the violence in Ireland, but I cannot help but feel greater parliamentary control and more just taxes would create a fairer system."

"Is that so? Well, I wouldn't go braying that abroad, especially not to Father."

A few weeks later, news filtered out from London that the Grand Remonstrance had been passed by a narrow majority in the House of Commons. By December there were rumours that the Queen, with her dangerous loyalty to the Catholic faith, was to be impeached. The year turned, and on a bitterly cold January day in the new one of 1642, Will rode into their local town on an errand for the manor house. Snow threatened from a gun-metal sky.

Martha had given him a list of items to purchase for the household. Once he'd completed this, he headed for a tavern on the square he knew to have parliamentary leanings. He needed to find out more about the latest story from London. He'd heard a tall tale he could hardly credit to be true and he was determined to get to the bottom of it.

Ordering a meat pie and jug of ale, Will positioned himself near the huge fire on a wooden settle, confident he would soon be joined by someone willing to gossip. A boy in a leather apron plonked down his simple meal and Will paid him a few coins. The pie smelt good and the icy temperature outside had sharpened his appetite. He bit into the savoury filling, burning his mouth a little.

He was just finishing the last piece of piecrust and preparing to lick his salty fingers, when a couple of prosperous looking merchants came in, calling for ale and heading straight for the blazing fire.

"Good day to you, sirs." Will nodded at them over his tankard.

"Nothing good can come of this day, my lad." The taller man took his tankard from the pot-boy and swigged a great gulp down.

The other man took off his hat and threw it down on the fireside settle. "Ay, grave news indeed."

"Can I ask of what you speak, gentlemen?" Will indicated the spare seat on his bench.

As he had hoped, the tall man, having roasted his rear, duly sat next to him. "The news hasn't reached you then?"

Will shook his head.

The shorter man took up the tale. "I've never heard the like of it. Can you read, lad? Well this is the pamphlet we've just picked up." He handed it over to Will, saying "The King has gone too far this time."

"How so?" Will stared at the crude cartoon of a throne-like chair with five birds flying above it.

"His Majesty only took an armed guard into the Commons chamber in Westminster where our MP's were gathered and going about their legitimate business."

The other man nodded and took another draught of ale, burping slightly as he set his pewter mug back down on the stained table.

"The King took the Speaker's chair as if it was his own throne." His drinking companion pointed his finger at the pamphlet. "Then his Royal Majesty commanded the poor man to point out the five members he had threatened to impeach the previous day." The man shook his head in disbelief at his own words.

His companion chimed in. "Except they had been tipped off and had very sensibly already left and were getting away in a boat on the Thames."

"So then the King said, to save his face, 'I see that all the birds have flown' and took himself back to Whitehall."

"Ah, I see, that explains the birds. Who are these Five Members?" Will was agog for more.

"John Hampden, Denzil Holles, Sir Arthur Haselrig, and, damn me, who were the others, John?"

John picked up the pamphlet and read from it. "Says here, Montagu and Strode, I think, the writing is very poor."

"Ah yes, all good men and true. Unlike our sovereign. How can you trust a ruler who forces his way into Parliament demanding its members be arrested because he doesn't like their criticism of him?"

"That Queen of his will be behind it with her Catholic sympathisers." The tall man drained his mug of ale.

"Want another, young man?" The choleric shorter man said.

"Aye, and I'll pay, if you'll keep talking." Will spilled some more coins on the beer-stained table.

John nodded and called the potboy for three more tankards. "And the worst of it all, for me at least, is that the King has shown himself to be a coward by scuttling off to Hampton Court before the apprentices beat his door down."

His friend let out a harsh laugh. "Aye, you speak truth, John, but at least Pym and his cronies can get back to work now his Majesty has cleared off."

"Aye, that is so but do not forget the King declared them traitors before he left." The shorter man scratched his head.

"But with the Queen now running back to France, where she belongs, and the King gone from Westminster, Parliament can regroup and collect its wits again."

"Not if the apprentices can help it. Roundheads they call 'em because of their thick, shaven heads. They're  rousing a rabble any chance they get and shouting 'Privilege' about the King, trying to stir things up even more." John lowered his voice and added, "not that I'm blaming them for that."

His pint-sized friend nodded. "Ay, John, I'm with you there but now barricades have been put up all over London to quell the riots."

"Perhaps things will settle down as a result?" Will looked from one to the other of the older men.

"Settle down? 'Tis more likely than ever the country will be divided, perhaps even by the sword."

All three men drank their ale in silence at the prospect.

Will rode home under darkening skies with flakes of snow the only speck of brightness. He turned his collar up against the icy blast from the north wind and nudged his horse's sides into a brisk trot. However cold he was, it didn't stop his mind from teeming with bewildering images of his King striding into Parliament and trying to enforce his will upon its members. He suspected both his father and brother would admire this show of strength, but to Will, King Charles appeared both reckless and foolish. Such intemperate behaviour did not demonstrate wisdom but unbridled willpower. Did their sovereign never stop to reflect before taking action? Did he think the only way to achieve his ambitions was through force rather than reasoned debate and dialogue? How could war be avoided if he trumpeted his way through the Commons with an armed guard at his heels, expecting to wave an imperious finger at its rightful Members?

The ground was white by the time he reached Meadowsweet Manor, laden with Martha's shopping. The snow continued to fall for a week and it was some time before any of them could get abroad for further news. Ralph was the first to venture out through the drifts of snow that had accumulated on the rutted roads. When he returned, looking as frozen as the ground, he told them King Charles had retreated again, this time to Windsor, while the river workers had risen up and gone to Westminster. According to his sources, London now seethed with Parliamentary revolt.

"The King's hopes lie in Scotland, I heard in The Woolsack Inn, and he's trying to broker peace with Pym's Parliament but that twisted sorcerer isn't having it. He doesn't know the meaning of compromise."

Sir Edward nodded and listened before making his own retreat to the fire and his bottle of brandy. Later that chilly month, Will had mixed feelings when he heard that the King and the Commons had a rare moment of agreement in raising a million pounds to suppress revolt in Ireland, rewarding those who invested in the scheme with the 10 million acres of the best Irish land, confiscated from its native rebels.

His great consolation through his mental turmoil was, astonishingly, Rose. More and more these days, she was turning to Will for advice on the commotion unfolding around them, as Ralph was often from home training the Militia Band he'd joined. Ralph talked of nothing else, especially after he met the Lord Lieutenant himself and had been noticed by the great man. It all served to make Will feel more redundant than ever, as he could not bring himself to join the King's side. He became more estranged from his father, who could not and would not understand his reluctance, calling him a coward and a wastrel. After one particularly ugly scene, Will made a point of rarely sharing a room or a meal with him.

This distance from his father's scrutiny released him to spend more time with Rose, and the confidence she placed in his judgement and opinions made his tormented heart swell with pride. He noticed that she'd taken to wearing more modest clothing, without the gaudy colours she'd flaunted before. To his eyes, this new modesty only made her lovelier, leaving no jarring note to distract from her natural beauty.

They developed a custom of walking or riding in the woods where they had met the day Rose accompanied him to Stickerton Common. Will would never, not as long as he lived, forget that pivotal day when Rose had begun to see their topsy-turvy world through his eyes. The lovely glade had become as sacred to him as any church.

The ancient oak tree at the centre of their special place was just beginning to unfurl its tender green leaves one day in early spring. They sat on its gnarled roots together, as had become their habit.

Will was still perplexed by the reports from Ireland, which had not improved since the winter. He told Rose, "I can see that the wretched Irish rebellion had to be stopped but they've virtually put the whole of Ireland up for auction to the highest bidder. I see only trouble ahead for that woebegone country as a result of this. Where do they expect the rebels to go?"

"Will it not lead to further conflict, Will?" Rose rested her lovely eyes on his face, as she so often did now.

"Ay, Rose, it will. Conflict, poverty, refugees - everything will unravel now."

*"I have you, wherever you go. There is no escape."*

Over lunch, mine a steak and kidney pie with some excellent chips, Percy's a beetroot soup with courgette bread, we discussed our next line of enquiry.

"Let's try the museum," suggested Percy, delicately wiping dark red marks from the corners of her full lips with her paper serviette.

"Worth a go, I suppose."

The museum curator, a grey-haired tweedy lady reminiscent of an earlier age, although perfectly friendly, informed us within five minutes of our arrival that the museum was shutting early due to essential refurbishment.

"Tea with the vicar, or even Miss Marple, more likely," I whispered behind my hand.

Percy pinched me to shut up.

We left empty handed. "There wasn't anything relevant anyway. Nothing but fossils. All way too far back in time."

Percy nodded her agreement. "How about the bookshop?"

"Good idea."

The doorbell of the large bookshop trilled a jaunty welcome as we entered its cavernous bounty. I inhaled the unique aroma of books. My shoulders might be outsized but they always relaxed with that smell. Silently, we both gravitated to the history shelves. My hopes weren't high after the disappointment of the museum but, on the very bottom shelf, I spied a drawing of a plumed hat on a thin, tall book over-topping the others. I swooped down and found to my delight a large A4 book, obviously written by a local enthusiast, describing in minute, heaven-sent detail a battle that had taken place just above Devizes on Roundway Hill.

"Percy, look what I've found."

Percy peered over my shoulder and her face lit up. "Wow! What a find. We must buy it right now."

"You know I've been so flipping dumb. Of course - the battle of Roundway Down. I remember touching on this at school, very briefly. How could I have forgotten?"

We rushed to the till and Percy paid with trembling fingers. "That seems very reasonable."

"Peanuts for treasure." I couldn't wait to read it. "Come on, let's go to a café and peruse our perfect find."

"Not the same one again, please! And I'm still full from lunch."

"I'm sure you could squeeze in a herbal tea, Percy."

"Oh, alright then. Look, there's a coffee shop there. That'll do."

I ordered an espresso coffee for me and a peppermint brew for Percy. I tapped my feet with impatience while the barista fizzed and popped the coffee machine. It smelt divine but it always took so damn long. Eventually I carried the tray to where Percy had grabbed one of the few tables left. She was squinting over the pages. A soothing babble of conversation reinforced the normality of our coffee-break.

"The chemist next, Percy." I placed the tray down on the little circular table. As always in these places, the tiny table wobbled and her tea spilled on to the saucer.

"Careful! Why do we need to go to a chemist's, Fay? Aren't you well?"

"I'm fine, although I am going to stock up on first aid kit and plasters, just in case you come at me with another rose bush or, God help us, a sword or something. No, the other thing is reading glasses for you, you chump."

Percy mopped up her spilt tea and smiled. "You are quite right, Fay. Luckily the print in this amazing book is quite large and there are lots of colourful pictures. They are quite childlike, look."

"Maybe the school got involved. Bound to be on the local curriculum." I slurped my coffee. It tasted really good. Thick and strong as treacle. Within five minutes the caffeine had fired up my flagging, overworked brain.

Percy opened the pages to show maps of the battle. "Look, Fay, it was obviously quite a fight and with a cast of thousands of men. It says here that the Parliamentarians were camped up on the downs and some of them were firing down on the town of Devizes below."

"Good vantage point by the looks of it, where was it?"

"It's called Jump Hill, I think." Percy traced the map with her finger.

"Couldn't have been much fun being on the receiving end of that barrage." I tried to picture the scene.

"No, but then the Royalists came swooping down here and engaged with them on the lower plateau," Percy frowned over the little crosses and boxes on the map.

"Come on, drink up and let's get those glasses. Then I think we should drive up to Roundway Hill." Only the dregs of my coffee stained my little espresso cup now and with brain awake, I wanted to discover more. "It's quite restful to do some conventional research and not be fighting in a virtual battle. Thank God our old friends left me alone in here." I got up to go.

Percy left half her tea and followed me out of the modern café. She picked out some trendy tortoiseshell specs from the rack of ready readers in the chemist shop.

"What do you think, Fay?"

"Very fetching. Point is, can you see better? Can you read these tiny letters on the sample?"

Percy took the card and read out the bottom line. "Clear as a bell! Goodness, what a difference!"

"Well worth ten quid then. Hurry up and pay and let's go exploring."

I knew the way up Roundway Down but it had been many years since I'd ventured there. Not since Robin's death had I felt the remotest desire to revisit the massive hill. Many walkers had done so in the meantime and there were well worn footpaths, rutted car tyre-tracks and signs describing the local flora and fauna all along the approach road. Much more organised nowadays than that midsummer's night when I had been sixteen and in love.

I had not told Percy the details of that night and I had no intention of doing so now. She was concentrating on driving along the narrow lane up the very steep hill, so my silence went unremarked. I was struggling with an overwhelming sense of claustrophobia in her flash sports car. I lowered the electric window, gasping for air. My heart thumped too rapidly and it wasn't all down to the caffeine in that espresso.

Percy had to pull in to allow a car coming the other way to pass. She yanked on the handbrake and looked at me. "Fay? Are you alright?"

I swallowed the lump constricting my airways. I could only nod and tried to smile. Percy didn't drive on when the descending four-by-four passed us by, without bothering to wave any thanks.

"Fay, what is it?"

I regretted that coffee now. Adrenaline coursed through my veins, making my breathing quick and shallow. I couldn't squeeze a word of reassurance through my tight throat.

Percy reached out and touched my knee. "Are they back again? Have you gone back in time?"

I shook my head and turned to her kind, concerned face. "It's alright, too much coffee, that's all." My words came in staccato gasps. Embarrassing really and the feeble excuse of coffee would hardly explain my panic.

"Do you want me to turn back?" Percy's new glasses glinted in a shaft of sunlight that shone across the top of her auburn hair where they perched, like frog's eyes.

Did I want to turn back? Hell, yes.

I took a gulp of windswept hillside air, swallowed its oxygen, and straightened my spine. "No way. Now we're here, let's see what we can find."

We bumped along the muddy track and parked up in a make-shift car park on the brow of the hill. To our right, there was a huge field, with cropped wheat stalks stretching for acres and beyond that, a sweep of rising ground crowned on the horizon by a clump of beech or oak trees, still in leaf. I couldn't tell their variety from this distance, which I guessed to be around four miles. On our left was a straggle of woodland bisected by an inviting footpath.

"I don't have my walking boots with me." Percy switched off the engine.

"Just have to get messy shoes, I guess." The way my knees had turned to jelly made dirty shoes a petty concern. I'd be grateful if I could just put one foot in front of the other and propel myself back into my personal nightmare. How often had I dreamt about this place? And I always woke up sweating and fighting bedclothes that threatened to suffocate me. How could I face it now?

Percy had got out of the car and was rummaging in the boot. "Aha! A cagoule." She held the coat up triumphantly. "There's a brolly too. Would you like to borrow it?"

"Thanks." I had little hope an umbrella would cope with this wind but it might be a useful weapon to fight any demons hiding in the menacing dark spaces behind the straggle of blackberry bushes.

We climbed over a stile and entered the woods. A few early autumn leaves littered the wide path and trickled down from the stately beeches, reminding us that September would soon be here. The wind whipped through their trunks, catching us in sporadic gusts and making the fallen amber foliage eddy around our ankles.

"It's so beautiful here, isn't it, Fay? Hard to imagine men killing each other in such a peaceful place."

It was no good. I couldn't chat. I walked faster. I had to be alone. Percy took the hint and stopped to take some photos on her mobile, briefly charged up in the library. I marched on, not thinking, not remembering, but concentrating on building up a brisk pace. The trees petered out and I found myself, once again, on the edge of the escarpment. My memories didn't match the view. It hadn't been here. I couldn't be sure, it had been so dark that awful night, but no hackles rose on the back of my neck. My breathing calmed and when Percy caught up with me, I was able to gaze at the tremendous vista with impartial objectivity. Below us huddled Devizes; from its centre, arteries of tarmac hosted satellite villages in all directions. Steam rose from the brewery chimney and a faint waft of malt hung on the air. The flat river plain stretched beyond the town towards Bath but mist obscured the line of the distant horizon. It could have been the sea with that bluish tinge blurring into the pastel sky.

"What a sight. You can see for miles and miles." Percy took out her new book and flicked the pages. "Ah, yes, no wonder the Parliamentary troops camped up here. It's easy to see why. You can view all the countryside around pretty much in all directions."

"Yes, ideal strategic position," was my pleasingly rational reply. I had finally got a grip. "Let's compare the map with the landscape. Together, we traced the positions of the troops.

"So, the Cavaliers came thundering down from over there, um, Roughridge Hill, it says here. You can see why they'd get up a good gallop, coming down that slope." Percy traced the map with her finger but her kind face looked sad. "Those poor horses. What must they have gone through."

I shoved my hands in my pockets, alarmed to find my silver chain felt very warm. We walked on and turned sharp right, away from the edge of trees and towards the battle scene indicated on the map. Halfway along the hedged field, I began to feel strange. Nauseous. Sweat pricked out along my hairline on my forehead. Just like the moment before Robin cried out, before he.., but worse, much worse.

The weather changed. Rain spattered my clammy face. For a second I thought I really had heard Robin's voice but then it became muffled, indistinct, as many voices drowned out his beloved one. Now they were shouting. Hoarse men's voices and then thunder. No, not thunder. Hooves. Hundreds of them, bearing down on me, drumming in my ears.

My knees buckled and I hit the ground, grazing my face on wheat stalks.

Someone screamed nearby. A lone female voice among the myriad male ones.

"Fay! Why are you screaming? Oh, goodness!"

Then some gentle hand was wiping my mouth with a tissue. No wonder. I'd thrown up my generous lunch. I gagged on the acrid taste of vomit and sat up. I had no idea where I was.

"Fay, dear. You've been ill. Here, let me help." Percy patted my shoulder.

I hung my head between my knees and clutched the softer grass under the hedgerow. It wasn't wet. It wasn't raining. The grass was dry, bone dry, under the strip of hawthorn. The breeze was cool and sprightly and stroked my face when I lifted it up again. My ribs ached from contracting my stomach. "Gotta go."

"Of course, but don't you want a moment to come to, Fay?"

I shook my head, "Gotta go. Car."

Percy tucked her slender arm under my robust one and heaved me to my feet. My shoes, liberally smothered in clay and other blobs too gross to think about, were almost too heavy to lift, but somehow we made it back to the car. I sat in the passenger seat, still dizzy, still confused, and closed my eyes.

Percy's compassionate silence undid me. Big, fat tears rolled down my mucky face. Still she said nothing.

I broke the silence. "Let's go home, Percy, and I'll explain everything."

She flicked on the ignition and the engine purred into life.

When they met one August day, some months later, Will brought Rose the communication they had both dreaded.

"Well, it has finally happened, Rose. Ralph was full of the news last night. He honoured us with a rare appearance when he supped with us at the manor. In truth, I do not often sup with my father these days either and I did not relish his bragging at the table, but Father drank in every word my brother spoke."

They were strolling in their secret glade, talking quietly. Will found it very restful and soothing to his troubled spirit.

"What has happened, Will?"

"The King has raised his standard in Nottingham."

"What does that mean?"

"I am sorry to say it means, Rose, we are at war. At war with each other." He kicked a tree root, hurting his toe and relishing the pain.

"But I thought, last time we met, you said the King had been refused arms with which to fight, at - Hull - was not it? How can he now declare war, if he has not arms to fight with?"

"You speak truth, Rose. Aye, Sir John Hotham stood up to his Royal Majesty at Kingston-upon-Hull, like the stout Parliamentarian he is but, despite his lack of arms, our bloodthirsty king has declared war on his own people, using the old Commission of Array to do so."

"How many soldiers does he have, do you know, Will?"

"Close on two thousand cavalry and Ralph is itching to join them."

"Two thousand men and horses. I cannot picture so many together. They will take a great deal of feeding." Rose looked thoughtful.

"A wise remark, Rose, and a womanly thought that does you credit. Aye, the countryside around will be stripped bare for his royal army and I dare say our king will claim the victuals are his by divine right." Will rubbed his forehead. He'd not slept much the night before.

They walked on in silence. Rose pecked him on the cheek, for the first time, before parting. Will, though still sad at heart, was yet uplifted by the reluctance Rose seemed to feel on leaving him and touched his hand to his blessed cheek all that afternoon.

Ralph surprised him by still being at Meadowsweet Manor when he returned home and launched straight into an attack on his brother before Will could absent himself.

"Nay, Will, biding still at your father's hearth? Is it not time, brother, for you to join the Trained Band and fight for your royal sovereign, now that he has raised his standard? God's blood, there are boys younger than you eager to fight. And we have arms for all, at last, thanks to the silver Father and other loyal squires in the county have generously donated."

Will, caught unawares, struggled to answer his brother's direct demand and gave no answer.

"Have you no stomach to fight, little brother, is that it? Tongues are wagging about your reluctance amongst my men." Ralph stood, legs apart, challenging him like a rutting stag and barring his way into the great hall.

"There is more than one way to fight, Ralph." Will faced his brother and stared deep into those bright blue eyes.

"You speak truth, I grant you. There are muskets as well as swords, but I see you do not carry either, even in these uncertain times." Ralph barked a laugh at his own joke.

"Nay, I do not." Will gave no answering smile.

"And what would be your shield, if attacked? Your piety?" Ralph's hand strayed to the hilt of his scabbard and hovered over it.

Will's eyes never wavered from his brother's challenging stare. "Aye, my faith."

Ralph gave a great shout of laughter, dropping his hand and bringing his other up to clap both together.

"Your faith! Aye, Will Sobersides, that will afford you a fine protection." Ralph cuffed him lightly around the ear. "Why, little brother, I do fear for you, if you think your God will stop a sword and protect your tender flesh. Sweet Jesu, I have no time for this mealy-mouthed nonsense. I'm off to Charlton House to visit my betrothed. I've a mind to call the wedding forward. I shall be off to war soon, Will, and wish to secure my bride before I depart for battle. In truth, I have seen little of her of late."

Before Will could stop him, Ralph disappeared, as swift as a swallow in summer. Everything Ralph did, he did in haste and with vigour and his parting words left Will in no doubt that he would act upon them with his usual speed and determination. And he had no means at his disposal with which to forewarn Rose of her betrothed's arrival.

*** 

Rose was lingering in the garden, gathering flowers for the table, putting off the moment of returning to the house, so she could school her face back into the bland mask she wore these days before her sharp-eyed mother.

The summer was fading. August blooms wilted in the dusty heat, not yielding their scent willingly until dusk. Only the roses looked fresh and new and Rose was drawn to her namesakes. She took a sharp knife from the still room, along with a willow basket, and decided to pluck from the climbing rose that clambered over the arch at the entrance to the square rose garden.

This rose was in a second flush, so its delicate blooms grew less profusely than in May, but still it provided an arbour of the palest pink bunches that drooped and dipped on their rustic poles. Rose tilted her head back to inhale their aroma, delighting in the fragrance of the open flowers. She bent down to place her basket on the path but gasped in shock when a strong hand cupped her buttock and swung her around.

Before she could speak, she was silenced by lips sealing her mouth with a deep kiss. Strong arms kept her pinioned to her assailant long enough for her wicked body to respond to his knowing skill. She felt desire flood her bones and soon gave up the struggle to resist; answering kiss for kiss and forgetting everything and everyone else in the world, and dropping her knife to the ground in order to grip his waist instead.

Her breath was coming thick and fast before Ralph withdrew; that hated, familiar and complacent smile on his face, his eyes alight with a passion she suspected was matched in her own. She had not wanted him to stop kissing her, and he knew it. A deep-throated chuckle emanated from deep in his chest and he threw back his head and laughed like a lion.

"God's teeth, Rose but you are the most passionate woman I have ever kissed and I love you more for it. Come, let us not tarry. I'm for war. The King has reached the next county and I mean to join him, but before I do, let us be married and have done with this child's game we have played for too long. I need you more than ever, Rose. I do not wish to risk my life before I have tasted all of you."

Rose was having trouble controlling her rapid breathing. She had known this day would come; that Ralph would come and claim his betrothal rights but she had not reckoned on it so soon. Damn the king, damn him into hellfire, that he should force her hand before she had made up her mind as to which Foulkes brother she wanted most. She wanted this dual game to go on forever. She liked the power it bestowed on her; she enjoyed receiving the different types of loving from both these handsome neighbours of hers and she was not yet ready to give up either of them. She turned her head away, that Ralph might not see the heightened colour she knew she displayed. His ardour had unmasked her and she still longed for him but that would not do; that would be defeat.

And Rose preferred to win.

"I am not yet ready, Ralph. Yes, you are comely enough, I grant you, but have a care to my person."

"You are nineteen now, Rose. More than old enough to be wed and of the age we agreed. I can wait no longer to bed you. You know that, surely to God?"

Rose turned away, picked up her blade and basket and resumed cutting the roses from the arbour. She needed to gather her wits.

Ralph grasped her arm. "Leave that, woman! And look at me. Tell me you do not care for me? Hah - silence - for I know you do. Your lips, though silent, have given their answer in their kiss. Come then, let us be married forthwith."

"No, leave me alone, Ralph. You cannot force me to wed you."

"Can I not?" Ralph shoved her against the prickly rose, making the poles of the arbour shake against her back. Thorns dug into her flesh, making her cry out, but Ralph ignored her protests and once more brought his mouth down upon hers. She felt blood trickle down her back, as a barb cut deep, but he had pinned her so she was unable to move her face away from his. Her hands were free though and she brought up the one holding the knife and jabbed it into his upper arm. The gasp of breath he released when she pierced him exploded into her own mouth but he let go of her and clamped his hand over the wound she had inflicted.

Blood seeped through his shirtsleeve. He stared at her, silent in his disbelief of what she had done.

"Fiend! Harpy! You have wounded me true. And I not yet in battle. You have gone too far, Rose. If the thought of wedding me is so abhorrent to you that you stab me and draw my life's blood, then I shall release you from our betrothal. I take my leave, Rose. I would not wed a shrew."

Ralph turned on his heel and strode away, his spurs catching on the stones of the gravel path and sending them flying.

Rose looked down at the knife in her hand, from which Ralph's blood dripped. When he was no longer in sight, she longed for him to return. "Ralph! Come back."

But he had gone.

***

Ralph rode back to Meadowsweet Manor furious that he had not persuaded Rose to capitulate into an early marriage ceremony. The strength of her resistance had confounded him. He had not known she possessed such willpower, although it only made him desire her more, but he was damned if he'd crawl back and beg her to wed him now. The quicker he joined the army, the better. She'd soon want him back when she missed his kisses.

He dismounted in the stable yard and Young Peter came running out to take his horse's reins.

"Rub her down, Young Peter. I have ridden her hard."

"Aye, sir."

Young Peter led Lodestar away. Ralph noticed that the mare was trembling slightly and sweat foamed along her neck. He frowned. He would need a different horse in battle. Lodestar had neither the stomach nor the stamina for hard fighting. He would go to market this week and see about another mount. God's teeth but he had wanted to mount Rose Charlton this afternoon. He still seethed with desire for her. He might admire her spirit until Christendom but that wouldn't ease this powerful aching want that drove him mad.

"Sally!" Ralph called as he entered the wide doorway into the great hall. "Come hither, girl."

Sally, the scullery maid, duly appeared, straightening her coif, her docile, bovine face pink from running.

"Come with me, Sally, my pretty poppet. I have something for you."

Next market day, Ralph found a horse to satisfy his wanderlust, if not his desire for Rose. Sally was an obliging wench but fondling her did little to assuage his appetite for finer fare. The bidding was fierce for the handsome white stallion but Ralph, whose purse had been supplemented by his fond father for the occasion, had enough funds to top them all.

The stable lad brought the beast around after the bidding had ceased. The big white horse was having none of it and the lad was struggling to hold his massive head, which reared up and shook from side to side in an effort to break free.

"Hallo there, lad. Give him to me, I'll hold him alright." Ralph held out his hand.

"Be glad to sir, he's a might strong for me and I'm used to nervous horses." The boy held out the reins.

"Nervous? Nay, this magnificent beast is not afraid, he just wants to break free. A good gallop is what he needs." Ralph took the reins off the stable-boy.

"God speed ye, sir, I'd not dare to ride him, meself." And the lad quickly retreated as the stallion lashed out with his hind hooves.

Ralph laughed, recognising a fellow spirit in the animal. The stable lad slung his saddle across the horse's broad white back and tightened the straps, while Ralph held on to the horse's bridle, whispering soothing words into the horse's twitching

161

ears. Then, with the boy holding the reins like grim death, Ralph swung himself up on to the saddle,

"You may let him go free now, lad, and here's a groat for your trouble."

"Thank'ee sir. God speed ye."

The boy scuttled off, looking well pleased with his coin.

Immediately the horse reared up, neighing his protest at Ralph's weight.

"Aye, you want your head. Then have it, brave heart, but take me with you." Ralph loosed the reins and they shot out of the yard, onto the cobbled street. Peddlers and basket sellers hopped out of the way smartly, as the big horse immediately broke into a canter. Soon they were out on the downs and Ralph let the horse have his head, only just managing to keep his seat, despite his excellent horsemanship.

They galloped over the common land towards Roundway Hill and Ralph marvelled at the speed of his new purchase.

"God's blood, but you are fleet of foot. I'll call you Mercury, for you are as slippery and fast as quicksilver."

Ralph rode all afternoon until they had both quenched their restless spirits and Mercury responded to his rider's commands. There was nothing now to stop him joining the King, who had reached the adjoining county of Gloucestershire. He could be proud with this fine beast under him and lead his militia with confidence against the Parliamentarians who had turned the country against itself. He'd met his match in Mercury, as he felt he had in Rose, but it was far easier to buy one's heart's desire than to be given it.

## *"Silver is stronger than it looks."*

For once, I wasn't hungry and refused the egg on toast Percy offered me when we got back to the kitchen at Meadowsweet Manor. Just the thought of a sulphurous egg made me gag, just like my memories. Percy's patient forbearance impressed me more than any gushing sympathy could have done. Within that quiet space our tentative friendship deepened to a new level.

I did accept a cup of tea. Limeflower. Never tried it before but it turned out to be both delicious and soothing. By the time I'd drunk half of it, my tummy had stopped churning. A soft belch escaped me before I could hide it but Percy only smiled, a motherly, Madonna-like smile (and we're not talking breast-cones here) that comforted me as much as the herbal tea. Cocooned in this new sensation of trust, I spilled the beans about Robin.

"I know you heard I lost Robin on that hill, Percy, but perhaps you don't know the details; it might explain my reaction on Roundway Hill today. When he died, I was sixteen and in love. We both were truly, madly, deeply in love."

Percy's previously impassive face registered surprise.

Am I really that unattractive, or did she privately suspect I wasn't interested in the opposite sex? I couldn't stop to ask now. "Robin was the only one who understood I could see and hear those on the other side. I'd never trusted anyone else enough to confide my secret in - not till now, that is."

Percy smiled her acknowledgment of the compliment.

"You see, I'd been increasingly plagued by the spirit world around that time, whilst trying to sit my GCSE's, not ideal timing. So we went up the hill to see if we could lay my ghosts," I chuckled softly, "as well as each other. We did a lot of that." That damn rock stuck in my throat again. I swallowed it down with a sip of my calming brew. It helped, a bit. "We were going to camp up there because I'd heard and felt lots of lost souls around that hill. It was a good excuse to have a midsummer adventure under the stars. Robin was such a daft romantic. A proper softie."

I stared at the little thread of white steam curling up from my mug. "We didn't get very far. I still can't understand why someone as sure-footed as Robin got caught out. I thought I'd heard a horse galloping and I've always wondered if..." I sipped my tea. I didn't want to sound so fanciful. I had no evidence. I carried on, sticking religiously to the facts. "He went on ahead into those woods, the ones we turned away from today. I couldn't face them, coward that I am, although I know the energy is strongest there. You see, that night, I got left behind and Robin...Robin, well, he fell. Broke his neck. The police found him. He had this in his hand."

I drew out the silver chain he'd been clutching when he died. The chain that had started the whole sorry business. Although it had been me who'd been drawn to it in the first instance, it had been Robin who'd insisted on taking it back up the hill that night. I laid it on the table.

"May I?" Percy picked up the chain and fingered the entwined silver circles. "It's beautiful. So delicate. This is wonderful workmanship and I should think it's very old."

"Do you know about jewellery? I've no idea. I just always carry it around in my pocket. I've never worn it around my neck. I don't know why, it would be easier, but somehow I never could bear it against my skin. It always felt hot somehow and it did today, up on the hill. I've never shown it to anyone else." I stared at the familiar piece of silver as Percy threaded it through her hands, appreciating its texture and beauty afresh through another's eyes. The delicate metal strand had almost become a part of me, I'd guarded it so long. My talisman; my only tangible relic of Robin's final hours.

"I don't like it, I won't wear it!"

I looked up. Percy's face had changed and her tone was shrill, sharp even. Her green eyes sparked anger.

"Percy? What is it? No one's asking you to wear it!" Her rapid mood swing had shocked me out of my maudlin state. To my surprise, she stood up so abruptly, she almost knocked her chair over. It rocked twice, then settled back upright.

"This silver bauble is worthless to me!" She was almost shouting now and her voice had risen an octave, making it sound hysterical.

"Oh, I don't know about that. Looks antique. I reckon it would be worth a bit." I strung her along, desperate to find out more.

"Oh, yes the finest Italian craftwork, I know, and the missing pomander even more valuable. Well, you can keep it. I never want your necklace round my neck again. It chokes me!" And she flung the chain straight at my face. Already on the defensive, I caught it. The metal was warm, almost hot. It felt alive.

"Sit down, Percy."

But Percy stood, her hands on her slim hips in a most uncharacteristic stance. Her chin was held high and her eyes still sparkled with hatred. She didn't look like my friend anymore. "I will not!"

"Who do you think you are?" I didn't use her real name and spoke in a soft, neutral voice. This wasn't Percy talking.

"I am Rose, Rose Charlton, as you well know, Ralph Foulkes, and I do not belong to you! You cannot buy me with this trinket."

"Do you not love me, Rose?"

"Nay, I do not."

"Who do you love, if not me?"

She clammed up at this interesting point. Frustrated and still living in the present, I could rationalise. This was a golden opportunity.

"Do not tease me, Rose." I hoped that sounded conciliatory, inviting.

"Do not flatter yourself, Ralph."

Not working then. I tried a different tack. "Forgive me," I began.

"Never! There is too much to forgive, Ralph, how could I ever forgive what you have done?"

If only I knew what crime she alluded to. I tried humility next. "I am sorry, Rose."

Percy crumpled into tears and slumped back on her chair. I was just glad she didn't miss it and fall on the floor. I went to console her and gingerly put my arm around her back, now shaking with sobs. As soon as my fingers touched her jumper, she flung out an arm, winding me in my already traumatised stomach.

"Ugh!" My breath was forced out of my lungs and I fell back against the wooden kitchen cabinets. It took a moment to steady myself and when I looked up, Percy's head lay across her sprawled arms on the table. Her eyes were shut and she looked like she was asleep or unconscious. With even more apprehension than before, I touched her back, glad to feel the gentle rhythm of her respiration.

Enough. Let it go. I needed a break.

Satisfied she was okay, I put the kettle back on the Aga hob and sat back to reflect. At last we'd got somewhere in piecing this jigsaw together. Rose's surname was Charlton, Wasn't that the neighbours? And we now knew that Rose didn't love Ralph, hated his guts in fact, even though he'd given her the silver chain I had carried around in my pocket for more than ten years. No wonder I had been pulled into this old house.

Percy stirred and sat up, rubbing her eyes. I stood well back, out of harm's way. The kettle began to sing its readiness and I made fresh tea, builder's this time, good and strong.

Percy looked glazed and sleepy and took the mug from me without a murmur. We sipped in silence. When the filmy look had left her eyes, I brought her up to date with a brief resumé of our last exchange.

"Well, that confirms what we suspected then. Fay," she said, when I had finished.

"Yes, it does, but I, for one, have had enough for one day. Think I'll have an early night - in my own bed."

"You're not leaving?" Percy looked quite distraught, and as tired as I felt.

"No, that wouldn't be very kind would it? And you've been so kind to me today, Percy. No, I meant upstairs." Any bed would be a welcome sight right now.

"That's a relief. Would you like a bite to eat before you go up?"

"Not really hungry, for once, thanks, Percy."

"A bit of toast or some soup?"

"Oh, alright, just a little." I didn't really want any food but Percy seemed to need to do something mundane and ordinary and I was all for that.

"I'll raid the freezer." Percy went to the utility room and opened the white door of her massive freezer. "Oh, no!" she wailed.

"What, now?" I got up wearily and joined her. The freezer was in a sorry, soggy state with melted bags of colourful goo sagging on its shelves.

"I'll have to sort it out tonight or it will stink. Look, here's some spring vegetable soup we can have tonight. I'll put it on the hob and after we've had it, I'll sort it all out." Percy reached in and brought out a Tupperware box.

"Are you sure you've enough energy to tackle that lot, Percy? Do you want a hand? You look pretty whacked yourself."

"No, Fay, you look done in and it's the sort of job I enjoy getting stuck into. And anyway I need to keep busy or I can't cope with all this stuff. This will stop me thinking too much."

I wasn't going to argue. I've never been domesticated. All I've ever used a freezer for was microwave dinners. We ate our soup and, although I hadn't been that peckish, its delicate flavour was gratefully received by my wounded insides. The food made me sleepy and I was very aware I needed a wash and brush up. "I'm going up then, Percy. Good luck with the freezer."

She smiled back and took a couple of tea light lanterns into the utility room with a very determined look in her eye. I carried a jug of hot water from the kettle and the candelabra up with me and climbed the stairs with leaden legs. I lathered myself in Percy's expensive silky soap and gave myself a good scrub. It had been a very long day. I lay in bed, trying to research the Civil War on my phone but my eyelids refused to stay open. I gave up, carefully switching it off to save the battery, only half charged up in the library earlier, and sank into oblivion.

The rain lashed at the narrow window of Rose's bedchamber. This room had been the extent of her world after she had been confined there by her mother.

Now she sat in the window seat, watching the drops of rain weave their weary way around the mullioned panes, this way and that, before pooling on the stone windowsill outside. When enough water had gathered there, it broke through its meniscus, cascaded down on to the gravelled path below and escaped. Two days and nights of solitude made her long to escape her chamber too and, like the rain water, flow out into the garden beyond. Her mother knew her well. She knew she hated her freedom curbed above all things. When she was little, Agatha bade her father chastise her for wrongdoings, of which there were many but she had never cared, or mended her ways, because of the mere sting of his cane. Pain would always fade in time and she'd got used to it. She had always considered it a small price to pay for the soaring thrill of adventures; the lure of breaking rules she did not respect or consider worthwhile. Rose preferred making her own rules and Agatha knew imprisonment was the only way to tame her.

Later that night, when the household was abed, she opened the window and climbed out on to the stone sill as she had done many times as a girl, unbeknownst to her parents. With the ease of practice, Rose slipped down the ivy covering the old stone walls, wincing as the wet leaves brushed her bare legs. The night air, though now dry, was cold. September had brought autumn early this year and a mist was already forming in the valley below.

Rose let go of the ivy and jumped the last few feet on to the gravel. That was always the most vulnerable time, as the little stones made such a noise when displaced by her feet. She stood holding her breath for a moment. An owl hooted down by the river but there was no other sound. A bat flew silently past her; its delicate wings quiet even in flight. Sensing she was indeed alone, Rose walked quickly away from the house into the orchard, where she stopped and inhaled the sweet night air.

Yes, she had escaped but where could she go now? Rambling through the garden, swishing her feet through fallen leaves, yielded no answer. She munched on a ripe apple, plucked from the tree. Her stomach had been rumbling for hours. Agatha had allowed nothing to be served in her room but thin gruel and dry bread. She thought about appealing to her father for leniency but quickly disregarded the idea as pointless. Now she had lost one of them, the game of brother against brother had also lost its savour, much like Agatha's broth. Rose sighed and retraced her steps to the house. She climbed back up to her room, none the richer for her escapade, which now seemed foolish, childish and had achieved nothing.

Above all things, she hated to be impotent.

She climbed into bed and drew the covers over her cold body. Her mind was clear now, as clear as the stars she could see out of her window.

Suddenly, she knew what to do.

## *"Do not follow a false trail."*

I came downstairs the next morning to find Percy slumped at the kitchen table, looking despondent. Refreshed from my night's sleep, I tried to cheer her up.

"Good morning, Percy. Having slept like a top and feeling fully energised, I'm going to try a different tack in our search today."

"Oh, yeah?" She looked up at me, her face drawn and tight.

"Yes, definitely." I poured myself a mug of coffee without ceremony and sat down opposite my new friend.

"Had some ideas in the night, did you, Fay?" Percy yawned.

"It's a major breakthrough having Rose's full name confirmed yesterday, when you held the necklace in your hand." I took a sip of the hot coffee. Delicious.

"That's true." Percy fingered her throat.

"And we now know that Rose blames Ralph for something he did."

"Also true."

"So, how about we investigate where Rose lived? It might reveal something about why she hates him so much." I stroked Arthur, who was sitting expectantly on the chair next to mine.

He started to purr in response.

Percy smiled at her old cat. "I'm not sure how to find out where that is, Fay. Have you got any ideas about that?"

"In that first trip back in time I had here, Ralph was sent off to ask his neighbours to Sir Edward's birthday party, wasn't he?"

"I can barely remember." Percy yawned again and stretched.

"No, well, you didn't see it like I did, but Lady Eleanor said the neighbours were the Charltons. They must have had a big house too, I reckon, and it can't be far away, if they were the closest family and it stands to reason that Rose Charlton lived there."

Percy sat up straighter. "Good thinking, Fay."

"A bloody genius, that's what I am. Just feed me up and I'm good to go."

"Go where?"

"On a discovery tour of every big house in a five mile range."

"I'll make some toast."

We set off straight after breakfast. Percy had dug out an ordnance survey map and I spread it out over my knees in the passenger seat.

"Now usually, big houses have symbols on the map, don't they?" I took a pencil from my handbag and drew a large circle around Meadowsweet Manor.

"Only if they are hugely significant."

"Your manor has one, look." I prodded the map with my finger.

Percy swerved slightly as she looked down.

"Actually, just take my word for it, Percy, and keep your eyes on the road." I hadn't forgotten my near miss a couple of months ago and had no wish to repeat it. "Just keep driving and I'll keep looking out for a biggish place."

I looked out of the car window. It was a bright, showery sort of morning and it felt good to be away from the manor house again. Of course, we now knew that nowhere was safe, but Percy had definitely cheered up and she hummed a tune as she drove.

We had been driving for an hour, exploring every lane and solitary house we came across, when, having exhausted the countryside to the west of Percy's house, we drove past Meadowsweet Manor and carried on towards the east.

Only a couple of miles later, we turned up a little lane towards a bungalow, perched on the edge of the road on rising ground. Nothing unusual about it, except it was nestled behind some large, very old gates, with stone pillars on either side. As we drew nearer, my feet became increasingly chilled, until they felt like solid blocks of ice.

"Stop!"

Percy obeyed so abruptly, my seat belt dug into my shoulder and the map fell off my knees.

"What is it, Fay?"

"Look at those gates."

"What about them? Hmm, they do look a bit out place for that boring bungalow." Percy screwed up her eyes as she looked out of the window, now liberally spotted with raindrops.

I got out of the car, dodging the puddles, and went up to the stone pillar on the left. There were letters carved into the stone, worn with age and indistinct. I pulled away at the ivy growing across them and studied the inscription.

Percy got out of the car and joined me. "Look, there's a capital 'C'."

I scraped some lichen away with my fingernail. "And an 'h' straight after."

A chilly breeze blew around my neck and I wound my scarf tighter against it but it could not stop the whispering.

"*No longer...*"

"What did you say, Percy?" I slewed around to look at my friend.

"I didn't say anything."

"Yes, you did. You said 'no longer', I think."

"No, I didn't. Listen, I'm not going to ruin my nails. I'll get the window-scraper from the car."

"*Not here...*"

"Percy?" Again I turned around, but Percy was rummaging in the glove compartment on the passenger side of the car. I didn't want to hear Rose and yet I knew, with deadly certainty, it was her high, strange voice in my reluctant ear.

## Charlton House and Meadowsweet Manor 1642

Rose crept out of bed just before dawn, dressed in her russet riding habit, which she had laid out in readiness the night before. Catching up her skirts, she opened the window, cursing as it creaked on its hinges, and stealthily clambered across the stone sill onto the ivy clinging to the walls of Charlton House. She descended quickly, following the twisted branches almost to their base, so as not to make too much impact on the traitorous pebbles on the path. Pleased to have made little sound, she tiptoed on to the grassy sward at the path's edge and ran along its silent carpet to the stables. Even the stable boy was not yet abroad and she saddled up Inkwell herself, stroking the horse's velvet nose to soothe her into conspiratorial silence.

Using the mounting block in the yard, she climbed onto Inkwell's saddle and settled herself on the leather. Its creaks sounded like gunshot in the stillness of the pre-dawn darkness. Patches of mist clung to the countryside beyond the boundary gates and she knew a moment of thrilling fear as she entered the white clouds of moisture and they obscured her way forward. What if she got lost? What if Inkwell stumbled into a rabbit hole she couldn't see and she fell? She might break her leg, or worse, her head.

But anything was better than the bruised pride she had suffered during her imprisonment over two whole days. Peering across Inkwell's withers, her eyes began to adjust and the sun, although not yet bright, began to awake, casting an eerie grey gloom over the fields and helping just enough to light her way.

She chivvied Inkwell into a trot as soon as they were out of earshot of her home. The mare whinnied her protest of the early ride without breakfast but Rose cajoled her out of her bad mood and soon they were cantering along steadily towards Meadowsweet Manor, with the dawn chorus willing them on.

She reached her neighbour's house much too early so she retreated to the manor's woods, on the south side of the big Elizabethan house. Rose had planned her foray carefully and had saved some of her meagre bread ration from last night's supper. It was dry and she was thirsty but her hunger had to be sated. She dismounted and let Inkwell eat her fill of grassy tufts between the trees.

Rose could see the manor from her hideaway but chuckled at the thought that no-one could see her, or even guess where she might be. Her mother, once she found out she had gone, would be furious and that pleased Rose deeply. It would take a while for the discovery to be made, as she had bundled the bed covers into a heap to resemble her sleeping form, and the servant was too timid to try and wake her if she thought she was deep in slumber. Last time it had been attempted, she'd given the silly girl a sharp slap.

She sat back against the scratchy bark of an oak tree and contemplated her quarry, content to wait; content to be free and following her own will at last. Slowly, very slowly, the dawn light crept up the bricks of the manor's walls until they glowed. It was time.

Young Peter, sleepy and tousle-haired, took Inkwell from her as she entered the stable yard and promised to feed the gentle horse.

Rose thanked him prettily and the man's eyes sparked awake in appreciation of the attention. Emboldened, Rose walked out of the yard and approached the massive front door of the imposing manor house. Her mother would have to listen to her commands when she was mistress of this place; a prospect she relished, if she could bring her plan to fruition.

She rapped on the door with her riding whip. It took a few moments for one of the servants to answer her knock and she knew a momentary misgiving. What if neither of the Foulkes brothers was home? She needed both of them to be present if her scheme was to work. It would be no use teasing and flattering Will if his brother was not there to witness it. She needed Ralph to become so jealous he would realise what - and whom - he had rejected.

Thinking of Ralph made her stomach lurch in the most peculiar fashion. Was this how love felt? She couldn't be frightened of him, could she? Her back had hurt as she leant against the trunk of the old oak tree. The puncture wound of the rose thorn had not yet healed and reminded her daily of Ralph's physical strength. Or did she just want him to renew those exhilarating kisses and bestow this magnificent home upon her? She had never appreciated the place so much as when watching the dawn enlivening its terracotta façade with brilliant sunshine this very morning, making her acknowledge what a prize she might lose if she didn't tread carefully.

At last the door was unbolted from the inside and old Peter, now bent with age, stood blinking at her in the sunlight.

"Why, Mistress Charlton. You be up betimes."

"I give you good morrow, Old Peter. Aren't you going to let me in?"

"Aye, sorry mistress. You are welcome in but I'm not sure the family be abroad yet."

Rose entered the house, and went straight to the great hall, where already a fire blazed in the huge hearth opposite the minstrel gallery. The flickering flames beckoned her inside the big room and she went to sit on the settle next to the fire, holding out her hands to warm them.

"Fetch me some fresh bread and ale, would you?"

The old man nodded and scuttled off into the kitchen but it was Martha who brought the simple food and placed it before her. Rose salivated at the sight of the golden butter in its stone crock next to the fresh loaf and longed to feast upon it. Another bowl held a honeycomb. Her stomach growled loudly.

Martha looked at her as sharply as her mother might have done, seeing far more than any servant had a right to.

"You're up early, mistress Rose."

"What if I am? I had a fancy for a morning ride."

"Must have been dawn when you got on your horse, I reckon."

Rose was silent.

"Well, there's some vittles for ye. I'll tell Sir Edward ye're here but he don't get up at this time of a morning these days."

"It is Ralph I have come to see." Rose reached for the bread and smothered it in butter and honey, biting into the slice with some vigour, delighted to find it still warm and the butter melting inside.

"He will not be here for many a long day. 'Pon my faith, I only hope he returns at all."

The bread stuck in Rose's throat and she had a job to swallow it down.

"What do you mean, Martha? Where is Ralph? He has not left yet to join the King's army, has he?"

"Aye, that he has, and the place is a mite too quiet with him gone."

"And Will, has he left too?"

"Nay, Will bides at home yet." Martha shook her head from side to side, as if puzzling why.

"I see. Then I'll wait for Will."

"As ye wishes." Martha turned about on her clogs making the rushes kick up dust and the fire to belch smoke in the updraught of her skirts.

Rose munched, forgetting how creamy the butter was, how sweet the honey, how fresh the loaf. She had to plot a new strategy now that Ralph had gone. The platter was empty before she could think it all through and Will stood before her looking as surprised as he was delighted.

"Rose! 'Tis good to see you, but I confess to be surprised at your presence here. I thought..."

He trailed off when she frowned her annoyance. Did he know she should still be under lock and key at Charlton House? How much had Ralph told him? Had he seen the wound on his brother's arm?

To gain time, she poured out some ale and extended the cup to Will.

He shook his head. "Nay, I thank you. I broke my fast in the kitchen, with the servants."

Rose sipped from the cup and drank her fill. She still had a thirst. "Will you not sit with me awhile, Will? Martha tells me Ralph has left to join the King in Gloucestershire."

"'Tis true. He left two days since and in some haste. Rose, forgive this trespass, but I must know the truth. Ralph told me, before he left, that the betrothal betwixt you and he is broken?"

Rose saw no advantage in denying it now. She could still play her game; it would just take longer, that was all.

"Aye, 'tis true, 'pon my faith." She sighed."Ah, Will, you know your brother well - that he is hot-headed and quick to temper. 'Twas he who broke our troth. He wanted to bed," she

176

sneaked a meaningful glance at Will, satisfied he'd heard the slip and was shocked by it, before continuing, "I mean, wed me before leaving for war but I am not ready, Will." Rose fluttered her eyelashes, trusting her cheeks had coloured from the warmth of the fire, then lifted her eyes fully to Will's, gratified to find them fixed on her face with an intense gaze. It gave her strength, so she raised her head and bestowed a tentative smile in reward for his attention.

Will smiled back, just a little.

When Rose returned home, Agatha was beside herself with fury. The only way of abating her mother's anger was simply to lie.

"I went to Meadowsweet Manor to beg for Ralph's forgiveness, Mother. I know I have done wrong and I also beg you to forgive my trespass."

It was satisfying to see the wind escape her mother's sails then. When she told her mother that Ralph had already left to join the King, Agatha could not place the blame upon her daughter because Ralph had left his home to go warmongering.

Over the next few days, Rose let her mother believe that concern for Ralph's father prompted her frequent visits back to Meadowsweet Manor and accepted praise for it with due humility. She basked in her mother's praise for her charity and enjoyed the resulting liberation from the habitual maternal nagging as a result. How she relished her freedom from then on, meeting Will in the woods when she could and even occasionally actually visiting his father at the manor, just to be on the safe side.

Will never attempted to kiss or even touch her hand when they met, even though they were alone and private. He always kept a polite distance and she found the only way to really hold his attention was to listen and comment on his extensive soul searching as he questioned his political beliefs but never, she noticed, his faith. That was a subject upon which he had no doubts and she found his views on both genuinely fascinating. Will's enquiring, intelligent mind made her own wake up and ask some questions. And so, despite herself, she was drawn into the politics seething around them. Sometimes she even forgot to flirt with him, so interested was she in things abroad, as he conveyed news bigger than either of them.

The first reports of the battle of Edgehill arrived via the knifegrinder, who called every month to sharpen Martha's kitchen knives and Old Peter's outdoor tools. The tinker travelled widely and had proven himself a reliable source of gossip over the years, if given to some elaboration, ensuring a willing audience around him as he ground their blades on his wheel.

"So what did that old Irishman have to report this time, Will?" Rose asked as they rode out to Cousin Margaret one day.

"That the two armies have finally clashed."

"'Pon my faith? Where?"

"The King had gathered a full army in Warwickshire, by all accounts, and decided to head for London to force Lord Essex into a confrontation. He succeeded much earlier than he expected."

"How so?" Inkwell stumbled on a tree root and Rose patted her neck to reassure her.

Will smiled his approval but his face remained even more serious than ever. "Near Banbury, I believe."

"And which army was victorious?"

"Neither, as far as I can gather, but that doesn't mean no-one was wounded. I fear for my brother." Will looked into the middle distance, his eyes shielded by his hat so Rose could not read them.

"Aye, Ralph may well have been there but Will, he only left a few days ago. He might not have reached the King before the battle began."

"'Tis true, forsooth, you speak wisdom, Rose. Perhaps I am overly concerned. Knowing Ralph, he will be triumphant in a fight in any case."

"I am sure Ralph will be well. He is very strong and hardy."

Will looked at her then, searching her face for a trace of giveaway emotion but truly, she felt none.

## *"The trail lies elsewhere."*

"Oi! What do you think you're doing?" A man in his mid-sixties, his face red and bellicose, was scrunching up the drive towards us. Dressed in a tweed cap, wellies, and a waxed jacket, he looked as if he'd stepped out of a country casuals catalogue but I didn't really register his outfit, just the shot gun nestled in the crook of his arm.

I was slow to react, I have to admit. Unclear as to which century I was in and suffering from numbing chills, I was relieved when Percy broke into her disarming smile and greeted the gruff stranger.

"Good morning!" Percy extended her hand.

The man hunched his gun higher and kept his other hand in his pocket. "Do I know you?"

"I'm sure we've met somewhere, haven't we?" Percy kept smiling.

Most men would have melted by now. I wished I could and began to shiver.

"I live in Meadowsweet Manor, not two miles down the road. Didn't we meet at the hunt ball?" Percy kept her hand outstretched.

The man scowled but he reached out and gave Percy a brief hand shake. "Possibly."

"I'm sure we did. Paul Wade, my husband, loves to hunt, although he keeps his horses in livery. He's away at the moment and my friend, Miss Armstrong and I, are doing a little bit of local historical research. About the manor, you know. It's so interesting!"

The man's face paled slightly and he looked slightly less hostile but not as much as I'd have liked. I stayed silent, marvelling at Percy's charm offensive; knowing I couldn't improve it, charm not being one of my talents, and besides, I was concentrating on preventing my teeth from chattering.

"So, what are you doing here, if you are investigating your own place at, where was it? Meadowsweet Manor? Oh, yes, I know it. Big old place. All thatch, red brick and beams." He was thawing, I could tell.

"That's exactly right, Mr?"

Clever girl, Percy.

"Matthews."

"Mr Matthews, of course! I should have remembered. Well, Mr Matthews, we've discovered that way, way back, hundreds of years ago, there was another house, as big as the manor probably, quite nearby, and the two families were friends." Percy nodded and smiled through her words.

"Dare say they were." Mr Matthews looked up at the sky as spots of rain speckled his shoulders.

I shivered again, longing to return to the warm car. I could see that Percy was beginning to lose patience, but she battled on with remarkable restraint.

"We think, Mr Matthews, that the family's name was Charlton, and we couldn't help noticing that your stone pillar here seems to have the name Charlton carved into it."

Mr Matthews nodded. "Yes, it was called Charlton House, I believe, a long time ago. I bought the land as a building plot and had my home built here, back in 1983."

"Did you have a hand in designing it? It's lovely, and such an attractive setting." Percy nodded towards the bland façade of the ugly building, standing like a square peg in a round hole, against the undulating landscape.

I could see Mr Matthews softening. Go to the top of the class, Percy. He leaned his gun against one of the dark, trimmed conifers lining the drive and opened the gate before joining us in front of the pillar. "Yes, you're right. Charlton House did occupy this plot but it burned down, oh, at least four hundred years ago. During the Civil War, I believe."

Percy's false smile slipped. "Burned down?"

"Yes, I don't know the story, so I can't furnish any details but the ruins are still in the grounds." Mr Matthews looked at me and frowned. "Is your friend alright?"

"I'm fine," I said. I had warmed up a bit. The silver chain in my pocket had heated up to such an extent I could no longer keep my hand over it. Now it was warming my thigh through my jeans and my shivering had stopped.

Mr Matthews shrugged. "If you really want to see it, you can climb over that gate there in the field next to my garden and you'll find it about two hundred yards further on, down in the dip."

"Oh, yes, we'd love to do that, Mr Matthews, how kind you are."

"Yes, well, just make sure you don't trespass on my garden. You can see my boundary is defined by the Leylandii hedge all around it." Mr Matthews went back through his iron gates and shut them.

"Yes, your hedge is quite a landmark, Mr. Matthews." Percy smiled, a little less warmly.

"Best to be secure, I find." Mr Matthews picked up his gun and stared back at us.

"Come on, Percy," I said. "Time to go."

"Goodbye, Mr Matthews." Percy didn't extend her hand in farewell. "Thank you for your help."

"Goodbye, Mrs Wade, and please, park your car away from the gates. I might want to go out." He was obviously going to make sure we left before he stopped staring.

Percy got back in the car and parked out of view on the other side of the gated field. I jumped up and down and rubbed my arms, to restore some feeling in them while I waited for her.

"William! Will! By thunder, where is the boy?"

Will heard his father's bellow reverberating through the house. He couldn't remember his father calling him by name for many a month and was instantly on the alert. The terrific commotion emanated from the stable yard, so he went to the window of the upstairs morning room to see what the fuss was about. Will had been reading the poems of John Donne and had been lost in a sensuous reverie, dreaming of Rose.

One look through the mullioned panes made him discard his slim volume onto the window seat and he ran down the broad staircase as fast as his father could have desired.

"Ah, at last, Will! Come quickly, your brother is returned from fighting and he's wounded! We must get him inside."

"Wounded? Where?"

"I don't know yet, damn it. Mercury came pounding through the gates just now with Ralph slumped over him. There's another of the King's soldiers with him too. Come on!"

Will stepped out into the autumn drizzle. A young man wearing a red sash across his breast held Mercury's bridle. His own horse looked as travel worn as he did.

"Is this Meadowsweet Manor? I have Ralph Foulkes here, wounded, shot in the leg. My name is John Courtney and we both fought in the battle of Edgehill. The surgeon patched him up but he's in a bad way."

"Thank 'ee for bringing my boy home, sir." Sir Edward said briefly, before turning away to stare at Ralph. Both Peters were lifting Ralph from Mercury's broad back. Will grabbed the bridle of the big horse and stroked his nose. Mercury was breathing hard and his massive white shoulders were caked in sweat and blood. His breath came in exhausted lunges, filling the stable yard with great clouds of steam.

"There, there, boy." Will laid his face against the horse's long nose and was nuzzled in return.

"God's truth, William, never mind that confounded brute! Look, your brother's been wounded in the leg!"

Will looked up but carried on stroking Mercury's velvety white face. Ralph's was no less pale and a crimson stain across a large bandage around his thigh explained why. Young Peter was taking Ralph onto his own bent back, helped by his father, Old Peter. Sir Edward was pulling at Ralph's arm in the most unhelpful way.

Ralph was ominously limp and unusually silent. Once his brother's body was transferred from Mercury's back onto Young Peter's, Will let go of the bridle and gave it to Old Peter.

"Take Mercury into the stable, Old Peter. Feed and water him well and check him all over for wounds and bruises.

Old Peter nodded and led Mercury away, "Come on, old boy. Chuck-chuck."

Mercury's hooves lifted reluctantly and slowly towards his old refuge. Will hoped the brave stallion would survive his ordeal. He looked utterly spent. Will had seen how Ralph had bonded with Mercury in a way he never had with any other horse, and had been glad to see how he spared the big stallion his spurs. He turned towards his brother, now slumped over Young Peter's back, who was heading inside the manor house, Sir Edward hopping with anxiety alongside them.

Will turned to their neglected visitor, who had dismounted and stood, looking a little lost. "And you, sir, will you not take refreshment? We are much in your debt."

"I will, I thank you, but I shall not tarry. Once my horse is rested I must return to rejoin the King's army, who are headed for Oxford."

"Of course. Please go with Abigail and she will give you food and anything else you might need. Old Peter will take care of your horse in the stables. You both look in need of it. I must tend to my brother, if you will excuse me."

"Aye, go to him. His needs far exceed mine own." Abigail took Courtney off to the kitchens and Will followed his father and brother into the great hall.

"Martha!" yelled Sir Edward, panic in his loud voice as he disappeared towards the kitchen.

"Lay him down in front of the fire, yes, here in the hall, Young Peter," Will commanded. "On the table would be best. Wait, I'll get a rug to go underneath him."

Will fetched a rug from the fireside chair and laid it on the refectory table. Young Peter was sweating now under the weight of his immense burden but he waited patiently, strong and silent as an ox from the field.

Will put his arms under Ralph's legs and took some of the weight. Between them they raised him up onto the table. Ralph lay perfectly still. Will leant his head against his brother's chest. It rose and fell slowly in time with his laboured breath.

"Here's Martha, she'll know what to do! Oh my boy!" Sir Edward had returned, dragging the boys' old nurse by the arm, making her run. Releasing Martha at the table, Sir Edward withdrew to the fire, throwing himself into his favourite chair and reaching for the brandy that always stood in readiness next to it. He swigged straight from the bottle, muttering to himself all the while and running his fingers through his long hair.

Martha was a lot calmer than her master and quickly ran her hands over Ralph's inert body.

"He's alive, Martha. See, he breathes and I heard a heartbeat," Will said, standing back in respect for Martha's skill.

"That's good, Master Will. Now, Young Peter, go to the kitchens and wash your hands then get Abigail to come with clean clothes, liniment, and scissors. You bring me a pitcher of hot water from the pot over the fire. Cook will pour it for you. Hurry now, lad!"

Young Peter scurried off.

"What can I do, Martha?" Will wished he'd been sent off with an errand too.

"Have you a blade?"

"Aye." Will showed her the dagger he had finally taken to wearing lately.

"Cut off his clothes, Will, and let's see the damage."

"Shall I pull his boots off?"

"No, cut them. We don't know what lies beneath."

Will removed the spurs from the heels of Ralph's wide boots and sliced through the leather. His knife was sharp and he made short work of them and the leather breeches above. Martha had already cut through the fine linen shirt and taken off the large bandage around his thigh. Ralph lay naked, white and bleeding on the table.

"'Tis only his thigh, see, Will?"

"A bullet wound!"

"Aye but is it still in there?"

Abigail arrived laden with white linen, embrocation and scissors, closely followed by Young Peter, lugging the pail of hot water in abnormally clean hands. When Abigail caught sight of the naked Ralph she threw her apron over her head and started having hysterics.

"That's enough, Abigail. You'll have to see a naked man sometime before you die, child. Now get a hold of yourself." Martha was already tearing the linen into strips.

Will wished the last servant girl hadn't left under a cloud. Sally had been plump and pretty and always ready with an obliging smile. He had never fathomed why she had been dismissed. Perhaps it was because she had got so fat. She had certainly left in a hurry.

Frowning at the young girl, who'd lowered her apron and was peeping at Ralph's still form with one eye, Martha turned to Young Peter. "Good lad, put it there." Martha was totally in command of the situation. Will felt a swell of love and admiration for his old nurse. She would have made an excellent doctor. He wondered that his father hadn't sent for one but maybe even he could see that Martha knew what she was about and old Doctor Blake lived seven long miles away. Will reckoned his brother had lost enough blood without Doctor Blake's blood-letting.

"Abigail, fetch me the lavender oil from the still room with some yarrow flowers. Boil the flowers in a pan, strain it and bring it to me. Fast as you can, girl."

Abigail scuttled off, her eyes now wide with fright.

Martha washed Ralph's body down. Will held Ralph's shoulders, as he had begun to moan. "It's alright, Ralph. You are home. Martha's just cleaning you up."

Ralph's head lolled from side to side and his eyelids flickered but did not open.

Abigail returned and Martha took the bowl of yarrow water and started swabbing the gaping wound.

"Hold him hard, now, Will. This will hurt."

More moans issued from Ralph's slack mouth and beads of sweat broke out on his newly washed forehead.

"Is he coming round?" Sir Edward said, from the fireside.

"No, Father." Will held his hands firm on Ralph's shoulders and tried not to squirm, as Martha parted the flesh and searched for a bullet.

Suddenly she gave a triumphant shout. "I have it!" She held up a small sphere of lead in a bloodied hand.

Sir Edward rushed over. "By God, woman! You would make a fine surgeon! Ah, but what a mess his leg is in. My poor Ralph, my dearest child. Will he walk again?"

"Oh, don't fuss, Sir Edward. 'Tis only a flesh wound. As long as we keeps it clean, Ralph will be up and about in no time. He's lost some blood alright but he'll make that up again, with good vittals inside of him."

Will wished he could share Martha's confidence. Ralph looked paler than ever. He'd even stopped moaning and lay quiet and immobile. Will laid his head on his brother's chest again, now bare. The sensitive skin of his ear touched the flesh of his kin and he knew, in that moment, how much he loved his brother. A fainter heartbeat was still thumping the blood through Ralph's veins. He wanted Ralph to live. He might not agree with his dashing off to war at the first opportunity, or the side he fought for, but he was his brother, his only sibling. There were times, God knew, he'd hated him. Hated his strength, his assured confidence, his bragging and bullying. Will hoped that strength, that magnificent physique, would pull him through now.

But then Ralph might renew their betrothal and marry Rose, dashing all his hopes. Rose. How he longed for her. But not at the expense of his brother's death, easy though that would make things. If Rose chose him it must be because she loved him more, not over his brother's corpse.

All these thoughts flashed through his mind in the short time his head lay against Ralph's torso. No-one would have guessed. Will had long ago learned to school his face to hide his thoughts. Traitorous thoughts; thoughts in direct conflict with Ralph's and Sir Edward's ideals; in conflict with the King himself, on whose royal behalf Ralph now lay wounded - thoughts of rebellion.

"Well? Does he live?" Sir Edward's anxious voice broke through his turmoil.

"Yes, Father. His heart beats strongly. Not as strong as normal but he's very much alive."

Sir Edward ran his meaty hand over his red face. Every line had deepened and he looked ten years older than he had earlier that morning. Will smiled at his father, who did not notice. Sir Edward's eyes never left Ralph's ashen face.

"A needle and thread, Abigail. From the sewing box over there. Thread it with the finest silk and take it to the kitchen. Dip the thread and needle into boiling water, with a few drops of lavender oil in it and bring it straight back. Fast as you can, child." Martha had finished cleaning the wound and was now trying to staunch the blood, drawing the edges of the flesh together.

Abigail ran off dutifully. When she returned, Martha stitched the wound together. Will held down Ralph's lower leg and watched her skilfully ply her needle in swift darts of silver. When she had finished, a jagged red line ran along Ralph's thigh about six inches long, puckered up like the edges of a crimped pie crust.

"Sir Edward? Pass me that brandy bottle. Ralph's needs are greater than yourn."

Will, smiled at Martha's bold truthfulness and strode over to snatch it from his father's lips, wiping the neck with one of the linen cloths Abigail had brought. Martha nodded in approval. She poured a generous glug into the little bowl of spare yarrow water.

"Lift his head now, Will. Gently does it." Martha tipped the bowl into Ralph's mouth but the liquid just poured uselessly down his chin. "Open his mouth a little, Will."

Will inserted his little finger into the corner of Ralph's mouth and eased his teeth apart. Martha took a spoon and trickled some of the warm liquid in over his tongue.

"Ah, see him swallow it down? That's good. He'll draw strength from this."

"What's the yarrow for, Martha?"

"Staunches the flow of blood, see? Inside and out, and strengthens the heart."

She poured more liquid into Ralph, who began to show a little colour in his face.

"Look, Martha!"

Martha's frown of concentration, worn from the moment she saw Ralph, eased into a glimmer of a smile and she nodded. Will met her eyes, and smiled back. Together they poured more brandy and herb tea into Ralph until he spluttered and coughed. Ralph's eyes flickered open. Blank and cloudy at first, they cleared after he blinked a few times and recognised his brother.

"Will?" Ralph's voice was no more than a croak but it brought his father rushing to his side.

Sir Edward elbowed Will out of the way, forcing him to drop Ralph's hand. Sir Edward clasped it tight.

"Ralph? Oh, Ralph, my son. You're alive!" Tears tracked down Sir Edward's raddled features and disappeared into his wide moustache.

Will stood apart from the scene. The status quo had been restored. He left the room without anyone noticing and went to thank John Courtney for the safe return of his brother.

***

No-one, not even Martha, could believe how quickly Ralph recovered. Only Will wasn't surprised.  Sir Edward treated him like a hero, which in a way, Will supposed Ralph was, if you believed in the cause he fought for.

Which he didn't.

But his father did. Most emphatically and very loudly. Sir Edward told everyone he knew that Ralph had fought at the battle of Edgehill. To hear his father speak of his eldest son's bravery and in such detail, you would have thought he'd been an eye-witness. But 'twas ever thus and Will knew it would never change.

Ralph was soon sitting up at the table and Sir Edward insisted he regale them with the details of the battle. Ralph, usually so impatient and quickly bored, seemed willing to sit and tell his tale at some length.

"As soon as I heard the King was drumming up an army, I mounted Mercury and set off in search of him. It wasn't hard to find out where he was, once I reached Gloucester. It was all anyone could talk of in the taverns. I headed north and soon fell in with some other men loyal to the throne. They'd heard King Charles was in Shrewsbury so we kept on northwards as far as Banbury."

"Weren't you worried you'd meet some of the Parliamentary troops on the way and be cut to pieces?" His father asked.

Ralph squared his shoulders and said, "We'd have given them a fight they'd never forget, if we had!"

His father nodded and nudged Martha, who'd stayed to listen with some of the other servants.

Ralph carried on, "Twelve thousand men had gathered around the King by the time we found him. I never saw so many people together in one place."

Ralph continued his narrative; his audience rapt and silent. Sir Edward never took his eyes off his eldest son. His face, flushed with wine, had softened since the day Ralph had returned wounded but he still looked much older. Will returned his gaze to his brother.

"We met up with Prince Rupert - now there's a fine figure of a man - and the rumour spread that he'd seen the Parliamentary troops a few miles to the west. The whole body of men and horses duly headed that way. We only found out later that the turncoat, the Earl of Essex, had been marching the parliamentary rabble parallel to us twenty miles hence for days!"

A gentle murmuring laugh amongst the company encouraged Ralph on. Will doubted he needed it.

Ralph's voice grew stronger as he reached the climax of his adventure. "The King ordered us to deploy up on a high ridge, called Edgehill. We could see the village of Kineton huddled below and I could see his reasoning. It would be a damned hard climb up for Essex to reach us from down there but the cowards never came close. They settled on the plain two miles away. Well, we weren't going to let them get away with that so we marched up and tackled them head on.

"I was with Prince Rupert's pack of horses and we charged Sir James Ramsey's cavalry. One look at us and the whole lot of them turned and fled and we chased them all the way to Kineton. One of the brutes turned in his saddle and discharged his musket into my leg at that point so I never had the chance to return to the battlefield."

"It might have gone better, if you had, my lad!" Sir Edward's words were a little slurred.

"Aye, it might at that, Father," grinned Ralph. "My friend, John Courtney, got me to the field doctor who patched me up. I am much in John's debt for I doubt I would have survived if he'd not brought me back here. I don't remember much about that part of it until I woke up and found Martha had been practising her embroidery down my leg."

A round of applause rippled round the table and Sir Edward stood up. "A toast! I propose a toast to my son, Ralph! The returning hero!"

A chorus of "To Ralph, and hear, hear," echoed their host.

Ralph raised his tankard, though he didn't get up. "To the King! Victory to the King!"

Will had willingly drunk the toast to his brother. He couldn't repeat it for his sovereign.

But he wouldn't declare his intentions yet. He would have to bide his time.

# *"Back, back, go back."*

"You know, we should each copy the elegant Mr Matthews and invest in wellington boots." I pulled my trainers out of another cow pat and watched a big black cloud approach out of the lowering sky.

"Yes, you're right. Luckily, these walking boots I'm wearing are waterproof." Percy had not only cheered up, she was positively cantering across the muddy field.

And I'll bet those leather boots weren't cheap, either. Neither were my trainers and they would need replacing after this. I winced as I stepped in a rut and the puddle at its base rose up, spilling its disgusting brown water inside my shoe. Bloody Rose Charlton. Not content with hurting my body, she was now making inroads into my wallet. Instinctively, I thrust my hand into my jeans pocket. As I thought, the necklace was hot again.

"Come on, slowcoach!" Percy was yards ahead but I couldn't increase my speed, my legs felt like lead and the deep mud didn't help.

I put my head down against the cold wind and plodded behind Percy's sprightly form. The field was level here but dipped at the end. As we approached, we could see how the land fell away, displaying a splendid view of patchwork fields stretching into the distance. In the foreground stood an overgrown orchard and we could just see the tips of some stonework above it.

"Look, Fay, can you see the old house behind those trees?" Percy pointed at the ruins.

"Yes, must be Charlton House, I suppose."

"No suppose about it."

By the time I'd caught up with her, I wasn't feeling too good. The heat radiating from my jeans pocket was the only warm part of me and the contrast made me feel slightly feverish and very apprehensive.

"Oh, look, there's a little lane leading back to Mr Matthews' bungalow." Percy nodded in the direction of the rectangle of conifers.

"Yes, his beautiful creation lies in the path of the house and gates, where the Charltons must have ridden to and fro. Lovely spot. Look at that view." I stood gazing at the vista, trying to focus.

"Lord knows what possessed that stupid man to block it with his wretched evergreen hedge." Percy stood beside me to take in the panorama.

"More money than sense. I'll bet he's a townie who made his money in the city and is now trying to become a country squire by hunting, shooting and fishing anything that moves."

"Probably. Judging by his taste in houses, he's not exactly fitting into the landscape, is he?" Percy agreed.

"Shall we have a poke about these ruins, then?" I didn't really want to, if I was honest.

"It would be interesting." Percy started clambering over the ruined walls.

I followed, willing myself to continue, against my better judgement.

We wandered about the ruins, and I started to relax, as we discovered nothing but broken stones and heaps of debris.

"I wonder which was Rose's bedroom?" Percy stood, looking up at a fireplace in the second story. Only one blackened wall was left, its interior exposed and vulnerable to the elements. "To think she must have looked out over this view as she was growing up. Sort of makes her more real, doesn't it?"

"She's already a bit too real for my liking." I couldn't wait to get away from the place.

"Look, these must have been the stables." Percy was out of sight now, behind some crumbled outbuildings, away from the square foundations of the main house.

I joined her. Some cobblestones peeked through the grass and weeds under our feet. I could picture washdays here, with maids sloshing the sheets in tubs with red-raw hands. It must have been a busy place then with the number of staff needed to run a household of this size. I sat down on a low wall in the yard, speculating on which building housed what.

I had just decided which ruined rectangle had been the old wash-house when someone thumped my back so hard, I fell, sprawling onto the cobblestones, narrowly avoiding hitting my head by saving myself with my hands. It took me a moment to come to and get my breath back. I rolled over onto my back and sat up, picking bits of mud and grass from my filthy palms.

Percy looked down on me with narrowed eyes; her mouth turned down at the corners by a sneer.

"Get up and be gone from my house. You will not find him here."

She didn't sound at all like Percy. I knew that high strange voice; I recognised that country burr.

Rose was the last to hear of Ralph's return. She, who should have been the very first person to have been apprised of the peril he'd been in, had she remained betrothed to him. As soon as she heard the news, via a travelling tinker, not a formal message from the manor, she ordered Inkwell to be saddled up and rode over to see him, taking a basket of gifts from her parents. Her mother sent her best calves' foot jelly to help him mend, while her father gave a book of poems Ralph would never open.

At least now she knew why Will had not met her in their glade of late. She'd not visited the manor house since Sir Edward had scolded her for her rejection of Ralph. The old squire's words had found their mark on that occasion, when he'd almost shouted, "And you sent Ralph off to war without your blessing? You should be ashamed, girl. What reason could you have for rejecting him thus? Fie on you, any maid would be glad to have him, aye and all he brings."

She could not deny this truth but when she had told him it was Ralph who broke the betrothal, Sir Edward was less easily convinced than his youngest son.

"You lie, Rose. More like Ralph wanted to make haste!"

Having no answer she was willing to give to his perceptive statement, Rose had left and had not been back until the news of Ralph's return had percolated through to Charlton House. She knew it would be awkward meeting Sir Edward today but it would not help her cause to seem disinterested in Ralph's welfare now he was wounded.

Old Peter admitted her into the house and she was thankful to learn that Sir Edward was from home meeting the County Lieutenant. She found Ralph alone, sitting in state by the fire in the great hall, his hounds curled around the foot that rested on the floor, while his other leg was propped up on a stool. He was dozing, covered in a blanket, for the November day was dark and dismal outside. Asleep, he looked childlike and vulnerable; so unlike his usual dynamic self. Everything that normally defined Ralph was absent - movement, action, vigour, haste and noise. He sat silent, pale and passive. Rose had never seen him thus before. It didn't suit him at all.

He stirred when she approached as one of the dogs looked up and growled, waking Ralph.

"Steady, Hector." Ralph raised sleepy eyes to her. For one moment, he looked pleased, then a mask came down over his face, making him seem gaunt, and older than his years.

"I give you good morrow, Ralph. We were all sorry at Charlton House to hear of your misfortune. Look, Mother has sent jelly and Father a book for you to read."

A glimmer of a smile at the book made Ralph look a little like his old self. "I thank you, Rose. That is most neighbourly."

"Neighbourly! You give a cold welcome."

"Not nearly as frosty as our last parting, Rose, or had you forgotten?"

She turned away, fussing the dogs, who had ceased growling on Ralph's command.

"May I sit, or am I too unwelcome?"

"I pray you, do sit. Your face is no less fair even though it is no longer promised to me."

Rose sat. "Are you in pain?"

"Nay, not so much now. Martha has patched me well and I am mending fast. I shall soon be back with the King's troops again. They are wintering at Oxford so I may as well bide my time here as there."

"Oxford is not so far."

"Quite."

A silence stretched between them, making Will's entrance even more welcome than it already would have been.

Rose turned to him gratefully. "Why, it is Will! Why did you not tell me of your brother's misfortune? If it had not been for a travelling tinker, I would still not have known of his injury. 'Pon my truth, I thought we were better neighbours than that."

Will went straight to her side and bowed, sweeping off his hat. "I beg your forgiveness, Rose. I have been occupied tending to my brother, as you can see."

"And you could not spare an hour for me?" Rose gave Will her very best smile, peeping across at Ralph to see the effect and pleased to see colour rising on his pale cheeks.

Will also glanced at his brother and looked discomforted. "What have you brought in your basket?"

Rose, glad of the diversion, brought out her gifts.

"That is right thoughtful of your parents, is it not, Ralph?" Will looked across at his brother.

"Mighty considerate." Ralph shifted on his seat and instantly, Will went to him, helping him get comfortable again. Rose remained seated.

Martha bustled in with a bowl of broth. "Time for your gruel, Master Ralph."

"Nay, Martha, not gruel again, I beg you. I'd far rather a good rib of venison. That would set me up more than this pap."

"You shall have venison very soon, I promise, Master Ralph, but for now you must eat this."

Rose seized her opportunity. "I shall leave you to it, Ralph, but I shall visit often and my parents will come too, when you are stronger."

She thought she heard Martha grunt but perhaps it was one of the dogs.

"Let me attend you." Will joined her as she got up from her seat. Ralph missed his spoon and some broth trickled down his chin until Martha mopped it up. A muscle twitched in Ralph's jaw.

"Fare you well, Ralph." Rose smiled at him but took his brother's arm.

The following week, her parents visited the invalid and came back with glowing reports of his improving health.

"You would do well to make the most of this opportunity with Ralph while he is idle and resting, Rose. Perhaps he would take you back, if you were humble and attentive enough." Agatha's whole physique bristled with resentment. It had been her fondest wish to unite the neighbouring estates and she was bitterly disappointed the betrothal had not been reinstated.

Rose did not need telling she needed to get Ralph back, but humility was not part of her strategy. She visited him again, taking a basket of pine cones she had gathered for the manor hearth and saffron from the autumn crocus growing in her mother's garden. The threads of saffron had to be painstakingly removed from the little flowers and were always appreciated by Martha, who wielded much influence in the manor's household.

It was one of those rare autumnal days when the sky was cornflower blue after an early frost and the wind, though cold, was dry and invigorating. She found both brothers walking in the manor gardens, Ralph with a stick and Will supporting his other arm. Ralph was limping still but obviously pleased to be ambulant.

"I see my mother's reports of your progress have not been exaggerated, Ralph. It is good to see you out in the fresh air again." Rose curtsied to them both and smiled at each man in turn.

"Well met, Mistress Rose. I am, as you can see, once more abroad and walking. This time next week I shall throw this wretched staff away and mount Mercury again." Ralph waved his stick in the vague direction of the stables.

"Methinks riding should wait awhile, brother." Will smiled through his concern.

"I'm sure Will is right, Ralph. He is wise in most things." Rose nodded at Will, broadening her smile.

"Is he indeed? That is news to me. However he makes a good prop."

"Is not Will good at many things? I have found him to be so."

"He can prate and preach at some length, that I grant you. I have had no means of escape from all his radical ideas and theories these last two weeks." Ralph turned around back towards the manor house.

"And I have found Will's thoughts to be stimulating and very interesting and have learned much. We have had many long conversations about the King and Parliament, have we not, Will?" Rose took Will's unoccupied arm, so Will was between her and Ralph, exactly where she wanted him.

"Aye, Rose and your questions have prompted me to search my own heart and mind more thoroughly. Rose has a brain equal to many men, Ralph." Will looked from side to side to include them both.

"You had better leave politicking and bible thumping to men, Rose. Women are made for gentler occupations." Ralph winced with pain.

"Are you weary, brother?" Will was immediately concerned and, to her annoyance, dropped Rose's arm in favour of slipping it around his brother's slim waist.

"I am ready to return to the fireside, aye."

Rose contained her anger and schooled her face not to show it. At least Will respected her intelligence and, as soon as they had reinstated Ralph in his fireside chair, she turned away from him.

"Is it not a lovely day, Will? Ralph looks settled by the fire, will you not accompany me back home? The days are shortening fast and I would be afeared to ride alone in the twilight."

"If my brother does not need me, I should be honoured to escort you home, Rose."

"Oh, don't mind me," Ralph waved them away. "Martha has promised me a meat pie tonight and that's enough excitement for one day."

"It is good to hear you jest again, Ralph." Rose went to kiss his cheek but at the last moment withdrew, mimicking his own teasing when they were betrothed. Ralph had inclined his head to receive it and looked very discomforted when her lips did not touch his skin.

"I shall be quicker on my feet for your next visit, Rose." Ralph said, without a flicker of a smile.

"I shall be ready for you." Rose curtsied to him and took Will's hand in her own, leading him out of the hall after a backward glance at his brother, who, she was pleased to see, was now scowling.

Ralph was indeed quicker on his feet the next time Rose visited, so quick, he was in the stable yard preparing to mount Mercury, who had also made a miraculous recovery. All the new tired lines on Ralph's face vanished under his grin once he sat up on the big white horse, towering above Inkwell and Rose.

He looked down at her. "See, Rose? I ride once more and it does feel good to be in the saddle again. Care to ride out with me?"

"You look very well, Ralph, but I must take these possets to Martha."

"If those milk puddings are intended for me, you have wasted your time. I told Martha I would thrive on venison and good English beef, and so it has proved. I haven't looked back since I over-ruled her fussing and ate red meat again."

"I'm very glad to hear it and hope you continue to recover well."

"So, let one of the servants take your basket and ride out with me."

Still Rose hesitated. She wasn't sure she was ready to be alone with Ralph. He did look strong enough to attempt anything. "Were you intending to ride alone, this first time?"

"Nay, Will is coming."

"Oh, in that case, I would be delighted to accompany you both."

Poor Mercury. Ralph dug his heels into his sides and the big horse snorted and reared his protest. Ralph laughed, keeping his seat with ease and looking entirely his old self.

Will came hurrying into the stable yard. "Sorry to have kept you, brother, I had to see Father about estate business. Why Rose! How lovely to see you again." He doffed his hat at their visitor and Rose nodded her pleasure.

Ralph settled Mercury, who was pawing the ground with impatience and said, "Come on, Will, get on your horse and let us be off."

Will mounted his piebald mare swiftly and they cantered out of the yard and onto the lane beyond.

Any conversation Rose might have liked was quenched by Ralph streaking ahead in a gallop, shouting his joy out loud. Inkwell had no chance of keeping up and Rose settled her little mare back into a trot, letting Ralph disappear into the distance. Will looked torn between care of her and of Ralph.

Rose saw his dilemma. "I am quite safe, Will. You had better keep up with your brother. He is a fine horseman but he may tire and a fall would not help his recovery. I have delivered my packages so I shall return to Charlton House."

"Are you sure, Rose?" Will looked anxiously over her shoulder at Ralph's fast disappearing form.

"Yes, indeed. Now go!"

Will galloped away on his piebald mare and Rose was left to trot home alone, with only her bad mood for company.

Another opportunity to goad Ralph was not afforded her. She rode over to Meadowsweet Manor in early December to find only Sir Edward in the great hall, still none too pleased to see her. He tersely told her that Ralph, fine soldier that he was, had fully recovered and had left to join two cavaliers, Digby and Wilmot, in sacking Marlborough on the Wiltshire Downs. They hoped to block the wool trade upon which Parliamentary funds depended.

"And Ralph wasn't going to miss that sport so close to home."

"Will he be back, do you know?"

Sir Edward snorted. "Once he's tasted some proper fighting among the King's men, I don't expect to see him until his Majesty is victorious. Nor would I want to. If only both my sons would give me the same pride." Sir Edward stomped off, not looking as pleased as he claimed.

Left to her own devices, Rose sought Will to find out more and found him up in the morning room, deep in paperwork, his fingers stained with ink and a frown on his thoughtful face.

"Am I intruding, Will? You look much occupied."

"Nay, I am glad to leave off this tedious task. It is always good to see you, Rose."

"Your father has told me that Ralph is back with the King's Army."

"Aye, strangling the wool trade. Only poverty will result in the long run but that is what war does. Strips the heart out of the land." He laid down his quill.

"Do you not wish to join the fight?" Rose knew she was treading on dangerous ground in asking this.

"May I speak plainly?"

"Please do."

"I cannot support our King, Rose, but fighting against him would be the same as fighting my own family, who as you know, are staunch Royalists. But a man must follow his own conscience. This king is so wasteful of people's hard-earned groats; so blatantly disregarding of the needs of the common man that I cannot fight his cause. You know my beliefs about all men being equal in the sight of God, we have discussed it often enough. The time is fast approaching when I must live up to my fine words."

"So, is it justice you seek?"

"Aye, but not for myself; for all. Parliament has its faults but at least it attempts to ease the plight of the poor. Only this week they have issued an Ordnance to relieve soldier's families in distress, showing their care of those worse off than themselves but, true to form, the King has denounced it." Will shook his head.

"I heard that Prince Rupert is raiding all the towns and villages around Oxford to feed his Majesty." Rose sat in the window-seat within the recess of the big window.

"Aye, and what is left for those he has stolen from? By thunder, it enrages me that these royals feel they can plunder where they like and leave families starving in their wake." Will got up from his littered desk and paced the room.

"Does the King join his nephew in these raids?"

"He eats the results."

Rose had never seen Will so stirred up but his words sparked a seed of rebellion in her own breast. She could see the logic of his thinking; she liked the promise of radical change he implied.

"Do you see a time when Parliament might rule without a king?" Rose knew she had crossed a boundary with her question and found the dangerous conversation exciting.

"That would be radical indeed, Rose, and there are some who speak of it, but only behind closed doors, for this is no less than heresy and I counsel you not to say anything similar outside of this room. I do not think it should go so far as a republic but if King Charles would just be less intransigent, more willing to co-operate and change his high-handed ways, all this conflict would be avoided."

"But Will, is it not already too late for that?"

Will looked up at her from his study of the floorboards he paced. "Aye, clever Rose. I fear so."

Christmas came and went without celebration that year. The looting breaking out all over the countryside undermined any seasonal joy and in the new year Parliament issued a General Order to sequester all Royalist estates. The looters now considered themselves entitled to help themselves to houses known to favour the king and all trust between neighbours became slowly eroded.

Early in the spring, committees were set up to raise funds for Parliament and when Rose discovered her father had issued money for it, she understood how committed he was to defeat their sovereign. To appease Agatha, Roger also gave money to the Royalist cause, though considerably less. Both sides were now frantically raising money. The King's chaotic followers were disorganised and sporadic in their methods of raising a levy and made Rose wonder if Parliament, by sheer efficiency and numbers, might indeed win the day. All around her, the country people looked hungry as their coffers were raided. Old feuds between neighbours broke out anew and, time and again, Will's dire predictions of a torn landscape and impoverished people played out before her.

Her father confessed his fears to her one day, when she brought him some food to eat, while he worked on his accounts in his chamber.

"I am being badgered on both sides for funds, Rose, and yet how can I sow the fields when my best men are away fighting? And now that wretched Marquis of Winchester has given his entire fortune, yes and his mansion on the London Road, to the King's cause. The place is a fortress and blocks all trade for wool from Wiltshire to London. As you know, we rely on that trade for a greater part of our own income and I do not know what's to become of us." Roger ran his blackened finger down a column of figures and sighed.

"If it's any consolation, they are also suffering at Meadowsweet Manor, even though Sir Edward refused to pay the Committee for Sequestration." Rose put down the tray she'd been carrying.

"How do you know of these things?"

"Will tells me all."

"Does he now?"

And Will did. Rose saw him often these days, her old game of using Will to taunt his brother forgotten in the desperate reality surrounding them. She had come to share his aspirations of a better way of life after witnessing the despair of the country-folk around her. She found herself agreeing that no one man had a divine right to impose poverty on this scale, to undo the very fabric of society. Her world had turned upside down and she was forced into changing with it.

## *"I must, I will, see him again"*

It might not have been wise, but we did return to the manor after Percy, presumably acting as Rose Charlton, had commanded we do so but not before we had continued our search among the ruins of Charlton House. Eventually the threatened rain appeared and we retreated to the car. It was quite late by the time we got back and we were both too tired to do much except read the few books we'd borrowed from the library about the Civil War. Disappointingly, we discovered that Charlton House had simply burned down after it had been struck by lightning in a storm a year after the war had ended. No exciting battle had been to blame, after all.

After a simple supper, I had grumpily retired to my bedroom for an early night. How long I had been asleep before my dreams took on an unearthly clarity, I shall never know. I remember stirring as I heard Percy come upstairs a while later and use the bathroom, but it barely registered. I snuggled back under the duvet, luxuriating in the comfort of what must be a memory foam mattress, so deeply had my weary bones sunk into it.

"I tell you, sir, my horses are needed here!"

Rose stood next to her father in the doorway of Charlton House as Sir Roger addressed the hungry-looking troop of Cavaliers, some sitting astride their big horses. Many were on foot and all looked very weary.

"And I have to inform you, sir, that your King has need of them." The leader of the horsemen had an arrogant countenance, one not used to being refused.

"They cannot be spared. It is harvest time for the hay," Sir Roger replied.

"Harvest, you say? That is good news. We have need of provisions also." The cavalier looked across at Rose and removed his feathered hat, swishing it downwards in a wide circle. "What have you in the larder, fair lady?"

Rose looked at her father before speaking. He looked nonplussed so she answered for him. "We have only enough for our own family and none to spare."

"Nonsense. I'm sure you are welcome." Agatha joined them on the step, pushed Rose out of the way and swept up to the young man on his black horse. "Dismount, sir and come in for refreshments, yes, and your men. Anyone who fights for our dear King is welcome here, isn't that so, husband?"

Rose looked at her father. He had gone white with anger but she knew he would never stand up to his wife. Those who had horses dismounted and their leader bowed to Agatha, sweeping off his headgear again, this time scuffing the dusty ground with its plumes. "James Bridges, at your service, madam. You are the lady of the house?"

"I am that, sir, and loyal to the King. Away inside and I'll summon the stable lads for the horses."

"Gladly, madam."

Agatha bustled past her daughter, still standing in the doorway. Rose frowned at her mother, whose face had gone even redder than normal as she made eyes at Mr Bridges, who must have been less than half her age.

Their guest stopped as he passed Rose and, ignoring Agatha, he pinched Rose's chin and had the cheek to finger the corner of her lips. Such trespass only infuriated her further.

"What? No welcoming smile from your daughter? Why, madam, I see she follows you in looks. Rarely have I seen such beauty on such a solemn face. Are you not glad to welcome us preservers of law and order in this upside-down world? Come, let us see these lovely lips parted in a smile."

He lingered over the word parted. She flattened her lips in compression.

The cavalier laughed. "I shall get a smile out of you before we leave and that's a promise! Pray what is your name, my beauty?"

Agatha stepped in quickly. "This is Rose, sir, my only daughter."

"Have you sons?"

"Aye, sir, we have four."

"Four! and you so youthful yourself, good woman."

Agatha, to Rose's shame, actually simpered. They walked into the hall and Agatha clapped her hands for the servants. The steward came immediately.

"Andrew! Bring wine, bread and yesterday's cold beef from the kitchen for these loyal gentlemen. There is some cheese, I believe and bring any fruit we have in the larder that's suitable."

"Aye, ma'am."

The cavalier sat at the long table, and angered Rose further by taking the chair at its head, her father's chair. Where was he? Roger was nowhere to be seen and Rose felt ashamed of one of her parents for the second time that day. Her father must have made himself scarce rather than face out these noisy intruders. Or were her suspicions about his Parliamentary leanings the cause of his absence?

"How old are your sons, madam? What is the family name?"

Agatha curtsied. "Agatha Charlton is my name and my eldest boy is twenty-two, the youngest only seven."

"One is no longer a boy at twenty-two! That young man is more than old enough to fight. Is he here?"

"I will have him fetched, sir." Agatha spoke to one of the serving lads who ran off with the message.

Rose's embarrassment now turned cold and hard inside. How could her mother sacrifice Tom to these soldiers? He could so easily be killed if he went off to fight. Rose went to follow the lad and warn Tom but Mr Bridges grabbed her arm, none too gently.

"Stay, mistress and keep us company while we drink your father's wine. Where is he by the way?"

"I know not, sir."

"Then sit with me and take his place." The man's steely arm pushed her down into the seat next to him.

The soldiers fell on the food Andrew brought and made short work of the flagon of wine. Tom, his eyes shining with excitement, drank and ate with them and so did their mother but Rose abstained. After a particularly lewd joke at her expense, she could stand no more and excused herself, dodging Mr Bridges's hand neatly. He was now quite drunk and much less nimble than before. Rose ran to her father's chamber. She knew he'd be hiding in there.

"Father! How can you skulk in here when those greedy men are eating everything we've got?"

"I will not bear them company, child."

"So, is it as I thought, Father, you do not support the King's cause?"

"Careful what you say, Rose. In times like these it is usually best to say nothing at all."

"Is that so, even when they're taking our Tom with them to fight for the King? Are you just going to sit here and let that happen?"

"What? They can't do that!"

"And Tom has agreed to go with them. One would think spring had come early to look at him. Oh, Father, cannot you stop him going? He is so young still. What if he was killed?"

"He is fully grown and his own master now. If he has volunteered, child, there is little I can do." But Roger looked troubled and stroked his chin, deep in thought. "I will speak to Tom and try and dissuade him from combat but do not interfere,

Rose. It would not do to declare the family against the King, especially while his supporters are under our roof. "

Her father got up, wearily, as if he had aged ten years in ten minutes. He turned back, his hand on the door latch. "Say nothing of this to your mother."

She watched him leave, his footsteps slow and dragging. Would he really stand up to those boorish cavaliers?

Rose wished Will was here.

Will! If these men went to Meadowsweet Manor, they'd press Will into joining them, as well as Tom. They probably already knew Ralph from his celebrated skirmish at Edgehill. In a sudden flash of recognition, Rose knew which of the Foulkes brothers she truly loved. She'd been flirting with Will to annoy Ralph, teasing him as Ralph had teased her, playing with his affections. Now Will was in danger, for the first time she understood and felt the pain love brought. The game was over. His plain and simple sincerity, his integrity, his intelligent quest for truth, his genuine, undemanding love for her - she had fallen in love with every aspect of the man but hadn't known it until this moment.

She walked quickly to the stables. "Alfred, saddle Inkwell for me and be quick about it."

Rose mounted her black mare and took the back gate out onto the road. She galloped the two miles to Meadowsweet Manor, giving Inkwell over into Old Peter's capable hands. Saying nothing of her mission, she simply asked where everyone was.

"They be in the hall, missie, having their midday repast, I b'lieve."

"Thank you, Old Peter."

God's truth. That meant Sir Edward would be with Will. How could she impart her news and save Will from conscription?

With no answer presenting itself, Rose trusted to fate and entered the hall. The fire was roaring away up the chimney and the two men had obviously finished their meal and were arguing, as usual.

The talk stopped abruptly at her entrance. Although her eyes flicked to Will's, it was his father who welcomed her in, without enthusiasm and bade her eat. She still wasn't hungry, despite her hard ride.

"To what do we owe the pleasure of your company?" Sir Edward said, pouring some ale into a pewter mug and passing it to her.

Rose sipped the liquid, to gain time more than from thirst. She looked across the table at Will, whose big brown eyes, soft with love, gazed at her. He was silent but she could hear his thoughts clearly. Thoughts of love, intense and true and sincere. Oh, why had she not felt this before? Why had she not known which brother to love until now?

Rose set her tankard down."There are Royalist troops at our house, Sir Edward. I thought to apprise you of it."

"Are there, by God? I thank you for telling me, Rose. What troop is it? Who do they serve under? By thunder, I'd be glad to ride out with them, were I younger. Do they stay long?"

"I know not, they have only just arrived but they have already eaten half our winter's supplies."

"Fighting men will always have hearty appetites." Sir Edward belched softly, one hand on his paunch. "We should billet them here, do you not think, Will? We have more resources than Charlton House and could easily house a few of the King's men. After all, your brother is now a captain in His Majesty's army and we should act in his honour. How many of them are, there, Rose?"

"No more than ten, I think, sir," Rose said.

"And are they gentlemen?"

What could she say to that? She'd thought them lascivious louts. "They seemed very well dressed, sir, but they had need of more horses. Their spokesman was named James Bridges."

"Bridges? Why, Ralph spoke of him being at the battle of Edgehill and said he was a fine soldier. I'll send Young Peter over to Charlton House right now. Will you ride back with him, Rose?"

"I think I need to rest awhile, Sir Edward, after my ride." Rose darted a look at Will and was rewarded with a gleam in his eye but still no word.

"This time you shall join his Majesty's army, William." Sir Edward had sobered up and now looked sternly and uncompromisingly, at his younger son.

"I, I'm not ready, sir." Will sat up very tall in his chair.

"Not ready? What do you need to be ready? You are fit and old enough. Of course you must fight for your King in this damnable war. I'll not have a Foulkes be labelled a coward! Go and tell Martha to prepare for guests and make your mind up to be civil to them when they arrive!"Sir Edward's voice had become very loud.

Will got up from the table and stood to face his father. "I shall not fight for the King, Father. If I fight for anyone, it will be for the Parliamentarians."

Rose took a sharp breath. She now regretted bringing her news. She had not meant to precipitate this announcement.

Sir Edward sat in suspended animation, his tankard held halfway between table and mouth, which gaped open. "What did you say, boy?" he growled.

"I said, I'm for parliament. This King has wasted our money, taking more and more in taxes and thinking he rules by Divine Right, as if he is Christ risen from the dead and descended direct from God. I believe every man alive should be free to worship as he thinks fit. Everyone has the light of God within their souls and deserves the chance to live freely and be rewarded for honest hard work, whatever their station."

There was a moment after Will's speech when Sir Edward continued frozen in time. Then, with a roar, he threw his tankard at Will, catching him on the cheekbone and cutting the flesh.

"I'll have no preaching Puritan in my house! Get out of my sight, William Foulkes. You are not my son. I will have no mealy-mouthed Parliamentarian under this roof. Be gone, be gone forever. I hope I never see your miserable face again." And Sir Edward stood up and drew his sword, pointing it at his youngest child.

Will never moved or flinched throughout this tirade.

"Very well, Father. I thought you would react like that and I understand why. I'm sorry to go but my faith must not be denied. It feels good to be honest at last and declare my intentions. I will leave this house, my family home and I doubt I will see it, or you, again. God bless you, Father."

"I don't want your false God blessing me, boy," Sir Edward's voice was shaking now but whether from emotion or anger, Rose couldn't tell. She looked directly into Will's eyes, which now rested on hers. She nodded; giving him a little smile.

Will turned from his father to her. "Rose?" He held out his hand. She took it. How had he known she loved him? Had he divined this truth before she knew it herself?

"What's this? What new treachery is this?" Sir Edward looked from one to the other, looking more astonished than ever, if that were possible.

"Tell this to Ralph on my behalf, Sir Edward. It is Will I love and his cause I espouse." Rose took off the silver pomander and chain around her neck, relishing the freedom from its weight. "And you may give him this." She placed it on the table in front of Sir Edward.

"Good God! You are a little viper! Two turncoats I have harboured. Aye, if that is the truth, go with this coward before Ralph comes home and kills you both. Now that *would* have my blessing."

Rose took Will's trembling hand and grasped it with all her strength. She walked around the long table to his side, without releasing its clasp.

"Get out!" shouted Sir Edward and slashed his sword before them. "Before I run you through, as I long to do."

Unhurriedly they walked, side by side, though Rose knew Will's heart was beating as fast as her own from his rapid breathing. But her heart felt light. Lighter than it ever had. Truth had a beauty that transcended the mind games she'd always enjoyed playing. Her female charms had bestowed a power upon her she'd used skilfully all her life but none of her little victories had felt like this.

Her sorrow at leaving this beautiful house for the last time pierced her pure, unalloyed joy. A house she had known all her life and where she had been welcomed all through her childhood. Her destiny had been to be its mistress, its bearer of descendants. Now she was exiled from it forever. A part of her would linger in this house. Meadowsweet Manor had always meant more to her than her own home but, in leaving this beloved place, she was shedding the suffocating lies she had been labouring under as Ralph's bride-to-be.

She was free. Free to love and worship as her heart dictated and with the man whose soul matched her own and to join in with the rapidly changing world around them.

Rose gave one glance back at the grand hall, taking in the minstrel gallery, the huge fireplace, barely noticing the red-faced man glaring at them.

The bones of Meadowsweet Manor whispered to her to return.

*"How I long to see him again, touch him, feel him."*

Maybe it was the dawn chorus that triggered the dream, because the surreal scene was accompanied by a symphony of birdsong. At first I could only see the dappled leaves, through which strong beams of sunlight filtered, while the birds chirruped their cheerful tunes. Like a baby in a pram, I looked up through the oak trees, delighting in their merry dance, as the sunshine baked their spring-green backs and a gentle warm breeze lifted their deeply serrated skirts. Blossom frothed in the nearby hawthorn trees; mayflowers, that only bloom in the prettiest month of the year.

I saw two lovers, standing before an altar made of oak wood, decorated with dark green ivy and spring flowers. A solemn, pockmarked man, looking somewhat grubby, stood on the other side but there were no walls to this church. They stood in a clearing in a forest of living oaks with only a couple of people witnessing some sort of ceremony. Everyone looked very solemn.

I saw a ring exchanged and, as the couple turned their faces towards each other, I recognised them as Will and Rose. So she married him, not Ralph! That was a turn up for the books after he'd given her the silver chain. Little minx, she must have led them both on at some stage. They kissed, their faces still serious, and the preacher blessed them both, placing their hands together on a bible with delicate reverence.

The ceremony seemed to be over and the party broke up without applause. Rose and Will walked away, hand in hand. I felt an intruder then, as I watched them eat a modest picnic, feeding each other daintily before lying back in a mossy nook and kissing tenderly. Such gentle lovers until their passion mounted. What a gooseberry I felt then. I didn't want to spy on this honeymoon; I wriggled in my bed, the scene slipping away; the faces blurring and disappearing. Now I was dreaming that Robin was with me; that it was us canoodling. Oh, it felt so good to touch him again.

What was that noise? Cries of fear? Of pain? I woke, bewildered and disturbed, my body thumping with erotic desire, to the sound of guttural shrieks. I shook my head free of sleep, thinking they were part of the paradise of my dream. No, they were still there. Alarmed, I grabbed my candlestick, struck a match with shaking fingers and lit all three candles. Not bothering with a dressing-gown, I ran out of my bedroom in my pyjamas and down the corridor towards the eerie noise.

I stopped in front of Percy's ancient bedroom door, hesitating. Another groan from within its beamed walls decided me and I opened the latch to find Percy writhing on the bed, legs akimbo and arms wrapped around her bolster.

"Percy? What's the matter? What's wrong? Are you ill?"

She was too far gone to hear me and kept groaning and yelling. Only when she said, in a sigh of ecstasy, "Will, oh Will, how I do love you!" did I realise, with a rush of blood to my face, what was going on.

Hell's bells, this was a highly embarrassing situation. What should I do? Leave her to have her pleasure with a flipping ghost, or intervene? I hope she didn't realise I'd already witnessed this intimate scenario. I couldn't watch any more, as her gyrations became unmistakably passionate.

I retreated to the window and opened the curtains, resolutely looking out instead of in, and cringing as I remembered my dream - seeing the overwhelming desire between Will and that perplexing woman who had only recently, through Percy, wounded me for life. My arm still ached constantly and the open cut refused to stop weeping. Through the old, flawed glass, the dawn plumed pink and lovely across the eastern sky and Percy's noisy sighs drew to a shuddering halt.

"Thank goodness for that," I whispered and leant my head against the cool glass diamonds of the mullioned window.

I tiptoed back towards the bed but kept to a safe distance, holding my candelabra aloft to gaze at its occupant. Percy, whose skin shone in the candlelight with a becoming glow of perspiration, was sound asleep with a fatuous, and very satisfied, smile on her face. I decided that discretion trumped valour and crept away.

In my own room, I drew back the heavy curtains and sat bolt upright in bed, afraid to succumb to fatigue in case my dream returned and I, thinking I was Will Foulkes, newly married and randy as hell, sleep-walked back to Percy and did something unspeakable. The dawn treated me to a display of the most wonderful palette of colours as a reward for my vigil. The early pink deepened to cerise, then violet, before the warmer hues of red, orange and finally yellow burst across the panorama. The sun may have risen on the other side of the house but it generously enveloped the entire sky in its glorious rebirth. A celestial blue irradiated the heavens before I could drag myself away from the free show to seek the more earthly comfort of the Aga downstairs.

I fed the impervious Arthur, envying his insouciance, as he barged through the cat flap and sat washing himself with effortless ease in a pool of morning sunlight, just outside the back door. I joined him on the flagstones and sat on the old mounting block, nursing my tea, glad of the warm rays on my sleep-starved face, musing on how the hell I was to explain the goings on in the night to my new and obviously extremely sensuous friend.

Awkward or what?

I hardly knew where to put my face when Percy arrived in the kitchen an hour later, just as I was refilling the kettle, her serene glow betraying her recent amorous dreams. She glided into a chair and picked at some grapes from the fruit basket, with a silly smirk on her lovely countenance. Her long wavy hair was tousled but it only made her prettier. Gawd, this was getting complicated.

I plonked a mug of tea unceremoniously in front of her. We were well past the prospect of juicing spinach and carrots now. In fact getting downright intimate, not that Percy knew that. Should I tell her?

"Sleep well, Percy?" Skirting around the issue might yet yield some clues.

"Marvellous, thank you, Fay. I feel wonderful this morning." Percy stretched out her lissom arms, cat-like, and yawned. She picked up her mug and sipped the tea absent-mindedly; I'm not even sure she registered its plebian taste.

"Er, that's good then." I turned and slapped some bread that we'd bought in town yesterday on to the hot bakestone of the Aga.

As it curled and browned, its comforting fragrance permeated the warm kitchen. "Mmm, that smells divine, Fay. I could eat a horse."

Funny how people change.

I used tongs to put the hot toast on a plate and bunged it in front of her, watching with some amusement as Percy lathered on liberal quantities of butter, which melted instantly. She topped that with some set honey, its waxy fondant waving across the buttery broadside in thick sweet furrows. Percy clamped her mouth around the confection with a vigorous bite of her unbelievably even white teeth.

"Had a swim before breakfast today, Percy?" I couldn't resist.

Through the food in her mouth she said, "Nah, couldn't be bothered, to be honest. I feel deliciously lazy after my deep sleep. Is there any more of that toast?"

I cut two more rounds, one for me, one for her, and decided to keep last night's foray to myself. She had no idea I knew about her nocturnal pleasures and it didn't seem right to confess to spying on her intimate moments with Will. I buttered my own toast and took a bite. Sawdust. I left it on my plate and Percy looked quite cross that I'd wasted it.

"Still not hungry, Fay? What a shame."

She put her hand out to take it from my plate but I snatched it away. "You don't want that, Percy. I was sick yesterday, remember? Could be a bug."

"Oh, yes, I'd forgotten. Oh, and how are your poor hands? " She still wore that daft, dreamy expression.

"Surprisingly okay, thank you. Right, I'll go and get dressed then. See you later." I tightened the cord of my fleece dressing-gown.

"What? Oh, okay."

I left her to it.

*** 

I ran the tap, cold of course, we still had no hot water, into the sink of my en-suite bathroom and squirted in some antiseptic lotion. The wound in my upper arm was even more tender today and throbbed with an ominous, persistent ache. Not much, but enough to set alarm bells ringing. Bracing myself, I ripped off the plaster and was dismayed to find the scab came with it, making the cut bleed all over again. Somewhere, in the dim, tired recesses of my mind, I remembered someone saying that blood is clean and washes out toxins. Well, as the hole in my arm now gushed red arterial blood into the trendy glass bowl, presumably it would clear up any brewing infection. I swabbed it with the dilute antiseptic, wincing with the pain and sheer panic that rose as the bleeding persisted. I'd never had clotting issues before. There was no history of haemophilia in the family. This was an entirely new and scary experience.

I grabbed the box of plasters I'd bought yesterday and ripped open the cellophane with my teeth. The uncovered gash pumped more blood. I tore the wrapping off the biggest plaster and after mopping the cut with a dry flannel, quickly pressed the dressing over it, making sure I sealed all the edges. I held my arm aloft and gripped the basin with the other. Feeling nauseous again, I stared at the mirror. I've never been vain, well, not since I lost Robin and stopped fretting about all the other girls in school but I was shocked at the face staring back at me. My hair needed a wash for a start but it was the bags under my eyes that concerned me most, emphasised by the fading bruises, now a sickly yellow colour. I've always had a ruddy complexion and used to despair over my red cheeks but I never would again. The pale face in the mirror looked far too ethereal to ease my disquiet.

What was that old comedy programme? 'One Foot In The Grave', that was it. I shivered and turned away from my reflection.

I lay back on the bed, keeping my problematical arm above my head. Gradually, the pain eased. I gazed out of the window, which looked out over the walled garden. In the corner the big old willow stirred in the morning breeze, its long fronds wafting gracefully, like a giant Hawaiian grass skirt. I looked beyond its green curtain at the little ruined chapel. Why did that area smell so much? Was it simply bad drainage or could it be decayed remains? Surely not our lively spiritual companions? They had died nearly four hundred years ago. They *should* be nothing but bones. But there were no shoulds in this situation, were there? My cut arm should have healed up and stopped bleeding long since. I should have gone home after that game of squash. I should be in my somewhat grotty flat, sleeping the sleep of the just every night during my week's holiday doing DIY. Somehow that still didn't appeal. No, I wasn't sorry I was here but it was about time we got to the bottom of the mystery and that stink out there had to be worth investigating. After all, there had been no Charltons or Foulkes in the village graveyard; their old carcasses must lie somewhere.

Satisfied my arm had stopped bleeding, I got dressed in my only remaining clean pair of jeans, pulled on a shirt and jumper and brushed my teeth, revived by the fresh mint taste in my dry mouth. I went downstairs. Percy was still mooning about in her floaty silk dressing-gown.

"Percy, I think we should have another poke about in your grounds, by the little chapel. Are you game?"

"What?"

"Come on, Percy. Brace up. Time for action. Go and get dressed and meet me out there, by the ruins."

"You're very bossy this morning." Percy pulled her silken robe around her slim body and pouted, yes pouted.

"Just want to move things along. Coming?" It was no good, looking at her in that turquoise garb, locks all flowing down her back, just brought my queasiness back. I went to the back door and opened it. "See? Lovely morning. Too nice to stay indoors. I'm going to investigate. See you later."

Thinking some time alone was just what I needed, I struck out across the manicured lawn towards the gate in the wall. The rust on the ancient hinges gave way more easily this time. Once through, I looked about and sniffed. Nothing yet. The morning smelled delightfully pure and brand-new. I loved this time of year just before the torpor of August bowed out to the rigour of September, hinting at the change of season to come.

I inhaled the cool, clean air and filled my lungs with it. Breathing more deeply, I caught the whiff I'd been both dreading and seeking. I followed its reek, not surprised to find it came from the direction of the little church. The roof had long since caved in and the grass grew tangled and thick around its base. The closer I got, the worse the stench became, until I had to cover my mouth with a tissue. Surprisingly, the door was still intact. Pocketing my tissue, my mouth firmly shut against the pong, even if I couldn't shut off my offended nostrils, I gripped the circular iron door handle and turned it. It took two hands to shift it but eventually it groaned away centuries of disuse as I forced it to turn clockwise. I shoved at the oak door with my shoulder but it opened only an inch. I applied my knee as well but something was jammed against the wood on the inside. Probably one of the fallen roof timbers. I gave up. It would have to wait until Percy joined me, if she ever got dressed, and with the fetid smell stronger than ever inside the church, I was content to wait. Cursing my weak will, I cravenly withdrew from the porch and clambered around the church walls, searching amongst the tufty tussocks of couchgrass for - what? Gravestones, I suppose, but really, anything to clue me into the history of the place and unlock its secrets.

My lurid imagination was getting the better of me, I have to admit, when a shout startled me back to the present with a jolt.

"Cooee!" Percy was tripping lightly across the tumbled grass, elegantly avoiding the spikes of marshgrass growing on the wettest areas of the boggy ground.

I let out a sigh of relief and greeted her with a smile. "Good afternoon, Percy."

"Don't be sarky, Fay. Have you found anything?"

"Not yet. I tried to force the door open but it's stuck fast. Want to help?" I knew Percy's slenderness belied her steely strength from the way she whacked a squash ball.

"Okay, but I wish I'd brought gloves." Percy eyed the mossy oak panels with distaste.

"Get over yourself, woman. You can always wash your hands later. Come on, heave-ho."

We pushed together, on a count of three, and the door retreated a good six inches under our combined weight.

"Again, Percy! One more shove should do it."

We pushed again and suddenly, the door gave way and we fell in, Percy on top of me in a heap of pastel chino and cashmere; me taking the brunt - again.

"Ow! Bloody hell. I'll be lucky if I get out of here alive at this rate." I investigated my perennially sore arm, terrified the plaster had come away and it had started bleeding again. Despite its pulsating pressure, it looked surprisingly okay.

Percy scrambled to her feet and pulled me up to mine. I felt slightly dizzy, and held on to her for a moment, while my eyes adjusted to the dim interior of the chapel.

Percy let go of my hand and brushed off her pale lemon jumper. She screwed up her nose. "Ugh, it stinks in here!"

"Yes, doesn't it just? Unfortunately these rafters are in the way but I can step over them, I think. " I could see more clearly now and the sunlight filtering through the smashed stained glass windows illuminated a sorry sight. Not quite hidden by the rafters was a substantial table in the centre of the little church. Its back was broken in half and it had collapsed in on itself.

"That's funny." I pointed to the sturdy table. "Aren't altars usually at one end?"

Percy dusted her hands off and looked up." I suppose so, the eastern end isn't it?"

"Yes, normally. I have never seen an altar in the centre like this." I climbed over the tangle of rafters and got closer. As I suspected, the table looked as if it had been chopped in two by an axe, or some other sharp, heavy instrument. The wood was robust and even falling roof timbers would not have been able to divide it. This had been rent asunder by an act of violence. "Someone carved it up in a bit of temper, I think. And look at those windows. I don't think the elements broke them either."

"And, see here, Fay." Percy had turned back and stood in the corner to the right of the door where a statue had been reduced to a mere stump at its base, surrounded by plaster rubble.

"This place has been well and truly trashed. Either they had a wild party or some religious nutters had a bit of a paddy and smashed everything in righteous wrath."

"I think that happened a lot in the Civil War," Percy nodded. "I was reading about it in one of the books from the library. The Roundheads didn't like the old Catholic ways with ornaments and wanted everything simple and plain."

"And like all converts, their zeal carried them too far. Not the Christian values I got taught in school."

"Are you Christian, Fay?" Percy turned back to me, her eyebrows raised.

"Nah, I think it's a load of baloney, myself. Not sure what I believe except in life after death. I think the hippies have got nearer the truth. You know, we all return to some collective consciousness and then have another go as someone else."

"But how do you explain all these restless ghosts, then, Fay?"

"Not sure I can. I know they exist and many's the time I wish they'd bloody well leave me alone and I know, no, I hope, we can help let them go into peace, but frankly, Percy, I'm way out of my depth here."

For the first time since we met, I saw real panic on Percy's face. Damn, perhaps I shouldn't have let her know I was winging it. After all, I have had experiences and it wasn't true I didn't believe in anything. Oh, it was hard to put into words but there *was* something else. There was both good and evil. Of that I was quite certain.

In the end, I fudged it. "It's too early for philosophical debate, Percy. Let's solve this little mystery before we embark on the deeper ones that have had better brains than mine confused for centuries."

"I can't stand the smell in here anymore, Fay. I'm going back outside." Percy picked her way through the broken plaster and wooden beams and disappeared through the front door.

I stayed back a moment. I had sensed a presence in here and I needed to listen to the message they were trying to convey. I perched on the fallen edge of the table, checking first it wouldn't give way and rested my haunches. I settled my mind and then emptied it before closing my eyes.

And then I waited.

The first thing I was aware of was the shouting. Great roars of outrage. I couldn't see anything at all. I tried to concentrate, forcing my inquisitive brain to be silent, receptive. What was that? I caught some words in the confusion. There was some argument about the very table I was resting against. I could hear glass smashing too in tinkling waterfalls of sound. The air around me cooled and swirled angrily against my legs. The wood beneath me shuddered. I leapt away from its solid support and as I opened my eyes glimpsed Will's face. His brown eyes looked at me beseechingly, wide with distress, fierce with anger. He was dressed in that long white shirt again, the cut on his face and his bruises still not healed. I could see his mouth open in protest but then all the noise diffused into a muffled roar and fell silent.

I blinked and looked at the table, scarcely believing it had not moved. I could have sworn it had been torn away from under me. But no, there it still stood, the two halves making a v-shape and its upturned legs pointing uselessly out at a forty-five degree angle into the fetid air.

I felt the ground with my feet. Solid, and just as real as the overwhelming smell. I had to get out or I'd choke. I clambered over the jumble of wood, bruising my shins carelessly in my desperate flight, I reached the door and squeezed through the aperture. Gaining the fresh, well relatively fresh, air, I inhaled, only to be further disturbed by the distinct fragrance of roses; their flowery fragrance mingling unpleasantly with the whiff of bad drains.

*She* was here too.

I scrambled clear of the porch and cast about for Percy's chic outline. I couldn't see her anywhere. If Rose was here, she could be in danger. Or more likely, I was. Rose certainly had it in for me. Against my will, my better judgement, I followed the sweet over-powering aroma of roses. My nose guided me around the tumbledown building to the rear of the chapel and there I found my friend.

Percy was squatting next to a gravestone, squinting - where were those blasted glasses - at the lichen-covered writing etched into the stone. Behind her, flowering in a profusion that belied the season, a pink rambling rose covered the entire back wall of the church and its branches grew along the ground, just like a bramble. The creeping branches, interspersed with beautiful blooms, encompassed the grave around which Percy kneeled. She held a plucked rose stem in her hand.

"Hello, Fay. Look what I've found."

I hadn't realised how I had tensed my whole body until it relaxed at the welcome sound of her normal, twenty-first century voice. So Rose hadn't taken her over - yet.

"What is it?"

Percy scratched away at the lettering with her rose branch. She was getting to be a dab hand at that. I looked down at my arm, dismayed to see a red stain creeping through the wool of my jumper outlining the neat square of plaster. The nearer I got to Percy, the more it throbbed but there was no choice but to go on. As I approached, the scent of roses around the grave overwhelmed me. I questioned again how bountifully the flowers cascaded from the chapel walls with all the exuberance of June, not the tatty exhaustion of the last days of August. The plant now completely encircled the gravestone and Percy knelt within it. Amazed, I watched as the tendrils grew faster and faster around my friend. If I didn't act quickly, she would be trapped inside. I lifted my feet over the flowery border but some forceful energy stopped me entering the rosy halo surrounding her. Curls of rose briars encroached on my feet like little fingers, clawing at me.

I gave up; tried to stay calm; to connect with Percy without alarming her. "Can you read the inscription, Percy?"

Percy didn't look round at me. She seemed unaware of the peril she was in and peeled away a section of lichen. "Ah yes! See? I can just make out the name, Eleanor, I think it says."

"The lovely Lady Eleanor, I presume, who died in childbirth."

"Yes, must be. Oh, look! Underneath are the names of her daughters. Poor thing, so many snuffed out at birth. I can't make out their names but we have them in the bible indoors." Percy continued to scratch at the faint letters, blissfully ignorant of the leafy cage building around her.

I tried not to panic, or at least let my panic show in my voice. "Yes, poor woman, but at least she appears to be at peace. Come away, Percy. I don't like the way the roses are growing around here."

"Oh, I hadn't noticed them." Finally Percy stood up and looked around her. "But, Fay, these weren't here before! There was just one climbing rose against the chapel wall. Oh my God! I'm going to be trapped soon."

"Yes, come away, Percy, please!" I put out my arm, the good one, to grab her hand. She reached out to mine and I tried to pull her to me.

We stood with the rose briar between us, now waist high, preventing contact, arms outstretched but not able to touch.

"Fay, I can't get past this damn rose bush!"

"You must, Percy. Don't let Rose take you over now. She's trying to hold on to you but you must be strong. " I leant forward and managed to connect. "Don't let go of my hands." My arm throbbed with pain and I felt sweat break out on my forehead. The ground beneath me felt too soft, almost as if it was giving way, sucking me in, drawing me down to the bodies below.

I looked into Percy's green eyes. "Look at me, Percy. Stay in the present. This is dangerous. Now, come on, step down onto the branches. That's it, we'll both stamp on them."

I lifted my leg as high as I could and slammed my trainers down onto the thorny briars, hoping like hell their thorns wouldn't pierce the rubber soles. Percy did the same with her leather loafers and we both forced our shoes down to the ground, as if we were putting out a bushfire. Frantically we jumped up and down until eventually the briar was beaten down under our crushing feet. As soon as it was low enough to the ground, Percy lunged out and stepped clear.

We hugged each other, gasping for breath. I closed my eyes with relief, determined not to the let the tears pricking the back of them expose the depth of my fear. I felt something soft brush my hot cheek, light and cold as a snowflake. I opened my eyes and thought we were caught in a snowstorm. But it wasn't snow whirling around us. A pink tornado of rose petals spiralled up in a column, pinning us inside. The air was thin within the spinning confetti, too fragrant, sickly sweet, sucking upwards and drawing the breath from my lungs up towards the sky with the rose petals.

Percy clung to me within the vacuum, gripping my forearms with white fingers. Her face was screwed up, her mouth tightly drawn in a grimace of pain. I thought my lungs were going to collapse from lack of oxygen. I had to open my mouth and get some air. Risking a mouthful of roses, I opened it and yelled, "Percy, we've got to jump out of this together! Come on, on a count of three!"

Percy nodded, and, still hanging on to me, nodded towards the direction of the house, which we could barely see through the veil of flowers.

"One, two, three!" I shouted, letting go of one of Percy's arms and punching the air in front of me with the other, while simultaneously thrusting my body forward and kicking out with my legs. Miraculously, we landed on our bottoms a yard distant, the boggy earth giving us a soft, if damp, landing.

I sprawled on the ground, one hand propping up my head, and saw the weird spiral of petals disintegrate. Some fell to the earth and some blew away in the wind but the transition was fleeting. Within a minute, no more, all the petals had dried up into tiny shreds and then disappeared before our shocked eyes.

When they had all gone, we turned and looked at each other. I'm not sure which one of us trembled the most. Percy extended a muddy, shaking hand and pulled me once more to my feet.

We looked at each other and said, with one voice, "Rose."

"Where do we go now, Will?" Rose slid her hand into his. Her neck now felt bare without the familiar silver chain around it and her chest almost too light minus the pomander that had lain against it for so long.

She felt a little disorientated; lost. Her triumph had been short-lived and now, despite the man riding so close to her, she felt abandoned.

Will smiled at her, dispelling her fearful mood. "Do not fear, Rose. I know exactly where we will be welcomed."

"Where is that?"

"We shall go to the forest."

"To be with the outlaws? Oh, Will, I'm not sure I want to do that." Rose turned back but the warm red bricks of Meadowsweet Manor were already gone from view.

She faced frontwards again. The two horses jogged on, as if it was just another day.

"You will find friends among them, Rose, my love. Ah, Rose, my dearest dear, I cannot believe you have chosen me. Are you sure?"

"About you?" Rose looked at Will's profile.

As if drawn by her stare, he turned to look back at her. "Aye, of course about me. Are you quite sure you love me, Rose? We have never spoken openly of our feelings and you were betrothed to my brother for a very long time."

"That is true, dearest Will. I never knew how much I loved you, until the Royalist soldiers came to my house today and I knew they would pursue you and make you join the King's cause. Knowing your heart, as I feel I do, I knew you could not obey. When I realised the danger you would be in, my heart spoke true of my love for you." Rose did not flutter her eyelashes this time. Perhaps for the first time in her life, she spoke simply, from her heart.

"Then I am deeply flattered and honoured. I have always loved you, Rose, and I always will." Will leant across from his horse to hers and held her hand, dropping it only when they saw distant flames through the trees.

"God's blood, what is this?" Will nudged his piebald mare into a canter and Rose reluctantly followed suit. The fire was no more than half a mile away.

"But this is the inn we were to rest in! I know it of old and it is staunchly for Parliament. The whole place is afire!" Will jumped off his horse and cast the reins to Rose. "Stay back, Rose. Whoever has done this could still be here."

He ran towards the inn, whose thatched roof was ablaze, and wrenched open the door.

"Will, no! You will be burned alive!" Rose watched in horror as Will tried to beat the flames down and enter the building, immensely relieved when he gave up.

"I'll have to try around the back. Follow at a distance with the horses, Rose, but please, be careful!" Will disappeared around the side of the building to the stables, which were not yet on fire.

Rose had to encourage Inkwell to approach, which wasn't easy with another horse in tow. Both animals were frightened of the fire, as was she. Rose skirted around the stable block at the rear of the inn, staying well back from the heat, finding some shelter behind a low wall that confined the yard.

She heard a whimpering noise and looked around. Huddled behind the wall was a boy. He was hugging a small dog, a mangy old thing. They both looked terrified.

Rose dismounted from Inkwell and approached him.

"What has happened here, boy?" She kept her voice low. Anyone might still be lurking in the trees surrounding the stable yard and she had no wish to meet them.

At first the boy was struck dumb, presumably with shock.

"Speak, child, I will not harm you. Tell me, what has occurred here?"

"Cavaliers, at least twenty of 'em. They did set fire to my father's inn when he refused to serve them."

"Cavaliers? You mean the King's men?"

"Aye, they were like demons, mistress. Possessed of the devil. They must have been. They, they...my mother. My poor, poor mother." The boy, who couldn't have been more than ten, began to cry and the little dog licked his face, leaving white patches on his smoke-blackened face.

"What happened to your mother?" Rose knelt down to him. He smelt of soot and sweat-soaked fear.

The dog snarled at her, defending the lad. "Steady, old Bodger, the lady don't mean no harm."

The boy looked at her, his eyes wide, tears welling up in them. "They ripped her dress off, mistress and they took her, there and then, on the floor." He sobbed. "She was screaming and my father, he tried to get in the way, but they ran him through."

"They killed him?"

"Aye, mistress. Three against one, all armed with sharp swords and he with none. Then they turned on my mother. She see'd me, she did. I saw the look in her eye, telling me to go, to save meself but I saw the first man on top of her before I got away. I couldn't stand the screaming. Oh, mistress, I should have saved her, I should have saved my own mother." The boy clawed at her dress, his sobs violent now.

"You could not have saved, her, boy. She was right. She would be glad to know you are safe. Is she still inside the inn?"

"As far as I know. I ain't left my place here behind the wall. The men, they drank everything we got, shouting and swearing. I've lived here all me life and seen drunkards aplenty, but I never did see nothing like this afore."

Rose could think of no words to console him. There was a huge crash and the blazing inn roof collapsed in on itself. Where was Will? Rose stood up, searching frantically for any sign of him.

"Will, where are you?"

Will came running up to them. "Rose! Rose!" he shouted, his face also blackened by soot, came over to her, catching her up in his arms. "Thank God you are safe."

"What has happened, Will?"

"I got the woman out, but she's in a terrible state, choking on the smoke and injured too. There's no sign of her husband and I cannot go back in there now." He turned to the boy. "Do you live here?"

The lad nodded. "My mother? Is she alive?"

"She is in a bad way, boy. I'll take you to her. Leave the horses and come with me, Rose. I will need your help." Will led the lad back to the rear of the inn.

Rose looped the reins of both horses over the branch of a nearby tree, well away from the roaring flames. The two animals were restless and pawed the ground, fretting at being tied up, but she had no time to reassure them. She turned and followed Will and the boy. Away from the burning house, but near enough to feel its heat, lay a woman, half naked, her clothes torn, her skin a strange bluish colour. Her face was bleeding and bruised under her pallor. The boy rushed to her side, and knelt down next to her.

"Mother, oh Mother, dear." He held her face next to his and kissed it.

Will and Rose stood nearby. Rose whispered, "Will she live, do you think?"

Will shook his head.

The woman's lips moved. "Save yourself, son." She gave a rattling last breath and her head lolled to one side.

"Mother!" The boy shook her but the woman did not respond. He threw himself against his mother's body, his breath coming in great rending sobs.

"Will, is there nothing we can do?" Rose could not bear the sound of the boy's cries, louder even than the thunderous roar of the fire behind them.

Will shook his head. "All we can do is get the boy away before we all roast alive."

"But his mother?"

"No-one can help her now." Will found some sacking beyond reach of the fire and covered the woman's body. He turned to her son, who had stayed on his knees, staring in silent disbelief.

"Come, lad. Come with us, away from here. We will protect you. I am sorry for your mother and father and what you have witnessed, but you cannot stay. Your home is burnt down and you are now an orphan. I will take you to people who will look after you."

The boy wiped his snotty nose with the back of his hand and nodded. He got up slowly from the ground where his mother's body lay. His little dog barked.

"Aye, Bodger. We have no home now."

"No, but you have friends. Pick up your dog and sit before me on my horse. We will find you refuge." Will held out his hand to the lad.

"But who will bury my parents? Who will say prayers over their bodies?"

"What is your name, boy?" Will asked.

"Edmund."

"We shall say a prayer now, Edmund." Will held his arm about the boy and spoke the Lord's Prayer.

Rose echoed the familiar words, trying not to break down. Her legs wouldn't stop shaking, despite the fierce heat emanating from the burning building.

Sobbing more quietly, the boy allowed himself to be led back to the horses, who waited in the cool of the trees.

Rose followed, silent in her shock; still trembling from it.

"We must get away from here, in case the Royalists return to plunder what's left." Will lifted the boy on to his saddle, the dog in his arms.

"There'll be nothing left." Rose mounted Inkwell, and looked back at the inn.

The front wall had now collapsed. By tomorrow it would be nothing but a smoking ruin.

## *"You will not escape me next time."*

We reached the refuge of the kitchen in record time, without a single further word exchanged. Once inside its haven, Percy slammed the door shut behind us.

"Silly, really," she said, with a lopsided grin, "We're not safe anywhere, are we?"

I shook my head, too out of breath to comment, and flung myself on to one of the horsehair sofas. Seeking reassurance, I clutched a cushion to my stomach and hugged it, burying my face in its velvet patchwork.

Percy, being that much fitter than I, regained her composure more quickly and soon had the kettle singing on the hob. I watched while she slung more coal into the obliging Aga, grateful for her competence. Whilst waiting for the water to boil, she swung into action, renewing the candles in the tea lights, before lining them up on the worktop with military precision. *My* trembling didn't stop until I had a mug of hot tea in my hands and had warmed them on its heat.

"You look a bit better now, Fay. You didn't look too clever earlier." Percy sat on the other sofa, set at right-angles to mine, opposite the Aga.

"Clever would certainly not describe how I'm feeling right now, in any shape or form." I took another sip from my steaming mug, enjoying the sensation of warmth as it reached my grumbling stomach. "We need to protect ourselves before proceeding further, Percy. That was some display out there, stronger than anything I've ever encountered."

"Yes, you frightened me when you said you were out of your depth, Fay. You've always seemed so confident, so in control before."

"That was an illusion, I'm afraid. My previous experiences had nothing on this situation. If only we could get on the computer and find out a bit more about the history. Do you think the electrician will turn up tomorrow?"

"Yes, I'm sure of it. I'll text him to make sure. He won't like it on a bank holiday but that's just tough."

"Is it Monday? I've completely lost track. No chance of him turning up today then."

"No, we'll just have to glean what we can from that book I bought. I don't want to use my phone for internet browsing and run the battery down. You never know when we might need it. Hang on, I'll fetch it from the study." Percy downed the rest of her drink and vanished into the hall, coming back a few minutes later with the slim white tome and thankfully, her new glasses.

Percy put on her ready readers and opened the book, which looked thinner than ever, not much more than twenty pages stapled together. I didn't have much confidence it would yield the information we needed.

"Shall I read it out loud or do you want to sit up at the table and look at the pictures with me?" Percy looked very owlish as she peeked over her tortoiseshell frames at me.

"Can't move, I'm too comfortable. Read away, Percy." I closed my eyes so I could listen with full concentration.

Percy began to read aloud. At first it was a general introduction, interesting enough in its way, but not pertinent to Meadowsweet Manor. As I listened to the account of the reign of Charles the First, I couldn't help but be struck at his infamous arrogance but even more, by his incredible stupidity.

"What a meddling fool the king was," I murmured over my cushion, still held as my bulwark against invading ghosts.

"Wasn't he just?" agreed Percy. "His stock answer to everything was to try and force it through with the aid of his army."

"You can easily see why his daft policies led so inevitably to civil war. The wonder is that everyone joined in, one fellow countryman against the other."

"Yes, listen to this bit; it demonstrates your point exactly. Apparently the battle on Roundway Down was led on each opposing side by men who used to be the best of friends."

"What a sorry state of affairs."

"I know, there is a very moving letter written by one of them, Sir William Waller, to his friend Sir Ralph Hopton, just before they became adversaries." Percy read out the letter, her voice straining with sadness. It ended on a very poignant note. *"'...We are both upon the stage and must act those parts that are assigned to us in this tragedy. Let us do it in a way of honour and without personal animosities. Whatsoever the issue be, I shall never willingly relinquish the dear title of your most affectionate friend and faithful servant, Wm Waller, Bath 16th June 1643.'"*

"That choked me up, Percy. To think these old buddies must try and kill each other. I wonder if they did? What side was Waller on?"

"It says here he was in command of the south-west of England for Parliament and Hopton had the same position for the Royalists, so that's why they had to fight each other. How tragic."

"And what was the date of the letter?"

"June 1643."

"Hang on a minute." I abandoned my cushion comforter and sat up. "What was the date of Roundway's battle?"

Percy flicked through the pages. "13th July 1643."

"Only one month later than the letter, then." I stroked Arthur, who had seized the opportunity afforded by my discarding the cushion by promptly taking its place. He began to purr; a deep rhythmic vibration that gave me far more comfort than had the inanimate cushion. I settled him more centrally on my lap and leaned my head back again on the arm of the sofa, trying to resist my fatigue and the ever-present pain in my arm.

"Shall I carry on reading?" Percy looked over her specs at me again.

"Definitely, I'm engrossed. Thank you, Percy. You read beautifully, by the way."

"Thank you, Fay! You are kind."

"Not at all, I'm enjoying it."

Percy cleared her throat and I could hear the proud smile in her voice as she continued. She related the battle of Lansdown Hill in Bath, a place I dimly remembered from a visit there with my parents when I was a child. We had picnicked up on the hill from where we had admired the panoramic view of that beautiful city. I recalled the gracious curves of the Regency streets, as I listened to the sad tale, remembering the same spot but imagining it instead littered with soldier's bodies, as each side tried to dominate the other.

"What a crazy business war is," I said.

"Sadly very true, Fay, but listen to this next bit. Hopton gets blinded by an ammunition wagon accidentally being blown up by his own troops, while Waller steals off the same night, leaving camp fires burning so Hopton's soldiers think they're still there. When they wake up the next morning, the Royalist army find not only is their leader terribly injured but their opponents are nowhere to be seen!" Percy laid the book aside in her astonishment.

"And Waller's the Parliamentary one who wrote that emotional letter?"

Percy nodded and sipped a glass of water to soothe her throat.

"Bloody hypocrite. I call that betrayal. What happened next?"

Percy picked up the book again. "Seems the Royalists, led still somehow by the blinded Hopton, went to Bristol to get more arms and food supplies and then headed for Oxford, where the King had his headquarters."

"Huh, bet his royal majesty kept himself safe and sound, skulking within the city walls."

Percy read on, "They never made it that far. They had some skirmishes between them but then Waller blocked their path to Roundway Down, which was on their route to Oxford. Hopton retreated to Rowde and they had a minor battle before *he* sneaks off this time and manages to get to Devizes town."

"Real cat and mouse stuff." I could picture the scene really well now, this game of give and take, strike and retreat. What a farce.

"And where did the Roundheads go, whilst the Royalists were no doubt feasting in Devizes? I wonder if Wadworths brewed their excellent beer way back then? If they did, they probably got roaring drunk that night."

"Do you know, I've never tasted Wadworths' beer?"

"What? Never had a pint of 6X? We must sort that out and soon, Percy. You know, we could go to a pub for lunch today.

Get warmed up and have a good feed. Would stand us in good stead."

"Feeling better then, Fay? You haven't eaten much since you were poorly up on Roundway, which by the way, is where the Parliamentarians went. They camped up there at the top."

"Oh, so that's why it's called 'Oliver's Castle'. Funny how you never question some phrase you hear every day."

"Oh, yes, I have heard that name too. Must have been a bit bleak for the Roundheads. Ironic - Roundheads on Roundway Hill. Maybe that's why it's called that."

"I think the name goes further back but who knows? But you haven't mentioned Oliver Cromwell before. Do we definitely know if he was there?"

"I don't think so. He doesn't seem to come into the fighting at this stage. From what I can remember of Paul's old school book about the whole duration of the war, Cromwell only takes charge much later."

"Ah, I see. Funny it's called 'Oliver's Castle' then, if old Wartface wasn't there. I wonder if Will was amongst the Parliamentary soldiers camping up there? I'm sure he would have been on that side, not the Royalists."

"Do you mean *my* Will?"

"Steady, Percy. Will belonged to Rose, remember, not you." We must not let those boundaries blur across time. I must remain vigilant but oh, I was so tired.

"You're right, Fay, he's not mine." Percy wriggled on her sofa, as if she was physically uncomfortable, but I suspected it was her thoughts she was re-arranging.

To divert them, I applied the conventional English tactic. "Does it say what the weather was like that night? After all, it was mid-July, so chances are it would have been a lovely balmy evening."

Percy took the hint and smiled, "No, the weather was anything but balmy. Apparently it was chucking it down."

My mind flicked, reluctantly, to Roundway Hill in the rain. Not the best spot to camp out all night in bad weather. Percy began to read aloud again and despite all my efforts, after a few minutes, I drifted off.

In my sleep, I saw Roundway hill decked out in canvas tents which billowed in the wind hunkered down against the rain. Somehow the soldiers had managed to light fires which afforded mini-beacons of light amongst the huddles of men crowding around them.

"Took a while to get the fire going through this rain, Master Foulkes."

"Call me Will, we're all equals in God's eyes. You've a good blaze now, Jack." Will held his hands out to the flames, glad of their warmth while the rain pattered relentlessly on to his back.

"Ay, we'll have this rabbit stew bubbling soon."

"And I shall be right glad of it."

"You travelled far today, brother?" Another trooper addressed him, while scraping his blade with a sharpstone. The sound grated on Will; made his teeth ache.

"No, not far. I have come from Savernake Forest."

"Be there fighting there then?" Jack, the swarthy man who'd undertaken the role of cook, stirred the greasy slop in the cauldron over the smoking fire.

"No, I had some business to attend to. Private matters."

"Oh yes? Surprised you had time. We've been kept busy bombarding Devizes with our cannon."

The scraper butted in. "And that was a right waste of bloody time. Cannon firing way too short on Jump Hill. We gave the church a scratch but t'wasn't no use; we wasn't even close."

"Fair play to Waller though, he had a good go at storming the place by the church but them barricades was too strong and our horses couldn't jump the ditches they'd dug so quick." Jack added grudgingly, "Them Royalists can't half shift theirselves, I'll say that for 'em."

The trooper spat on his sword. "Ay, well they're well fed, ain't they? We got them supply carts, though, didn't we? Good grain too."

"Yes, they take anything they want wherever they go." The image of the burning inn flashed across Will's mind.

Jack stirred his pot, which showed no sign of coming to the boil, as far as Will could tell. "Hopton weren't having no truce though; he had too much ammunition left to want to parley. That's why we's up here in this Godforsaken spot. Rain's coming slantwise now, we's so high up. Bad as that hill in Bath.

I suppose you never went to Lansdown either then, young Will?"

"No, but I've heard all about it."

"You should have seen old Waller, grinning like a pauper with a fistful of hot pie." Jack licked the twig he'd stirred the stew with.

The other man joined in with a rough laugh. "Aye, he stole off that hill like a nipper stealing apples from the orchard. We come away, see, leaving them camp fires lit up like beacons. Them stupid cavaliers never suspected nothing." The sword sharpener held his blade to the fire. It flashed silver and very sharp; lethal. He grunted his satisfaction but didn't stop his noisy scraping.

Will wasn't too sure how he felt about Waller's deception in Bath, pretending they were camped on Lansdown Hill like the Royalist troops but quietly retreating in the dead of night. It didn't seem honourable to him. Such double-dealing pricked his conscience but then he remembered the blazing inn and poor Edmund's mother. He stood up. "How long before supper's ready, Jack?"

"Give it an hour, young Will and this rabbit will be tender as a lamb."

"I'll be back then, be sure to save me some." Will smiled his thanks and wandered off towards the trees at the edge of the field.

A few other soldiers were relieving themselves on the roots of the tall beech trees and ignored him. His bones ached with fatigue and his stomach growled with hunger but his heart still sang with joy, despite the tragedy he had so recently witnessed. In the distance, some men were singing hymns. Their deep voices rose and fell on the sombre words, as befitting the eve of another battle, but Will did not share the general mood of foreboding. All the men were tired, probably far more than he, having marched from Bath and lost some of their fellows along the way. The last three days of skirmishes must have exhausted them all. He felt a fraud for a moment, having not yet fought for the cause he believed in, but his guilt was fleeting. He had at least rescued one life from the pillaging of cavaliers.

Edmund had remained silent all through their long ride into the outlaw's hidden camp deep in the forest. He'd questioned nothing and Will had handed him over to Brigit, one of the wives who lived there. Brigit was a tough but motherly woman. Will knew Edmund would be safe with her, though he doubted he would ever recover from the horrors of that night.

Witnessing the destruction of the inn had brought Will to a decision sooner than he had anticipated.

He had taken Rose to one side, away from the motley collection of rebels who had gathered at the camp in the forest. Out of earshot, he told her he had resolved to join the Parliamentary army.

Rose had been livid. "But, Will, what will become of me? You cannot abandon me to these, these vagabonds!"

"We shall be married directly, Rose, which will afford you protection from any men here. They may look rough and ready but they all abide by a code of honour, unlike the Royalists. You saw what they had done; you now know the sorry state of our divided nation. I cannot wait longer. I must defend our country from these wanton cavaliers who are raping and plundering everywhere they go. And you must go home to your parents' house afterwards, for I will not be able to watch over you personally."

"No, I will not!" Two spots of pink and personal rebellion had flared in her lovely cheeks. How he had longed to kiss them.

"I insist, Rose. Unless you stay here with the outlaws in the forest, you will not be safe, but Charlton House would also afford you refuge until my return."

Rose had looked about her then; at the rough bivouacks hewn from the branches of the oaks around them; at the primitive beds made of bracken on the earth floor; at the smoking fires and the cauldrons of simple food stewing above them.

Slowly she had nodded her consent. "Very well. I shall keep our marriage a secret from my parents, Will, but return to their protection. Promise me you will return as soon as may be, so that we can begin our married life together."

Will was relieved she had capitulated so quickly but doubted she would fool Agatha for long. "I'm glad, Rose. And, are you sure, really certain, that you want to be wed before I join up?"

"I am certain."

The preacher they had seen on Stickerton Common had been sought and found at daybreak, and a plain gold band purchased from one of the widows amongst the outlaw fraternity. The ceremony had been simple but what followed changed Will forever. The memory of it came soft and full into his mind.

He had waited so long for his beautiful Rose. All those years he had struggled to accept he would only ever be her brother-in-law were over. Now he had gloriously claimed her for his own and such rapture it had it been. Truly, his marriage was nothing less than miraculous and he thanked God for it.

And he really believed she shared his faith, though she had never said so outright, he had to trust in it. Had it been that gadding sermon on Stickerton Common that had begun the reformation of his beloved? Or the poetry of George Herbert that her father loved so much? He and Rose had read the verses aloud to each other, just as Eleanor and Roger had done before them, as part of their wedding vows. Since her death, he was never without his mother's favourite book and, after a fractional hesitation, Rose had joined him in the exchange. Or was it his own words, his own conviction that everyman had the light of God in their souls? That each had a right to the bounty wrought from this beautiful earth, not just the landowners and their henchmen who forced tenants into labouring to put food on his table before their own? Was it his own sincere belief that all men were truly equal in the Lord's eyes that had persuaded Rose finally to reject Ralph's earlier claim upon her? Or did she simply love him for himself, as she claimed?

Savernake forest had harboured them in their night of wedded bliss; protected them with its natural fortress of oaks. And such bliss. Now, in this quiet moment before his first battle, he allowed himself to remember it all. How Rose had held his hand. Hers had felt small and tender in his fist, soft against his roughened woodcutter's palms. They'd walked in the glade alone, talking of the outlaws who guarded it, who had witnessed their blessed union. The gadding preacher, who had inspired them both with his potent words, had married them that morning under a cathedral of tall oaks, so they could stroll, man and wife together, blessed by God if not by their families, in the gilded forest.

Will had wanted to say so much, but his heart had been too full. He'd squeezed his wife's hand instead and the instant returning pressure of hers had shot up his arm and spread throughout his body in a wave of fresh happiness. Rose had stopped walking then and turned on tip-toe to kiss him. They had never kissed like this before. Will knew a moment's jealousy feeling her mouth on his, her tongue licking his. Rose knew what to do. She had experienced this before, and with his own brother. A jumble of emotions welled up in him then. He was a traitor to his own flesh and blood. He had taken his brother's bride for his own and was about to fight against him, against his king, against his own father. Will had pulled away and tried to ignore the hurt in Rose's big brown eyes; eyes lit by desire - for him.

"Will?" Her voice had been as soft as her eyes but he could hear the injury of his rejection within its gentle timbre.

"How can mayflowers look so enchanting and yet smell so vile?" Will had hated himself for his anger, yet could not quell it.

"They need to attract flies to fertilise."

"A dirty trick."

"Perhaps. Come, husband, and take my hand once more. We do not have long together."

It had been too true. Will was determined to join the Parliamentary forces the very next day.

"Will, do not spoil this precious time, this sacred moment. Is it Ralph who has turned your thoughts from me?"

Will had nodded. Of course she'd understood. His anger had vanished as quickly as it had come. He'd turned around and scooped his new wife into his arms, bruising her rosy lips with his own. "Forgive me, dearest one. My heart is sore that we are married thus, clandestine and in secret. I would have it otherwise."

"But hasn't God blessed us, Will? Isn't that enough for you? You, who love simplicity. Our wedding could not have been more in keeping with your beliefs, surely? Here, let us break our fast. I have cheese and bread in this basket. Brigit gave it me as a wedding favour. And there is ale, and apples. Come husband, let us share the first meal of our married lives."

Rose had pulled him to a mossy alcove, lined by limestone boulders. The little nook caught all the sun and the ground felt warm and dry; a softer mattress than any bed. The bread had been dry too and Will suspected much more than a day old, while the cheese had been over salted. The apples, after a winter in someone's barn, were wizened with age, but he would not spoil their wedding day with complaints.

"I would have given you a feast, if I could, Rose, but any food eaten in your company is as good as nectar. The ale is very good, and tastes more like mead, as if the bees have given it their honey."

"Yes, Will, it is sweet and true, like you, my love."

They had lain back on the velvet moss. Their simple meal soon forgotten as they feasted on each other's bodies. Will wondered why he had worried about his ignorance. Desire had swept through him and guided him into her with such fluid grace until he felt they were but one person, melded together by love and bound together by God, as indeed they were. He had finally found his heaven on earth.

He fondly remembered the curves of his wife's young body; the eagerness of her hips as she pressed them into his; the secret parts of her snow-white skin that the sun had never caressed. He had kissed every inch of it. Unlike that worm of doubt about her faith, she had given him no reason to doubt her passion. Now he understood all those sonnets about the ecstasy of union.

And their union was lawful, blessed by God himself. No-one could tear them asunder again. Not Agatha, not Sir Edward; not Ralph.

Only death could part them.

## *"It is I you must see; I, and no-one else."*

I woke up with a start. My feet and hands were freezing cold, only my middle was warm, and that was down to Arthur's feline body, now curled into a contented ball on my lap. Instinctively, I pulled the blanket from the back of the sofa over me and huddled under its woollen shroud. I looked at Percy, her mellifluous voice still flowed on unchecked. She had become totally absorbed in her book. How long had I been asleep? The kitchen looked just the same, Percy looked just the same and the clock, run by batteries presumably, ticked on. Five minutes had passed. Just five, and yet I had travelled back for centuries. I rubbed my weary eyes. They were so gritty and sore and the cat fur didn't help.

Percy was reaching the bit about the siege of Devizes town, where the blinded Hopton was issuing orders from his sick bed. My eyelids drooped again. Arthur twitched in his sleep. His dreams must be vivid too.

"What are our orders, Sir John?" Ralph thought he might go mad with all this hanging around. The bombardment from Jump Hill thumped away constantly in the distance. The only break had come for a sombre reason. Hopton and Waller had agreed a six hour truce so that Sir Grenville's brave body could be escorted back to his home in Cornwall. But now those Parliamentary guns pounded out unceasingly again. Surely they could steal around the back of those Parliamentary gunners and ambush them from behind; stop that infernal fusillade? After all, they only reached the outer defences. The craven bastards didn't dare come closer. Typical.

Byron nodded in his peremptory fashion. "I give you good day, Captain Foulkes. I will go and ask Prince Maurice what Hopton's planning."

"It would be good to know, sire. But, forgive me, is Sir Ralph Hopton well enough to issue orders? Should not Prince Maurice assume command?" Ralph knew it was presumptuous to ask but inaction was anathema to him. Frustrated by the Parliamentarians creeping away in the night on Lansdown Hill, the cowards, and the inconclusive result in Rowde, made him long to settle the outcome, once and for all.

Byron disappeared into the inn Hopton had claimed for his own. Rumour had it that Hopton lay reclining on a bed, his head bandaged all around and bloody. Brave man to withstand that pain, to be able to command others, even in his agony. Ralph had glimpsed his commander's burned skin with his own eyes. He quaffed his ale and ordered a pie from a streetseller doing a roaring trade among the ravenous soldiers. Lord knew what meat it contained but it tasted alright, savoury and hot, almost too hot to eat, but he was so hungry he wolfed it down and chased it with more of the excellent local ale.

Sir John Byron returned, grinning. "Seems we've to raid every house in the town and demand the bedcords from under the mattresses of the goodwives of Devizes! That should give good sport."

"Bedcords? What on earth for?"

"We're out of match, young Ralph. The bedcords will serve, once dipped in resin. Come on, let's set the men on to it, then you and I, my lad, are going to scale the roof of St John's church here and relieve it of its lead. Then we might have some shot to load."

"What about powder?"

"Seems we have enough to get by but only for a day. We must get a party to ride to Oxford for reinforcements from the king but first, match and shot." Byron strode off quickly towards the market place, where soldiers were gathered, warming their hands on braziers. Ralph had a job, despite his long legs, to keep up with him.

The lead came away easily from the church roof. It was soft but incredibly heavy. Ralph used the blade, then the scabbard of his sword to peel it away from the ancient stone. There was plenty of it and it would soon be turned into a useful amount of ammunition. He threw it down to the grassy graveyard below, shouting for anyone below to get out of the way. The stuff was heavy enough to flatten a man. When all the lead was laid out on the ground, Byron grabbed his arm.

"We can leave it to the others to transform this lot into shot. Come, gather a few of the best men under your command, Ralph, we're off to Oxford. Waller's up on the hill there but we're outnumbered and need more troops."

"How many men has he got, sire?" Ralph followed his senior officer out of the churchyard.

"I've heard reports of five thousand." Byron's young face looked grim.

Ralph was rendered silent. They were lucky if they could round up three thousand Royalists. They strode into the stables of the Bear Hotel, where their horses were quartered. Mercury greeted Ralph with a friendly whinny and nuzzled him while he strapped on his saddle.

"Ready for a good gallop, Mercury? I hope they've given you some oats, you're going to need them."

Ralph swung into the saddle, eager to be off; proud to be amongst those chosen for this vital task.

Prince Maurice was already mounted on his stallion and addressed the three hundred cavalrymen gathered in the yard.

Lord Hertford and Lord Carnarvon flanked him on either side. Both looked very serious.

"My good fellows, we are to ride to Oxford this night and get reinforcements. The Parliamentarians have the advantage of us up on that damn hill and we can't have that, now can we? We're going to head out in the direction of Salisbury to act as a decoy. If we encounter no Roundheads, I'll give the command to veer back to Oxford, so stay close together, men. God save the King!"

A ragged cheer went up.

"At the gallop, then!"

Three hundred horses' hooves clattered on the cobbled yard as they set off. Ralph fingered Rose's silver chain and pomander in his pocket, as he now liked to do before meeting danger. The anger that flooded his body every time he touched it fuelled his need to kill.

## *"Good, I have you close now."*

Suddenly I felt hot, burning hot, and the source of the heat was coming from my pocket. I woke up, sweat beading my brow and my heart pounding in my chest. Half asleep, I threw off the blanket. Poor Arthur, startled out of his slumber, arched his back and hissed at me before leaping off the sofa and walking off, hackles raised and tail vertical, his exposed arse clearly displaying his disgust at this rude awakening.

Percy was reading no longer. She was standing above me, peering down, her green eyes once more narrowed with hatred. My heart pumped even more violently as I tried to come to. I blinked, erasing the crumbs of sleep from my eyes and begging my brain to clear. I hardly knew now which century I was in.

"Rose, I..."
"I know what you are about, Ralph Foulkes." Percy's voice had lost all its fluid poetry. High and harsh it came, barbed on rose-thorns.

Instinctively, I lifted my good arm to protect my face. Just as well, as Percy's hands had curled into claws, her long, sharp nails clearly aimed straight at me. She lunged but I ducked out of the way and landed on my knees on the floor. The hard fall jolted me back into the present and I crawled away, before scrambling to my feet and reaching the sink. I grabbed a jug from the draining board and splashed tap-water into it. Percy came at me again, clawing the air, trying to rake my face with those long, vicious fingers. As soon as she was close enough, I threw the water over her.

Percy's hands relaxed immediately. She brought them up to her own face and dashed the water from her eyes. She shook her head and her beautiful hair scattered drops of water in an arc around her. Some of them caught my hot skin, making it tingle with delicious coolness.

Percy, gasping with the shock of her cold shower, turned towards the Aga and grabbed a tea-towel, hung out to dry on its rail. I watched, still coiled in defence, as she swabbed her face with the cloth. Only when she stared back at me, looking like Percy again, did the muscles in my stomach, not usually taut, return to their normal, flaccid state.

"Oh, God, I'm sorry, Fay!" Percy panted out her apology.

"We can't go on like this." I slumped against the butler sink.

"But how can we stop it?" Percy schlepped to her sofa and flopped back against its myriad cushions.

I shoved my hands in my jeans pockets to stop their shaking but quickly withdrew the right-hand one, where I kept Rose's silver chain. "Ouch!"

"What's the matter now, Fay?"

"That bloody chain. It's red-hot in my pocket. I've just burned my hand on it."

"Oh no, poor you. You've got so many injuries. If I'm Rose, it's my fault, I'm so sorry." Percy sounded on the verge of tears. She was such a gentle soul but the woman she was hosting obviously was not.

"It's *not* your fault, Percy, because you are *not* Rose. You are simply the vessel through which Rose is acting. And she's not trying to hurt me, she's going for Ralph. Every time I see Ralph, she has a go at me. It never happens when I see Will. Look, there's stuff I haven't told you. I'll make a brew and bring you up to date." I spilled water as I filled the kettle with my trembling hands. The water dripped down the outside of the bright red enamel kettle and sizzled on the top of the Aga. It was a wonder my hand hadn't made the same noise when I touched that burning chain. I sucked my fingers where they still scorched with heat.

"Run it under the cold tap, Fay, it's the only cure for a burn."

I did what I was told and held my hand under the ice-cold stream for as long as the kettle took to boil.

"I'll get some lavender oil and we'll pop some in a bowl so you can dunk your hand every time it hurts." Percy rummaged in a wall-cupboard and fetched out a tiny brown glass bottle.

She poured some drops into a Pyrex bowl and held it under the running tap until it was full. The aroma of lavender quickly filled the room and calmed my harried, weary mind.

We took our mugs of tea over to the sofas and Percy placed the lavender bath next to me. Every time my fingers regained their stinging heat, I immersed them in the cool scented water until the pain melted away.

"Why don't you take the chain from your pocket and put it somewhere safe, Fay?"

Percy's wonderfully rational question was entirely reasonable, so why did it make me instantly cross? "I have a very good reason to hang on to it, thank you very much."

"I'm sorry, I didn't mean to offend. I had forgotten about your Robin."

"Forgive me, Percy. That was rude. It's a touchy subject."

"Of course it is, Fay. I was being thoughtless."

"Not at all, your suggestion was very sensible. I don't know why I *don't* stick it somewhere safe under lock and key but I can't help hoping, silly I know, that it connects me with Robin." My composure deserted me and I caught on a sob. "I miss him so."

"Oh, Fay, you poor dear." Percy got up and came and hugged me. Instead of comforting me, I recoiled from her touch. She, or Rose, through her, had hurt me once too often for physical contact.

I pushed her away. "I'm fine. I'm tired, that's all."

Percy didn't prevaricate. She seemed to sense I needed some distance. Maybe she did too. Being as we were both permanently on guard, how could it be otherwise?

I sat up straight and took a deep breath. "Let's do that recap, whilst we are both 'compos mentis', for once. I tell you what, Percy. I'm frightened to go to sleep at all now. I just get transported back in time whenever I drop off."

I told her what I had 'seen' whilst she'd been reading.

"So, you saw the action from both Will's and Ralph's perspectives?" Percy no longer looked like the vacant bimbo I had written her off as at the squash court. With her reading glasses perched on the end of her nose and her forehead creased into a frown of concentration, she looked more like an intellectual than the airhead I'd taken her for.

"Yes. Now, we need to piece together all that we have learned and slot it into the information in your history books; see if we can work out what these players got up to and why they are not at peace. For that is our task, Percy. We must lay these spirits to rest."

"I'll get some paper." Percy left the room. I sat back against the arm of the sofa, feeling the prickles of its horsehair scratching the back of my neck, glad of its tangible rough texture. I clung to the irritating sensation, using it to stay awake until Percy returned, armed with a loose-leaf notebook and a couple of biros.

"Why don't we sit up at the table, Fay? You're less likely to fall asleep and we can spread out our papers. Come on, I'm going to draw a time-line of events."

I got up. My limbs ached. They felt as heavy as that lead Ralph had heaved off the roof of St John's church. Funny, I could gauge its weight exactly, as if I held it in my own hands. I tottered, feeling the mists of time drawing me back.

"Fay! Come here!"

My eyes snapped open again. Percy had me by the arm and was pulling me towards the kitchen table. She plonked me down unceremoniously and stabbed her finger at the empty sheet of paper before me. "Write it down, Fay. Come on, stick with me, now."

I obeyed her command, scrawling down the story in a chaotic strand of uncoordinated memories. They came in a rush, too fast for me to write. Who was controlling my hand?

# Oxford, July 1643

Ralph swayed in the saddle. Sleep beckoned and Mercury's rhythmic stride lulled him. He must keep awake. He shook his head free of slumber and Mercury responded with a whinny. Even Prince Maurice had noticed his horse and admired him. He loved this horse, how could he not? Brave as a lion in battle, Mercury was loyal too and his noble spirit had chastened Ralph into handling him softly. No more digging in of spurs, as he had done with his previous horses. He was ashamed of that now. Mercury had no need of rough manners, his intelligence picked up the most sensitive of cues from his rider. He had even brought him home when he'd been wounded. There was no parting them now.

Mercury's white ears stayed pricked up and alert as he cantered through the night. There was no moon to guide them, just a miserable pouring rain which obscured all the landmarks. Ralph had long since stopped worrying about their direction but blindly followed his peers, trusting they knew the way to Oxford, and their king. They reached a clearing in the forest by a river and Prince Maurice called a halt. He dismounted and swept off his plumed hat, raking his long hair with gauntleted fingers.

"We'll stay here until dawn, men. The horses need to drink and rest awhile too. Dismount and see to your needs and theirs. We'll set a watch. Volunteers please."

Ralph didn't volunteer. He knew he couldn't stay awake for more than five minutes. He quickly dismounted and stroked Mercury's long nose, laying his brow on the horse's snow-white forehead. They stayed like that a long moment, then he led Mercury to the river to join the other horses and drink his fill. While Mercury extended his long neck to the water, Ralph mixed up some oats and water into the nosebag he carried and slipped it over his head when the horse had quenched his thirst. He walked him back to a likely spot under a broad oak tree and looped his reins over one of the lower branches. Mercury chomped on his food, one leg resting on its hock. Ralph eased off his saddle, and took the heavy weight of it onto his own shoulder.

Ralph checked his men had all they needed, then slung down his saddle and flopped back against it. He'd filled his flask from the stream and glugged down half of it. Such thirst. No-one spoke much, the fatigue on their faces spoke for them. Ralph rammed a couple of oat biscuits and a lump of cheese down his throat, then willingly gave himself up to slumber, placing his large, feathered hat across his face to blot out the drizzle dripping through the oak leaves above him. He'd just have to trust those on watch didn't do the same.

At dawn, a grey unpromising morning, the order went up to remount and ride the last leg into Oxford. A quick breakfast of more cheese and biscuits and they were off again, thundering through the valley. "You've the right mount for this place, Captain Foulkes," called the man at his side, Geoffrey.

"Why's that? And please, call me Ralph."

"Don't you know? This is the Vale of the White Horse. Mebbe you should be leading the way on that brave steed of yours. If ever you sell him, I want first refusal."

"Mercury will never be sold while I'm alive."

"Then let us hope you live long, Ralph."

"In war, who knows how long any of us shall live?" Ralph replied.

"I don't hold with such paltry talk. We are the King's men, and as such, we have Divine Right on our side. God save the King." Geoffrey spurred his tired horse into a gallop and put distance between them. Ralph let him go.

Aye, Geoffrey, and God save *us*. Ralph no longer trusted the sanctity of Divine Right. His fight was deeply personal.

*"The veil of time slips between us and I have all eternity to lure you back."*

Cramp stopped my hand in the end. The muscles in my arm contracted painfully and I let go of the pen with a yelp. I clutched my biceps with my left hand and massaged the rigid muscle until it relented.

"What have you written, Fay?" Percy stared at me, nonplussed.

"I have no idea, and right now I don't bloody care. Now *both* arms are killing me."

I carried on rubbing my arm and feeling sorry for myself until Percy stood up and massaged my neck from behind. At first I tensed even more, half expecting her to strangle me, but eventually her strong fingers manipulated my shoulders into descending to their normal position. Pity she couldn't re-arrange their width. I laughed out loud at the familiar, forlorn hope.

"What's so funny, Fay? Have I hit a ticklish spot?"

"Ah, don't stop, Percy. It's wonderful. No, I just had a delightfully normal thought, just like my old self. I'd almost forgotten that feeling."

Percy patted my back softly and sat back down. "Well, that's a relief. Good to have you back. I never know who you are these days."

"Well, it's not exactly a large cast of characters we're dealing with, now is it? You're Rose and I'm either Will or Ralph. Wish I could control which and then we might get somewhere."

"You know, you're onto something there. Could we induce them into taking us over, you know, sort of stage manage an encounter? I mean, if we could consciously coincide, we could ask questions of each other and find out what is driving Rose to all this violent hatred." Percy chewed the end of her biro.

"That would be scary."

"Hmm. It would, but I'm game if you are."

"Maybe, Percy, but how could we remember it afterwards? I mean, I do, because mostly I see it as a film, but you don't always remember what you do as Rose."

"No, that's true. You would have to be the one in control. I suppose you could strap me into a strait-jacket?"

I attempted a laugh. "Or a kid's playpen? Possibly, but let's see first if we can decipher this scrawl of mine - not even mine really, doesn't even look like my handwriting."

Percy popped on her reading glasses and peered at the reams of scribble marching across the pages in front of me. "And you've written in old-fashioned English with weird spellings, see?"

We worked away at the chaotic script for a good half an hour to no avail.

"It's hopeless. I can't make head nor tail of it. How frustrating. Listen, Percy, how about that pub lunch? I need a break."

Having thrown up the day before and not eaten much since, my normal voracious appetite was kicking in with its usual vengeance.

Percy chuckled. "I haven't known you properly for very long, Fay, but it's good to see you back to normal! Come on, we'll take my car."

The day was bright, with scudding clouds, the sort of freshly laundered day when anything seems possible. Downright cheerful in fact. And so was lunch. We were greeted by a fire burning in the grate of the old inn on the London Road but that was the only old-fashioned thing in it. Normally I hate themed pubs that have had their souls ripped out of them by some shallow designer, but today I loved the bland, branded look. I'd had enough of authentic history lately.

Lunch was equally bland and predictable. Nothing special, just a roast dinner but it filled the vacuum in my belly. They did have 6X beer though, as well as the regulation keg crap and we both had half a pint each.

"Sticky toffee pudding, I think." I put down the plastic menu. "How about you, Percy?"

"I think this is a chocolate situation. Brownie for me, please."

"I have lead you astray, Percy."

"I know. I'll have ice-cream with it as well." Percy grinned and waved a fiver at me, which I ignored.

We scoffed in silence. "Coffee?" I put my spoon down in my empty bowl.

"You don't want to leave either, do you, Fay?" Defeated by the stodgy dessert, Percy had left half her brownie and I gave myself strict instructions not to offer to finish it off.

"No, I can't say as your house is the alluring prospect it was when I first set eyes on it."

"Was it really only last Thursday? I feel I've known you a lifetime." Percy burped discreetly into her napkin.

"Does Meadowsweet Manor seem like home to you, Percy?" As the words left my mouth, a cold draught swirled around my sturdy calves. I decided to take that as a warning.

"No, do you know, it never has, although it is so beautiful and I do love it? Paul wants to start...." she stopped in mid-sentence before changing tack and carrying on. "I mean, he's hardly ever there and it's too big just for me. Really, it's too big for the two of us." She gave a heavy sigh.

"Except you're not alone."

"Quite." Percy sipped her cappuccino, letting the mention of her husband fade. "It's very cold in here all of a sudden."

"Yes, time we changed the subject, I think."

"Ah, I see. Talking about the manor has clued her in, perhaps. Rose, I mean."

"No perhaps about it - and I know just who you mean. Tell me about your Paul instead. When do you expect him back?"

It worked. The cool air gradually warmed up around my legs, as Percy doggedly rabbited on about her absent spouse but avoided concluding her earlier remark about him wanting to start something. A family perhaps? Instead, she only repeated what I already knew. Did she really love him? If she did, or even if she didn't, it was none of my business.

We went to the bar and settled the tab, which I insisted on paying. Percy only conceded when I pointed out I'd been living off her for days.

"I don't think we can put off the evil moment of departure any longer, do you, Percy?"

I retrieved my credit card from the machine and nodded my thanks to the smiley, heavily made-up barmaid.

"Don't use the word evil, Fay. It gives me the shivers." Percy lifted the latch on the pub's old front door.

"Fair point. I shall avoid it like the devil from now on." We walked to the car park in the breezy sunshine.

"Fay! There you go again. Have a care." Percy clicked her high spec Mini-Cooper open with the electronic key. My old Polo still had a key you had to shove in the lock and that always stuck. Paul might not sound the most sensitive guy on the planet but he obviously provided plenty of financial security.

We drove back along the winding lanes; it only took fifteen minutes, not nearly long enough for me. I was dreading our return. The wheels of Percy's car scrunched on her drive and my stomach turned over with nerves at the prospect of entering Meadowsweet Manor once more. Who knew what might happen next?

"You're very quiet, Fay." Percy changed down into second gear and drew the car to a halt. We sat facing the front of her house. Meadowsweet Manor stared right back at us with its deceitfully innocent façade of beams and thatch.

"I'm digesting."

Percy laughed. "That doesn't take brain-power. You don't fool me. Are you as scared as I am?"

I nodded. "Bloody terrified, especially of going to sleep." I still hadn't told her about Will and Rose's honeymoon. It was just too embarrassing to confess that I'd witnessed her writhing in ecstasy in the privacy of her own bedroom.

Neither of us made a move to get out of the car. It was nice and modern; I liked being surrounded by four well-engineered metal walls; I liked the radio twittering on; the heaters, the lights; all the gadgets of a twenty-first century machine. The attractions of the seventeenth century, with its vicious civil war, paled in comparison.

But it must be faced. These unhappy spirits needed us. I turned to Percy. "I don't want to go inside, Percy, it's true, but I think we have been drawn here by these poor, tortured souls for a reason. Whatever it takes, we must bring them peace. I'm sick at the thought of what that might entail but I think only you and I can resolve this."

Percy nodded, her oval face anxious and a little wan. She switched off the engine, rendering the cheery radio silent. "I agree. I feel such pain from Rose. All that anger, anguish even. She could go on for eternity in this purgatory. Although she's screwed up, I think it's with grief and I must admit, I've come to feel a little sorry for her."

I patted Percy's slim thigh. "Come on, then. Let's tackle those scribblings of mine, see if we can make sense of them. The nights are beginning to draw in but we should have enough light for a couple of hours."

"Yes, I got a text back from the electrician earlier. He says he'll be here first thing in the morning." Percy, now out of the car, clicked the remote lock and it pinged a lovely, reliable reply back.

I never knew how much I loved modern technology till that moment. When this was all over, I was going to treat myself to a new car with every gizmo going.

The smell of beeswax on the wainscot greeted us in the hall and instantly transported me back to a time when, I imagine, mob-capped maidservants polished its oak panels until it shone. Now the wood was layered in a lacquer of the honeyed stuff, built up over hundreds of years. There wasn't a single gizmo in sight. I sighed, bracing myself for whatever was to come.

Arthur chirruped as we entered the warm kitchen. I was surprised he never seemed affected by the energy of the old souls patrolling the place with such vengeance. "Has Arthur always lived here, Percy?"

"Oh yes, she said, carefully hooking her car keys on the key rack by the door before rattling cat biscuits into his little dish. "He's an old cat now, about seventeen, I believe. He was here long before I was."

"Hmm, maybe that's why he's so unfazed by all the poltergeist behaviour. Unusual."

I sat down at the table, determined not to succumb to the intense desire of a luxurious afternoon nap. I pulled the scrawled notes towards me and scrutinised them. If I hadn't known I'd written them with my own hand, I would never have recognised the wobbly lines as mine.

"Where's that old bible, Percy? That had old-fashioned lettering too but was far more legible. If we compare the two, we might be able to figure out some of the words."

"Good idea, I'll fetch it from the study."

By the time she had returned, reinforced by my full belly, I had already begun to get the hang of the 'f's and 's's and to be able to distinguish them.

"I think this was coming from Ralph, rather than Will, because he talks about King Charles all the time. And someone, hmm, looks like, Byron? Wasn't he that rakish romantic poet from a later century? Ah, now here - there's something about riding to Oxford. That's an easy word to pick out. See?" I pointed to the name of the town.

Percy put down the heavy bible and opened its yellow pages. "Ah yes, those letters are the same here. Tell you what, Fay, how about I try and write through Rose while you pick away at Ralph's words? I'll see if I can hear her."

"Don't bloody sit near me, then."

Percy laughed and went to sit at the other end of the long kitchen table. "Don't worry, Fay, I can't reach you from here."

"Then make sure you stay put!" But it was I who left, I'm not sure when, but the lines of uneven scribble soon blurred into horses galloping across the page.

Ralph cantered into the quadrangle of Christ Church College, Oxford, on Tuesday morning, the 11th of July, having ridden all the previous day and most of the long, wet night. Lord Hertford looked almost dead with fatigue and grey-faced. He and Prince Maurice, with the other leading men, Wilmot, Byron and Lord Carnarvon, swiftly dismounted and disappeared into the building surrounding the square yard. Ralph had never seen such a beautiful building. Carved golden stone graced every corner. A fit home for the king's headquarters but he had no time to dwell on its magnificent architecture. He ordered his men to dismount and see to their weary horses, letting his deputy, Richard, take Mercury to the stables, while he waited for instructions from Byron with the other captains.

A manservant came hurrying out to them wearing a stained leather apron and a harassed, lined face. "The King has already departed with Prince Rupert but has left instructions all his soldiers should receive refreshments. Please follow me into the lower hall, gentlemen. This way, if you please."

"No audience with his Majesty for the likes of us, then." Geoffrey entered the refectory alongside Ralph.

"Did you expect one?"

"No, not really. Have you ever seen our King, Ralph?"

"Aye, but only from a distance at the battle of Edgehill before I was injured."

Ralph couldn't believe the largesse spread out before them. Sides of beef, hams and pies jostled with a pyramid of apples and pears on enormous pewter platters. It seemed the King's headquarters were better victualled than the rest of his unfortunate country. They fell on the food, as did the other men, and the atmosphere lightened considerably. An hour later, with still no word from their seniors, many of the men dropped off to sleep and soon snores emanated from several corners.

Eventually Byron found them and addressed the room at large. He had bad news. "There are only eighteen hundred cavalry left here in Oxford. The King and Prince Rupert have taken the rest up to the Midlands to escort the Queen."

"That will still level the odds on Roundway, my lord." Ralph was secretly impressed by such a number.

"Aye and they are rested and well-armed which is just as well, as we must hurry back tonight. We cannot risk Waller taking advantage of our poor numbers at Devizes and Hopkins is in no fit state to lead the field. Let your men rest while they can and see they are briefed while we marshal the troops."

Ralph joined in the unanimous chorus. "Yes, sir."

Ralph thought his limbs might creak out loud as he remounted a tired, surprised Mercury later that night and headed out of golden Oxford to retrace the route of the morning. Lord Hertford had declared himself unfit to return and stayed back safe within the university spires. There was some muttering about that, but for the rest of them it was heartening to have fresh men following behind as they galloped back towards Wiltshire, and Ralph took comfort from the thunder of thousands of hooves in his wake.

# Charlton House, July 1643

Rose's secret had supported her return home like a second spine. She'd relied upon its structure to keep upright, to keep sane. And at first, her parents never suspected her changed status, though she went about her normal routines more quietly than before, hugging her memories of Will close to her newly awoken body.

This rapturous state was a revelation. She might have hungered for Ralph's vigorous attentions but could never have guessed that love could be sublime like this. When she had lain with her husband, his tenderness had melted all her remaining defences and she had given herself up to him entirely, simply because she felt so safe. She trusted this gentle man as she had never trusted anyone before, including herself, perhaps particularly herself, knowing the game she'd been playing. Will was so thoroughly good, so strong in his beliefs and had such integrity, she could let go in his arms. Through this security she found true love, not lust, not lechery, not physical desire alone, but love, real love just like those in the sonnets of Shakespeare and the poems of John Donne Will read to her in his rich, deep voice.

Oh! how little time they'd had. She prayed daily after her return home, she, who had never really believed in God, who had gone to church simply because she must and had fretted at the tedium of it. Now she started and ended each day on her knees, pleading for Will's safe return.

"Please God, O heavenly Father, bring him home safe from war. Please send us years of bliss together so I can show him I understand now what love means. Let me bear his children, dear God, so I can give back to him some of the joy he has given me."

When the rumour of her marriage reached her mother, much quicker than Rose would have liked, Agatha's rage knew no bounds. She threatened to thrash her daughter herself but Rose was as strong as her mother now and, when appealed to, Roger refused to do it. A different war broke out at Charlton House; a cold, internal one. No-one spoke to anyone else and Rose retreated into her memories, eating her food alone in her room. Now it was no longer secret, she placed her wedding ring back on her finger, twirling it round and round constantly to remind her of her love. It was a simple band of Welsh gold, instead of the two-piece gimmel ring she had expected but its simplicity reflected the character of her husband and she wore it with pride.

The real war had come so close now, with daily reports of fighting and even more stories of hardships and cruelties, that everyone went soberly about their business. But it wasn't that for her. To Rose, the outside world had receded and only her inner happiness, her very core, was truly alive. She lived in her recollections of that wondrous honeymoon night, when she and Will had only the stars for company and had needed no other.

It was her brother, Tom, who broke the spell. He clattered into the courtyard of Charlton House one wet July day full of news.

"Mother, Father! Are you about?"

Rose came rushing out to see him. "Tom, how are you?"

"I am well, I thank you, sister and camped very nearby. We have had a close shave in Bath, by God! And now we are only a few miles away, in Devizes. I've come to steal some food for my men from Mother but I must return forthwith."

Tom dismounted from his horse and the stable boy took the animal away to be fed. "Feed him up, lad!"

"Aye, Master Tom."

"Come inside, out of this wretched rain, Tom and tell us all your news."

They went into the dining hall of Charlton House and found their parents had gathered there, with their younger children, to greet their son.

Avoiding her only daughter, as had become her habit, Agatha went straight to Tom, kissing him soundly and holding him close, dabbing her eyes when she released him.

"Ah, it is good to see you, my son." Roger clapped Tom on the back, his eyes moist too.

"Brother, are you hungry?" Rose said, after also hugging him.

"Ravenous!"

"I will go to the kitchen and bring the best of whatever we have left." Agatha bustled off, brushing past Rose roughly and jostling her.

"Are you short of food, Father?" Tom discarded his hat on to the table.

"Aye, Tom, we are short of everything. The Parliamentarians insist they have the right to anything we own and have even taken my best plough horses. We live off last year's stores but they are not infinite."

"I am sorry to hear that. I was hoping to conduct a raid of my own." Tom threw himself down on the settle near the meagre fire.

"But tell us about the fighting, Tom. You were in Bath, you said?" Rose was desperate for news of Will.

"Aye, we crossed the river at Bradford-on-Avon and met the Parliamentarians at Monkton Farleigh and by God, we beat them back there."

Agatha had returned and was spreading platters of cold meats and cheeses, more than the family had eaten in a week, before her son. "Bravo lad, what happened next?"

Tom snatched up a lump of cheese and said through it, "Well, we camped at Batheaston that night while Waller withdrew up to Lansdown Ridge so next day we drew him off the ridge - didn't want him looking down on us, you know, and he followed us to Marshfield. Damn cold spot that."

Agatha carved up a side of beef and smothered his pewter platter with it, adding some mustard. "Go on."

Tom chewed a hunk of meat, then continued. "It was the Cornishmen who saved the day. Waller's musketeers were popping away at our cavalry but they stuck it out and we managed to gain the ridge after all and capture their cannon. Took three goes though and we lost Grenville. A fine man."

"Were there many injured?" Rose's voice had gone husky and she cleared her throat.

"Some, many, if I am honest, and would have been more but Waller did the most cowardly thing!"

"Typical Roundhead," Agatha almost spat out her words.

"Aye, Mother, you have the right of it. Those Parliamentarians stole away in the night on Lansdown ridge.

None of us King's men suspected a thing because they left all their camp fires alight and made not a sound. Ah, it was a strange sight come morning, a deserted camp with nothing but wisps of smoke and corpses to show anyone had been there." Tom shook his head and took a swig of ale before ramming it down with some bread and more cheese.

Corpses! Pray God Will wasn't among those. "But where are you going now?" Rose longed to ask about the Parliamentarians' fate but didn't dare.

"We were for Oxford to make for the King but poor old Hopton fell foul of a powder-wagon. Damn thing blew up in his face and he is sorely burnt so he's laid up at Devizes, while Prince Maurice, Hertford and Lord Caenarvon are leading some cavalry to Oxford to ask for more help from the King, as the Parliamentarians are camped up on Roundway Down in great numbers. So that is why I am here now, while we wait for their return." Tom stopped eating then and his voice went husky. "Mother, Father, who knows what will happen in the next battle? I made sure to see you again, being so close."

Agatha rushed over to him, spilling his tankard of ale and wouldn't let go of him.

But soon he had gone, taking a ham and a sack of flour for his troops with him. Agatha was distraught and disappeared into her chamber. Roger, though as silent as ever, went with her.

Rose was left to help clear the table and contemplate their lean larder, now even more depleted, while all the time she longed to gallop to Roundway Down and search for Will amongst his fellow Parliamentarians. Despite every fibre of her body screaming to leave, she mastered it over the next day, hating the inactivity, the wondering, the speculating.

Ralph recognised few of the waymarks on their return from Oxford but followed his leaders, blinded by exhaustion and the shock of his news. Despite his fatigue, he slept only fitfully, dwelling obsessively on the new status of his brother. Tom Charlton had sent him a message about the snatched wedding through a courier with a message for the king who had arrived in Oxford that morning and sought him out before they left for Roundway.

Thoughts of Rose with Will now intruded on every waking moment, however much he batted the images away. He and his brother had always been of widely different temperaments. He took after their father and Will after their mother, but he had never expected Will to steal Rose from under his nose. Oh, he'd seen the changes in her, but his visits home since the war began last year had been fleeting, once his leg had mended. The world was changing rapidly around them. Life had become serious for all and he'd put her more demure way of dressing and her new solemnity down to that. He'd never suspected she'd turn Puritan. Not giggling, fun-loving, hard-riding, deep-kissing, Rose.

He should never have allowed her to put off their wedding. A short engagement, as he'd wanted, would have sufficed. He cursed his softness in being persuaded otherwise by her pleading sweetness. Ralph remembered their stolen kisses, ardent kisses; urgent fondlings. It hadn't been easy, holding back from taking their caresses to their natural conclusion, and now he wished like hell he hadn't been such a gentleman. That little Rosebud had wanted him just as he had burned for her. He'd tasted her lust, for all her recent show of piety.

Ralph licked his parched lips. Oh, yes, Rose knew desire alright. But it had been simpering love-lorn, poetry-spouting Will she'd given everything to. *Married* him, for God's sake! And not even in a church, he'd heard. Maybe it wasn't legal? But no, Tom had written that Agatha had was spitting fury and he'd seen the wedding ring. It was real alright.

And he hadn't even known how much he'd loved her until he knew she was married. Another man's woman. His brother's woman! He hated Will with every fibre of his being, with as much passion as he still felt for Rose. These conflicting emotions now occupied his every thought. God, if he met Will in a fight in this damn war, he'd soon make her a widow. Who would care if he slew his own brother? Every family was split asunder now, there would be no dishonour in it. It wouldn't be cold murder but a fair kill on a battlefield.

All's fair in love and war.

And with one husband gone, Rose would need another.

As before, they stopped to rest in the darkest hours of each night of the two day journey, so it was afternoon of the Thursday before they reached the village of Bishops Cannings, high above Roundway Down and viewed the enemy camped on the rough, grassy sward beneath them. By then, even Mercury's great lungs were heaving from the long ride. They paused as their leaders surveyed the scene and Ralph patted his horse's long white neck. Mercury snorted his protest. Ralph dismounted to offload the pressure of his body weight and instructed his men to do likewise. Some of them looked as if they could barely stand from fatigue.

"If only this accursed rain would stop," Geoffrey said, gulping water from his leather flask.

"Aye, the ground is soft. Makes it even harder for the horses."

"I confess I feel in no fit state to fight, Ralph, and my mare is as tired as I am," Geoffrey whispered, under his breath, into Ralph's ears alone.

"You have no choice, Geoffrey. Look below you. There are thousands of Parliamentary troops just waiting for us and see? They've spotted us and are making ready for battle." And Ralph hoped that Will was amongst them. His lack of sleep had blackened his mood into a single, obsessive desire for revenge. He could think of nothing else but the pursuit of his rival. His gritty eyes raked the field below for a sign of his brother, but the men appeared as small as toy soldiers from this distance and unrecognisable.

Sir John Byron rode up to their troop and addressed his soldiers. "I know you are tired, men but the enemy is before us and we must attack immediately. Draw on your reserves of strength, for we are going straight into battle. We're to form up the left wing, gentlemen. Lord Wilmot's cavalry will take the right. Jump to it now! God save the King!"

"No rest for us or our horses, after all, Geoffrey."

"God pity us all." Geoffrey put his boot in his horse's stirrup and heaved himself onto his mare's saddle, muttering curses under his breath. Ralph, exhilarated by Byron's call to fight, clambered more readily onto Mercury's broad back and followed his leader, impressed by the disciplined way the king's army regrouped and quickly formed three distinct blocks with Lord Crawford's body of horse in the centre, supplemented by two cannons and the two wings of cavalry on either side.

Ralph felt proud to be a part of it and his fatigue melted away, leaving behind only the determination to seek and kill his quarry. He instructed his men to follow and they gave a ragged cheer.

As they galloped down the hill towards their opponents, Geoffrey, his face drawn and gaunt, yelled, "My God, Ralph, we're facing Waller himself on our wing! I'd know the scoundrel anywhere after seeing him at Lansdown."

"And by thunder he's approaching fast!" Ralph winced as musket balls flew through the air in both directions past his ears. Mercury faltered and he was terrified his horse had been wounded, but it was just a rabbit hole, and they pounded on unscathed.

"What is Waller thinking?" Ralph shouted to Geoffrey as a small force of foot strode forward to harass their advance. Brave soldiers these, to walk headlong into the might of galloping horses, but their pikes looked vicious and he feared for Mercury's unprotected hide.

Sir John Byron swerved around in front of them, brandishing his sword towards the centre of the field. Ralph followed him and, in searching for the quarry of his brother, saw Wilmot's right wing doing the same on the opposite side. The Parliamentary foot soldiers didn't stand a chance as the pincer movement caught them broadsides and many fell to the sword.

The leader of the Roundhead dragoons, Haselrigg and his famous Lobsters, so swathed in metal armour Ralph wondered how their steeds could take their weight, muscled in behind their butchered pike-men. Byron and Wilmot tightened the pincer movement on to Haselrigg's armoured horsemen and, under the dual pressure, they retreated back to their line, but not before his fellow Royalist, Captain Atkyns, whom Ralph had always written off as a braggart with no real courage, turned him into a liar. As Ralph and his colleagues beat back the dragoons, Atkyns spotted Haselrigg himself and made a bee-line for the Roundhead general. Haselrigg discharged his carbine at the young captain but missed and Atkyns chased on regardless, getting close enough to fire his pistol at the Parliamentarian. Haselrigg's comprehensive armour proved its worth and the bullet simply ricocheted away.

Ralph rode behind Atkyns to support him. If their leader fell, the dragoons would lose heart and they would have the advantage. Atkyns had now made contact and was slashing away at the Roundhead with his sword. There was no sign of Will amongst the dragoons; he must be in the Parliamentary cavalry that had yet to charge. Ralph swore he'd have his brother yet, but first he'd help to see off this ludicrous man encased in enough armour to furnish an entire troop of horse. He spurred Mercury on. Damn it, he couldn't get near enough to do any damage.

Then the Parliamentary general demonstrated the ruthlessness behind his steel by lashing out at Atkyns' horse, cutting its nose wide open in a deep, fatal gash. The horse screamed with pain and fell, dislodging his rider. Ralph had no time to waste staring at the writhing creature as some more of the heavily armoured cavalry came to assist their general. He fired his pistol at one of them but it was useless against these tin-plate soldiers. Ralph drew his sword and aimed at the only place not covered in armour, the man's knees, but it was too small a target. Dodging the Roundhead's sword, he glanced across to see Atkyn clutching his arm, which dangled uselessly at his side, having been crushed under his wounded horse, but

Haselrigg looked injured too. Blood streamed from his ear and arm and he slumped in his saddle.

"Foulkes, help me here!" Atkyn's cried. "We have him!"

Ralph went to grab Haselrigg's bridle but two more dragoons galloped up and barged him out of the way, dragging Haselrigg's horse back to their line before Ralph could reach him.

"Leave it, Foulkes, we've lost him. Here, get me up on your horse." Ralph helped Atkyns up on to Mercury's saddle and took him back to the rear of the field. Atkyns slid off and waved him away with his good arm.

"Thank you, Captain Foulkes. Now go and finish what I could not."

Ralph turned back and rejoined Byron's cavaliers, who were now proceeding at a sedate trot towards their Parliamentary counterparts, right into the path of their cannon.

Ralph caught up with Geoffrey. "How goes it?"

"I've notched up two kills so far and am eager for more."

"I cannot claim any."

"But you got damn close to Haselrigg behind Atkyns there?"

"Aye, but the bastard wriggled away before I could grab him. He was in a poor state though." Ralph settled Mercury, who had skittered away from a cannon-ball, falling too short before them.

"They're wasting a great deal of shot with those guns." Geoffrey said.

Sir John Byron rode up the line, shouting, "Hold your fire, my lads! I want no man to discharge a pistol until the enemy have spent all his shot. Remember, hold your fire until we are within range!"

Ralph had reloaded his pistol when he took Atkyns back but it took all his courage not to fire it when the Parliamentary musketeers let forth a volley from their carbines. As they drew closer, another round whistled towards them from the enemy's pistols, but Byron had been right. The Roundheads fired too soon and there were few casualties among the Royalists. One by one, Waller's men began to fall back. He could see their faces now, white with fear, mouths open in horror.

Byron, fearlessly leading the field as ever, raised his arm. The cavaliers fired their pistols into their enemy's white faces and the few Parliamentarians who had begun to ride away were suddenly joined by a surge of retreating horses and men who also turned around to flee.

"We have them! Charge, my brave cavaliers!" Byron broke into a gallop and Ralph nudged Mercury, already eager, into following. They roared across the downland, chasing the Parliamentary cavalry at full pelt.

Mercury's legendary speed took him ahead of the pursuing pack. Ralph felt a thrill of triumph as he stood up in his stirrups, yelling his head off at the rumps of fleeing horses before him.

They chased them for some distance, faster and faster as the ground levelled out under the thundering hooves and Mercury proved his immense stamina and strength. Ralph was gaining all the time on the enemy. He could smell their terror. One Parliamentary rider turned in his saddle and looked back at him, just before entering a straggle of trees.

Ralph's heart missed a beat. He knew that face, he should do, he'd grown up alongside it. Those brown eyes, that white skin, that broad forehead, belonged to none other than his own brother, Will. And, in that single moment, all his obsessive desire to kill his sibling vanished. With a shock, he knew that he loved his only blood-brother, perhaps even loved him more than Rose herself.

He did not want Will to die.

Ralph stopped his yelling. He sat back in the saddle, tried to check Mercury's powerful stride, but the big horse had the bit between his teeth now. He was enjoying the chase, Ralph could not hold him back and other Royalist riders flanked him, catching up alongside as Mercury slightly slowed in response to Ralph's body slackening in the saddle. His fellow cavaliers stared in horror and yelled at him to keep going. If he arrested Mercury's gallop they would both be trampled by the Royalist cavalry bearing down behind them.

No, he could not stop Mercury's galloping dash, even if he wanted to and *how* he wanted to. Maybe he could protect his brother if he did catch up with him. Stop his fellow cavaliers from slashing Will with their sharp swords? Yes! He stood up in his saddle again and spurred Mercury's willing flesh on and on.

Will looked back again. Ralph saw his terrified face change, saw him mouth his name, Ralph? And something else. What was Will trying to say? But Will could not stop either. His brother was a mere ten yards ahead now, no more. Pistols were firing erratically from cavaliers who had kept back their firepower till this crucial moment.

Ralph wanted to stop them. Wildly he looked around, desperately wanting to call a halt to the chase after several Parliamentary horsemen cried out as they were shot and fell, only to be trampled under horse's hooves. Horses fell too, their screams joining with those of their dying riders. And still they galloped on, pell mell, en masse, no way of stopping until, suddenly, Byron held up his sword and yelled, "Halt, halt, I say!"

Ralph watched in horror, as horses shuddered to a grinding stop all around him while the Parliamentary horses plunged over an abyss before his eyes. He could see Will's horse, a singular piebald, unmistakable even amongst so many others, disappear into thin air.

Madly, roughly, Ralph pulled on Mercury's reins, jerking up the poor animal's neck, checking his speed at last but it was too late. In front of him, dropping away like a cliff before the sea, was a sheer escarpment down which tumbled the Roundheads and their fated mounts. In agony, he watched the piebald mare somersault over and over, an unearthly screeching sound coming from her open mouth and her rider crumpling beneath her.

Byron's horse stood next to him, panting as hard as his rider. "They are gone, Ralph. Gone. What a way to die! Thank God our cavaliers could arrest their charge in time. No horse or rider will survive that drop. Come, we must away and finish off their exposed foot soldiers. The battle is ours for the taking!"

But how could he follow his leader, when his brother lay dying hundreds of feet below him?

## *"I will have my revenge."*

A shattering shriek brought me out of my trance. Startled, I opened my eyes to see Percy still sitting at the head of the table, gripping its edges with those dangerous hands and glaring right at me with her unsettling green eyes. Dread pitted my stomach. I could only be grateful that the solid wood of the table barricaded her from me. Outside, the twilight had stolen in, making the kitchen gloomy and full of shadows.

I had to think quickly, had to take control, had to remember what I'd seen; had to remember the real truth.

Boldly, before fear stilled the ragged remnants of my courage, I stood up and squared those big strong shoulders of mine. I had already witnessed one battle; now I must fight another.

"Hold up, Percy." I held my hands up to stop her approach, as she had already half risen from her seat. How could I snap her out of it this time? I had no water to hand.

"Rose? Did you see the battle too?" I decided I might as well accept her slip into the past.

"Aye, I saw you kill him; I saw you with your sword and pistol. You murderer."

Percy's face had done that weird transformation again. Her eyes had become slits, her voice an octave higher, her lips, usually full (whether naturally or not I no longer speculated) drawn into thin rosy bars over her white teeth. I preferred the modern, enhanced version to this menacing harpy. Randomly, I wondered what Will and Ralph had seen in this spectre to drive one of them to attempted homicide. Focus, I must focus.

Luckily, my instruction to stay put had held. Percy didn't stand up but returned to her seat, so the table still stood as a reassuring bulwark between us. I leant down, placing my sweaty palms on its solid surface. "What do you remember, Rose? What did you see?"

"Horses, hundreds of them and my Will, waiting, waiting in the rain. Soaked through he was. Gunshots, smoke, men screaming, blood." Percy trailed off.

She ran her hand across her eyes and when she drew her hand away, Rose had gone. Somehow her features had softened into Percy again and became once more the ideal of modern beauty.

I sat down with a thump and exhaled. "Thank God that's over. Are you alright?"

Percy rubbed her face, making it pink up and erasing all vestiges of Rose's malevolent countenance. "I, I think so. What happened?"

"Not much, don't worry, I'm unharmed, for once."

Percy gave a weary smile. "I don't *mean* to wound you!"

"I know, and I also know exactly how Will was killed."

"Really! Wow, that's fantastic. I don't remember anything."

I related the scene of the battle and the fatal headlong fall of the Parliamentary cavalry down the suicidal drop on Roundway Hill.

Percy dragged the book about the battle towards her and flicked through its pages. "We hadn't got to that bit, but yes, that's exactly what did happen. It says here that the Royalist cavaliers chased the roundheads across that field where you were sick and they were all going so fast they were driven off the edge of a particularly sheer escarpment at Oliver's castle. Fay, I vote we visit it tomorrow and check it out in daylight."

Could I really face going back to where Robin had died, knowing that had also been Will's fate?

"I know you're right but it's the last thing I feel like doing." I sighed, feeling completely overwhelmed and exhausted. "Listen, I've had enough for one day, Percy, how about you?"

"Definitely, but tomorrow, we'll see the electrician first and then go straight out to Roundway Hill and do a bit of grocery shopping on the way back, now the bank holiday's over."

Night now enfolded the manor house. Percy got up and drew the blinds on the kitchen window and lit several tea lights.

At once the room was transformed from a treacherous trap of uncertain shadows into a cosy, ordinary kitchen.

"I'm so knackered, Percy, but I'm terrified to go to sleep."

"You've had one undisturbed night here, haven't you?"

"Ye-es and I could really use another." I got up, scraping my chair on the flagstone floor. "I'm going up anyway. I'm so tired I should sleep through whatever Rose wants to cook up."

"Shove a chair against your door handle in case I go sleepwalking as Rose, oh, and keep a light burning. Here, take this tea light lantern I've made."

"Right you are, goodnight, Percy."

I'd almost called her Rose. Careful.

I did as she'd suggested and fortified my defences with the chair against the door in my modern bedroom above the pool, leaving the candle burning safely in its jam jar on the chest of drawers opposite my bed. Too tired to think or analyse, sleep came swiftly and I did not resist its seduction.

It's amazing what a good night's repose can achieve. I slept around the clock and woke to find the sunny morning had broken long since. I stretched my arms above my head. Even that sickly wound in my arm didn't hurt quite so much. I got up, drew back the curtains and gazed out at the world. It appeared pretty normal; green countryside spread unchecked before me, flecked here and there with amber on the chestnut trees, always the first leaves to turn. Birds trilled away in their branches, chattering to each other about flying somewhere warmer. And who could blame them with winter round the corner? My stomach grumbled its demands in a delightfully familiar greeting.

For the first time in days, I felt good. Today I had awoken as Fay Armstrong, sensible woman and happy glutton. Me, in fact. I slung on my clothes and descended the stairs.

"Morning, Fay." Percy looked much brighter too and what was that hum? It seemed to be coming from the fridge. "Look! We have power again. The sparky's come and gone already. Just needed to do something with the fuses and the trip-switch apparently."

"Didn't we try that?" It seemed a long time ago now but I distinctly remembered how carefully I had checked them.

"Yes but he had the magic touch and the bill wasn't too bad either. Coffee?"

No use worrying about that now. I caved into the prospect of renewed home comforts.

"Lovely. Did you sleep well, Percy?"

"Like the proverbial log, how about you?"

"Same here. The world looks like a different place this morning. Fancy tackling Roundway Hill?"

"Absolutely."

We set out as soon as I had gobbled some toast and upped my game with some caffeine. By the time we'd parked up on the hill the sun had ebbed away, as it so often does when it's too bright too early.

"Looks like rain's on the way," Percy said, as she pinged the lock on her Mini. I was getting fond of her smart car and wondered again if I could afford one of my own on the never-never.

"You could be right. Let's get on with it then."

We walked along the narrow path which hugged the edge of the woods and I tried not to look down to the yawning drop below on the bare backside of the hill. Most of the time shrubs of blackberry and sloe hid the danger from view, so it was a shock when we came to the precipitous slope and the trees gave way to the heady exposure of the chasm below. It took all my strength not to hang on to a tree trunk, as a dizzy wave of the all too familiar nausea made me sway and lose my balance.

"Steady, Fay. I've got you." Percy grabbed my bad arm, making me wince.

"It's a long time since I was here last. On that occasion Robin and I climbed up the steep slope from below. I remember I heard her then."

I stood still, transfixed by the spot where the police had found Robin.

"Who?"

Percy still had me in her grip, held fast and for once, I didn't shake her off, despite my arm beginning to throb again.

"Do you know, I think it was Rose, even then? Of course I didn't know it at the time; how could I? But now, I wonder if she's orchestrated my meeting you and my coming to

275

Meadowsweet Manor through all these past years, or is that just too crazy?"

I planted my feet wider apart and nodded to Percy she could let go.

"Nothing's too crazy about this peculiar situation. Are you sure you'll be okay if I release you?"

I nodded. "Yes, I'm fine now."

I walked to the very edge, wary of the crumbling crust of earth there, held together by mere clumps of couch grass. I peered down the sheer drop and a shiver of fear whisked down my spine. My guts performed a somersault, leaving my stomach much too high up; it pressed on my windpipe and I swallowed it down. It didn't shift much.

I wrenched my eyes away from the ground hundreds of feet below and cast them across the landscape. Sleepy villages clustered here and there. A tractor ploughed some wheat stalks into the chalk, chased by a flock of hungry birds but no birdsong surrounded us from the woodland on the hill. The silence pressed in, making my head ache. The clouds sank lower, patterning the pretty view with gloomy foreshadows of rain. I shivered again but it wasn't that cold, not really.

"I'll have to sit down, Percy. I'm afraid of falling if I go into a trance."

I plonked straight down where I stood and Percy quietly knelt a little way from me, watching my every move from a safe distance.

"Is it coming, Fay? Can you see anything?"

I couldn't answer for the roaring sound in my ears. I shut my eyes and pressed my hands into the rough, damp grass, clutching at the knobbly roots, trying to stabilise, seeking anchorage.

# Roundway Down, 13th July 1643

The rain was falling harder than ever. Ralph had been swept up in the final triumphant charge that routed the Parliamentary infantry but he had not joined in with the whoops of celebration when the battle was over. Under cover of the gloaming, Ralph turned Mercury's exhausted head away from the cheers of his fellow Royalists and found a gentler slope down that treacherous hill.

A grim sight greeted him there. Most of the dead Roundheads sprawled on the ground, their necks broken. Their brave steeds lay mangled up amongst them, twisted into unnatural, grotesque contortions. How could they not, after the cascade of flesh and bone down the side of that murderously steep slope? Some men groaned in agony as they lay, trapped under the weight of their horses but already the camp followers were scrounging for gold rings and teeth, coins and food. Ralph had pulled his hat down around his face and had taken off his tell-tale coloured sash. Hopefully no-one would question his loyalties in this dark aftermath and if they did, he could simply speak the truth: he was looking for his brother.

It was ridiculously easy to spot the piebald mare although she was buried under two other horses. The markings of her hindquarters were unmistakable. Ralph dismounted and looped Mercury's reins over a blackthorn bush, continuing on stealthy feet to the tumbled mound of corpses. Will had been thrown some distance from his horse and lay, a little apart from the heap of bodies, face down, legs at strange angles and his arms thrown up at either side. As if that could have saved him. Ralph looked back up at the huge hill above. It must be three hundred feet at least. They'd had no chance of survival and the Royalists would have been killed too if Byron hadn't stopped them. At this precise moment, Ralph would have preferred that he had not.

He knelt down next to his brother's body and turned him over. Will was already purpled with bruises, especially around his neck. Ralph hoped it had broken instantly. Will's head lolled without restriction when he lifted it and he shuddered at the loose feel of it, laying it back down on the grass with the instinctive recoil of the living for the dead. Will's eyes were open and wide with terror, the whites showing too much, their spheres streaked with blood. More blood had oozed from his nose and his mouth but no longer flowed. A half healed scar slashed his cheekbone. Already his brother's body had begun to cool and stiffen out here in the rain.

Ralph pulled down the lids across Will's eyes and his brother's face instantly took on the peace of terminal repose. Ralph felt bereft, knowing Will's soul had already departed and he rested his head sideways, one ear flat on his brother's chest, just as Will had done on his after the battle of Edgehill, but no answering whisper of a heartbeat came.

He let go of his brother's body and sat back on his heels to gaze upon him. A rage unlike any other he'd known surged up in him. Ralph fingered Rose's pomander and chain in his pocket. Rose would now be alone, a widow. She would never see or touch Will again. He wept out his remorse over Will's body and yielded to the barren wasteland ahead.

## *"I will let nothing come between us."*

It was the tear meandering down my face, tickling me, that brought me round and another hand, not mine, gently wiped it away. I reached out to grab it but no-one was there. Percy sat too far away to touch me and she was rummaging in her bag for something, not even looking at me. I looked down at my hands, still clutching blades of coarse grass. They had not moved. Perhaps it had been the wind, now picking up and drawing the threatening rain-clouds nearer.

So, I realised, it wasn't raining in the here-and-now. It had been when Ralph had found Will's body. As the name Will threaded through my fuddled brain, I heard a whisper through the reedy grass. Was that Rose? I looked at Percy but she was busy sketching in her notepad and didn't look up.

It came again, the merest suggestion of sound but, no, how could it be? I strained to listen to the distant male voice. It wasn't speaking in that old-fashioned incomprehensible English either. No, this was a voice I knew, a voice I trusted above all others. A beloved sound that made my lonely heart leap. I'd know that Yorkshire accent anywhere.

"Fay, love. Finally, I've made contact with you. Let me help you. You're in danger... danger, Fay..."

The voice trailed off. I looked around frantically searching for any visual clue, any movement in the woods, down the hill, anywhere.

"Fay?" Percy looked up from her notepad. "What's up?"

I couldn't speak and shook my head in the negative. Percy returned to her sketching. My Robin was here, I was sure of it. Here, where he too had fallen in a gruesome repetition of Will's death, hundreds of years later than the sad scene I had just witnessed through Ralph Foulkes. And he still loved me, still wanted to protect me, as he always had. I gasped out loud, reaching out with desperate hands that clutched at empty air pockets and water vapour. Nothing solid; nothing alive; nothing I could touch or kiss or hold.

Nothing.

I glanced across at Percy, still engrossed in her drawing. How could she be unaware that my heart, closed for business for so long, was now singing with joy? She appeared entirely oblivious, taking quick peeks at the landscape, then eyes down to draw it. The sketch looked good too and accurate. Was there no limit to her skills? She was wasted as a housewife, that was for sure and I wouldn't disturb her concentration now.

My revelation, my reconnection to my dearest love, was a private wonder and not for sharing. I clutched it to me, hugging the memory, reliving the cherished sound of Robin's deep voice whispering in my ear. It was enough to remember the timbre of his words and I forgot their meaning. I longed to hear him again and closed my eyes, willing my mind to retreat back in time once more where there might be a chance, however remote, that I could listen to his voice again.

The ceaseless rain pattered on Ralph's hands as he lifted up the dead weight of his brother's body and carried it, staggering a little, to Mercury. The big horse whinnied in sympathy as he laid Will across his wide back. Mercury looked round at the lifeless corpse, sniffed it and snorted. He pawed the ground. Could an animal know who this was? Ralph shook his head in disbelief and climbed aboard, chucking Mercury into a walk. He had some strange looks from Parliamentary soldiers as he walked past a gaggle of them, piling muskets from the dead into a heap of jagged metal. Killing tools.

One Roundhead came towards him, a truculent question on his swarthy face. Ralph didn't wait to listen to the man's terse words but nodded a silent greeting and kicked Mercury into a trot, pulling his hat down even more. No-one pursued him and he was soon clear of the Parliamentary camp. Having informed Byron of his intentions, Ralph set Mercury for home. Will belonged at Meadowsweet Manor now, which lay a mere ten miles to the east. He trotted clear of the battlefield and slept as he had for the last four nights under an oak tree. His brother lay next to him, still and forever silent.

## *"I am reaching you, I know it."*

Real raindrops roused me this time and they may well have been mixed with more tears. Whether for the tragedy I'd witnessed or because I'd not had more longed-for contact with Robin, I wouldn't like to say. In any case, the cold drips brought me round and I blinked them out of my eyes. Percy, efficient as ever, was quietly slipping her sketchpad into a waterproof poly-pocket before stowing it away in her bag. That girl would definitely make an excellent scout.

I shivered as more rain slithered down inside the neck of my coat, waking up my spine in the most unfriendly but very effective way. I stood up, easing my stiff legs with a little shake.

"All done, Fay?" Percy strapped up her rucksack before rising to her feet.

"Yes, thanks. Let's get out of the rain and I'll tell you all about it."

We walked back to the car in silence, heads down against the hefty shower. Having delayed so long in venting, the rain now pelted down on our unprotected heads and, without discussion, we both broke into a run, reaching the car in double-quick time.

Once inside our metal refuge, Percy switched on the engine and revved it. "Let's get straight home, Fay. I'm soaked."

It was true. In barely five minutes, despite my cagoule, I'd got drenched. A rumble of thunder in the distance confirmed why the rain had come down with such a wallop. Percy didn't talk as she drove home, she was concentrating too much with the wipers on superfast speed and water sheeting across the windscreen. I also had too much to think about, too much to salvage and treasure, to want to chat and I wasn't thinking about those wretched Foulkes brothers either.

It was still bucketing down when we got back to Percy's home. We legged it, hoods up over our heads, into the manor house and Percy slammed the door shut against the foul weather. More thunder rumbled, closer this time.

"Bloody hell! I had no idea we were in for a storm. Let's hope your power stays on through this one. I'm going straight up to change." I took off my coat and slung it over the banisters to dry.

Percy followed me up the stairs and we parted on the landing. I peeled off my wet things and hung them over the shower to drip into the tray beneath. Shrugging on the clothes that had dried there, I blessed the fact I'd brought several changes with me. Who'd have thought chasing ghosts would be so messy?

Back in the warm kitchen, Percy rustled up some hot soup from a few root vegetables she'd ferreted out from her larder, as we'd forgone the grocery shop on account of the weather. While she chopped and sautéed, I recounted what I'd witnessed in the aftermath of the battle of Roundway Down. Percy's sympathies were once more aroused but Rose, thankfully, didn't make an appearance.

We slurped our soup from colourful pottery bowls and the warm savoury broth chased the chill from my bones.

"Lovely, Percy, and very welcome." I laid my spoon down in the twice-emptied bowl and ran my fingers through my damp hair.

"Glad you enjoyed it, Fay. I've found a packet of biscuits too. Fancy one?"

I didn't bother to answer that question and with practised ease whisked open the packet of chocolate digestives and took two, just for starters.

"So, we know that Ralph brought Will's body home here." Percy broke a biscuit in half, crumbling it on to her plate but not eating it.

I felt no such restraint and took a third. "That's right. At least, that was his intention. I wonder if Rose knew how much remorse Ralph felt, how much he regretted it and mourned for his brother?"

"There's only one way to find out, isn't there, Fay?" Percy popped a morsel of biscuit in her mouth and chewed it slowly.

"Are you sure you want to?"

She nodded. "We have to finish this."

"Alright. Let's plan how we're to go about it then. And try and safeguard the process as much as we can."

"How?" Percy took another digestive and bit into it with those immaculate white teeth. Seems she'd stopped counting biscuits too.

"We need to see where Ralph took the body. My guess is that Will is buried here, by your stinking chapel, not in the village churchyard, where there is a distinct lack of gravestones showing the Foulkes family name. Agreed?"

"Agreed."

"So, I suggest we go into the garden and back to where you found Eleanor's gravestone."

"But she's not really involved. Eleanor died years and years before the battle."

"True but there may be other graves nearby we haven't found yet." I took my fourth digestive.

"Okay but we can't go out in this thunderstorm." Percy wetted her finger and pressed it, damp, into the dry crumbs on her plate then licked it.

"You're right there. As we still have electricity, why don't we check the forecast?"

Percy pulled her phone out of her jeans pocket. The chinos hadn't made an appearance today, I noticed. She thumbed the screen. "Says here, the storm will be over by early afternoon."

"That gives us an hour. Show me your sketch, Percy. I noticed you drawing up on the hill."

"Okay. It's nothing much, just capturing the lie of the land, working out what happened."

We spent a relaxed hour or two going over a map and her sketches and fixing the topography in our minds. We checked out the battle of Roundway Down in Percy's book and compared it to the account on Wikipedia on Paul's computer. Nice normal research stuff, twenty first century style. Killing time, seeking respite and for my part, psyching myself up to face whatever seventeenth century terrors lay in the graveyard outside.

About an hour after we'd finished lunch, the storm hiccupped a last shower of hailstones and then rapidly disappeared, allowing the sun to break through and change the tenor of the afternoon.

Heartened by this, I abandoned my scouring of the internet for morbid details of the battle of Roundway Down and switched off the computer.

"Come on, Percy. Time to face the music in your garden. Looking at screens and books isn't going to lay these wandering souls to rest."

The computer clicked off, leaving only its pilot light glowing. I decided to unplug it from the mains, just in case.

"Alright, Fay. I could use a break." Percy pushed her reading glasses onto the top of her head and rubbed her eyes.

"Can't guarantee a break but it'll be different." I stood up. "Looks like the weather's cleared, so no excuses."

Percy looked out through the mullioned window and nodded. "Yes, I suppose we'd better get on with it but I can't say I'm looking forward to searching for graves."

We went into the kitchen and armed ourselves with torches, jam-jar lanterns, spare matches and tea-lights and put our trainers and cagoules on. Percy went into her utility room and came back with a garden trug full of useful-looking tools.

"Should we take a bible, do you think, or a crucifix?" Percy looked anxious.

"Do you believe in all that really? Or are you just remembering some old horror movie? I personally don't put much store by using accessories. These people weren't evil, just tragic. What they need is love and compassion and above all else, a way of communicating with each other.

"But..."

"Look, Percy, we're not about to perform an exorcism." I sounded cross, I knew I did but truth was, her anxiety was transferring to me and fear wouldn't help either of us.

"Aren't we?"

"No! Now come on, let's simply go exploring and see what happens. Try to be calm and centre yourself."

"Centre myself?" Percy seemed perplexed by this command.

"Yes. Look, let me show you. It's important we stay grounded in the present. Some people do use symbolic tools like joss-sticks or crystals, it's true, but I think all you need is to be focussed and calm. It might help to envision yourself with a shield around you, a sort of cloak of protection. Call on angels or God or anything else that you feel is a benign power. Personally, I ask for help from spirits I have loved and who've passed on, people I've known in my life that I still feel connected to." No need to mention names or that I'd heard the voice of the most treasured person I'd ever lost that very morning up on the hill, warning me of the danger I was in.

In a small voice, Percy said, "Do you mind if we say a prayer?"

I squirmed a bit, then relented. "Go on then."

Percy almost whispered the Lord's prayer. She spoke out loud but if I hadn't had the familiar words drummed into me as a child, I would have struggled to catch them.

"Our Father, who are in heaven, hallowed be thy name...".

With her long hair bundled up in a pony tail, head bowed and her hands together, Percy looked about five years old which I suspect was her age the last time she'd recited the old standard prayer. Good memory, if that was the case. I used the time to ground my feet, connect to the inner core of the earth through them and to the heavens above through the top of my head. I'd practised this when going through my Tai Chi phase and always found it helped. I sensed friends from the other side gathering around me in a protective mob of spiritual bouncers and I no longer felt alone or scared. Well, not *so* much.

We walked across the sunny walled garden. Diamonds of leftover rain sparkled in the neat, fading flower borders and as we passed the weeping willow, its fronds swished a frisson of water across my recently dried cagoule, smattering it once more with dark streaks. Percy wrenched open the ancient wooden door in the wall and its hinges complained loudly, rustier than ever from the storm's drenching. I forced my legs to continue their reluctant march towards the little chapel, which looked deceptively benign in the afternoon sunshine.

We squelched across the marshy ground, burdened by our motley collection of equipment and went straight around to the rear of the little church. The fetid stench enveloped us in a miasma of decay. I was curious about the climbing rose that had so effusively flowered around Lady Eleanor's grave last time we were there. No sign of the scrambling branches now. Its single stem hung against the church wall, drooping modestly like a neglected wallflower, an unwanted maiden at her first ball. However, the thorns on its bare branches looked as wickedly sharp and strong as before. Maybe it was Percy's recital of the Lord's prayer but I had the fanciful idea of the skeletal rose resembling Christ on the cross, emaciated and spent. Proper daft.

"Come on, Percy, let's see if we can find other gravestones beyond Lady Eleanor's."

We cleared the undergrowth of meadowsweet and brambles, she with her hand scythe and thick leather gardening gloves; me with a blunt pair of secateurs and bare, easily scratched hands. The meadowsweet was still in flower; soft clouds of vanilla scented blossoms. They were going over and shed their petals all too readily, making me sneeze. They seemed to have dried very quickly after the heavy rain.

Percy was scratching away at Lady Eleanor's headstone as she had before but this time she had the advantage of her hand-hoe, selected from the various garden accoutrements in her trug.

"Well done for having the foresight to bring some tools."

I went over to see what her scrapings had revealed under the lichen.

She gave a brief smile. "See? Sir Edward is buried with her. I think it's his name above, look there's a capital 'E' and a lower case 'd' at the end of the name. How sad when you think of all those babies in with them too."

"Man on top, typical." I peered at the barely discernible carved names. A long list. "No sign of the two brothers, though. Let's go a little further afield."

We left the marital burial site and Percy slashed away with her hand scythe at more brambles and I followed, taking out the taller branches with snips of my secateurs. We came to a particularly thick bramble patch, covering about twenty feet in thick briars.

"You must have a good crop of blackberries here." I started to clip the thorny stems.

"Strangely, we never do. It's mostly wild roses anyway," Percy paused in her slashing.

We looked at each other, each thinking of our quarry.

"Ouch!" I pricked my finger on a blackberry thorn. At least it wasn't a rose but weren't they from the same family? My finger dripped blood and I sucked it. It was more painful than it had any right to be and set my old wound off into throbbing again. I'd forgotten how sickly that felt.

"Eureka!" Percy had gone to the right hand edge of the bramble patch and, as she'd had the good sense to wear gloves, could plunge her hands into the mess of weeds with impunity. She swiped the brambles and some tatty goose-grass with her sharp scythe and it rang against another headstone.

I checked the ground for further hazards before gingerly kneeling next to her and examining her find. Time had almost eroded the words some ancient hand had carved into the stone but we could just make out:

## Here lies William Foulkes
## 25th September 1622 - 13th July 1643

"He was just twenty. So young to die." I shook my head at the waste.

Percy got up and moved to the left-hand-side of the tangle of thorns and started hacking away at the bushes there. Sure enough, another headstone emerged from the undergrowth.

I joined her at the graveside. "Ralph was a bit older. Look, he was born in August 1618."

"Yes, we knew that from the bible. I suppose the big gap in their ages, four years, was down to those poor girl babies in between." Percy scythed the last bramble away from the stone so we could read the date of Ralph's death lower down.

"He died only a year later, 2nd July 1644, but look - there's more inscribed underneath."

I read out the words. Again, we had to trace the outline of the letters with our fingers to be able to read the faint script, and there was more of it this time.

Here lies Ralph Foulkes,
beloved first-born son of Sir Edward and
Lady Eleanor
Loyal to the end

"Loyal to the end? What does that mean?" Percy ran her fingers along the lines etched in the fine marble.

"Well, Watson, I deduce that Ralph's dad was also a Royalist. Hence the fancy marble and the lovey-dovey stuff. Poor young Will's grave is marked by common-or-garden limestone and the inscription couldn't be plainer, but then, if he had turned Puritan, I suppose that would have suited him."

"There's a big space between them." Percy had gone pale. I didn't like the look of the odd gleam in her eye. She stood up and started slashing like fury at the dense knot of dog-roses that grew between the graves we'd uncovered. In fact, she looked quite demented.

"Take it easy, Percy."

"It's here, I must find it. It will give me the power I need."

I could barely hear her fevered whispering. "What did you say?"

Suddenly, she paused in her scything and stooped to pick something up from underneath the mesh of plants.

I sat back on my haunches, as I watched her scrabbling in the undergrowth, hoping she'd unearthed another clue and content to let her get on with it. So I was caught completely unawares when Percy came at me like a banshee wielding her sharp hand scythe.

After that tortuous day of waiting, listening to her mother's weeping and wailing, Rose could stand it no more and saddled up Inkwell, the day after Tom's visit, saying she was riding out to check on cousin Margaret. She made sure to tell the servants, instead of her parents, who were sure to prevent her going anywhere with the fighting so close, but she could wait no longer.

She rode to Meadowsweet Manor to see if they had news. She dreaded seeing Sir Edward after the last time he had banished her from the place, but she was now desperate. She'd try Martha first, she decided, go round the back. That was it.

She dismounted Inkwell quietly and gave her over to Young Peter, thankful he had not enough wit to understand the complexity of her situation. Ignoring the front door, she went round to the kitchen entrance.

She found Martha stirring a stewpot over the fire. She looked tired, thinner too, but then they all were these days.

"I give you good day, Mistress." Rose hoped her politeness might win the older woman over.

"Mistress Rose. What be you doing here? Thought you'd made your bed and would be alaying on it by now."

Rose flushed at her accuracy. Was the woman a witch with that uncanny knowing she had about everything? She wouldn't be surprised. All that herbcraft she knew. People did whisper about Martha and her doctoring of Ralph's leg. Thoughts of Ralph brought home the awkwardness of the situation but then she remembered his brother; remembered why she was here and she squared her shoulders, entering the kitchen with a smile.

"I came to ask after the family."

"Why didn't ye go to the hall then? Sir Edward's there, hunkered over the fire, worriting and fretting over his boys."

"I...I wasn't sure if..."

"I know he sent you off with a flea in your ear, girl. Well, which of our boys is you asking about, anyways?" Martha slammed another pot on the hearthstone and poured some milk from a jug into it before turning to face Rose, hands on hips.

"I am concerned for both of them, of course."

"Not what I heard from their father. I heard you jilted our Ralph and took young Will instead." Martha took the pan off the heat and cracked six eggs onto the warm milk. She beat the custard with a birch whisk, hard enough to splatter Rose's skirts.

Rose backed away a little. She didn't have to give an answer to a servant. "I know there has been fighting near Bath and now both sides are gathered in Devizes, Martha. Do you know if either Ralph or Will are there?"

Martha slapped down her pot of milk pudding and dashed her broad hand across her eyes. "No, Mistress Rose, I do not know and 'pon my faith, I wish I did."

"I see, then I bid you good day, Martha and take my leave. Please give my good wishes to Sir Edward."

"Tell him yourself, you little troll." Martha had spoken under her breath but Rose caught the words. So that's what people thought of her. A sob caught in her throat and she walked away briskly, calling for Inkwell.

She rode home, the lump in her throat swelling into tears now and then. She tried to go about her tasks normally the next day but it was hard to concentrate on anything.

Two days passed, no, they dragged on minute by anxious minute, until the knifegrinder turned up. He set up his wheel in the kitchen yard and, as usual, the servants gathered around to hear the latest gossip from his slippery Irish tongue.

Not having a roof over his head, old Flynn couldn't wash very often. Not many people did, but Flynn had a particularly acrid odour that signalled the monthly knife sharpening ritual. Rose caught a whiff of him while gathering herbs in the kitchen garden. She dropped her willow basket and ran to the backyard.

Flynn was in full flow and all domestic work had come to a halt as he ground their implements into good cutting edges again.

"They says Sir Edward's gone quite demented. Bad enough having each of his lads on different sides. 'Course he was never the same after Lady Eleanor died but that was years since. God's truth but he was a rare one in his youth."

Rose burst through the huddle of servants and demanded. "Of what do you speak, man? Has anything happened to the Foulkes boys?"

"Morning, missus." Flynn touched his filthy cap. "Haven't ye heard? 'Tis all over the county. Young Will Foulkes was killed on Roundway Down, not ten miles from here and it was his brother, though he be Royalist, brought the Roundhead home. Why, 'tis nearly two days' since."

"You lie! You stupid tinker, this cannot be true!" Rose refused to believe the stinking old man. He was always exaggerating the truth and this must be false. She wouldn't let it be true.

"Nay, Mistress, begging your pardon, but I just come from the manor, see. Meadowsweet Manor where the Foulkes do live and I'd not tell a lie about something so tragic as that. That place is cursed, I swear. Never has no luck, that family, never did."

Rose went to hit his dirty, lined face but the tinker was quick and he held up the knife he was sharpening.

"Steady, mistress, this knife be ready for cutting now."

"You old scoundrel!" But Rose stopped lunging at him and turned away, dispersing the gaggle of servants standing with their mouths open. "Aye, you can stare! Stare all you like." She walked away, muttering, "Idiots, the lot of them. It cannot be true, I do not believe it. I would have known. I would have felt it if he'd died. Died, oh God!" Sobbing, she ran to the stables and saddled up Inkwell with fumbling fingers. Telling no-one where she was going, she climbed on to the mare's back and kicked her into an immediate gallop. Inkwell neighed in surprise but responded gallantly and she rode as fast as the mare could go to Meadowsweet Manor.

Rose leapt off the horse's back in the yard and ran the few steps to the front door, hammering on the old oak panels with her white knuckles.

Ralph answered the door, his face stern.

"Rose! You have heard our news, then."

"It is not true. That wretched knifegrinder said Will was dead but it is not true. I will not believe it."

"Come inside, Rose." Ralph shut the heavy door behind her and drew her into the great hall, by the fire.

She refused to sit. "I just want the truth."

"Do you? Or would you prefer a fairy story? God's truth, Rose, do you suppose I want to believe it myself?"

"Tell me straight what has happened."

Ralph's already pale face blanched bone white. He looked away into the roaring flames. "I didn't know it was him. I would have avoided it if I could."

"What are you saying?"

"We were on Roundway Down and we'd routed the Roundheads. It was a mighty battle, Rose. They had been bombarding us from Jump Hill for days, then I rode with Prince Maurice and some other cavalrymen to Oxford for more men and horses. I was exhausted; I no longer knew what I was doing. No-one does in the thick of battle and we were winning at last, after all we'd been through and Mercury is such a fast horse. None faster. I couldn't stop him. He had the bit between his teeth and was flying like the wind and then I saw..."

"God's teeth, Ralph, what are you saying?"

"I saw him at the last moment, Rose." Ralph looked at her then, his eyes unseeing, bleary with unshed tears, his countenance riven with grief. "Will looked at me and I recognised his face, even under his helmet. He looked at me with those sincere brown eyes and I swear, he saw into my very soul in that moment. Aye, and in that moment, I knew," Ralph's voice caught and broke, "I knew I loved my own blood and kin more than I love any damn King of England."

Ralph turned away, dashing his hand across his eyes. Rose noticed in a blank, numb moment that his hands were latticed with scars, still red and unhealed. It distracted her for a few precious seconds before the pain struck.

"No! Will was saved. He must be safe. You have not truly said he died."

"Ah, but he has. I wasn't alone in the charge. Thousands of horses alongside me rushed into the Parliamentarian cavalry and they had no choice but to flee from us. And then, God save me and then... they disappeared into the air. There were a few trees and at first I thought they were hidden from view but as I drew closer, I could see the awful truth."

"What? God's bones, tell me!"

Ralph swallowed. "They fell to their deaths over the sheer drop at the top of the hill. 'Tis a strange place, as if God himself has carved the earth in two and taken one half away. No horse or rider could have survived it."

"And Will was one of them? You drove them off this cliff and your own brother was one of them?"

"Aye, God help me, he was."

Rose felt all the breath leave her body until she was gasping for air.

Ralph came to her and held her but she could not breathe. She felt her body go limp and her eyes lose focus. If this was death, she welcomed it.

When she opened her eyes again, Rose looked up at the minstrel gallery. She could swear Will was standing there, smiling down at her with his eyes as serious and loving as ever.

She reached out her hand, "Will, my Will."

Another, much bigger hand, drew hers back down. Rose went rigid. She blinked and opened her eyes to see Ralph looking back at her anxiously.

"Rose?"

Rose inhaled deeply, filling her lungs with air, expanding her rib cage before she exploded her rage.

"You murderer! You killed your own brother. Take your filthy hands from me."

Ralph let go of her so suddenly, she dropped like a stone on to the rush-strewn floor.

Rose looked up at him, "I will not believe it until I see his body."

"Then come with me."

She followed Ralph up the steep ladder to the minstrel gallery. He went with measured steps and she wanted to dash past him. She had seen Will there, hadn't she? She knew he was there and not dead but very much alive. He had smiled at her, for God's sake!

When they reached the top, Ralph stood back so she could see her husband.

Will lay on the table that ran the length of the gallery, hidden from view in the hall. His eyes were closed and he was stock-still, dressed only in a white shift. His skin was not much darker, except around his neck where it was purple, even black in places. Rose traced his jaw line with a shaking finger, feeling where it was misshapen and swollen. She ran her hand across the scar on his cheekbone, donated by his father, after Will had declared his love for her, and for Parliament. It had formed a jagged scab already. She reached inside his linen shift and placed her hand over his heart. His skin was cold and it did not move. No heart pumped life around his beloved body. Rose bent over and kissed the icy lips, even now wondering why they did not respond. Will's mouth had been so generous in his loving, sensuous yet kind, eager yet respectful. How could they now feel lifeless?

She drew herself upright again, pulling away with effort, with reluctance. When her vision cleared, she saw Ralph standing in the shadows against the wall by the ladder.

Ralph had snatched away her husband, this man more precious to her than her own life. The man who had made her a better woman. Her restraint broke and she flew at him, her hands outstretched like claws, ready to tear the flesh from his hated, handsome features.

Ralph was quick to respond and stopped her arms, pinning them to her sides effortlessly. She spat in his face.

"Do not do this, Rose. I see you loved Will truly but he is gone." He let go of her hands.

"I still have our pomander, Rose. Let us honour Will by marrying yet and share our love of him."

Ralph placed the necklace around her throat where it used to lie, and left his hands resting against her chest. She snatched at it, at him, screaming, "No, never!"

She kicked his shins with the points of her riding boots and bit his arms, anything to get free of him and the necklace.

"Rose, hold fast. Stop!" Ralph wrestled with her, pushing her against the railings of the gallery. She gave him one more savage kick, high up this time. Ralph gasped, then doubled up and let go of her, losing his footing on the top step and falling back down the ladder, rolling over on to his front, hitting his head on the wooden steps, but his hand was still hooked inside the pomander chain and he pulled her down with him. Rose's skirts tangled up under her, she tried to grab the newel post at the top of the stairs but the chain caught around it. It cut across her neck, strangling her, the weight of Ralph's body pulling it taut. She felt it cut through her skin and then she was over the gallery rail, dangling her feet into the air, unable to get a foothold. She couldn't breathe. She clutched at Ralph, who lay above her on the stairs, trapping her with the necklace. The more she scrabbled at her neck, the more the chain got caught up in her collar. The fine white linen tightened further around the chain. Now she couldn't see. She couldn't swallow. She felt her eyes bulging; the pressure built in her head. If only she could free the necklace or get a foothold. Will's face swam before her but then he was gone and everything went black.

## *"I have you now and I will have my revenge at last."*

"Of course Will wants it plainly writ! His God needs no idolatrous marble to demonstrate faith but you, Ralph, never understood that. You put your faith in the King, but he's nothing but a mortal man, and a vain one at that." Percy seemed to have grown in height.

She towered above me as I knelt vulnerable beneath her, my hands upheld in supplication. So this is how a mouse feels when an eagle swoops down to kill its prey. Funny how I always have these totally irrelevant thoughts when I'm up against it.

Percy's scythe glinted in the setting sun on its rapid descent towards my head. That focussed my butterfly brain and I rolled out of the way, drawing my feet up into a foetal position. She was above me again in an instant, brandishing her sharp weapon with the ease of a practised warrior. I had a flashback to the squash court and remembered how well she could smash that dead-ball against the wall.

I sank my energy back into the earth, imagined a beam of light connecting me to the spirit world above and pleaded for assistance to any benign souls who might be bearing me witness. Immediately a warm, invisible hug encircled me and I huddled into its shelter. I had a strong sense of Robin around me, oh, if only he was.

"Percy, you're acting as Rose. Try to remember who you are! And I'm Fay, not Ralph." I rolled to my right as the hand scythe plunged into the earth where I had just lain, missing me by a fraction.

Percy took no notice. Again all the softness had left her face, now distorted by blazing rage. Ninja-like, she lunged at me, swinging her scythe sideways and down, straight at my neck. I kicked out and made contact with her shin, seconds before the blade reached me. She yelped and dropped her arm, taking the lethal scythe out of range, but not out of her grip.

Seizing the brief respite, I turned away and scrambled to my knees, ready to stand up but, before I could get upright, I felt a shove between my shoulder blades. I slewed my head around to see a vague outline blocking Percy's attack. Who the hell was this? Taking advantage of this surreal cover and using the headstone as leverage, I stood up, breathing fast after the hard push to the back of my lungs.

I spun round and will never forget what I saw. Percy seemed to be wrestling with the scythe as if fighting some unseen warrior. Percy looked unrecognisable, her eyes wild, her hair, free of its band, whirling around her head, and her mouth opened in a piercing scream, not of terror, but of anguish.

"Unhand me! Ralph does not deserve to live. He took Will from me so cruelly."

Years of discipline had made Percy physically very strong but it seemed to be taking all her might to grip the scythe and hold it aloft. Who was she fighting? Whoever it was, she was fully engaged with her opponent and I took advantage of their grappling to run out of reach and cravenly hide behind one of the gravestones. One of us had to stay in the present, had to remain neutral, or we'd never resolve this. Standing inside my protected space, I could observe, though perhaps not objectively - that would be impossible - but I could watch as they battled it out, maybe intervene if necessary.

Something forced Percy's hand back and held it down by the wrist, shaking it until she loosened her grip on the hand scythe. It fell to the ground, clanging on Ralph's marble headstone on the way down until it lay across his grave. Percy's face had transfigured into Rose's ravaged one again but I still couldn't see who had been fighting her. There was no sign of them now.

With the scythe out of reach, Percy turned back to me.

"Give me the chain." Her voice had risen again; taken on that terrifying country burr.

"Why?" I could feel its heat against my thigh from within my jeans pocket.

Percy held up her other hand. In it was a round, metal object, tarnished but recognisably silver. "Because I have its partner. Give it to me!"

I looked around wildly for support but could see no-one. Being unable to think of an alternative, I thrust my hand into my pocket and drew out the silver chain.

"Ouch!" The chain was so hot it scorched my hand and I had no choice but to throw it on the ground in front of her.

Percy fell on the chain. Kneeling, she picked it up and held it, with no sign of it burning her. She began to clean the silver object. I could see it now, round and intricately worked. It looked like a locket of some sort, but a very large one; it must be a pomander.

Percy seemed satisfied it was clean enough. It did look shiny, far shinier than it should have done without a good scrub with silver polish. But there was no logic in this situation. She fiddled with a catch and the round lid sprang open. Why wasn't it silted up with mud?

I smelt a waft of sweet fragrance emanating from inside the pomander. Roses, of course.

Percy lifted the open silver bowl to her nose and inhaled deeply. A deep chuckle escaped her. She snapped the lid shut again and threaded the pomander on to my chain. The setting sun's dying rays caught the metal and it shimmered in the golden light. Still smiling, Percy lifted the necklace over her head and let it fall on to her chest, then she lay down on the half-hewn briars she'd cut with her scythe. It was only then I noticed the edge of another grave, set squarely in the middle of the other two we'd uncovered.

Percy lay as one dead on this central grave; with the necklace gleaming on her chest and her eyes shut, she appeared to be sleeping, silent and inert. I started to get up and go to her, to check she was alright, when out of her body another woman's shape rose up. I did a double take. Percy was still lying quietly on the ground. I focussed on her chest, relieved to see it rising and falling in regular waves. Thank God for that. I had barely registered this fact when the amorphous female figure, who had emerged from Percy's prone body, began to solidify and take form.

I could see this virago was definitely not Percy. A mask of hatred morphed her features into a spitting fury of revenge. This woman's hair was also long but it was raven black and wavy. Her full length russet gown was old fashioned, of the same era as Ralph and Will's, of that I was sure, and as surely, this had to be the real Rose. I was glad her blade lay across the other grave.

Rose's image grew stronger, more definite, less diaphanous, making her look more real, more alive, more earthly. She threw back her head, her mane of hair spreading out behind her in a great black veil and she laughed. A huge growling laugh, coming deep from her belly. My skin crawled in fear. Rose seemed to grow larger until I felt she was twice my height, but it was her overwhelming presence that had dwarfed me.

"I have you now, don't I? You're in my power. I can do anything, as I have the necklace." Rose's high voice had also grown terrifyingly stronger.

"What do you want to do, Rose?" My own voice had a decided quaver.

Something moved behind her and I strained to see past Rose's shimmering figure.

Percy was coming towards us, from the grave, where she had lain.

"How did you do that? I thought she needed your life force to manifest." I hissed out of the corner of my mouth as Percy approached, stealthy as a cat.

"I don't know. I just woke up. Watch the necklace, Fay!" Percy pointed to Rose.

"Can you see Rose too?"

Percy shook her head. "Only the necklace, suspended in thin air."

I looked back at Rose, who now towered above our crouching figures. I had to think quickly. Where was her energy coming from? If not from Percy, then what?

Rose was looking about her, searching for something, or someone.

As I was no longer mesmerised by her black stare, I studied the rest of her. The necklace and its pomander shone as bright as diamonds. That was her energy source. It was obvious the second I realised it. We had to get it away from her. But how, when it lay around her scrawny neck?

She laughed again and turned away, still apparently searching for something. I looked at Percy, and beckoned her with my finger, whispering, "Percy, we have to get the necklace off her and destroy it."

"How the bloody hell can we do that?" Percy whispered back.

I had no idea. There was no way we could grab it off her. I tried to think, desperate for a solution. And then it came. So simple, as the best ideas always are.

"Rose Foulkes!"

Rose turned back to me, triumphant and strong.

I drew myself up to my five feet, two inches. I took a deep, shuddering breath and squared my broad shoulders.

"I know what you want, Rose. And I can give it to you." I hoped I sounded more confident than I felt.

"You do not know what I seek." She hissed the words.

"Ah, but I do. Didn't you bring me here for the purpose yourself? I am here to bring you peace. Rose, you cannot have revenge but you can have eternal peace with your husband. Isn't that what you want?"

Rose seemed to shudder. "You speak of my husband? You can reach my Will? Can you truly do this?"

"I can, if you will let me. Would you allow it, Rose? Can you let Ralph go, so you may be with Will?"

Her ravaged face softened, giving me a glimpse of the girl she used to be. "Let me see Will."

"You must give me the necklace first." I held out a tremulous hand.

"No!"

"Then I cannot help you." God, this had better work.

"It is mine." Rose flicked back her long, black hair in a defiant gesture.

"Finders keepers, Rose. You left it for me on Roundway Hill, remember? Percy, over there, found the pomander just now. You can no longer claim it as yours." I knew I had to have that chunk of ancient silver.

"I will never give it up." She placed her hands on her hips.

I withdrew mine. "Then you will never see Will, never be with him again. Which do you want, Rose?" Out of the corner of my eye, I saw Percy come forward, nodding me to go on.

Rose hesitated and touched the pomander on her chest. Instantly her outline grew stronger again, confirming the source of her energy.

I had to get it away from her. "See, Rose, I can bring Will to you, if you give me the necklace. I say again, isn't that why you brought me here?"

"How do you know this?"

I could hear doubt in her voice; not as loud as that in my terrified brain, but I had to go with my gut instinct. "Give it to me and I'll show you." I held out my hand again.

Slowly, painfully slowly, Rose put her other hand to the necklace and lifted it back over her head. She placed it into my outstretched hand, with reluctance, as well she might, as her image instantly faded and she looked ethereal once more. Ethereal, but not gone. Not yet.

"Thank you." I tried not to wince as the silver burnt into my hand, and raised my voice. "Please, come forward, Will Foulkes."

A shape emerged from the grave nearest me. Horrified that my command had been obeyed, I watched a man's form peel away from the wet ground and slowly rise upright. I was aware of how immensely strong he was, how tall and muscular, every inch the soldier, dressed in old-fashioned battle gear but with his long hair uncovered. He turned his face towards me and I recognised Ralph Foulkes. Damn it, I thought I'd called for Will! Too late, I realised I was standing next to the wrong grave.

Ralph spoke, and not through me, thank God. His voice was as strong, as manly, as his body and held a charismatic power, instantly commanding attention.

"Rose! Listen to me. It is I, Ralph." His imperious tone was compelling. "Come, Rose, come and avenge yourself on me. You have the right but you must know, I did not kill Will with my own hand."

Rose's answer was to spit in his face. A corner of my mind registered that she had more passion for hating Ralph than for loving Will.

"Ralph Foulkes! I damn you now to eternal wandering. May you never find peace." Rose sneered at Ralph, her eyes dark with hatred.

I stepped forward. "Rose. You have no right to condemn anyone to eternal damnation."

"Do I not? Who is to stop me?" She turned back to Ralph. "Don't expect me to believe you grew a conscience then or now, Ralph! You hated him because he loved me and I chose him. You hated him from the moment I rejected that silver bauble." She pointed to the silver pomander in my hands. "But I have brought you here by its power." She reached out, fingers curling into claws, aiming for Ralph's face.

Ralph gripped her arms. "Yes, Rose, I hated you then, and Will too."

The pomander and necklace weren't just hot in my hand, but vibrating as well. I could barely hold them. I had to think. Rose said Ralph had given her the pomander and it was he who had been summoned by its power, because it connected these two. But Rose evidently didn't want Ralph, except to hurt him. If any healing was to occur, I must bring Will here, somehow.

The heat in my hands was unbearable. I looked down at the source. Would the necklace have enough power to reach out to Will? I turned to the third grave, the plain one bearing his name but no endearments. Leaving Ralph and Rose arguing amongst themselves, I crept over to the grave and knelt down, placing the necklace on its weedy surface, dreading that I might lose control over the situation by parting with the strange thing.

"Come forth, Will Foulkes, and claim your bride." I added silently, "before she's the death of us all". Percy followed me, skirting around Rose and Ralph, keeping to the shadows. Sensible girl. It was comforting to have her near but I had no idea how much she could see.

The damp earth parted, revealing Will's slim form. Like Ralph before him, he emerged and brought himself upright in one graceful movement. As he stepped into the darkening twilight, ignoring both me and Percy, another shadowy figure, less easy to see, appeared behind him.

As Will stepped into the arena, his ghostly contemporaries, as well as the both of us who were still alive, fell silent. I watched, my breath held. Would Rose go to Will? But Ralph held her fast. In that frozen moment, only one voice could be heard, one I had never expected to hear again - my own Robin's dear, familiar voice, his Yorkshire accent unmistakable.

The faint silhouette behind Will slipped past him and smiled at me. I could barely discern him in the dim light, and yet... "Yes, Fay, love, it's Robin. I wasn't going to stand by and see you hurt."

My heart lurched violently inside my ribcage. How could this be? Had it been Robin who had come to protect me when Percy was trying to take lumps out of me? I went to stand up and go to him but Robin lifted his hand to halt me and turned away to look at Will, who had now come forward and was speaking.

"It is I, your husband, Rose." Will's deep voice was as calm as ever, soft with love as he addressed his wife.

"Will, you are here at last! Oh, my love, how I have longed for you, searched for you." Rose started forward towards Will, but Ralph kept her pinioned.

All my attention was now on Robin, who looked less solid by the second; his shape oscillating in the gloaming, so I could barely see him. I wanted to run to him, and forget about everyone else.

Will continued talking in his mellifluous voice. "Yes, Rose, I am here."

"Then let me go, Ralph! Unhand me, that I may be with Will, whom you killed, you murderer."

"You are wrong, Rose, I did not kill my brother." Ralph still held her tightly by the hand, though Rose struggled to be free.

Will came closer, but not yet within Rose's reach. "Ralph is right, Rose, my love, he did not kill me. I knew he tried to save me on the battlefield but it was too late. Our flight, our retreat, was too swift and we could not halt our horses in time to avoid the drop off the hill. It was Ralph who found me and brought me home."

Rose was having none of it. "I don't believe you! I've been back many times to that hill, after Ralph told me you'd died there, to see for myself. I've wandered all over it, searching and searching. I even left the silver necklace there. I knew it was imbued with my death throes and would be strong enough to pull *you* in." She looked directly at me then, her eyes almost black, and quite merciless.

Then she looked over at Robin, my Robin. "Once, I thought I saw Ralph, walking on foot but it wasn't him. I knew it when that man fell, and anyway, he was blocking *her*, whom I needed." She transferred her gaze back to me.

I yelled, "You bitch! *You* killed Robin that night, ten years ago. It was *your* voice I heard. Not content with ruining two men's lives in your lifetime, you've taken the only one I had!"

Robin's shadow shimmered and moved towards me. "It's too late now, Fay. You can't change what happened."

"Oh, God, Robin. How can I bear it?"

"You must, Fay and you will. It was an accident." His voice had grown fainter, fuelling my rising anger.

"It was no accident. You could climb like a mountain goat. She must have chased you over that edge." I was now as angry as Rose.

But Rose, still held by Ralph, turned her warped, twisted face to me. "I wanted to kill him, I thought he was Ralph. I'd tried before but his silver chain choked me before I could do it."

"How could you? You harpy!" I lunged at her then, beside myself with the rage of ten years worth of loneliness.

It was Robin who came between us. "No, Fay. She is not really alive, remember? You will hurt yourself over someone who is long dead. Come away, love, over here." And he moved away from Rose. I followed him, drawn as to a magnet I could not resist.

"Fay, I cannot stay much longer. Don't be angry. What's done is done. Let us resolve this tragedy now and be free of them." Robin's voice was even weaker now. "Get the necklace, Fay. It will give you the strength you need to finish this."

Even moving two metres away from Robin almost killed me but I knew he was right. I left his side and quickly went to Will's grave, where the necklace still lay, the only bright object in the dark gloom. I picked it up and it responded like a live thing, warm, humming with energy.

Holding it high up in front of me, I turned back to Rose, with the thrill of its power surging through my arms.

"Rose. Look at me."

As she turned her head towards me, her eyes locked onto the pomander. She tried to wrestle her arms out of Ralph's hold, wriggling and squirming within his steely embrace.

I clutched it to my chest and its warm strength spread throughout my body. "Yes, Rose. I have your necklace now. You have wronged me, Rose. You have killed my love and yet you want to be with yours. You cannot be at peace; you cannot be with your Will, until you have repented for this great injury you have done to me."

Rose looked at me, her face a mask. Through thin, angry lips she spoke in her strange, high tone. "Forgive me for the loss of your friend. It was grievous wrong and I am sorry for it."

Robin, fading fast, said in a soft whisper I could barely catch, "Forgive her, too, Fay. For my sake, so I may also know peace."

"But does that mean I'll never see you again?" I'd forgive nothing rather than that.

"No, love, but it will heal your heart."

I dragged my eyes from his faint image and turned back to Rose. She looked strong and very much alive and I hated her with every fibre of my being. But I could deny Robin nothing.

"I forgive you, Rose Foulkes. May you rest in peace." The words found their own way out through my gritted teeth.

Ralph released Rose at last, sensing, as had I, that she had calmed, saying, "I am sorry that your friend was lost. It was completely wrong of Rose." Ralph turned from me to his peers and addressed them in his sad, solemn voice. "I have my own confession to make to you all. I survived that fall down the gallery stairs, though you did not, Rose. After you both died, Rose and Will, I buried you here at Meadowsweet Manor and I laid the pomander and chain upon you, Rose, in your grave. I no longer wanted to have it with me or to live without either of you. The King's cause was lost by the time we fought at Marston Moor and I rode into the thick of the cannon-fire, caring little for the outcome. Poor Mercury, he didn't deserve that."

I decided it was time to clinch the deal, resolutely putting my own deep sorrow to one side in order to see this wretched business through to its bitter end. "Come Ralph Foulkes, make your peace with your brother." I held the necklace up and they came towards me. I stood on tip-toe and held it above their heads. An aura of light shone out from the silver jewellery, illuminating the two brothers who embraced, then slapped each other on the back. I lowered the necklace but kept it in front of them.

Ralph released Will. "We are joined by blood, brother. Our dear mother would not wish us to be at odds for eternity."

"We often were when we were younger." Will's serious face broke into a smile.

I ventured, "But you are together in death, Will and Ralph Foulkes, and may rest here, near your mother and father, forever more. Shake hands on it."

The two men nodded at my words and extended their hands towards each other but before they could connect, Rose planted herself between them, where she had always been, I suspect.

"Not so fast. Have you no remorse, Ralph? You bullied and belittled Will all his life and you then deprived him of it. How can you forgive him, Will? When we had only one night together as man and wife? How can you accept your death at your brother's hand? We might have had many years together; we might have had," her voice broke at this point, "children. Children whose offspring would be living here now, at Meadowsweet Manor?" Rose started to sob openly. "Oh, Will, we could have been so happy."

Will, his face grave again, nodded. "Aye, Rose, we could have had all of that but fate decreed otherwise. We have no choice but to accept it."

"I won't! I refuse to let go into obedience. I want to live again. I want to lay with you again and bear your children. And if it wasn't for you, Ralph, that's what would have happened."

"You don't know that, Rose." Ralph spoke calmly but his emotion was evident. "Nothing is certain in life. You could have died in childbirth or Will could have been killed in another battle. Many were. Ah, yes, so many families were rent asunder by that wretched war. I lived on a while longer than you and I saw plenty of young men dying before their time. We are not unique in this."

Robin stepped forward. I could see right through him now. I lurched towards him but again he held up his hand to stop me.

"Wait, Fay, I can't do this for much longer. You must make her see they can be together only if she forgives Ralph."

I turned to Rose. "Rose, listen to me. Your life as Rose Charlton, as Rose Foulkes, is over, there's no going back from that fact. You and Will can be together, but not until you yield to your death as Rose and forgive Ralph."

Robin nodded and smiled at me in encouragement. How long had he got? That wretched Rose woman, she was stealing whatever time he had from *me*. "Robin?"

"Wait, Fay, just wait. Rose, do you understand?" Robin held both his nearly transparent hands out in supplication.

"Is it true? Can it be that Will and I can live again as husband and wife again in a different life, a new life?" Rose laid her hand on Robin's sleeve.

But it was me Robin spoke to. "Tell her, Fay, for God's sake, make her understand, they can have a future only if this healing occurs."

I gripped the necklace for strength, resisting the urge to grab Robin instead, as I longed to do. "Yes, Rose, you must believe this. Forgive Ralph and let him go in peace that he may rest. Rose, I command this!"

Robin held Rose's gaze as well as her arm, his outline transiently stronger.

"Please do this, Rose, then we can be together." Will added his melodious voice to the plea.

"That is what I want," Rose nodded slowly. She released Robin and turned to face Ralph, who stood a head taller than the rest of us, his feet planted a foot apart, his arms folded across his broad chest, his eyes serious and sad. "Very well, Ralph. I cannot forgive what you did but I forgive *you*. I see now that you do love Will, perhaps not as much as I, no-one could." She gave Will a little secret smile, a lover's smile.

Ralph's face looked solemn. "I loved you too, Rose. I knew it not until you left with Will and I know you were not willing to marry me and yet I kept you bound. It was not just lust, on my part. I loved you true. And, because of that, I release you to my brother. May you rest together in harmony and be reborn in a happier life. I promise I will not trouble you again."

Ralph took up Rose's hand and lifted it to his lips to kiss. Rose hesitated for a second, then she curtsied in acknowledgement. Ralph let go of her and went to his brother. They looked long into each other's eyes, then hugged again.

"We may never meet again, brother, but if we do, I hope we can meet as friends." Ralph clapped Will on the back.

"Aye, brother. Go in peace now. I bear you no ill-will for my fate."

"Nor I you for stealing my love." Ralph laughed, a deep rumbling sound from the depths of his ribcage.

Desperate for time with Robin, I decided to move things along. "Go now, Ralph. It is done."

They parted, and Ralph walked back towards his grave, looking less solid with every step. The night had fully descended now and water vapour had risen up from the marsh. Though I strained my eyes, I could no longer catch a glimpse of Ralph's tall frame as he disappeared, swallowed up in the swirling mist.

I went forward towards Will and Rose, even though I ached to be with my Robin. His outline was growing dimmer by the second. I had to hurry these two off or I'd miss my chance. "Will and Rose, you are together now and will remain so for eternity. Go in peace and know you are united now and for always." I put the necklace back into her hands, but she cast it aside.

"I have no need of that trumpery now. I have my husband at last. Our love is stronger than silver."

Will enveloped Rose in a deep kiss.

I turned away, turned to Robin at last, because I wanted one of those. He smiled at me and my heart melted. "Robin, how I have longed to see you again, connect with you again. Tell me this isn't a one-off?"

"I don't know, Fay, it's not easy coming back but I wasn't going to see you cut in two by Rose. My energy's draining fast, Fay. Know that I will always watch over you until we're together again."

Hang on, did that mean that Robin and I might have a future life together?

"Do you mean...?"

"Yes, we will be, Fay...I can't...Fay..."

"No!" Robin was disappearing before my eyes. I reached out to grab him but only clutched thin air. I whirled around to see Will and Rose but there was just Percy, standing where Rose had stood, her face uptilted, and blissful. I had not seen her take Rose's place but, judging by her beatific countenance, she'd been part of the last embrace between Will and Rose.

Percy blinked and lifted her hands to her lips; her full soft, rosy lips, still bruised from their crushing. How come she'd had that and I hadn't? I thought my heart would break. I had lost Robin all over again. I stepped forward into the spot he'd occupied, desperate to find anything tangible left behind.

And there was something, glinting dully in the darkness. I bent down and picked up the silver pomander, redolent of the sweet aroma of roses and threaded on my silver chain. I opened the catch and sure enough, it was stuffed with red rose petals, fragrant and fresh.

We left the garden trug and its motley assortment of tools, or weapons, more like, back in the misty marsh. Percy was very disorientated and I had to march her firmly back through the gate, across the lawn and into the house. Was I rough? A little; she'd been in Robin's arms. Okay, it had been a wrestling match rather than heavy petting, but still.

And Percy had been kissed, long and deeply by Will, though how ghosts made that kind of contact was beyond me. My lips were parched and dry; untouched. How many years had it been since they'd been kissed by Robin? More than I cared to remember. I should be happy that I'd seen him at all, I knew that, but losing him a second time seared my heart. Percy was silent on the way back and content to be led. I shoved her through the garden gate. There were no lights on in the house to guide us back but our torches lit the way in focussed rays.

We stumbled into the kitchen and I flicked on the electric lights, half expecting them to fail. But no, the room was instantly illuminated by the trendy spotlights concealed between the beams on the ceiling. Arthur leapt up from the sofa and curled himself around my shaking legs.

"Alright, old boy, give us a minute." I guided Percy to the warm patch he'd left behind on the sofa and she plonked down, still in a dream bubble. This only made me crosser than ever and Arthur didn't help with his loud miaows.

"Okay, Arthur, I heard you the first time." I poked around in the cupboard under the sink and retrieved a cat food pouch. I ripped it open and the revolting meat jelly splashed on my face. "Damn it!" I squeezed the smelly paste into his bowl and shoved it under his nose. Somehow he managed to purr and eat at the same time. If only my life was that simple.

I rinsed my hands and face with some tap water and filled the kettle, slapping it down on the Aga with an angry thump. That seemed to rouse Percy.

"Ooh, making tea? Lovely."

"Lovely? I'll tell you what would be lovely. Snogging my bloody boyfriend, that's what!"

"Sorry? I don't know what you mean."

I dropped a couple of teabags into two mugs, deliberately not looking at her. "Don't tell me you've forgotten already?"

"Forgotten what?"

"Oh, bloody hell!" I turned around at last and faced her, barely able to control my rage. "For heaven's sake, Percy, can't you remember anything that happened out there in your own backyard?"

A blissful smile played across her placid countenance. I itched to slap it away. The kettle broke into song and I turned back to the Aga, splashing water incontinently into the two mugs with an angry, quivering hand. It seemed entirely unreasonable to me that I could conjure up two brothers who'd hated each other and had been dead four hundred years when I'd had only minutes with my recently deceased lover and most of those had been spent focussed on that bloody cow, Rose fucking Charlton. I scooped out the teabags and flung them in the sink, splashing its pristine, white surface with streaks of brown tannin-rich tea.

It was quite satisfying, creating those stains. I sloshed some milk into the mugs and stirred them, then took one to Percy, just about holding off from pouring it over her tousled auburn hair.

"Drink this, maybe it will refresh your memory."

"Thanks, Fay. I'm chilled right through. All I can remember is you doing a lot of shouting." Percy took the mug and sipped it delicately. She'd never looked lovelier, damn her eyes.

I slurped my brew noisily, hoping to annoy her but nothing was going to penetrate her serenity. Unable to contain my temper, I asked, "So, not curious then? Don't you want to know what you've been up to while masquerading as that strumpet, Rose?"

"Strumpet?"

"Yes, bloody strumpet. She had those two brothers fighting over her all their short lives. A right prima donna, if you ask me - which you're not."

"I don't recall that bit. I just remember watching you talking to someone, as if it was Rose and then you seemed be talking to some other ghosts too. Were all three there, then?"

"Yes, the drama is now played out, I think."

"You mean, it's over?" Percy put down her empty mug and looked at me, interested at last.

"Yes, Percy, it's over. We can sleep tonight in peace and so will they. I don't think Rose will bother you again."

"Oh, Fay, that's marvellous," and Percy got up and hugged me.

The warmth of her spontaneous gesture of affection undid me. As I clung to her, my confused well of suppressed emotion erupted into messy, uncontrollable sobs.

"Oh, Fay. You poor thing. Was it so very terrible?"

"No," I gasped between sobs, "not really. It's not that."

"Then, what is it?"

"Robin, my Robin!" And I gave way to my despair in her arms.

Percy let me cry for a good ten minutes, until I got hiccups. She fetched me a glass of water and I drank from the wrong side a few times until my diaphragm reorganised itself. She sat back and watched me as I slowly regained my composure.

I relayed the entire scene I'd witnessed by the old graves and Percy listened round-eyed with wonder, as well she might. When I had finished, she said, "So, Robin came to help you, then, Fay? He must love you very much to do that."

The vice gripping my heart loosened its hold a fraction. I nodded, "Yes, I think he does. He said we'd be together again, in another life in the future but how am I supposed to get through this one without him?"

"Yes, that will be hard but how wonderful to have known love like that." It was Percy's turn to look sad and I wondered again about that patronising husband of hers.

We sat in silence for a while, each thinking about the absent men in our lives.

"I suppose it is a comfort to know that Robin came through for me." I acknowledged after a while.

"I'm sure he would again, if you were in danger." Percy patted my knee.

"Perhaps I should jump off Roundway Hill then. Seems all the rage around here."

"I don't think that would be a good idea." Percy got up and let Arthur out into the darkened garden. "It's going to be strange without Rose in the house. You are amazing, Fay, to get rid of her, I mean. Watching you with the necklace was incredible, even though I couldn't see the ghosts, I could see you were communicating with them. I can't quite believe she's gone. I do hope she'll find peace now."

"She will, I know it."

"And have we made ours?" Percy smiled at me, a nice everyday sort of smile with no hidden agenda.

"Okay, yes, of course. But if Robin does reappear, do me a favour and get out of the bloody way so *I* can snog *him* next time?"

How different I felt going to bed that night with no nocturnal prowling spirits lurking in the shadows. I gazed out across the garden before drawing the curtains, just to check no-one had risen from the dead, then turned back the covers on my comfortable bed and slid between them. I'd expected to drop off to sleep immediately, I was tired enough but my mind replayed the scenes around the graves. Starved of his love for almost ten years, I raked over the crumbs of my exchanges with Robin. Although he'd been ethereally faint, almost see through, I could remember his outline clearly and pored over each of his beloved features, wishing I could caress them.

All these years I'd not seen him and yet he'd come through when it really mattered. Those arid years, I regretted them now. If I hadn't shut down my intuition and my sensitivity, we might have corresponded under less trying circumstances, well before this traumatic experience had brought us together.

I sat bolt upright in bed. So, if I left my psychic door open a little, ajar, as it were, perhaps he'd come again? What was I scared about anyway? You couldn't get a more vicious spirit than Rose Charlton and I'd survived her visitations. Come to think of it, how was that old injury? I touched my wounded arm with the fingers of my right hand. It wasn't sore or weeping, neither was it hot and infected. I switched on my bedside lamp and pulled off my T-shirt. The redness around the plaster had faded right away. I got up and went into the bathroom, where I ripped off the beige dressing. You would hardly know my arm had been gashed. There was a small residual scar where the rose thorn had penetrated but other than that - nada. No swelling or anything. I chucked the old plaster in the bin and grinned at my happy, tired face in the mirror.

The spell was broken and I rather fancied my taboo on travelling between worlds was too. Hugging the memory of Robin's protective love around me as well as the duvet, I closed my eyes and slept with a smug smile on my face.

It was still there when I got up the next morning and checked in the mirror again. I wore a definite jaunty look and the marvellous thing was, I no longer felt alone. That hollow in the pit of my stomach that I had carried around since Robin's death like a camel with his hump had finally dissolved. The warm glow of reconnecting with Robin remained wrapped around me as I showered and dressed and I hoped it would never leave.

I clattered down the wide wooden staircase eager to greet the day, which matched my mood with bright sunshine and deceptive warmth. Summer had stolen a day back from autumn. By the time I had fed Arthur and nudged him outside with the toe of my trainers, Percy joined me, also fully dressed and looking refreshed.

"Sleep well, Fay?" Really, she was the most solicitous hostess when she wasn't hosting some raging ghoul from the past.

"Like a top. How about you?"

"Fabulous. I feel like a different person."

"Me too."

I drank my cup of tea but Percy refused one. "No, thanks. I think we should go back to the graves today and tidy them up, Fay. That is, if you would like to stay on?"

"Yes, I'd like that. It would be good to honour our old friends with a goodbye ritual."

"Maybe even see your Robin again?"

"That would be wonderful but do you know, I feel he's with me all the time now, since last night."

"I'm so pleased for you." Percy reverted to her old habits this morning and whizzed up some fruit in a blender. She drank the smoothie down, leaving a white frothy moustache on her face which she wiped off with the back of her hand. I was relieved to see that standards hadn't entirely returned to normal.

"That's the last of the fruit." Percy rinsed her glass under the tap. "We'll have to do some shopping today. We're out of everything, including cat food and Arthur won't tolerate that."

I laughed. "No, sharing a house with a hungry cat is never pleasant."

"So, would you like to stay for a bit longer, Fay? Once we've finished tidying up outside, I'd like to cook you up a storm this evening, as a thank you."

"If you do that, I'll never leave."

316

And, truth be told, I had no desire to go, although my holiday would soon be used up and I would have to return to the dreary office routine.

Percy looked delighted. "I shouldn't mind. Now, what's your favourite food?"

"Goodness me, Percy, how long have you got?"

After an earnest discussion about tonight's menu, we walked back out to the family graveyard.

"Do you notice something, Percy?"

"What?"

"There's no smell of rotten eggs. Have a sniff, see?"

Percy inhaled deeply, then grinned at me. "You're right! It's as fresh as a daisy. What a relief."

"So, it wasn't the marsh making the stink then. I wonder if the church smells as sweet?" I wandered over to the little stone chapel and poked my nose through the gap in the door. "Do you know? All I can smell is wood from the pews. Now, who'd have thought it?"

"I've been thinking about the family church, Fay. I think I'll get Paul to renovate it. Maybe get some builders in and restore it properly to its former glory. It could be really pretty, if it was done up."

"Great idea. Let's make a start by clearing the weeds around the graves."

We set to with the gardening tools, using them in the manner they'd been designed for this time. We worked away all morning until all the brambles, weeds and overgrown grass were cut back. Rose Foulkes' grave, lying between the two brothers, was the toughest one to tackle. Her headstone had been covered over with brambles and took some fearsome pruning to expose. At last the three headstones stood out, proud and unencumbered, their names, so familiar to us now, freely on view though faint with age.

We stood together reading them silently.

Percy spoke first. "I feel I really knew them, don't you?"

"Yes, I'm not sure I'd want to meet Rose again but both brothers were a tad gorgeous, I thought." But not as beautiful to me as Robin, I hastened to add privately, just in case he could hear my thoughts.

"Weren't they just? I wouldn't say no to either Ralph or Will Foulkes if they turned up again, in the flesh, I mean."

"Percy! And you a married woman."

She laughed at my mock horror. "Being married doesn't stop you fancying other people, you know. Come on, we've done enough here. Let's go into town and get the ingredients for a celebration supper."

I needed no encouragement for that errand. Once in the supermarket, Percy became very focussed and piled her trolley high with gourmet delights. I insisted on buying the wine and spent a happy half an hour debating whether to get a hefty Merlot from Chile or a refined looking red Bordeaux. I got both in the end, and a bottle of champagne to go with our starters. To hell with the cost. We'd just survived the most macabre days of my life. We deserved a party.

Percy also bought a shed-load of spring bulbs to plant around the graves. "Look, Fay - I've got daffodils, crocus, snowdrops and tulips."

"That will make a beautiful display come spring. Very cheering idea. I'll help you plant them this afternoon."

Percy shook her head. "I shall be in the kitchen this afternoon, preparing your feast."

We got to the check-out and started loading the belt. "Blimey, Percy, you've bought half the supermarket. I hope you're going to let me pay for some of it."

"No way. This is my thank you and you're buying some very nice wine, I see. Paul gives me plenty of housekeeping, so don't worry." The bill came to an eye-watering sum but Percy nonchalantly slipped her credit card in the machine without batting an eyelid.

"Well, thank you, Paul Wade," I said, as we loaded up the car.

"He can afford it and we've cleansed his precious manor of restless spirits, haven't we?" Percy giggled as she slammed the boot shut.

"Suits me." I got in the car beside her. "But I'll plant those bulbs for you this afternoon, while you're slaving away in the kitchen, if you like."

"Perfect. I hate anyone else in the kitchen when I'm concentrating on something special."

"It's a deal, sounds like I need to work up an appetite to do justice to your culinary skills." I licked my lips in anticipation.

"It will be a pleasure, Fay. I love to have a reason to go a bit crazy making something fancy." Percy switched on the engine and we roared out of the car park in style.

I had a happy afternoon, planting spring bulbs in the autumn sunshine. A choir of birds kept me company, their voices full throated in song. As I handled the bulbs, the sensation of all that potential bound up in the little corms of crocus, the fatter daffodils and the smooth, shiny tulips uplifted me still further. The snowdrops were so tiny I bundled them in together in groups of half a dozen in the hollowed out earth. It was a fitting homage to counter the cessation of life around them. I distributed them with scrupulous equality around the graves of Will, Ralph and Rose. These powerhouses of plant energy would push through the damp earth next spring, symbols of the ever turning cycle of life - be it flowers or people; all comes around again, if we can but wait.

I loaded the debris of the bulb packets and tools into the trug with hands blackened by dirt. Standing up, I inhaled the sweet air again, marvelling at its clean, fresh scent. Not a trace of bad drains.

I stood looking down at the graves to admire my handiwork, the grass surrounding them now spiked by little mounds of fresh earth where I had planted the promise of spring. They might have been dug by a small mole on a random spree. Hopefully, these flowers would multiply and form pleasing drifts connecting up these dead lovers for many years to come.

A lone robin separated from the rest of the natural orchestra tweeting around me and flew closer. He broke into song in the nearest willow tree amongst the strand of its cousins meandering along the marsh line. The solitary bird followed me back to the house and landed on the mounting block next to the kitchen door.

"Now listen, mate. That's Arthur's favourite washing spot. You be sure he doesn't turn you into his dinner."

The robin took my advice, spread his wings and fluttered away, back towards the weeping willow by the garden door in the wall. There it settled amongst the graceful green fronds and sang its heart out, so loudly I could still hear it indoors.

The glow of my reconnection with Robin shone within me all through showering and trying to make myself look half decent in honour of Percy's efforts. I washed my hair and even brushed it. I touched up my eyes with some mascara and daubed on some glossy lipstick I found lurking in the bottom of my make-up bag. I'd only brought jeans with me but I had a long black shirt that wasn't too shabby. I looked in the mirror. Still a bit drab. It needed some jewellery. I fished in the pocket of my jacket and drew out Rose's silver chain and pomander. The metal felt delightfully cool and inactive and the roses within the pomander had dried and shrivelled, leaving only a vestigial whiff of their heady scent. I slipped it over my head. It lay on my black silk shirt quiescent like any other necklace.

I decided to wear it.

Another glance in the mirror confirmed my choice. The silver pomander lay elegantly across my chest, its high quality workmanship would enhance any outfit. It was probably worth a bomb. However valuable it might be, I felt I had earned the right to wear it.

I went downstairs to find Percy, looking quite as elegant as the pomander, swanning around her kitchen. Mistress of her art, she had set the table with candles alight in the two candelabras we had found so useful during the power cut but had left the ambient light low. From the garden, she'd picked some late dusky-pink roses which sat, queen-like, in the centre. Crystal glasses twinkled in the soft light and white linen shrouded the table in soft damask folds. If a queen did turn up, she wouldn't look out of place.

"Wow, Percy. This looks fantastic and smells even better."

Percy, who had donned a simple but no doubt hugely expensive sapphire blue dress and whose hair was piled up on her head, laughed indulgently. "You deserve it, Fay. It's my pleasure to treat you. Before you came I was living in this great barn of a place in fear of my life. Now I've found a friend and there are no ghosts or ghoulies to frighten the wits out of me every night. It's the least I could do."

"Well, I think this calls for champagne." I went to the big fridge in the utility room where I'd put the bottle earlier. I popped the cork and poured the froth into the champagne flutes Percy held out. Just catching it before the bubbles cascaded over their rims, we chinked the crystal together.

"To Rose, I think?"

Percy nodded. "Absolutely, and may she rest in peace for ever more, for all our sakes. Is that her necklace?

"Yes, it's not reactive anymore so I feel it's a sort of triumph to treat it as an ordinary piece of jewellery." I touched the silver with my fingers.

"A kind of barometer?" Percy raised her perfectly shaped eyebrows.

"Yes, in a way."

"And it's very beautiful. It suits you, Fay. Looks great against that shirt."

A compliment from a model. I never thought I'd hear that.

I took my first sip of bubbly. "Oh, that's heaven in a bottle."

"And I have just the thing to accompany it. Fancy some canapés?"

When we were two glasses in and the canapés a fond memory, Percy declared it time to begin the main event. I felt quite giggly by then and hiccupped quietly as I sat to the table. She produced a fine salad of prosciutto ham nestled in fresh figs and ricotta cheese, resting lightly on a bed of soft green leaves.

"Hmm, this is delicious, Percy. What is in that dressing?"

"Secret ingredients but honey's involved." Her green eyes twinkled mischievously.

"It's just right."

The main course was my favourite, rack of lamb, so I stoppered the half drunk bottle of champagne and opened the bottle of red Bordeaux to accompany it.

"The sauce is based on balsamic vinegar and fine herbs." Percy divulged, as I scooped up the last dribble on my plate.

I was past caring how she'd arrived at such nectar and poured out the last of the wine in to our glasses.

"Another toast. To the cook!"

"Did you buy some Merlot, Fay? That would go well with the cheese."

"Cheese?" I groaned. "Give me a minute. I know I'm a glutton but even I must pace myself."

Percy laughed and cleared the plates with an enviably steady hand. "I'll open the bottle anyway and put the cheese on the table so they can both breathe."

"I need to do a bit of breathing myself." I surreptitiously undid the top button of my jeans while she fetched the next sumptuous course.

Somehow I managed to squeeze in various tasty chunks of cheese. Of course, I simply had to wash it down with the Merlot. By the time Percy placed a pile of chocolate profiteroles in front of me, I was decidedly tipsy.

She giggled. "Oh, Fay, the kitchen is beginning to spin around me! I think we'd better have coffee with dessert rather than more wine."

"Yesh, definitely." Not trusting myself to stand up, I watched her totter to the sink and fiddle with the coffee maker. I sat back in my chair, not thinking, just feeling mellow and content to let my digestion get busy while my mind went pleasantly blank.

Percy came back to the table and we waited for the coffee to brew and chatted over the past few days in a gentle alcoholic haze of mutual congratulation. Just as the coffee began to gurgle and splutter into its glass jug, there was a crash in the hall.

Instinctively my hand went straight to Rose's pomander. I expected it to be red hot but the metal was still cool against my silk shirt. Not Rose then, but who?

"Oh, God, don't say Rose has a successor. I'm in no fit state to tackle another ghost tonight."

My heart, laden with cholesterol and booze, lumped into a faster pace and my digestion stopped its contented rumblings. I felt a bit queasy, just like the other times when we'd had a visitor from the manor's history.

Percy looked just as alarmed, her heavily made-up eyes wide with apprehension. We both slewed round in our seats as the kitchen door burst open and a tall, fit-looking man, wearing a cagoule and beanie, stood in the doorway, his mouth dropped wide open."What the fuck?"

"Paul!"

Percy went to stand up but didn't quite manage it and fell back in her chair, only just managing to reach her target. She sat awkwardly on its edge and stared at the person I presumed was her husband. Neither looked particularly pleased to be reunited but what did I know? I'd never been married and I was far too drunk to be objective.

"So, who is this you're entertaining so royally in my absence? Is that a champagne bottle over there? Are you celebrating something?"

Percy made another attempt at vertical. "I washn't expecting you home for weeksh, Paul."

"Evidently. Sorry I've disrupted your intimate party. Aren't you going to introduce me?"

Paul darted a severe stare at me and I tried to cobble my brain back together but it stubbornly refused to comply and I couldn't think of a single thing to say.

"Er, yesh, yesh, of course." Percy turned to me and smiled.

Even my sluggish brain could sense she was frightened again and not by the undead, but the living.

"Paul, meet Fay Armstrong, my new friend and saviour."

"Saviour? Is she Jesus fucking Christ then?" Paul came over to the table and against all my instincts I extended my hand. He shook it briefly and sat down. His grip was strong and his hand cool.

"You going to give me some of that wine? I've been travelling for two days. Hmm, nice cheese. Come on, Phoney, fetch us a glass and a plate. Seems I've missed the main course. What was it? Smells like lamb."

Paul spoke in an posh old Etonian accent, despite his coarse language; perhaps that's how he got away with it, but it left me stone cold.

Percy scurried away to the cupboard for a fresh glass and poured him out a glass of Merlot right up to the brim. Her hand trembled slightly.

"So, what's the occasion? I feel like a bloody gatecrasher in my own house." Paul glugged back half a glass of wine in one go and cut a wodge of stilton.

There was a basket of leftover French bread on the table and he took four slices. Even I hadn't had room for that after all the other bounty I'd consumed.

Through the cheese and bread Paul said, "Come on, Phoney, tell me what this is all about, unless this is how you live every night I'm away? In fact, looking at you, maybe you do. You've put on a ton of weight."

Suddenly, his face softened and he added quietly, "Phoney, you're not, not, you know, pregnant - are you? Can it be happening at last, my darling?" He half got up from his chair and held out his hand to her. With his face and voice more gentle, I could glimpse why Percy had found him so attractive.

Percy, who had paled when her husband arrived, now coloured up and spoke in a small, compressed voice. "No, no, I'm not having a child, Paul. I wish I could make you happy that way."

The weathered lines on Paul's face quickly hardened up again and he dropped his hand.

Percy stumbled on her next words. "Um, Fay and I *are* celebrating something."

"Oh yeah?" Paul helped himself to a big slice of matured Cheddar and topped up his wine glass.

I sipped some water in a desperate attempt to sober up.

"You guys gay, or what? You having a lezzy affair behind my back, hey, Phoney? This has all the hallmarks of a romantic supper à deux to me. I can't remember the last time we shared one." He looked at me. "You don't talk much, do you?"

I cleared my throat. Despite the inordinate amount of lubrication it had received, it had gone horribly dry.

"I've been staying in your house for a few days. You weren't here to check that was okay. Percy and I have been dealing with some ghosts." Pleased I hadn't slurred my words, my complacency was soon squashed.

"Oh, my fucking God! Phoney hasn't been on about those bloody poltergeists again, has she? Load of neurotic nonsense. Are you going to eat those profiteroles, Phoney, because if you're not, and let's face it, you probably shouldn't, I'll have them. The food on the plane was as crap as ever." Paul reached over and swiped her dessert away, laying into them immediately with his spoon.

The fog in my mind cleared enough to register that the coffee percolator had stopped gurgling. Feeling in urgent need of some caffeine, I got up and brought the jug and three mugs to the table. Percy rewarded me with a wan smile. A smudge of mascara had smeared a line at the edge of her eye, making her look unusually imperfect.

"You've made yourself very much at home, I see." Paul scraped his bowl noisily.

My teeth shuddered at the grating sound.

I poured out a mug of black coffee and took a sip before answering. "Your wife has made me very welcome. You have a lovely place here."

Paul refilled his empty wine glass, shaking the last drops from the bottle. "Huh, that didn't last long."

"Would you like me to open another bottle, Paul?" Percy half rose from her chair without her usual graceful movement, scraping her chair on the flagstones.

"Nah, but you could fetch the brandy."

Percy immediately disappeared on her mission.

Paul drained his glass and turned to look at me squarely. "So, I'm sorry, I've forgotten your name?"

"Fay. Fay Armstrong."

"Oh, yes, the name suits you in so many ways. How did you meet my wife then?"

"We met through the squash league and played a match."

"Oh, yeah? Who won? Not Phoney, I'll be bound, Miss, or is it Mrs, Strong Arms?"

"Armstrong, Ms. It was a tough game. Persephone is a very good player."

"So, *Ms* Armstrong, would you say you were 'well matched', you two?" Paul laughed at his own joke.

The coffee was, thankfully, taking effect. It seemed to be resurrecting my adrenal glands and they had transferred their wake-up call to my hands, now balled into fists under the table.

"At squash, yes, very."

326

Percy returned with a bottle of cognac and a brandy bowl glass and placed both in front of her husband on the littered table. "There you are, darling. Can I get you anything else?"

I longed to suggest a knuckle sandwich but interfering between man and wife has never been my style, or popular.

"I'd ask for a kiss, but I'm not sure if you're in need of one. Come on, spill. Are you two having a gay affair? I'm up for a threesome, if you are."

Paul stoppered the brandy bottle after filling his glass. He swirled the amber liquid around the bowl, leaving streaks of alcohol clinging to its crystal sides.

I speculated what impact the brandy bottle might have on his skull, now he'd removed his black beanie. He looked like he belonged in the SAS rather than the sensitive photographic artist I'd been led to believe.

Percy spoke into the awkward vacuum following his lurid suggestion. "Paul, I think you've got the wrong idea. I, I know what it must look like but you're way off beam, darling."

I suppose it was the shock of her husband's return that rendered Percy so sober in her speech and I attempted to emulate it.

"No, neither of us is gay, Mr Wade. Persephone genuinely had problems with restless spirits in your house and asked for my help. Together, we've been able to get rid of them." My pomposity was punctuated with an unfortunate hiccup at the end and he laughed.

"Oh, yeah, that old story. Pretty feeble cover up because, I have to say, you do look a bit butch."

I stood up, pleased not to stumble. His rudeness had cleared my head as effectively as the strong coffee.

"Listen, I can see I'm intruding. I'll help you clear up, Percy, and then I'll get off to bed. I shall be off in the morning anyway."

"Oh, no, Fay. Don't go."

Percy looked genuinely alarmed at my announcement. Was this boor also physically abusive? I wouldn't put it past him and the doubt made me hesitate.

"Percy? Why's she calling you that? Sorry ladies but that confirms my suspicions. Why are you calling my gorgeous wife by a man's name?" He smiled in an unattractive leer.

"Come here, Phoney." Paul got up and pulled her to him, letting his hands linger around her waist. When he lowered his head for a conjugal kiss, I took my cue and left them to it.

She had married him after all. How could I interfere?

Sleep proved elusive. The mixture of rich food and alcohol, topped with a large amount of coffee, wasn't the only conflict I wrestled with. An hour after I'd hit the sack, I heard Paul and Percy stumble up the stairs and go into their bedroom. The walls of the manor house were thick but not quite thick enough. Just as on that night when Will and Rose had honeymooned in our heads, I could hear the guttural sounds of energetic sex permeating into my chamber. Even placing the pillow over my thumping head didn't blot it out. And it went on and on, just like that Paul Simon song; if it had been a competition, they were bound to win a prize.

The sexual marathon continued till three in the morning. The man had some stamina, if he'd been travelling for two days, but I heard no cries of female ecstasy this time. After the first session came to a grand finale, I decided to ram my bedroom chair under the doorknob again. It didn't sound like my kind of party and I dreaded an invitation to join it. I felt sorry for Percy and wondered what she'd seen in him to commit to being legally bound to the bloke.

At last the house fell silent, until snores reverberated along the corridor. Obnoxious man. Eventually even that annoying noise couldn't stop my eyelids from shutting and I dozed off. I surprised myself by waking reasonably early. I got up, washed quickly and quietly packed my belongings in my suitcase. I'd had plenty of sleepless hours in the night to plan my exit strategy.

I lugged my bags downstairs on tiptoe and left them in the hall by the front door. I went into the kitchen to find Arthur happily up on the table, licking cream off the dessert plates. He leapt down smartly when I appeared and sat on the sofa where he proceeded to wash in a leisurely manner, his replete smile reminiscent of his feline cousin from Cheshire.

The kitchen was a mess. Obviously Percy had been too busy to clear away. I didn't mind, it was the least I could do for my gentle friend. Within half an hour the room was back to its normal orderly state and the dishwasher hummed away, swishing debris from plates and glasses. I had learned where everything was housed in Percy's house and, with no sign of the other two appearing, carried on tidying until all the china and glass was back where it belonged. I'd opened the back door to air the place which had reeked of stale food and booze and Arthur, his ablutions now thoroughly completed, stalked out, tail in the air, in defence against any unfair criticism. I wasn't going to tell him off. I'd have scoffed the remains of the feast myself, if I was a cat.

Order restored, I joined Arthur in the garden. I wasn't going to disappear without saying goodbye properly and anyway, I might see the little robin, if I was lucky.

The morning was again kind and my aching head needed the soothing balm of its mild air. It wasn't too bright yet, for which I was truly grateful or sunglasses would have been required, but soft and hazy. September had arrived with all its promised mellow fruitfulness. I crossed the lawn, hoping to see the little robin in the sweeping green of the weeping willow by the gate but, apart from a blackbird trilling away, I saw no cheery red breast. Trying not to feel disappointed, I wandered on through the wet land towards the little church where our old adversaries lay.

I didn't expect to see them again but wanted to take one final look, just to satisfy myself they were sleeping peacefully under the green sward. The three headstones stood in a line, in a companionable sort of way, surrounded by my earthy scars of yesterday's planting. I decided to take a picture with my phone, just to remind me, as if I could ever forget, that I could communicate with souls that had passed over. There would be times, I knew, when I would doubt again, especially if Robin didn't put in an appearance when and if I ever needed rescuing again.

I pocketed my phone in my jeans and, in deference to my morning-after headache, sat down to rest in the sun-drenched chapel porch while I waited for Percy to emerge. It was still fairly early and I didn't expect them to rise from their hectic marital bed anytime soon. I closed my eyes against the glare of the sun, now dispersing the early clouds and warming the stones against which I leaned.

I felt sad that my stay with Percy had been truncated by the arrival of her uncouth husband. I suppose it must have looked a bit weird to him, coming home to us wining and dining like that. If you didn't believe in spiritual entities either, it would bring out the cynic in anyone to find your wife closeted with a psychic who claimed they'd cleared your house of an infestation of ethereal creatures, especially if you'd been unaware of them. Then my own inner cynic put the counter argument that Paul was dead from the neck up and hadn't noticed his own wife's recoil when he groped her.

Not your business, said my head. Poor Percy, said my heart.

I stretched out my legs and put my arms above my head to cushion it against the stone and looked at the manor house, now basking in sunshine behind the garden wall. Its many chimneys, as russet as its bricks, stretched up into a sky now displaying a lovely shade of cerulean blue. The warm brick walls, mellow with age, drank in the sunlight, as they had done for centuries. Had Percy seen this beautiful house before committing to marriage with its owner?

Voices wafted across from the house and the gate in the wall creaked open to reveal Percy and Paul walking, hand in hand, towards me. I scrambled to my feet, dusting debris off my backside as I did so.

"Oh, there you are, Fay!" Percy waved with her spare hand. "We thought we might find you here."

No accompanying wave from himself then. I raised my hand in greeting. "Good morning to you both."

Percy looked tired, as well she might, but also rather strained. It irritated me no end.

"I was just telling Paul about these three." Percy nodded towards the graves.

"I'd long forgotten these were here." Paul had found his voice but obviously had decided to dispense with courteous formalities.

"Look, Paul, see how we've tidied it all up? And darling Fay has planted spring bulbs. Won't that look pretty next year?" Percy pointed to the divots in the grass.

"Probably disturbed several habitats in the process with your suburban gardening. I hope you didn't clear that patch of nettles behind the chapel. Invaluable for butterflies."

"No, no, of course not, Paul. I, I'm sorry if we did the wrong thing."

My irritation increased with every faltering word Percy spoke.

"So, you reckon these corpses have been wandering around the manor, do you?" Paul looked at me directly, his eyes truculent and cold.

"Yes, I can assure you that's exactly what they've been doing, particularly Rose Charlton." I stared right back at him.

"Huh, load of nonsense, if you ask me. Rose Charlton, you say? Why is she buried here? I thought it was reserved for the Foulkes family." Paul peered at the middle headstone. "Yes, see? Says Rose Foulkes, not Charlton. You need to get your facts straight, Ms Strong-Arm."

"She married into the family, Paul." Percy spoke in a rush. "You see, the Charltons lived in the next manor and Ralph, Foulkes that is, the elder brother, he was engaged to her but she loved Will, the younger one. It was at the time of the English Civil War and they fought on opposite sides. It's a tragic tale."

"Phoney, you've been reading too many romance novels. Load of tosh." Paul moved across and inspected the other headstones.

"You can see that the names are correct, surely?" I wasn't going to stand for this negating of our triumph.

"What difference does that make? Any tale can be embroidered to suit the storyteller and Phoney is prone to exaggeration and stupid fears about things. I keep telling her to relax but she has far too fanciful an imagination." Paul tamped down an upturned sod with his shoe, leftover from my horticultural endeavours.

"I can assure you, Mr Wade, that your wife did not imagine Rose Charlton haunting your house. She was extremely frightened about being here on her own and, after I stayed just one night, I could understand why. Persephone has been very brave rather than stupid and you should thank her for ridding your house of malicious spirits. Far from whims of fancy, the undead are very real indeed and we were both in mortal danger at times." It was no good, he'd fanned the flames of my irritation into a burning furnace.

Percy leapt to my defence before he could answer. "It's true, Paul, darling, really it is. I was terrified before dear Fay turned up and do you know, she's psychic. It's amazing! She can see dead people and talk to them but Rose sort of inhabited me and although I can't remember it, I attacked her several times. Show him your arm, Fay."

I didn't like the sneer on his face. "Yes, Fay, *dear*, show me your arm. Let's have some evidence."

How could I explain the magical healing of my arm? Even the residual scar had now vanished. No way was that going to convince this sceptic. "I'd rather not, if you don't mind, Percy. You'll just have to take our word for it, Mr Wade."

"I knew it, load of bunkum. Honestly Phoney, get a fucking grip, will you?" Paul crossed his arms emphatically.

"Look, do you have to talk to your wife like that?" I went to Percy to comfort her.

"Oh, Paul, why don't you believe me?" Percy grabbed my hand and I squeezed hers back. "We've had the most bloody awful time and if it wasn't for us this place would still be haunted. The windows were being blown open, one of the mullioned panes broke in the spare bedroom, the furniture was moving about; we even had a power cut that lasted all weekend but when the electrician came out he said it was just the trip switch."

"Anyone could have told you that. Why didn't you flick the switch yourself? I've shown you how to do it countless times in case it happens while I'm away." Paul appeared unmoved at his wife's distress.

"But that's the point, Paul. We did try the switch but it wouldn't come back on."

"God, you're so thick. I mean, you've got other attributes, obviously, but let's face it, Phoney, you're never going to win Mastermind, now are you?" He'd uncrossed his arms and now stood, hands on hips, a sardonic smile lifting the corners of his smug mouth.

I'd had it by then and opened my own mouth to inform him about his wife's superior qualities but Percy beat me to it. Her fine-boned cheeks turned bright pink.

"You know what, Paul? You can stick your remarks right up where the sun don't shine. I've had it with you! Being with Fay has been such a contrast to living with you and your constant running me down. I'm not thick, actually, and there were ghosts here. I just hope they do return and haunt you, then you'll know what I've been through but I'm not hanging around to find out. I'm sick to death of you and your carping on at me; sick of your using me as an unpaid housekeeper and if you must know, I'm sick of your selfish demands for sex. You're a rotten lover, I've never had worse and if you ever call me Phoney again, so help me I'll..."

It was Paul's turn to redden up now; an ugly brick red. His face didn't even match his mellow terracotta house, it was a raw, unlovely shade, more reminiscent of the Victorian terraced street I lived in. He didn't deserve to live in this graceful old place. "Oh, yeah? You'll do what, exactly, Phoney?"

"That's it. You've done it now. I'm leaving you, Paul Wade and I'm never coming back."

"You little bitch!" Paul lunged at Percy and would have hit her had I not barred him. For once, my sturdy frame came in handy and I swung my arm out, making contact with his flushed cheek.

A small bird tweeted furiously above me, fluttering its wings before swooping down in front of Paul's face.

"What the? Fuck off, you stupid bird." Paul lifted his hands to protect his face as the robin dive-bombed his head.

I turned to Percy. "You sure about this?"

She nodded, eyes brimming with tears but chin firm. "Absolutely."

"Then let's go."

"Do you want to grab some stuff before we go? You know you're welcome at my place, don't you, Percy? It's not much but the couch is comfy." We walked swiftly across the lawn, past the conservatory housing the swimming pool and in through the kitchen door.

Percy, betrayed her emotions with a sniff. "Thank you, yes, Fay, I would be glad of somewhere to stay. Do you mind waiting for five minutes? I'll be as quick as I can. Will you be able to handle Paul?"

"Don't you worry about him. Go on, get your things. I'll put mine in my car and wait for you outside."

"Okay, thanks." Percy gave my arm a quick squeeze and leapt up the stairs, two at a time.

I picked up my suitcases and hefted them into the boot of my little hatchback, leaving the lid open for Percy's luggage. I unlocked both the driver's and the passenger's door and left the latter open for her before climbing in behind the wheel. I started the engine, just to check it still worked, as I hadn't driven it for a week. The engine chugged into life and I blessed my choice of a diesel engine. I left it switched on in an idling growl.

When I heard shouts from inside the hallway, I got out and stood in the entrance, poised for rescue.

Percy and Paul were standing facing each other, both shouting insults at full volume. To be fair to Paul, he looked as distressed as his wife. I had a moment's misgiving about the break-up of this marriage and hesitated on the doorstep. Was I to blame? Had they been happy before? Then Paul raised his hand and I waited no longer.

"Oi, you! Leave her alone!" I marched into the dimly lit hall.

"Get lost. This is none of your business." Paul lowered his arm but spoke through clenched teeth.

"Maybe not but violence won't solve anything. Perhaps you both just need to cool off, then you can talk. Percy can stay with me for a few days while you both work out what you want."

Percy threw me a grateful look. "That's right, Paul. I need some space. I'll ring you soon, I promise, but I just need to get away and sort my head out."

"Go off with your lezzy friend, you mean. I obviously interrupted something last night. Go on, then. You'll come crawling back when the credit card dries up." Paul folded his arms again, it seemed to be his habitual stance. Very defensive.

"Right, come on, Percy. The car's waiting." I hooked my arm under her elbow and she turned to me.

"Okay. Goodbye, Paul. I'll, I'll be in touch." Percy looked around at the wainscot hall, as if saying goodbye to the house, rather than the man, and followed me out to the car.

Just before getting in, Percy paused and surveyed the beautiful old manor. I wondered if this was the real parting for her. She wrenched her gaze away and clambered into the passenger seat, clicking on the seat-belt without prompting.

"Ready?" I put the car into gear.

"Ready." Percy nodded.

The gates already stood open and we drove between them. Percy never looked back, not once.

Percy remained silent on the journey to Swindon and I didn't feel I could intrude on her thoughts. I drove through the traffic and up the hill to Old Town and my flat. I drew up outside the Victorian terrace and squashed the car into a tiny parking space outside. It was supposed to be residents only but it was surprising how many residents had cars, if not stickers on the windscreens to legitimise their space.

"Well, Percy. This, such as it is, is it."

"Right, um, thanks."

"Bit of a come down for you, I know, but the kettle works."

She followed me quietly to number 34 and stood patiently while I fished for my Yale key. The communal door swung wide and we entered the scruffy hall, liberally marked by scuff marks, and squeezed past two pushbikes leaning against the wall.

"This is mine, Percy." I inserted my key into the internal door and let her go first. The flat smelt stale and dusty and looked drabber than ever. I never was much of a one for interior decoration. As long as the microwave and the telly worked, I wasn't too bothered about the aesthetics but now I felt embarrassed. It was tidy enough, I wasn't that bad but it could never be accused of having soul.

"It's lovely, Fay," Percy lied.

"No, it's not but it's a safe haven. I'll make some tea."

Percy sat on the Futon sofa in polite silence. I filled the kettle and switched it on before exploring the inside of the fridge to find a packet of cheese, left open so long it resembled yellow leather and a half carton of milk, smelling more like cheese than the dessicated cake of the stuff bearing that label.

"Ugh, I'll have to go to the corner shop and get some supplies." I poured the coagulated milk down the sink and used the boiling water from the kettle to chase it down the plug-hole.

"Do you want me to come with you?"

"Nah, shan't be a mo. What do you fancy for supper?"

"I really don't mind, Fay. Anything. You are kind."

Percy's chin began to wobble. I patted her on the back. "Have a good cry while I'm out. Do you good."

She nodded and reached for the tissues. I reached for the door. I felt distinctly bewildered wandering around the little Indian corner shop, lobbing comestibles into my basket. What a strange turn of events. When I had played that game of squash with Percy I could never have guessed the outcome. I felt very weary all of a sudden.

"Hello, Miss Fay. Been away?" Mr Singh shook his head from side to side and smiled his wonderful toothy smile.

"Yes, been staying at a friend's, over Marlborough way." I unpacked the items for him to zap them through the checkout.

"Have a nice time?"

"It was interesting." I punched my number into his machine and took the carrier bag he had packed for me so carefully, as always. "But it's nice to be back."

"Always good to see you, Missy."

"And you, Mr Singh. 'Bye for now."

"Good day to you."

He nodded me out of the little shop and all at once I was glad to be home. Familiar territory, even the long lines of terraced houses, was comforting, even through the steady drizzle that had now set in.

I let myself back into the flat and stowed away my purchases. "Nothing gourmet this time, Percy, but I took the precaution of getting some beers in. We can have the hair of the dog tonight and you can drown your sorrows."

Percy came over and helped me unload the shopping. "I'm not sad, Fay. No, I'm not sad at all. I feel free for the first time in ages. If anything, you know, I'm a bit excited. I don't know what I'm going to do with my life but the magnificent thing is, it's *my* life and I can do whatever I want."

I shut the freezer door and stared at her. "Really? I thought you looked pretty upset when I left just now."

"I think that was shock, to tell you the truth. Honestly, the way Paul behaved to you disgusted me and I knew then I wasn't in love with him anymore. I wonder if I ever was but, you see, when he was behind the camera, in London, I mean, when I was still working as a model, he was so charismatic. He's a different guy when he's working. He cajoles, cracks jokes and flatters you to get the best picture. That's who I fell in love with. We married in London but it wasn't until we came down to Wiltshire and moved into Meadowsweet Manor that he changed and I saw a different side to him."

Percy folded my carrier bags, far more neatly than I ever did. "He never used to swear so much before either, or raise his hand to me."

"A proper Jekyll and Hyde." I ran the tap into the kettle and switched it on. I was gasping for a cuppa.

"Not quite that bad, and I was still in love with him but, shall I tell you a secret? I'm almost ashamed to confess it." She stacked the folded bags one on top of the other, and smoothed the topmost one.

"Go on."

"I also fell in love with his house!" Percy laughed. "Such a divine place, isn't it?"

I laughed with her and the kettle chimed in. I made a couple of mugs of tea and opened a packet of fig rolls.

"Come on, let's sit down." I took the tea to the sofa and we sat at either end.

"But it's not enough to stay for a building, however beautiful and it never did feel like home to me. I'm not in love with Paul and I shall petition for a divorce." Percy spoke with a new, assured authority.

"I would sleep on that decision, if I were you." I munched on a fig roll. "It's a big one, not to be taken lightly."

"Good advice, Fay but I'm not going to change my mind."

"So, what will you do? Where will you go?"

Percy dunked her biscuit. "Back to London, I suppose. I can always get more modelling work, although I'm getting close to my sell-by date and that game is tougher than ever. It's hard to make decent money if you've taken a break."

"Nonsense. A good night's sleep will have you looking as stunning as ever. I just hope you'll be comfortable on this Futon."

"I'm sure I will."

"Tell you what, I'll cook you a feast tonight or better still, we'll get a take-away. Do you like Indian food?"

"Love it." We chinked mugs. There was no answering ring of crystal this time but I don't think my guest minded.

After we'd unpacked our things and I'd emptied a chest of drawers for Percy to use and brought it into the sitting room, we had a snack lunch and pretended to watch an old movie by dozing in front of it.

After dusk had fallen, I rang an order through to Singh Junior's restaurant and went to collect it. We drank beer from the bottle with our poppadoms and tucked into our curries.

"This is such fun, Fay. I can't remember the last time I had a take-away curry." Percy swigged from her bottle.

"Two parties, two days in a row." I helped myself to more chutney.

"And this is the best one."

"I'd better check my emails afterwards though, if you'll excuse me."

"Sure. Want another beer?"

"Why not?" I flicked on my laptop and waited for the spam to arrive. "You know what, Percy? We were pretty damn good at ghostbusting."

"Yes, weren't we? It was very scary at the time but it was the most interesting thing I've ever done. Did you say you used to have lots of experiences like that?" Percy gave a less than discreet burp. "Ooh, excuse me!"

I laughed. "You're coming down to my level very rapidly, I see."

Percy chortled as she flopped back on to the sofa. "Oh, it's so good to relax, Fay, and let go. Still, if I'm to return to the world of modelling, I'll have to get back on the straight and narrow."

"That sounds boring."

"It bloody is, I can assure you. Lettuce leaves for lunch, dinner and breakfast."

"Isn't there any other work you fancy?"

"Not qualified to do anything else, that's the problem. Not like you. I'll bet you have a sheaf of qualifications."

"A few, but I loathe and hate my job. It's the dullest existence you can imagine. Hmm, no emails worth bothering with and I don't need a Swiss watch and have no desire to fund an army in Timbuctoo, thank you very much." I deleted the whole lot, did the same with the junk folder and closed the email app. "Think I'll see what today's world has been up to while we've been wrestling with the past."

I scanned the news pages. "Instant depression."

"Oh, I know, there's never any good news is there? Perhaps I'd better look at the 'Jobs Vacant' page."

"Or, considering we're so brilliant at bringing peace and goodwill to restless spirits, we could set up a website and go into business as ghostbusters."

Percy giggled again and swigged more beer. "What a laugh. Why don't we try it, just for a joke, and see what happens?"

"Do we dare?" I looked at Percy in a new light. Was she tiddly from the beer or drunk on freedom? "Could be a whole new career for us both."

She grabbed the computer mouse. "Come on, Fay, let's do it! I'd love to see what happens if we try. How do you set up a website anyway?"

"Oh, that's easy, it would only take half an hour."

"You are so clever. Now, what shall we call ourselves?"

I took my mouse back and opened a website page, a free one. There were tons available and the process looked very straightforward. I chuckled and cast about for an idea. My eyes lit on my toolbox. "How about 'Spirit Level'?"

"Oh, Fay, that's fantastic! Come on, let's go for it."

"Get me another beer then." Within half an hour, Spirit Level had a presence on the worldwide web. I imported a beautiful picture of a lake, with white mist rising from it and two swans gliding across its serene surface towards each other. The strap line read, *'Do you want to reach out to a loved one who has passed over?"*

Together we composed a blurb beneath, explaining who we were and making all sorts of extravagant claims about our abilities to connect to the dead before laying them to rest.

By this time, whether through exhaustion, a surfeit of heightened emotions, or simply because of the beer, we were in fits of laughter.

"Can we really let this go live, Percy? I mean, it's all very well for a joke, but..." My hand hesitated on the mouse.

Percy reached over and pressed the 'Go' button. "What's the worst that can happen?"

# EPILOGUE

## My flat

I woke with a hangover headache for the second morning in a row. It took a minute to come to and recognise my old familiar bedroom. I exhaled with relief and stretched out in my bed. No place like home, however humble. I flopped out of bed and wriggled into my fleecy dressing gown. The route to the kettle was also so well known I could reach it on comfortable auto-pilot. The kitchen was housed in a corner of the sitting room and I aimed straight for the sink without hesitation or deviation. I filled the kettle and clicked it on to boil. It was only then that I remembered I had a visitor.

I rubbed my eyes and turned around to steal a glance at Percy's sleeping form on the settee. She looked out-for-the-count. I made my tea as quietly as I could, sat down at the dining table and flicked on my laptop. I sipped my drink while the machine whirred into life.

No interesting emails again. I remembered our mad enterprise of the ghost-busting website and navigated to the page. Hmm, looked pretty good, actually. Not bad for a tipsy evening's work. I scrolled down the page, smiling at our extravagant claims to help bring peace to restless spirits. I laughed quietly. Someone must have doctored that beer with hubris powder.

Then I saw something that made me put down my mug and focus my eyes on the monitor. There, in the enquiry section, someone had responded. I clicked on the box and opened it up to full screen.

I read the words, a few of which were spelled wrong. This sort of site was bound to attract weirdos.

"Can you help me? I gotta real problem up here in Anglesey. Bought a studio on an island to record me music and got some weird prowlers hawnting the place. If you guys can make them piss off, I'd be greatful. No expense spared. Contact this number or emale me on: rickoshea@email.com."

I stared at it until my tea went cold.

THE END

All Alex Martin's stories are available as paperbacks and make great gifts

Alex writes about her work on her blog in

# www.intheplottingshed.com

where she welcomes feedback and comments.
You can grab a FREE book there too!

Constructive reviews oil a writer's wheel like nothing else and are very much appreciated on Amazon, Goodreads or anywhere else

Go to www.intheplottingshed.com **online for** your *free* book

FREE

**A COLLECTION OF 3
SHORT STORIES
BY ALEX MARTIN**

The Pond
A Tidy Wife
The Wedding Cake

I hope you have enjoyed The Rose Trail.
If you have, I hope you might also like my other stories,
listed below:

Book One of The Katherine Wheel Series, DAFFODILS, drags Katy and Jem into the global arena of World War One and changes their lives forever.

Cheadle is a sleepy village in rural Wiltshire, England. Nothing much changes and little family dramas provide the only food for scandal and gossip. Then WW1 erupts into the lives of these country people, leaving no-one unscathed.
We meet Katy as a young maidservant, restless for more than domestic service can offer and reckless to a fault. We see her develop and mature, as life throws joys and tragedies across her path and the war lures Jem away. Another man tempts her to stay home but in the end she too signs up for the war and in doing so, finds her true self, and discovers that the only thing that really matters is, after all, simply love.

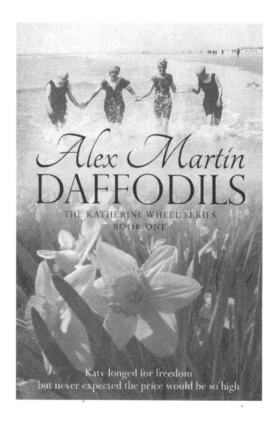

Katy trained as a mechanic during the war and cannot bear to return to the life of drudgery she left behind. A trip to America provides the dream ticket she has always craved and an opportunity to escape the strait-jacket of her working class roots. She jumps at the chance, little realising that it will change her life forever, but not in the way she'd hoped.

Jem lost not only an arm in the war, but also his livelihood, and with it, his self esteem. How can he keep restless Katy at home and provide for his wife? He puts his life at risk a second time, attempting to secure their future and prove his love for her.

Cassandra has fallen deeply in love with Douglas Flintock, an American officer she met while driving ambulances at the Front. How can she persuade this modern American to adapt to her English country way of life, and all the duties that come with inheriting Cheadle Manor? When Douglas returns to Boston, unsure of his feelings, Cassandra crosses the ocean, determined to lure him back.

As they each try to carve out new lives, their struggles impact on each other in unforeseen ways.

SPEEDWELL is the third book in the Katherine Series
and completes the story - for now.
(A fourth book, set in the 1940's, called Woodbine and Ivy,
may conclude the series but has yet to be written.)

Katy and Jem enter the 1920's with their future in the balance.
How can they possibly make their new enterprise work? They must
risk everything, including disaster, and trust their gamble will pay off.
Cassandra, juggling the demands of a young family, aging
parents and running Cheadle Manor, distrusts the speed of the modern
age, but Douglas races to meet the new era, revelling in the freedom
of the open road.
Can each marriage survive the strain the new dynamic decade
imposes? Or will the love they share deepen and carry them through?
They all arrive at destinies that surprise them in Speedwell, the third
book in the Katherine Wheel Series.

Alex Martin's debut book, is based on her grape-picking adventure in France in the 1980's. It's more of a mystery/ thriller than historical fiction but makes for great holiday reading with all the sensuous joys of that beautiful country.

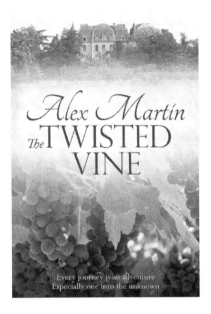

The shocking discovery of her lover with someone else propels Roxanne into escaping to France and seeking work as a grape-picker. She's never been abroad before and certainly never travelled alone.

Opportunistic loner, Armand, exploits her vulnerability when they meet by chance. She didn't think she would see him again, or be the one who exposes his terrible crime.

Join Roxanne on her journey of self discovery, love and tragedy in rural France. Taste the wine, feel the sun, drive through the Provencal mountains with her, as her courage and resourcefulness are tested to the limit.

Printed in Great Britain
by Amazon